THE VALLEY OF SAGE AND JUNIPER

SHAY GALLOWAY

RUNNING
Wild
PRESS

The Valley of Sage and Juniper text copyright © Reserved by Shay Galloway
Edited by Laura Huie

Published in North America, Australia, and Europe by RIZE. Visit Running
Wild Press at www.runningwildpress.com/rize Educators, librarians, book clubs
(as well as the eternally curious), go to www.runningwildpress.com/rize.
ISBN (pbk) 978-1-955062-60-2
ISBN (ebook) 978-1-955062-55-8

for Keili,
my own back-valley sister

GENESIS

The first time Daddy put a gun in my hand, I was seven. I'd been watching him and the ranch hands on Fourth of July, popping bottles and cans off fence posts. Daddy never missed a shot, even though the hands kept taunting him. I was fascinated by the bang, the smell of spent powder, and the echo of the shot ringing.

I asked Daddy if I could try, he laughed and beckoned me to his side, the hands cheering. Daddy traded his big Colt revolver for one of the hand's smaller Smith and Wesson. He knelt to my level, placed the wooden butt into my palm, the lacquer smooth and warm. It was heavy, smelled of oil and powder and metal. Daddy had to help me lift and aim, his hands rough and calloused but strong and gentle.

"Alright now, baby, it's gonna give you a bit of a jolt." He anchored his hands around mine, and I pulled the trigger. I felt the kick through my bones. The can on top of the fence was gone, flown somewhere into the field. My ears buzzed. The hands all cheered. I knew really it was Daddy who'd done it, but I was proud all the same. "Shoot like that, and you'll never need a man to save you," Daddy said.

Mama saw from the porch. She shouted for me to come in and made me read passages from the Bible while she muttered to herself about everyone working against her trying to raise young ladies. Across from me, Gramma winked. "Grampop would be proud," she whispered.

Mama and Daddy argued about it. Daddy said there was no harm in it, that if I wanted to be a sharpshooter, I should start now. Daddy was not a yelling man, not inside, not with us. But Mama could be. The hands out in their bunkhouse heard her carrying on.

That Christmas I got a pellet gun, a small oak-stocked rifle. Mama scoffed and told me to keep it out of the house. "When you get a little bigger, we'll get you a real revolver, like mine," Daddy said.

What dreams our mother must have had for us. She raised us proper, righteous, educated. She tried to, anyway. As if, by raising us on the straight and narrow, we could all atone for her father's sins. Every other night it was the Bible and the Classics. But you can't survive out here on the soft words of Jane Austen and Dickens. You can maybe survive on the brutality of Revelations, the stories of heads served up on platters, and women torn apart by dogs. This is the land for those stories, this land of sagebrush, black basalt crags, and scraggly juniper thickets, where the sky turns to rivers of blood at dusk.

What names our mother gave us. Sometimes I wonder what she was thinking when she named Isaiah. Maybe she had some premonition about her. Or perhaps in the fever of the birthing bed, she'd heard the midwife say *boy* instead of *girl* and was too stubborn to change it. Either way, Isaiah's name was marked on the doctor's register, born at our house, the estate of our famed grandfather.

I was too young to remember her birth, of course, but I can remember watching her looking at me from her cradle. I'd had to stretch up tip-toed to see her. I remember her dark eyes half the size of her round face, the thicket of crow-black hair on her crown. I remember she regarded me with silence, only the intensity of her gaze showing any sign she was aware of my presence. And then she broke her stare and giggled and reached for me.

"Grampop had black hair like that," Gramma told us. Grampop had been a rough rider in his younger days. He gained notoriety robbing and rustling. He was already old by the time Mama was born—nearly fifty. Gramma was twenty years his junior. She had her own sort of notoriety. There's a story she killed her father. "He was an awful mean man," she'd tell us.

Grampop was gone long before Isaiah and I came along. Mama resisted telling us anything about her pop. But we had Gramma around in our early years, and she told us everything Mama wouldn't.

"I was so young when I met him the first time," Gramma often said. She had only been seventeen. Her uncle was one of Grampop's gang, and they would often use her family's home as a safe house. "And he was dazzling. Gruff, lethal, dirty, but he was like fire. Something about him made you just want to be consumed by him, though you knew it'd hurt."

In the meantime, she'd shacked up with a boy or two and took men to warm her bed. "I was no holy angel when we married," Gramma once said. Mama told her off, and Gramma cackled, telling Mama not to be such a prude. "And then one day, he was tired and gettin' gray, and he realized he wanted to settle down, and I packed my bags and we bought some land and decided to live decent—put those days behind us. We even got married on paper, in front of a justice, like decent-folk."

Mama was nothing like Gramma. Gramma herself could barely read, but she and Grampop made sure Mama got as much school as possible. And with schooling, Mama learned about church and God, and Gramma and Grampop would get her to church on Sundays. "We were too far from God for too long," Gramma told me when I asked why she didn't ever go to church.

There's not much special about our land, the land Grampop settled on. There wasn't much to the land when he staked his claim, just sagebrush and scraggly juniper thickets, but there was a lot of it, and it butt right up against a rock gorge that passed into the jagged hills. Grampop set up his ranch, investing his money in it.

"He stole some, shot some men—never nobody who didn't deserve it, though. Many a man's got holes in 'em thanks to your Grampop. He done some things, surely, but he never disrespected a man that deserved it, and he was a charmer," Gramma told us secretly, nearly in whispers like a storyteller while we lay in our bed at night. "He never killed anyone of too much importance, so they didn't have much on him on that account. When they did manage to get him behind bars—he spent his fair share of nights in the jailhouse—he made good with the warden or the sheriff and he got out in little time. He was good at keepin' the other inmates in line, and every now and then he'd help the law catch some of the others. So they went easy on him."

And then he was done.

"The law started cracking down on his type," said Gramma. "By then, he'd started laying low, but they caught up with him. He spent seven years on a chain gang, and when they released him, he came to me."

He'd said he was ready for a wife, the way Gramma'd tell it.

"I'd been shacking up with another fellow, but I wrote that

nice young man a note, left him some cornbread on the stove, packed up my things and joined your Grampop at the courthouse."

"Wasn't he angry?" Isaiah asked once.

"Who?"

"The man you were with," I said.

"Nah," Gramma cackled, "Besides, I was known for being flighty when it came to men. After all, I'd left another man in the dust for that one. But I'd known your Grampop all my life, and he was the only man I ever felt something real about."

Together, they took all the money Grampop'd had stored away and they got this land, almost four thousand acres ten miles from town, and built a cabin that grew into a clapboard house and a ranch, where they bred and raised cattle and horses.

"He became a respectable man. The town knew him, maybe feared him a little on account of his history. But people out here, they take pride in their legends, whether they be for good or bad."

We're a family of legend, then, and this land of ours is hallowed ground. The first time I realized this for truth, I was ten. I was accompanying Daddy as he made perimeter rounds. We came upon a part of the fence that'd been cut—it was only barbed wire and rough posts after all.

"Damn treasure hunters," Daddy grunted and grabbed his rifle from the truck and soon enough we came upon a group of three or four men in a thicket, shovels in hand. Daddy cocked the gun. "You're either burying something you don't want found, or you're looking for something that ain't yours." The men climbed out their holes, hands and shovels raised in surrender. One of them started trying to make some excuse and Daddy steadied his rifle. "Or maybe you're digging your own graves?" He pulled the trigger, the men all jumped and one or two squeaked, but the bullet lodged in a tree. "Best you all get gone." And they scattered, leaving behind their shovels.

"Grab a couple of those," Daddy said, taking up one himself. We set them on the flat wooden bed of the truck.

"Daddy, what were they looking for?" I asked as we climbed back into the old Chevy.

Daddy laughed, "Everybody thinks there's treasure here."

"There's no money here," Gramma said. "It's in that barn, and this house, and the cowshed, and all those books your Mama loved to read, the cornbread and the bacon on the table. The money's in the land between all the fence posts we built ourselves. Your Grampop never owed anybody anything—except maybe his life a time or two."

Legend had it that Grampop had been sitting on as much as any of the Rockefellers and had buried it on his land. For a while, Isaiah and I took to becoming treasure hunters ourselves, as convinced as everyone else there were chests of gold coins hidden in some juniper thicket.

How could so many people make up such a story? we thought. We tried our hand at digging holes here and there about the property, but we realized we hated digging holes and no treasure was worth the sore backs and blisters—the pain that had to be endured just to prove a legend.

PART I

SUMMER 1928 - FALL 1932

ISAIAH

I don't like popping cans as much as Genesis, but she always tells me to come out and practice with her. She lets me have turns with her BB gun; Gramma sits on the porch and watches us, sometimes she claps and hollers when we make a shot.

"Next, Daddy's gonna get me a real gun," Genesis is saying, her eye long on the barrel of her BB gun. "Of course, it'll only be a little pea-shooter, nothing big like the old Winchester."

"Or the double-barrel," I say.

Genesis scrunches up her face, "Of course not. Daddy wouldn't get me a shotgun. I'm gonna be a sharp shooter for heaven's sake, Isaiah, not a hunter."

I shrug as Mama's shout comes from the porch. Gramma's sitting on the top step, a bucket between her knees catching peas as she pops them from the shells. Mama's standing behind her, her hand propping open the screen door as she calls out to us.

"What do you think she wants?" Genesis says, lowering her gun.

"Isaiah, Genesis! Girls!" She beckons for us. We don't go immediately, just watch as she waves. "Gene-*sis*, Is-*ai*-ah! Come on!" she shouts. Gramma puts her fingers in her mouth and whistles.

Genesis sighs and grabs my hand. "We better go see what she wants." As soon as Mama sees we're coming in, she goes inside. Genesis rests her gun against the porch railing. "What's Mama got for us to do?" she asks Gramma.

Gramma shrugs. "Dunno, but she's got the keys to the truck, so I expect she's headed into town."

In the kitchen, Mama's got tinfoil over three dishes. She glances at us. "Haven't you got anything else to wear?"

Genesis and I look down at ourselves in worn overalls. Mine are cuffed at the bottom and a bit more faded. We'd been doing chores before, but we weren't too dirty. I look at Genesis, confused.

"Something going on at the church or something?" she says.

"It's not Sunday or school," I say. "I ain't putting on any dress." Genesis elbows me. Mama sucks air through her teeth, and I know it's because I said "ain't."

"I am not gonna put a dress on," I correct myself. "What's wrong with what we're wearing, anyway?" Mama wears dresses and skirts every day, not just on Sunday. Even Gramma wears pants on the regular; there's work on the ranch that can't be done in a skirt.

Mama looks at the clock and sighs as she wipes her hands on her apron before she unties it. "Well no matter now, I guess." She lays her apron on the counter. "Each of you grab one of those," she says, nodding to the covered dishes. She grabs one herself and the key for the old truck.

"Where are we going?" I say.

"Taking dinner to Mary Hannigan."

"The preacher's wife?"

I don't want to go into town. The preacher died last week and now old Ms. Hannigan's always sad and even more cantankerous. She's old and she always scowls at me like I'm something a dog left behind. "She doesn't need all this food."

Mama sucks air again. "Isaiah, just—I'll let you get penny candy if you help without complaining."

"Can we stay in the car when we get there?" I ask as Mama grinds the gears, and we go bumping down the crunching gravel.

"Of course not, you've got to help carry it all in."

It's almost ten miles to town, with only one other ranch and a couple smaller homesteads between. The road's mostly packed rock and dirt until the edge of town, and dust billows up behind us. A few black and brown cows and horses and sheep stand out in the fields of sage and wild grass. Some of them hide in the shade of the scraggy junipers that dot the landscape. Evening's falling soon, and once the sun goes down, the night will cool.

There isn't much in town. There's the little school, the old church, Stevenson's garage and fuel station; Margaret's boarding house and diner, the feed and supply store, Knudson's Grocery, Feaney's Goods. There's the bank and the single-room dentistry, and the bakery, and the doctor's office, and the newspaper office all lined up together on Main Street. The town hall and the jail and post office are all just different rooms in the same building. The town's pretty much been the same since Gramma and Grampop settled here, she tells us so all the time. The only thing that's changed now is that the bar is empty— they're illegal now.

We park in front of the church; the Hannigans live next door. When Mama knocks on the door, it's not Ms. Hannigan who answers. Some woman about Mama's age is at the door. Mama calls her Lila and tells her we've brought some supper. "Girls, you remember Miss Lila."

Truth is, I don't, but Genesis says "Yeah" so I agree. When the grown ladies turn their backs on us, I lean to Genesis. "Who's that?" I whisper into her neck. It's as far up as I can reach with my own neck stretched.

"Preacher's daughter," she whispers back. "Hush."

Miss Lila has us put the dishes on the counter and walks us into the sitting room, so we can be presented to Ms. Hannigan. The preacher's old widow sits on her sofa dressed all in black, sleeves down to her wrists, collar up to her neck, and I think —*Heck, she must be hot.* Her hair isn't all the way white like some old ladies, so she's not all that old, really, but she looks stern and hard, which makes her seem older than Gramma, whose hair is all gray now. Her eyes move over us.

"Girls should be in skirts," the widow says.

"Ma, they just brought us supper," Miss Lila says.

"I apologize," says Mama. "They were out working, and I didn't give them much time to get cleaned up before coming." She places her hands on our shoulders giving a light squeeze, and we know we aren't in trouble for this lady's disapproval. "How are you holding up, Mary?"

"As well as a preacher's widow can, s'pose. Now this one wants to take me away with her," she motioned to her daughter.

"The home comes with the church, Ma, we discussed this," says Miss Lila. "And you're not going away to nowhere, Ma, you're going to stay with Joshua and his family."

"Why not you? You aren't married, you work, you've got money."

Miss Lila rolls her eyes, a thing we'd get our hands slapped for. I don't mind Miss Lila, but I don't like Ms. Hannigan, and sometimes it's hard for me to hide when I don't like something.

She's already said something that made Mama defend us, and all I want to say to Ms. Hannigan is that she's ungrateful and cantankerous, but the hope of penny candy keeps me on my best possible behavior.

"What's this one scowling for?" Ms. Hannigan says, pointing at me. "It's unbecoming. Heavens those black eyes of hers could take the Devil himself." She looks at Mama, whose grip has tightened on us. "Better watch out for that one, Adelaide, she's a little harlot in the making."

I don't know what a harlot is, but Mama's grip tightens so hard on my shoulder I can feel her nails through my top. Genesis takes my hand in hers and shouts, "You're just a dried up ugly old witch."

Miss Lila starts to smile but hides behind her hand. "We best be going," Mama says, sucking air between her teeth. She pushes us toward the door. Because Genesis shouted, I'm sure we aren't getting penny candy, but Mama parks right outside Feaney's shop and gives us each a penny.

I choose a lump of rock candy, and Genesis takes a rope of licorice. We push our pennies over the counter to plump Mr. Feaney and go sit out on the steps while Mama goes over fabric with Mrs. Feaney.

"If she'd given us a nickel, we could have gotten ice cream," says Genesis.

"Maybe next time. If you hadn't shouted, we might have got her to give us some." The rock candy's sweet, rough, good enough.

"Who's that?" Genesis says, and I look across the street. A man wearing all black—black shirt buttoned up to the neck and black trousers held up by black suspenders and a silly, soft-brimmed black hat—is making his way across to us.

"Afternoon, ladies," he says. He puts his foot up on the step between the two of us and leans on his knee to be level with us.

"Heard ya'll are in need of a new preacher," he says. The twang in his voice is different; he's not from around here.

"Old preacher just died, so I guess so," Genesis says, looking at him with her eyes narrowed. "We ain't no ladies."

"Are you a preacher? Is that why you wear all black?" I ask. "Our last preacher didn't wear all black except on Easter." He looks at me with green eyes, sharp as a wolf's.

He leans close and smiles. I can see one of his teeth is silver, but most of the others are yellow. His eyes slide over me as he strokes his stubbly graying beard. "Yes I am, and who might you be?"

I glance at Genesis, who's still scowling with her licorice dangling from her mouth. "Isaiah," I say, "and this is my sister Genesis." But he doesn't look at Genesis at all.

"Isaiah, yeah?" He laughs loudly and slaps his knee. "What's been planned for you with a name like that?"

Something about his laugh makes my stomach squeeze, and I set to scowling like Genesis. "It's just the name my Mama gave me." He leans in even closer, so he's almost nose-to-nose with me, it feels like. His breath smells sour. He shifts, lifting his hand from his knee and Genesis stands in one movement, her hands in fists at her side. The preacher man tilts my chin up with his knuckle.

"I hope to see y'all in church someday soon," he says, almost like a whisper.

"We've gotta go now." Genesis pulls me up, yanking on me. The preacher man straightens and laughs again, tipping his hat to us as Mama comes out with her arms full of fabric.

"Who was that?" Mama asks.

"New preacher," says Genesis, scowling after him.

Later, as we lie beside each other in the dark I say, "Genesis?"

14

"Yeah?"

"What's a harlot?"

"I don't know, Isaiah."

"Then why'd you get so mad at Ms. Hannigan for saying it?" I say.

"I just don't like the way she said it," she says. "It made Mama upset, so I knew it was bad." I snuggle close to her, and she puts her arm around me. "Oh, you ain't nothing."

GENESIS

After the new preacher set up in town, Mama took us to church. It had been the first time in months. Mrs. Hannigan and her daughter were there. Mama pushed us quickly to the opposite side of the chapel. All the town seemed to be there, ready to size up the new preacher. I'd never seen it so full. Even Daddy came along. It had taken Mama days of pleading to convince him to come. The fourth or fifth time, she said, "What will they think, me going alone with the girls when I have a good, God-fearing husband? They'll think you don't hold solidarity with me."

Daddy finally agreed. I think mostly so Mama would stop pestering him about it. No one was as God-fearing as Mama. Daddy's general philosophy on church had been—"Why do I need some high-collared, tender-palmed man to tell me about God when I can just as well read the bible in my own home?"

"Propriety," was always Mama's answer. She shuffled us into a pew that day, the four of us starched and pressed, bows in my and Isaiah's hair. When the new preacher got up to the pulpit, the congregation shifted nervously against their wooden pews, not quite knowing what to expect. The old preacher had been around so long—well over thirty years—it was a shock to see another man in his place.

The new preacher wore his black, wide-brimmed hat, even inside, which already set him apart from the last preacher. He was younger than his predecessor, but still older than Daddy. I had taken an immediate disliking to him the moment of our first meeting outside Feaney's. I was young, but old enough to have reason to my preference, and I could not quite pin what it was exactly about the preacher that irritated me. I just knew he rubbed me wrong.

"Brothers and sisters," he began. "Thank you for coming out on this lovely Sabbath morning, and for welcoming me and my family—" he motioned toward the front pew where a tight-haired woman with a face to match and a large handful of brown-haired kids sat. Half the children were older than me or about my age. There was one Isaiah's age and one younger—a little girl about three or four. The one Isaiah's age was a boy. The only one who was blonde, thin with his nose and mouth scrunched like he'd smelled something bad. He sat stiffly against the back of the pew. "—to this good Christian town."

The preacher talked of community and standing together in Christ against the evils of the world. Mama nodded along with every word. The preacher got more animated at the pulpit and sweat slid down from beneath the brim of his hat. Mama was so enthralled by his "passion," as she referred to it, she made a point to take us up after the sermon and properly introduce us.

"I think you've already met my girls, Genesis and Isaiah."

"Yes, ma'am," his eyes lingered over Isaiah a little longer than the rest of us, but Mama didn't seem to notice. "You seem to be a humble, devout woman, Mrs...?"

"Addie's fine," she said. I think she almost blushed. Daddy

was just outside the doors, catching up with one of the other men. I silently willed him to come in. He looked over at us, at Isaiah and me scowling while Mama held tight to our hands. He came in, placing his hand on Mama's back.

"It's time we get, isn't it, Addie?"

"I was just introducing myself and the girls—Pastor, this is my husband."

They exchanged "How do's," smiling pleasantly enough but their eyes challenged each other.

"Wasn't that a lovely sermon?" Mama said in the truck on the way home, us two girls smashed between our parents. "He's got such a passion about him."

Mama continued on in this fashion for a few minutes until Daddy finally said, "He sounds like a snake-oil salesman."

Mama was silent the rest of the way home. Before we exited she said, "Does this mean you won't come anymore?"

"You're welcome to go, take the girls if they want," was Daddy's answer.

ISAIAH

Each year, just as winter is ending and spring is starting, the bunk house out back fills up with ranch hands. Some of them come back a few years in a row. Some don't. But a lot of them like my Daddy, so they do. As winter comes back around —when the herds have been whittled down—most of the hands go; only a few of them stay.

There's one who stays on regular through the winter, a guy named Denney that's been around since before I was born, before even Genesis was born. He's got a pretty collie named Biscuit that follows him around everywhere. He and Daddy both started working on the ranch as hands way back when they were young, and they came back every year until eventually Daddy married Mama and took up the ranch like it was his own, even though it's really Gramma who owns it, being Grampop's wife.

Every year, when Daddy introduces us to the hands, or re-introduces us to the returning ones, Mama gives a little speech about welcoming them to our home and if they have any domestic problems, let her know, but she's not a maid so don't expect her to do all their ironing, though she's willing to wash socks and under-things and provide what they need to do the rest of their washing on their own. She says how she expects to be treated with respect, as well as us little girls, and to please remember to treat us like ladies. They all nod along and say "Of course, Ma'am" and then she brings out pies and a couple turkeys or hams and they all dig in.

When the hands all come back that means calving and foaling season is coming, and then the ranch is alive. Genesis and I go to school and sit in that boring old room with all the other kids from around town, and then we hurry home—or try to get Mama to hurry up in that old truck—so we can see any new calves or foals born during our absence.

At the beginning of summer all but two or three of the bull calves get bands tied around their dangling parts so that they fall off and they grow up to become steer instead of bulls. When it's time for the banding, all the hands laugh and joke and get worried about their own parts. And then Denney whistles and tries to remind them we're there sitting on the fence within hearing distance. He pretends he's stern, but he's laughing right along with them. "If you don't stop that, I'll tie you all up myself!" Denney says.

They holler and say "Well, start with Colman, he's got a baby in every town from here to Santa Fe!" And then they laugh and slap each other on the back and wink at us little girls sitting on the fence watching it all.

At night, they sit around smoking and playing cards. They mostly make their own food, except for when Mama's feeling generous. After supper, a lot of nights Daddy sits out with them. Sometimes a few of them come up around the porch where us girls and Gramma can chat with them. Sometimes they all stay down in the bunkhouse, and when Mama's not home, we'll go down there, too.

They like when Genesis reads to them from her big, wordy books. They ask me to read sometimes, too. My books are shorter and have pictures, but Genesis and Daddy tell me to go ahead and read to them, and they remind me to show them all the pictures.

Mama doesn't like us spending so much time with them, but she's been spending a lot of time at the church lately. The new preacher (who isn't all that new anymore), likes church so much that he holds extra meetings other days of the week, prayer meetings and bible studies and hymnal nights. Mama's gone sometimes two or three nights a week. Those nights, Gramma gets us sandwiches together, and we spend the night relaxing.

On the nights Mama's home, she calls us in before supper and sits us at the table with sheets of arithmetic problems and blank sheets of paper with the dictionary and the bible. I copy out three words from the dictionary—Genesis has to copy out five since she's older—along with the definitions.

Mama's favorite scripture she has us copy down—especially when we've spent a long time with all the hands or we've been shooting with Daddy—is Deuteronomy 22:5: *The woman shall not wear that which pertaineth unto man*...Mama often comes home at night from her church meetings humming hymns. One night she asks Daddy if she can take us girls to Sunday School. Daddy doesn't even look up from his food. "So you'll have to take the truck earlier?" he says.

"Just an hour," Mama says. "It would be good for them."

Daddy looks at us. He sits back in his chair with his hand on his full belly. "Do you ladies want to go to Sunday School?"

Genesis looks between the both of them. I know she wants to say no, but Mama's staring hard at her. Genesis doesn't like upsetting anybody, especially Mama, who always says no one is ever on her side.

"What is it?" I ask.

Daddy looks at Mama. "Well," Mama says, "It's like church, but for children only. There's songs and bible stories and—"

"Would we still have to go to regular church?" I say.

"Of course," Mama says.

"I don't want to go," I tell her.

Mama's mouth gets tight. "Isaiah..." she starts to say, but Daddy talks over her.

"The girl says she doesn't want to go."

Mama's fingers are turning white around her fork. Genesis sits up straight. "I suppose we could go just once, just to try it out."

"Just once," I agree. Mama nods and goes back to eating. She's taken us to church nearly every week since the new preacher came. Every week it's the same; the preacher gets so excited up at the pulpit that he spits, especially when he's saying we're all sinners wandering through this place of corruption called Earth and we're all doomed for Hell.

Mama takes us early to church the next Sunday. Sunday school is held in the preacher's house. Mrs. Hannigan doesn't live there anymore. Now it's the new preacher and his family that live there. Chairs are set up around the parlor when we get there. Already there's a lot of other kids sitting in them. Mama hands us off to the preacher's wife and goes next door to the church.

I sit next to Reuben, the preacher's son who's my age. He's got a sour face, and he swings his legs so he kicks me in the shin until I say "Ow!" and his mama snaps at him to stop. The preacher's oldest daughter leads us all in songs about Noah and the flood and tribulations of fires from heaven and blood filling the sea. All the kids are bad at singing, but Genesis and I don't even know the words.

We know a few of the kids from school, but most of them are new. When the Missus and her daughter go to get snacks, Genesis asks some of the other kids where they came from.

"We just moved out here," a girl Genesis' age says. "Came out following Leader—the preacher."

"You aren't Preacher's kids, too, are you?"

The girl shakes her head. "No, we've just got our Mama. Daddy was a drunk and a sinner. We left him back where we came from. Leader takes care of us now." A few other families had moved out recently, following the preacher it seems. "He called us out here to set up his promised land."

"What's a promised land?" I say, trying to shake off Reuben's pinching fingers.

No one answers my question; none of them really seem to know. "Well," says Genesis, "I don't think we've ever had so many kids in our school. Might not all fit."

The same girl shrugs "We ain't been to school since we took up with Leader and the Community."

"Our mamas all school us themselves," her little sister says.

Come to think of it, I never have seen Reuben or any of his brothers and sisters at school. We saw them every week at church and didn't spend long with any other children anyway. "Why do you keep calling the preacher 'Leader?' And what's 'The Community'?" I ask.

"It's the name of the church, The Community of the Promised Land," says the older girl.

"We've always just called it church," I say, pulling Reuben's fingers from my skin again.

"It's more than just church," the girl says.

Reuben leans in close and whispers in my ear, "You're the spawn of the Devil."

"What are you talking about?" I say to him.

"Your gran'pa was a wicked man," he says. "I've heard all

about him. And your Gran-mama was a whore." I don't know what a whore is, and I'm sure he doesn't either. It's just a word the preacher says a lot in his sermons. I'm sure my Gramma isn't one.

"You're crazy," I say and turn back to listen to Genesis and the older girls talking. He pinches me again and laughs. "If you pinch me again, I'll hit you in the face!" I rub my arm where he's pinched. "How do you know any of that, anyway?"

"Your mama always comes in and talks to Father about salvation for her demon-parents' sins." He pinches me again and then I'm on top of him, punching him in the face. He's crying out and his mama comes in and pulls me off by my hair and drags me to the back sitting room where she shoves me into a seat.

"You!" she says, pointing her thin finger in my face.

Genesis rushes in. "Hey, leave my sister alone!"

"I told him if he kept pinching me, I'd hit him!" I say. I rub at my head; it feels like she's just about ripped all my hair out. Next thing I know, she slaps me across the face with the back of her hand. I'm so shocked tears bite my eyes, but I bite my lip to keep them back.

"Your mother told me all about you and your belligerent, improper and faithless ways!" Preacher's wife shouts.

"She's eight!" my sister shouts. Reuben's sister has her by the arm; Genesis is trying to claw her fingers off. Behind them, Reuben's smiling. His mama and sister drag Genesis and me to a pantry just off the kitchen and sit us in there, telling us to stay until our Mama comes back. They shut the door, and the only light we've got is a dim bulb and we're surrounded by bags of flour and oats, tubs of lard, and buckets of corn meal.

When Mama comes to collect us for sermon, Preacher's wife opens the door, blabbing away. "Such insolence, Adelaide. You've spared them the rod, I can tell!"

Mama's mouth is tight as she looks at us crouched on the floor of the pantry. I know we'll be in a lot of trouble once we're home. "Yes, well, we don't normally have to—they're generally well-behaved—a little spirited..." She reaches for us and quickly pulls us to her side.

Preacher's wife makes a noise that's something like a laugh. "They'll never abandon this character unless you firm up with them! It'll only get worse from here, and then before you know it, they're out of control harlot-types. The little one, she smarted right up as soon as she felt the sting of discipline!"

Mama's face goes pale. "You mean you—?"

"Of course! She attacked my son. My daughters would never behave in such a fashion. They know—"

Mama starts walking us quickly through the house toward the door. "Thank you, Sister. I'm sure it won't happen again." She takes us straight to the truck.

"Mama," I say, "Reuben was pinching me. She even saw it! I told him to stop. I warned him. I didn't want to hit him. Well, I didn't at first, but then we—"

"Hush, Isaiah." Mama says calmly, but her fingers are tight on the steering wheel, and I'm afraid we're going to get home and Mama's going to give us the rod that Preacher's wife was talking about. I haven't quite worked out if I'm meant to stand and hold it for a long time, or carry it around for a long time, or if she's going to hit me with it. In that case, I hope it's a small rod. Mama's pinched our ears before, or smacked quick at the backs of our hands, but she's never hit us across the face like Preacher's wife. Mostly her tone gets sharp and we know to straighten up.

"Do we have to go back?" Genesis asks softly.

Mama sighs. "No."

There's no stern talking to when we pull up to the house, but Mama doesn't move once she's turned off the truck.

Genesis and I stay too, listening to the cracking of the cooling engine. After a while Mama says, "You girls go on inside."

"Mama..."

"Go on, I'll be in in a minute."

I go straight for the bible when we get inside. Gramma's surprised we're back so soon and she asks why. Genesis answers as I sit at the table with a new sheet of paper and a pencil. "Mama didn't say we have to," she says to me.

"I know," I say. I get through fifteen verses of Ezekiel before Mama comes in. She pats my head and kisses my hair but says nothing as she goes into the kitchen to start lunch.

GENESIS

Mama stopped making us go to church altogether after that, but Mama was more adamant than ever that we keep up our bible verse copying. She never "took up the rod" against us as Isaiah feared she would. However, Mama spent more of her own time in quiet pondering, more time at church meetings. We, on the other hand, spent more time with the hands and Daddy and Gramma.

I was in the kitchen with Mama when she cooked, Gramma when Mama was away. It was Gramma who told me any man could cook up bacon or steak, but real cooking required more than just throwing lard and muscle into a skillet. Gramma was not the cook Mama was; she didn't enjoy it and regarded it as a chore.

"I could hardly cook a thing before Grampop and I settled down," she told me. "Cornbread, I could do, but I burned potatoes, over-boiled corn, undercooked chicken. Your mama started cooking young and she liked it, so I let her have it, and I spent more time helping outside. She was hardly older than you are," she told me.

I wouldn't consider myself domestic. All my sewing ends up in knots if I do more than simple stitching-up. I detest dusting and scrubbing, but I did it because Mama instilled in us a respect for orderliness despite our tendency to appear rough on the regular. But cooking was the thing I did because I liked it —the feel of puffy dough, the smell of frying onions and steak.

I could slice open a tomato and anyone who crossed me the wrong way. Mama, I think, took some pride in that as well, whether she would admit it or not. "My pop taught me to shoot as well," she said.

"He did?" I said.

"I didn't take to it quite like you have. I was always afraid," she said. "Afraid of the gun, afraid I'd shoot myself in the foot, afraid I'd shoot someone else. Afraid I'd have to shoot someone else." She pressed her knuckles into the dough. "When Pop was gone, Ma'd have to chase off a few men herself. She'd got one once. She made me..." Mama bit her lip. She did not tell me the rest of that story. "My daddy would have loved you both." Mama brushed her finger along my cheek. "I just wish I could have given you better."

"We're pretty happy with what we've got now," I said.

She smiled sadly. "I know," she said.

Leader bought a ranch on the other side of town, and rumor was he'd started building what appeared to be a village. More families came, all of them coming to be part of "Leader's" congregation, taking up residence in the cabin-like structures on his ranch. Once Leader got a nice big house and chapel built, he and his family moved into it and sold the church house and chapel. The town never got a new preacher, most people went over to the next town north to attend church there; many of them had found Leader too fanatical and *too* preachy and had abandoned his congregation early on.

But Mama stuck it out, and even traveled out to the

Community—as Leader's village came to be known—and she came home enraptured. One day she came and, in fervor, removed all the photos from the walls. There wasn't much by way of artwork. A sketch or two gifted by hands passing through the years, but there were a number of framed photographs.

Grampop was removed, the photos of Isaiah and me in our baby gowns, Mama and Daddy on their wedding day. In the emptiness Mama nailed a large, rough wooden cross. The ghosts of what had hung there before stained into the wallpaper.

She took the books next. First she took the ones in the sitting room and tossed them in the burn pile. I quickly picked through for the ones I wanted and stashed them in our room. The only books left in the public areas of the house were the dictionary and the bible.

And then there she was.

I came into my room to find her flinging my books into crates. "Mama! Stop! What are you doing?" I screamed so loud, Gramma came running up to see what was wrong.

As fast as Mama was tossing the books away, I was rushing to them, trying to pack them all into my arms. Mama was in a frenzy, shouting, "Filth, lies!"

"Mama, you're being crazy!"

She turned on me, her eyes blazing. "You see, it's these books that make you talk to me like that. I should never have let you—" she tried to wrangle the books from my arms. I was near tears—tears hot with anger and disappointment and fear. Up to that point, though Mama had been gradually becoming more fervent, she'd pretty well left us out of her newfound rapture. It had been a year since she'd taken us to church.

Gramma shouted, causing Mama to pause, and then she spoke as though trying to talk down an injured dog. "Addie, I don't think it's harming anyone for Genesis to keep her books."

"You too!" Mama shouted. "You've been filling their heads with—with trash, feeding them tales of your and Pop's debauchery! Taking pleasure, even encouraging them, in their insolence and wild ways."

"So be it," Gramma said. "But you can't punish the girls for that." She stepped forward with caution. "Addie, let Genesis be. She's always been a good girl."

Mama sucked air, but she dropped her hands and strode from the room. Gramma and Isaiah helped me pack the books from the main house to the bunk house, where the hands ensured their safekeeping. Mama never went there.

That night Mama and Daddy fought, their shouts quaking through the floorboards. Gramma came in and held us in the dark. Daddy was shouting how Mama'd become too entwined in that church and was becoming maniacal. Mama shouted back just as vigorously that he was dragging this family to hell, and he didn't care about our salvation. Daddy never yelled at us, and he never physically lashed out, but his arguments with Mama were anything but quiet near the end, and we could hear his fist coming down on the table. Daddy took to spending the nights in a cot on the porch or in the bunkhouse.

Mama calmed down a bit for a while. Things almost got back to normal, though it seemed that our bible study seemed to last an eternity. I felt that Mama was going to have us transcribe the entire bible by the end of the summer. I did my best to appease her, to give her no reason to go on another crusade against us. As long as she let us keep doing as we wished about the ranch, I could bear her gradual descent into lunacy.

When I turned twelve at the end of spring, Daddy gifted me with a small .22 caliber rifle, just as he told me he would. He gave it to me out on the porch while Mama was inside putting the cake together. "It's not a toy," Daddy said. "It won't do much damage, but it can hurt like hell."

"I know, Daddy," I assured him, trying to keep the giddiness out of my voice, trying to show him I was mature enough for this.

"What's she need her own gun for?" Mama said. I had not noticed her come to the door.

"She asked," said Daddy with a shrug, "And I think she deserves it."

Mama said nothing, but her lips got tight and she went back inside. Daddy grunted and led me and Isaiah off the porch to go test out the new gift. The hands were there and they gave me their own gifts in turn, including a knife with an ankle sheath— an identical one would be given to Isaiah for her birthday a few months later—a whittled horse from Denney and a sketch of Isaiah and me sitting on the porch steps.

I spent most of my birthday dinner on edge, waiting for Mama to say something about our imperfections in the gospel, waiting for Daddy to get fed up and snap at Mama. But both were cordial, and I did my best to stay in neutral territory and to lead Isaiah there. I didn't even bring the gun inside that night. I didn't even suggest sharing the rest of the cake with the hands—Mama had taken to calling them godless roustabouts. Isaiah and I sneaked the rest of the cake out to the bunk the next day.

ISAIAH

I met another Isaiah. He's a new hand. Daddy brought him home from town one day. Of course I know about Isaiah in the bible, but I've never thought about that one since he was just a name on a page written years and years ago. But Daddy brings home this guy with my name—he's still a kid, younger than all the other hands, but a few years older than Genesis. Everyone calls him "Kid" all the time. No one really calls him Isaiah. Maybe because it's confusing with my name also being Isaiah. He's a knife fighter, and he's got a long thin scar down the side of his face. I asked him one day if he got it in a fight.

He laughed and said no. "My daddy gave me that."

I asked why. "Well I suppose I said something that he didn't like hearing." He leaned on his knees to get down to my level. "We Isaiahs tend to do that, say things that people don't much like to hear." He winked at me and ruffled my hair.

"He got that scar protecting his little sister," Genesis tells me later.

"How do you know?"

She shrugs. "He told me."

"Why?"

"Dunno," she says.

"Is it true," I say, "What he says about Isaiahs saying things people don't like to hear?"

"Isaiah's got a lot to say in the bible."

I never pay much attention to most of the bible. I just copy the words out like Mama wants us to. Mama's been gone more often than not, but she's still making us copy out bible passages every chance she can.

After Isaiah the Kid has told me about Isaiahs I actually start paying attention to what Mama's making us copy down. *The woman shall not wear that which pertaineth unto a man, neither shall a man put on a woman's garment for they that do so are abomination unto the Lord thy God.* We have to copy it every time we go out shooting. I don't know what "pertaineth" means, but I guess it's got to mean something like "belonging."

I put down my pencil loud enough against the table for Mama to hear and look up from her kneading. "Are you done, Isaiah?"

I'm not. I only got to the "a" in "wear." "What did you have to go and give me a boy's name for, if we ain't supposed to wear anything belonging to men?"

Genesis pauses, her pencil hangs over the page, her eyes moving back and forth between me and Mama.

"I gave you a name from the bible," says Mama. "Like your sister."

"Is Genesis a woman's name?"

"It's not really a name for a person at all," Genesis mumbles, but Mama doesn't hear.

"I've never met another," Gramma says, and Mama ignores her too.

"Isaiah is a boy's name, Mama. Even in the bible, it's a man," I say. "And it says, right here '*the woman shall not wear that which per-tain-eth unto a man.'* And I'm wearing a man's name, and you gave it to me. You broke a rule in the bible you love so much!"

Gramma's shaking silently behind her hands in her chair.

"Isaiah!" Mama snaps. "You! You are so—why can't you just—how dare you disrespect—"

She makes me so angry sometimes, saying what we can and can't do, saying all the time how we're running too wild, not proper. "You don't make any sense, Mama. And I think I'm done writing this verse forever."

Her hand comes across my face so fast and hard I'm knocked out of my chair. Genesis gasps, "Mama!" Gramma says, "Jesus, God!" It's a second or two before I realize I've bit my tongue and as the pain starts to burn, I spit blood on the floor, where it turns dark on the wood. I don't cry. I glare at Mama and she's glaring at me.

Daddy comes in and sees me on my hands and knees on the floor, blood dribbling down my chin. He sees the mark of Mama's hand on my face, and Mama and I glaring at each other. "What the hell's happened here?"

"Your wife doesn't make any sense!" I say, wiping blood spit from my mouth.

"Your daughter is belligerent, disobedient. We've been too lax with her. She'll be wild!"

Daddy picks me up off the floor and looks at Genesis. Genesis shifts and glances at Mama and back to Daddy. "Isaiah said she doesn't want to write the verses anymore," she says.

"It says not to take upon ourselves anything about men, and she gave me this name!" I say. "She broke the commandment herself!"

Mama's breathing hard and she starts shouting high and loud as Daddy motions for Gramma and Genesis to take me away. They clean me up and we shut ourselves inside our bedroom. All the while, Mama and Daddy are shouting and yelling. The shouting goes on a long time. It picks up and gets quiet and then they get louder again. Genesis and I lay on our bellies and listen through the floor.

Mama's saying how Daddy doesn't care, he's never really cared, not about her or salvation. Then Daddy says something in his low voice that we can't make out through the floor, and Mama answers back and they get a little louder back and forth until we hear Daddy say, "Who even knows what you get up to out there!"

"How dare you imply...I've always been a good wife..." Mama says back.

"I see you, Addie!" Daddy shouts.

Mama's voice is low again, so low we barely hear her speak at all. Daddy's voice comes back. I press my ear harder to the floor, but I can't hear. All I can hear is my heart thumping on the carpet. Genesis grabs my arm. "Come on," she says, and we get back into bed as Mama and Daddy start shouting again.

The next morning, Mama's gone.

GENESIS

In the days following Mama's departure, Isaiah became quiet, sullen. I guessed she felt it was her fault Mama and Daddy had fought. At first, it seemed that Mama was just spending a night away like she did, out with the Community. But she didn't return after a full week.

The Community was less than fifteen miles away; if we really wanted, we could have seen her, or she could have visited us. But she didn't.

Mama wasn't the only one from town who joined the Community, but those others had not abandoned their children. In town, we were given smiles of pity, people muttering to Daddy or Gramma it was such a shame "that charlatan" had come to town. "Their Grampop would never have stood for it," they said.

Time passed without Mama, and the ranch carried on. The hands all helped bring my books back in. The shelves were not as full as they once had been, many books having fallen victim to Mama's holy fire, but Daddy promised I'd collect enough to fill the shelves and then some.

Gramma removed the great ugly cross and replaced the photos. I'd never really looked at all the photos; they'd been there all my life. They had been just as much a part of the wall as the plaster and paint. Their new emergence allowed for fresh discovery. I handed Gramma an oval frame holding an old sepia-faded photo of a young woman with long dark hair and a long skirt, a rifle in her hand, and intense gaze in her eyes set stern and haunting. There, I saw shadows of Isaiah.

Gramma smiled with nostalgia at the photo. "I was so young then."

Isaiah scrambled up to her side, craning to see the photo as well. "That's you? How old were you?"

"That was taken not long after Papa died..." without another word on the photo, she hung it and moved on to the next. Gramma never came out and said she'd killed her father. "Papa died" was all she ever said. "He was shot through the chest." She was fourteen.

"My daddy wasn't a good man. Your daddy is. Mine wasn't. After my mother's brother took up with your Grampop, we were taken care of." Once I asked her if she was ever afraid of her father. She shrugged and said, "I could hold my own. I kept my sisters out of his reach, and tried as much for the boys, but they spent more time with him."

Gramma'd had three sisters and two young brothers. Within the five or six years after her father's death, all but one brother and one sister had perished, taken by fever, a rattlesnake bite, a tumble from a barn loft. Her sister married a clerk and moved across the country to Boston, and her brother made it to the age of twenty-two before he found himself gutted in a drunken bar brawl.

"I did what I could for them," she said. "My sister moved away and forgot about us, just as well for her."

In time, I'd find an old telegram in Gramma's things stating that her sister had died in childbirth, dated around the year my mother had been born. A letter, buried deeper, stated she'd previously had a healthy boy; and another letter from the sister's husband apologizing for not being able to send for Gramma for the funeral, and for the lack of correspondence over the years, but he assured her both children were fine.

"If you ever go away, write me every week," I said to Isaiah.

"I ain't going nowhere," she said.

"You might, when you're older."

"You might."

I laughed. "I can't, I've gotta stay here and take care of you and Daddy." I tapped her forehead and pulled her close.

"I'll stay if you stay."

The months passed and grew into a year. The hands came and went and soon it was like Mama had never been. It was us and Gramma and Daddy and the hands. There were the books and the cattle and the horses, the dust and the sagebrush and the juniper berries. The winds coming hot and dry through the summer.

With Mama gone, we were free to flourish among the dust of men and all their ways. Some of them, most of them, were God-fearing, their god the dust rising from the cracking earth, the lightning and the thunder, their pistols and knives, bacon frying in fat. God was in the small snippets of scripture left over from childhood, in the winds changing across seasons, the movement of men from one place to the next and back.

For every thing there is a season. I'd been aware of Mama's "monthly headaches." I'd seen her scrubbing the blood out of her under-things. She'd often told me that someday I'd understand and she'd explain it all to me. Instead, it was Gramma, and she held nothing back. She told me about men and women, about bodies and yearnings and the dangers that come with them as well as the pleasures.

She didn't send Isaiah away, and I blushed to think Mama would not approve. When Gramma saw my bashfulness, she told me to buck up. "This is your lot now. And Isaiah might as well know, the way she's growing, it'll be upon her soon enough," Gramma said. "Now you don't let no man take advantage of you, but don't you be ashamed of what God gave you. Loving a man's a spiritual thing in itself. Loving the wrong man's hell. You be the wolf, not the hare." She chucked me under the chin.

"Your girl's a woman now," she told Daddy at dinner.

Daddy, being a man, shifted uncomfortably, staring down at his dinner plate without taking a bite. He grunted and cleared his throat before looking up. "The Indians used to send their girls off into the wilderness by themselves, like a spiritual journey."

"Are you going to make Genesis go off into the hills?" Isaiah asked. Daddy laughed and said no.

Instead, Daddy led us girls and Gramma into the gorge. We rocked on horseback between the rough walls of stone, the scent of evening rising in the shadows cast the mountain. The junipers gave way to pines and willows, a stream trickled, growing stronger as we wound our way higher.

It wasn't our first time into the gorge. We'd accompanied Daddy as he'd chased down a roving calf or horse, but we were warned not to go wandering about up there unaccompanied, and never at night. The walls narrowed in places and the river dropped sharply, a cliff forming the banks. Grampop and his gang used to cache in the mountains through the gorge, where caves dotted the maze of rocky inclines and winter made the passes impassable. Snow was infrequent down in the valley where the ranch sat, only falling in the coldest of winters, but far up into the gorge and the hills it fell thick as anywhere in the rest of the Rockies.

Daddy led us over a gentle rise, away from the river where the ground sloped gently, and we made came in a thicket of pines. Soon a fire was smoking, and Gramma had bacon spitting in a skillet. Daddy had us frolicking around the fire, whooping like ghost-dancers and howling along with the coyotes.

Isaiah slept snuggled next to me just like in our bed, the stars above us twinkling white and milky in the thick blanket of night. Gramma brushed her hand through my hair, and we fell asleep to her low humming.

Then I was the woman of the house. Gramma technically was the matriarch, but I ruled the house for the most part. She left most of the cooking to me, though she'd shell peas and beans and shuck corn. She chopped heads off the chickens and plucked them clean, and I basted and baked them. She started to get silly not long after, though. She grew forgetful and bumped into things. She grabbed for things without reaching them. She very nearly cut her own finger off, unable to judge the distance from the blade to her flesh. In the end, her speech jarred and jumbled until all she could mutter was a slur of incomprehensible noise.

In another year, Gramma was dead.

ISAIAH

S he fell asleep and just keeps on sleeping and none of us
can wake her though she's still warm and breathing. I
touch Gramma, kiss her goodnight. There's something under
her skin, it wriggles and pulls at me, something both hot and
cold moving like a heartbeat or a snake in the grass. She's been
sick a long time; she's had fever for a while, and I've felt the
fever. But this is a different thing. Genesis doesn't seem to feel
it, and the next day Gramma stops breathing and goes cold.

Daddy and Denney make the coffin; Genesis and I wash
and dress her body. I'm eleven today, but there's no cake.
Instead, I see Gramma all unclothed. She isn't real. She's too
thin, skin sagging off her bones, lines along her tummy like
when rain runs over dry dirt. The blood lines in her legs are
swollen and blue.

"They're called veins," Genesis says. She wrings out a cloth
and wipes at Gramma's face.

"Are you going to wash her *everywhere?*" I'm trying not to
look at anything other than Gramma's face and shoulders. I'm
trying not to look at the hair sprouting between her legs, or the

grayish lumpy breasts on her chest. I've never seen a grown woman naked before. I'd never seen a man naked. The only person I've seen naked at all, really, is Genesis, and it's been years. She's got her own breasts now.

"She hasn't bathed in a week. We've got to, for the sake of dignity," Genesis says.

"I don't want to touch..." I say. She isn't real. She's all blue and gray. This isn't my Gramma.

"Then don't," she says. "I'll do it myself. Like I do everything."

"Are you angry?"

She sighs. She sighs just like Mama used to. "No." She's lying. I know she's lying. She keeps wiping away at the body. She's being so gentle. Why? It's dead. It's dead and cold. She's treating Gramma as if she's made of glass. Genesis hasn't cried. I feel like crying, but she doesn't, so I don't. Genesis pauses, Gramma's hand in hers.

"You don't have to be in here if you don't want to."

I don't know where else to go. I don't like being in Gramma's room with this copy of her, but I can't be anywhere else in the house alone. It's too quiet, too empty. I sit. Genesis goes back to wiping. I pick up Gramma's brush, the silver-handled one she got from Grampop. I brush her hair.

Gramma had a dress in her wardrobe. We never even knew about it until now. It's old. We get it on, but it's crooked, too small. It's all wrong. "Back in the bibs then," Genesis says. She smiles a bit. When we're done, the Gramma-doll looks right. Genesis puts her hands on her hips and nods like she's proud. Then she stops looking proud and wraps her arms around herself. "We should send for Mama." But we don't.

Gramma's buried beneath the big tree where all the other graves are. Right next to Grampop. There's little small stones in there as well. Those are the babies Gramma and Mama never had. There's no real preacher because the only one is Leader, and Daddy hates the man. So it's just Genesis reading out from the bible while we stand around the new grave. *A time to live and a time to die.* The men all have their hats in their hands, chins turned down.

All around, there's amens. I say my own "amen" and I toss dirt onto the coffin.

Gramma's died and I've turned eleven, but no one's noticed. Gramma's being buried made us all forget. Life goes on. Though the ranch gets a day of reverence, things still have to get done: stalls mucked, fences mended, dinner made. Genesis spends most of the day sitting in the chair on the porch, staring off into nothing. I stay next to her. She goes in to get supper together and Denney comes up. He's remembered my birthday. He pulls a little wooden animal from his pocket. We're too old for these now, but Genesis says it makes him feel good to make them since he's got no kids of his own. This year it's a beaver. I'll put it in the box with all the others. I tell him thank you and walk up the porch.

Genesis is standing in the door, staring at me, not moving a muscle in her face. "Isaiah..." she looks away from me, tilts up. "I'm so sorry, I—I'll make you a cake tomorrow. I promise."

"It's alright." I say, but I'm trying not to cry. I'm too old for crying. She didn't mean to forget. Gramma didn't mean to die.

I put the beaver in the box with the others. We crawl into bed at night. "Tomorrow, first thing, I'll make that cake, I promise," she says again. She kisses my forehead before she rolls over. I wake up in the middle of the night to hear her sniffling beside me. I pretend to stay asleep, but I snuggle up against her. Neither of us sleep.

GENESIS

Isaiah said she dreamed of a man hanging from a tree. We were sitting on the back porch, me with a Twain in hand—Huckleberry or Tom Sawyer—her with a stick, scratching at the dirt. "Like Judas," she said. I closed my book then but said nothing, wondering if, at any point, she'd ever actually seen a person hanged.

Are these the things she dreams of now? I considered for a moment what that could mean. She'd taken to wandering at night. I'd wake to find her missing and feel prompted to look out the window and see her shadowed figure moving about in the moonlight. Sometimes she'd just stand there staring at the moon. Sometimes she'd move into the darkness beyond my sight, and I was left to wonder. I thought of confronting her about it, but I couldn't. Or I wouldn't. She was always back in the morning, always there curled up beside me when I woke. If she didn't want to tell me, I figured "Alright, fine. I've got other things to worry about."

I had asked her if she wanted to move into Gramma's room.

It wasn't empty. We hadn't touched the room since she died. "No," Isaiah said. "I don't want to sleep in here."

I didn't either, so we stayed together in our bed as always. I spent lots of nights sitting awake in the dark either watching Isaiah asleep in bed or watching her wander beneath the stars, the moon hanging above the black mountain peaks.

We'd stopped going to school. I'd aged out of the little school house. I could have travelled over to the high school in the next town, but it was almost an hour one way in the truck. Daddy had taught me to drive, and no one cared back then if an unlicensed fourteen-year-old girl took her Daddy's wooden-bed Ford. No one else I knew was going—every now and then one or two people from our town would carry on to high school in hopes of continuing on to college and becoming doctors or something.

Most of us stayed doing what our parents before us had always done. We trained in the schools of our fathers and mothers; expertise was handed down like inheritance. It was rare if someone moved far—maybe one in a hundred—and became scholars. The doctor was the son of the previous doctor, and he was sending his own son to medical school, sure he'd come back and take up the mantle when the time came.

Some days I dreamed about leaving, of making my way through the mountains and the world beyond them. "From here to forever, it's much of the same," Grampop had said. He'd gone all over and when Gramma asked him about it he said most of it's all the same, just with flat places and high places in between.

I knew I wasn't going anywhere. Our school attendance had been sporadic at best when Gramma was still alive. She never remembered and we never reminded her. Mama had been the one who made sure we went regularly, but that was before the Community arrived and Jesus took her over.

Everyone in town knew Mama had abandoned us, and they knew Gramma died. When I went into town again I got the looks of pity, as though our lives were more tragic than theirs, as though none of the rest of them were scraping around in the dirt and the dust and the muck of livestock, darning their old socks and patching holes in their children's bibs. Though they gave their condolences and offered their assistance, I knew they went home and whispered their pities to each other. We were just another set of down-and-outs on a long list.

Isaiah was getting too old to be traipsing around in pants— I'd stopped wearing them soon after Mama'd left. But I didn't stop her. Gramma, after all, had spent most her adult life wearing denim overalls like a man. Isaiah was growing dark, dreaming of men hanging from trees, wandering about at night. Her black hair was often matted, tangled. Someone in the general goods store offered to buy us a brush with a look of shaded condescension at Isaiah. I declined the offer and made some excuse about the wind blowing through the truck.

When we got home, I asked if she wanted me to cut her hair so it'd be more manageable. She was mortified by the suggestion and nearly cried. Maybe she thought of Samson, losing his hair and then his strength and his life in consequence. She started brushing it then and I'd braid it in one long plait down her back; a black rope.

Sheriff Burnham came knocking on our door one evening, asking for Daddy. His brother-in-law, who was known for bouts of instability, was missing. The sheriff was requesting Daddy's help to form a search posse. Just as Daddy and the hands swung their legs over saddles, Isaiah called out to them, saying she knew where he was.

"You've seen him?" I said, my heart suddenly pounding. Though we'd never heard of him getting violent, I worried about her stumbling upon him alone in her night-time escapades. I'd read stories of girls getting lost in the woods and eaten, of wanderers stranded in the mountains.

"No," Isaiah said. "Yes."

"Which is it, girl?" Burnham said.

I knew, right then. She'd seen the man in the tree, but not with her eyes. She looked at me, hoping I'd be able to explain, but I couldn't.

"I just know where he is," she said. We'd heard of crazy people, read about visions and prophets that always ended in death and scorn.

"You're sure?" Daddy said. Isaiah nodded. The grown men looked at each other, and at her, raising eyebrows and shrugging shoulders, silently deciding between themselves whether or not to believe her. But Isaiah with her deep black eyes stood with her shoulders back, steady. Daddy nodded and pulled her up in the saddle. They went off into the evening and night fell. I sat on the porch, waiting. They came back in the dark. Isaiah had been right. They'd found him up in the hills, strung from a tree. Isaiah admitted she dreamed it.

I suppose every town needs their mystic, their legend. "Did you hear? She said she dreamed it up!" everyone said to each other. "Never would have found him if it wasn't for her!"

Three weeks later, playing piggy-back with Isaiah the Kid, she suddenly shouted to be put down, and refused to touch him again. She ran inside and to bed, her face in her pillow. He died two days later; the whispers really started then. The stories spread quickly, flowing fast like a spring river, about the girl and her dreams, about her brushes with Death. "Do you know when I'll die?" people stopped us in town to ask. Or, "I know my wife is dying, can you ask Death not to take her?" or "Touch my fevered child, touch his rashy skin, his measles, please, tell me he'll live."

I stopped taking Isaiah to town with me, but it didn't stop

the gawking or the whispering, or the requests that she be brought to touch the hand of a feverish child. I did not want her touching death; I did not want her catching it and bringing it home. But she obliged the requests, because she saw how it made people feel; somehow it calmed to know death was there or not. She never caught anything, and she never saw them die. They sent her home before she had to witness it herself. None of us knew what it meant, Isaiah's sense. It didn't seem she could do anything about it. She couldn't stop death; she couldn't pinpoint it to an exact moment. None of us can. We all know it's coming. She just knows it's coming sooner.

And then Mama was back.

ISAIAH

Daddy and Denney and me come in from the pastures with Biscuit to find Genesis standing at the bottom of the porch steps looking worried. "Daddy," she says. "She's back."

Before I can ask who, Mama shows up in the doorway. Her hair's pulled back tight. She'd always tied her hair back, but not so tight. Usually bits would be loose around her face like feathers. *Flyaways*, Genesis calls them. But now Mama's standing here with her hair pulled back tight and wearing a long blue dress.

"Addie," Daddy says, tipping his chin. He steps right past her into the kitchen, so he can wash his hands. Denney tips his hat to Mama then whistles for Biscuit to follow and they go back to the bunkhouse. Daddy sits in his chair and puts his hat on the table. He looks at Mama in her long blue dress. "I suppose this is just a visit? Or are you here to take the ranch back?"

Mama doesn't move, just turns to face Daddy at the table. "The ranch is practically yours," she says. I haven't heard her voice in two years. I haven't thought of Mama's voice much. She speaks tight, like she's going to get angry at any moment. "I won't take the ranch from you," Mama says.

"It's not you I'm worried about," says Daddy.

Mama sucks air through her teeth. "I'll get the papers written up and sign it all over to you. I've no need of it."

"You got something else to ask me?"

Mama doesn't answer him. She looks at me instead. "You've gotten tall," she says. That's not really true. I haven't gotten much taller since she left. Genesis has only had to let down my hems once. She turns to Genesis. "You've become quite the young woman." Genesis says nothing.

"Girls, why don't you go on ahead and get supper on the table," says Daddy. "Addie, you joining us?" Mama nods and Daddy kicks out the chair next to him. Genesis and I get supper on the table. I get plates and knives and forks; she gets the chicken and potatoes and biscuits.

We're all silent as we eat. Genesis stares down at her plate and pushes the food around.

"What are you doing here, Addie?" Daddy finally asks as he wipes his own empty plate with a biscuit.

Mama puts down her fork and straightens her back. "The girls are growing up."

Daddy pushes his empty plate and sits back, folding his hands over his belly. "So you've seen."

"And Ma's gone."

Genesis scoffs and pushes her own plate away. "So you did hear?" She crosses her arms. "Your own mother died and you wouldn't even come back to see her buried? Or to see her on her deathbed?"

Mama's eyes get hard on Genesis. Genesis is angry. I guess I'm a little angry too. Genesis is right, Mama wouldn't come to

Gramma's funeral. It's not like she was on the other side of the country, just on the other side of town. But we hadn't invited her. Do people need to be invited to their own mother's funeral? Maybe she hated Gramma so much she didn't care. They did used to argue when Mama was still with us. If Mama had died would the Community let us go to see her buried?

"Your mother was taken care of and laid to rest beside your Pop," says Daddy. "And now the ranch is yours in the state of law."

"I told you I don't want the ranch. I'll even go sign the papers tomorrow."

"What is it you're here for then?"

"The girls."

Daddy sits up straight, puts his hands on the table. Genesis starts swinging her head. "Addie," Daddy says softly.

"They're growing up, and Ma's gone. They're out here alone surrounded by men."

"What's wrong with that?" I speak up. But no one answers me. Daddy's looking at Genesis in a way I've never seen before. Like he's working out a puzzle, or a little bit afraid.

"But Denney and I..." Daddy shakes his head. "The men are all good. The girls are still young. We can keep an eye on them..." He sighs and sits back in his chair.

"You can't keep them all in check," Mama says. "It only takes one bad egg. And the girls won't be too young here in a little while. Genesis is almost a full-grown woman."

I've seen the looks some of the young hands give Genesis. They look at me like a little sister. They look at Genesis like a woman. Sometimes they get silly around her. But they've never done more than look at her as she walks by. If I've seen it, Daddy probably has, too. "Why can't you just come back?" I say to Mama.

"I belong with the Community," Mama says. "And you girls belong with me."

"Daddy, you can't let her take us!" Genesis yells. "I can take care of myself—and Isaiah. I have so far. You've taught us how to shoot, we've learned how to handle a blade—Mama, you can't just come in here expecting us to just come along with you because you suddenly want to play mother again! You don't really even care about us--"

"Genesis!" Mama snaps. She takes a deep breath and straightens herself. "You don't understand, you're just a girl."

"I understand you're crazy." Mama and Genesis stare at each other.

"Addie..." Daddy tries to say again. "This is the only home the girls have ever known."

"It doesn't have to be," Mama says, her eyes set on Daddy's. "The ranch can be yours. Tomorrow."

Daddy stands, picks up his hat and makes for the door. "You sign those damn papers first thing tomorrow." He twists his hat in his hands before he puts it on his head. He doesn't look at us. He slams the door behind him.

Mama leaves when she's done eating. "All you girls need to pack is underwear," she says. "I'll be back for you before lunch."

Genesis tells me to bathe and when I finish, I find her sitting on the bed, staring at a bunch of books spread out on the floor. "What are you doing?" Genesis hates leaving stuff in the middle of the floor. She snaps at me whenever I do it.

"Deciding which ones to sneak into the Community."

"You don't think they'll have books there?"

Genesis snorts. "Don't you remember when Mama came home and burned all those books? She got that idea from *them*."

"Oh," I sit beside her. There's *Huckleberry Finn* and *The Jungle Book* on the floor. She's read these both to me. But there's other kinds of books, too, books too grown-up for me—*A Passage to India, Siddhartha, Mansfield Park.* I point my toe at one with a pretty, dark blue cover. *The Painted Veil.* "How about this one?" She nods and puts it in her lap. "What's it about?"

She shrugs. "A woman having an affair in China."

"With a Chinaman?"

She picks up *The Jungle Book.* "No. But her husband takes her to some village and then she falls in love with him."

"Why'd she marry him in the first place?"

"To escape." I don't catch the name of the third book she chooses. "Alright, that's it."

"Only three?"

"I'll have to be able to hide them."

"What about all the rest?"

She scowls at the books left on the floor. "They'll wait for me here."

"How long?"

She wraps a book in a long ivory nightgown. "Until I can forgive Daddy."

"Forgive him for what?"

"What do you want to sneak in?"

I look around the room. There isn't much, just our bed and a chair, a wardrobe and a bedside table with a lamp. There's not even a mirror. Mama had been the only one with a mirror and it's still in Daddy's room. The knife Isaiah the Kid gave me is on our bedside table. "This?" I say.

"Sure."

I get on my hands and knees and reach under the bed. There's a couple boxes there. One's got a couple old dolls we don't play with anymore. Another box is baby clothes, and another is just mine, where I've kept all of Denney's carvings. I pull out the beaver he made for my birthday. And the wolf—the one he made when I was five. Genesis wraps my trinkets in some of my clean underwear and sticks everything neatly into a sack. She stacks all the rest of the books on the chair and starts undressing for bed.

In the morning, Daddy doesn't come in for breakfast, and he's not around when a truck comes up the road, dust trailing behind it. Denney's on the front porch. "Where's Daddy?" I ask him. His eyes follow the truck.

"He went up to the hills," he grunts. Genesis grunts as well with her arms crossed. She leans against one of the posts. All of us watch the truck roll up. Mama's in the passenger seat. Some man I don't know is driving, and the Preacher's wife is between them. The two women come out.

The Preacher's wife looks us all up and down, her thin mouth tight. Denney tips his hat to her but she just scowls back. Mama clears her throat. "Well, if you girls are ready."

Genesis unties her apron and goes inside. She comes back out with the sack we packed last night. She pats Denney's arm before she climbs into the back of the truck. Denney hugs me tight and whispers, "Come back whenever you can." He smells like sawdust and dry sweat and hay.

"Don't worry," I say. "We won't be gone long." This is our home, this is where we live. Mama can't mean to make us leave it forever. She'll see.

Mama clears her throat again and Denney lets me go. I scratch Biscuit's ears, and I climb up beside Genesis. The hands are gathering around the house, watching us leave.

We bump along in the dust all the way through town and back out on a gravelly country road. We turn off the main road and rumble along another long, empty dirt road hardly wider than the wheels of the truck. Finally, in the distance, gray-brown buildings grow out of the sagebrush. There's a gate across the road; two boys hardly older than Genesis stand on either side. They stare at Genesis and me as we pass. Genesis takes my hand, and we come to a stop in front of a big, plain church with a tall, brown steeple.

PART II: THE COMMUNITY

FALL 1932-SPRING 1933

GENESIS

It would be years before I understood why Daddy let us go, why he didn't fight for us to stay. I didn't fight Mama taking us because Daddy didn't fight for us to stay. Daddy was protecting our inheritance. If Mama took the ranch, the Community surely would have taken it; it was profitable with direct access to the gorge—where one can easily cache contraband and hideout from authorities. This, though, I wouldn't understand until years later. All I knew then was the discomfort of being taken into a communal bathroom, our clothes stripped from us and replaced with rough, homespun dresses with high collars and long sleeves like all the other girls and women in the Community.

My sack was taken from me. I tried at first to cling on to it, but in fear it would raise suspicion, I let it be taken. "It's just underwear. Our mother said that's all we needed to bring." I said, "And shoes," I added as an explanation for the weight. The preacher's daughter was among the women tasked with "communicating" us—the same one who helped lock us in the pantry three years before. She took the sack and opened it. My heart

59

fell when she put her hand inside to ruffle around the contents. But she nodded without comment and set the sack aside. Her face remained as blank as mine, though I knew she'd felt the books.

The women brushed our hair with rough strokes and braided it tight. Our mother had promptly disappeared when we'd arrived, telling us that Leader's wife and some of the other sisters would help settle us. Leader's wife took to laying out the rules for us. She was just as sour-faced as the last time we'd seen her, though my memory hadn't retained her being so pale and thin. "No man should see your hair loose," she said. "And it shall not ever be cut. Second to purity, it is the prime virtue of the woman."

My hair I'd kept long enough to tie back, but short enough not to get in the way. Isaiah hadn't cut her hair since before our mother left us. Her hair fell down her back like a sleek black snake whose tail brushed her bottom. "Isaiah's still a child," I said. The women all paused with breaths held. The one at my hair—a Sister Philippa—tutted. Leader's wife's mouth somehow drew tighter and thinner.

"She's old enough. And do not address your elders unless you have been spoken to first. It's uncomely for a young lady to speak out of turn." She carried on with her commandments. Among her list of contraband, as to be expected, were books, music, talk of topics deemed inappropriate, insubordination, ribbons, jewelry or any sort of "worldly finery" that could potentially distract the soul from constant heaven-ward thought.

I noticed Isaiah's eyes glaze over as she watched the old lady's lips move. I knew she'd already decided she didn't like the woman. I knew, too, that Leader's wife would find Isaiah a bane. The woman already had made her mind up about us, and we would hold that against her, living up to her opinion both with purpose and without. At last, she motioned to Judith, the daughter, to take us away.

Judith led us from the women's "washhouse" to a large, lodge-like building with a single door and no windows. The door opened to a wide hallway lined with flat white doors. "This is the women and children's house." Women meant women without husbands. Married couples got their own small, cabin-like houses scattered around the commune. "As Isaiah is still a child, she'll sleep here," she led us through the first door on the right.

The room beyond was large and open, small beds lined the bare, white-washed walls. The only colors were the drab gray-blues and faded greens of the quilts, with perhaps a small toy here or there. I thought of the workhouses in Dickens, of *Jane Eyre*. "We won't be staying together? We've never slept in separate beds...what about our mother?"

Judith's face held stern, but her words were soft and apologetic. "This is where the children sleep. When Isaiah is no longer a child, she can move into the girls-only dormitory."

Leader's tow headed son came in behind us. He'd grown since the last we'd seen him, but he still looked like a child, and his face held the look of perpetual disgust. Isaiah matched him pound-for-pound and inch-for-inch. "Reuben, you remember Sister Adelaide's daughters."

"Yeah," he scowled at Isaiah. "I remember. You punched me in the face."

"I'll do it again if you—" Isaiah began. I laid my fingers on Isaiah's arm, a warning to keep herself in check as Judith's eyebrows rose.

But Reuben deflected Isaiah's threat. "I'm too old for pinching and kicking anymore. Come on," he said. "There's a bed free by mine since Malachi's moved up." Isaiah followed him to the far end of the room.

"She'll be fine," Judith said. She turned and led me all the way down the hall, around the corner and to the final door. There were fewer beds here, only nine, placed precisely three feet apart so they filled the whole room, as if the room was built around the beds with wardrobes at the feet. A door centered the opposite wall, the wardrobe beside it flush against the jamb. "You'll rarely be here to do anything other than sleep. *Idle minds are the Devil's playground*," she said with mockery in her voice. "There are only about seven of you at the moment. There aren't many young women here to begin with, and then they tend to get married off around sixteen or seventeen."

Judith had been at least my age when they'd first arrived, but I spied no ring on her finger. "Which bed is yours?"

"My sisters and I sleep in Mother's house." She took keys from her pocket—I noted the lack of pockets in my own dress—and unlocked the opposite door, pulling out a set of bed sheets and two quilts. Blue and gray. Gray and blue. I felt I would never see any other color in my time there. I took the bed there by the linen closet, across from the small fireplace. Judith assisted me with the linens. It was a bed built for one, hardly more than a cot.

The church bell rang outside. I calculated this room was nearest to the chapel. "That's lunch," Judith said. "Whatever you've got stashed in there, you'd better hide it quick." She nodded to my sack. I stumbled for an explanation or excuse. "Everyone's got something. They pretend they don't, but they do. If we turned this room upside down we'd find hidden dime-novels and lipstick and ribbons, maybe even a Parisian post-card. But they'll snoop through your things and if they find anything, they'll give it up."

"Where?" I said, pulling my books from my bag.

She pointed to the side of the wardrobe against the wall. "No one ever thinks to look there. Or even thinks to hide anything there. There are only three beds in the room that have the wardrobe against the wall."

The gap was just wide enough. Judith watched longingly as I pushed the books in one-by one. "You locked us in a pantry once," I said when we were done.

"I know," she said with a shrug. She would become the only one who didn't scorn me. Each morning, we young ladies were up at dawn, herded to the kitchen, prayed with hands held and shifted to various breakfast-making tasks: frying sausage, flipping pancakes, kneading biscuits.

The older, single women rotated duties with us. My mother never did. Married women were responsible for their own allotted homes and weren't tasked with much other than childbearing. All their laundry came to us, all their mending. They weren't forbidden to come help us, to group with the other women, but they didn't. Mama wasn't one of *them*, either. Mama just seemed to disappear most of the day.

Judith was never directly relegated to anything like the rest of us, but she always chose to partner up with me, whispering and gossiping over the mundane tasks we were assigned; cooking, or laundering, polishing, or stitching. As we'd trudge to the mess kitchens to make breakfast, we passed by the young men on their way to milk the cows. The boys spouted remarks to me on the off chances I passed near them. "You Sister Adelaide's girl? Heard you were brought up by a whore and a scoundrel. We'll sure turn you right." Then they'd sneer and leer. To these remarks, I never responded.

"They're boys. Children. The only girls they ever see are their sisters and cousins—the same girls they've been seeing their whole lives." Judith would say. "For all the purity the mothers preach, men are still men."

At first, the other girls glanced at me and whispered. But when they did speak to me, it was scornful. "We're surprised you even know *how* to cook, or sew or clean or even brush your hair," they'd murmur. Judith's two younger sisters were the ringleaders. "Well you don't *look* like a heathen," they'd say. "But we heard you'd grown up in the proximity of only men, like some sort of brothel."

Men don't live in brothels, I wanted to say. "We had our grandmother," I said.

"Hardly," said Judith's sister Jerusha. "She was a whore in men's clothing. Harlots breed harlots." The other girls snickered.

"Well, let him without sin cast the first stone." I turned back to the garments in the steaming water, determined not to let my own anger rise to her provocation. I could quote the Bible with the rest of them, perhaps even better. The verses my mother had made us copy down were etched into the fabric of my memory, ready to call up when I wanted—and even when I didn't.

"We aren't tempted by sin here," came the reply.

And before I could stop my tongue, my thoughts escaped. "Because none of you are tempting." Judith laughed, but I knew the girls would not forget. And two days later, Leader's wife and Sister Philippa approached me before breakfast, before I'd even changed out of my nightgown. Sister Philippa held a candlestick; the commune had generators and electric lights in every room, thus, the candlestick raised my suspicions.

"Come," Leader's wife said. They never called me by name. The other girls watched with inconspicuous smirks. I had wanted to stay in the background as much as possible, but I swallowed my "insubordination" and followed. Down the hall, to a small room hardly larger than a closet, all bare except for a rough cross on the wall and a Bible on a low podium, a broomstick on the floor below it.

Sister Philippa lit the candle, and they ushered me in and

closed the door. We were left in the orbed orange glow of the single flame. "You have been making lewd comments to the other girls, you hinted at your *experiences*, and lauded them like some sort of common whore," said Leader's wife. I bit my tongue against my rebuttals. "We will not allow you to taint the purity of our community." She gave an exaggerated sigh. "But even sinners can be saved. In time, we will get your soul cleansed, despite your discrepancies."

I could hold my tongue no longer. "I've never told of any such experiences, because I have none to tell."

"You're saying my daughters are liars?"

"Lies have been told, but not by me," I said.

"Kneel." I did, my knees on the hard, rough floor, before the bible altar. "On the stick," Leader's wife said. I glared at her, but I shifted forward until my knees rested on the broomstick. "Sister Philippa will remain with you until you've completed." She left the room. Philippa stayed in the corner with her candle. I could already feel the ache in my knees.

"Proverbs," said Sister Philippa. "Aloud."

The fear of the Lord is the beginning of knowledge, but fools despise wisdom and instruction ...

I could barely stand fifteen chapters later, my knees stiff and bruised, my throat rough and dry. I had been denied breakfast and any light brighter than a single candle. Judith showed me how to wrap my knees so the aching abated. I vowed I'd never open another bible once I got out.

ISAIAH

In the mornings, we get up and wash our faces and dress for the day. Us older kids, like me and Reuben, are supposed to help the younger ones. Everyone over the age of five has to sleep in the dormitories—except for Leader's kids. Reuben could live in his mama's house if he wanted, but he says he'd rather be with the other kids. His sisters don't get a choice, Judith told us so.

At first, I wasn't so sure about Judith because I thought she was as mean as her mama. But then Genesis said she helped hide the stuff we brought. I get to keep my wooden animals in the trunk at the foot of my bed. Genesis said she'd better keep the knife for now and not let anyone know we've got it.

I didn't think I'd like Reuben either—and sometimes he makes me angry because he teases me or gets upset suddenly and calls me stupid because I can't do something right. But he showed me how things go around here. I'd never made a bed before, at least not alone. Genesis always made sure it was done. Reuben said I was stupid because I couldn't get the wrinkles out of the blanket.

I told him to shut up or I'd punch him in his stupid mouth and split his lip. He said he'd cut off my hair if I did. But then he laughed and helped me when the Sisters' backs were turned. And then he pulled my braid and laughed again. The Sisters don't let anyone help me. They just tut their tongues and mumble about how I was brought up by animals. I tried to speak up once and tell them to shut up about my Gramma and Daddy, but Reuben shook his head so hard I thought his eyes would fly out.

"They'll slap you right across the face if you talk back," he whispered later. "Mother says you need to have the heathen beaten out of you."

The old ladies always ask me questions I don't know the answers to in front of everyone. "See, children, this is what happens when you grow up without the discipline of the Lord," they say when I don't know how many seals there are in Revelations, or what happened to the harlot Jezebel. Sometimes the other kids laugh. Sometimes they look sad and just nod along. Most of the kids don't bother me, though. Reuben says they're scared of me because they believe I'm bad since I came from outside. At first, no one but Reuben would talk to me, but then the others started to when they saw I could do just as good as them at making my bed and doing the chores.

We eat breakfast in the big dining hall with rows of tables and benches. Genesis and Judith and the other young women usually have to get up real early to help get breakfast made for everyone, and Mama sits with all the other unmarried mamas at the head table. Married ladies get their own houses with their husbands and babies. When the babies turn five, they move into the dormitory with the rest of us. The unmarried ladies get their own rooms. The ones with children get dining tables in their room to have supper with their kids every night but Sunday or whenever Leader orders a communal supper.

I don't see Genesis much. The young ladies are always kept busy. Us kids have our own duties, too, but not as many. We clean off the tables at the end of meals, gather laundry from all over the dormitories, sometimes we help the muck stalls or milk cows or help keep the little ones out of trouble. We just get told what to do and where to go, and if there's nothing for us, we're kept inside to sing and learn bible stories.

Genesis is always sewing or cooking or washing. I don't know what Mama does all day. She doesn't have to help with the children like some of the other ladies, she doesn't cook or do laundry. I asked her once at supper what she does. We didn't do much talking.

"I help in the chapel," Mama said. She seemed proud of herself.

"What do you do?"

Mama sucked air and sat real straight. "I help Leader prepare for worship services."

I still don't know what she does exactly. She always leads the hymns, but all she does is wave her arm around, which doesn't seem like it would take too much time to learn to do.

On Sundays, it feels like we spend all day at church. There's sermon, then breakfast, then Sunday school. We have lunch and get an hour for "reflection"—that's mostly just being quiet and not being allowed to go anywhere outside the dormitory. Then Leader gives another sermon before we have supper in the dining hall. Leader's family sits at the head table. Then we have Benediction, which is just another month's worth of praying out loud and praising and singing and damning Babylon. Reuben and me usually slip out of Benediction because everyone's so fired up they don't notice we're gone.

We're not the only ones who do it. I know Reuben's brother Benjamin usually takes Brenda Peters outside and kisses her. We saw them once, but Reuben said we should leave before Benjamin saw us or he'd beat us. Or he'd tell on us for leaving Benediction and the old ladies would beat us.

I try to stay out of trouble—Mama and Genesis have both warned me to. But sometimes I just get so upset. In the morning when we're all getting up and dressed and making our bed, one of us kids that can read is chosen to read from the bible.

The bible they've got is big and floppy. I stand at the end of the room and Sister Agatha hands it to me. The page is open to the first chapter of second John, where we left off the day before. Before I get a good grip on it, Sister Agatha lets go and it tips. I try to catch it, but it's too heavy on one side. Before it even hits the floor, Sister Agatha's hand swings to my face. "How dare you drop the word of the Lord!" she shouts at me.

My face burns. The heat goes down my neck and up over my scalp. "It's heavy!" I try to say. But she doesn't listen or doesn't even hear.

"You've got the devil in you for sure, child! No respect for the Lord, can't even hold a bible without it trying to leap away from you—"

I can't stop myself. "Oh, why don't you go to hell?" Everyone in the room gasps. I brace myself for another slap. Let her beat me. Instead, she grips my wrist real hard and pulls me across the room, rambling on about my sure damnation. She pulls me into the room with a bible and a broomstick and pushes me to the floor. I think she's going to use the broomstick to beat me. She twists my braid around in her fist, pulling hard on my scalp.

"Knees on the stick." I move, just wanting her to let go of my hair. She does. "Isaiah," she says.

At first, I think she's saying my name. None of the old ladies ever call me by name. To them I'm only ever "child," "girl," or just "you." I look down at the bible and realize she's talking about the Book of Isaiah. She's got a hard smile, like she's just told a mean joke.

Afraid she'll pull my hair again, I turn to Isaiah. The last person sent here—most likely one of the boys—finished off at the seventh chapter of Romans: *oh wretched man that I am!* I get to Isaiah, the vision of Isaiah, son of Amos.

"Aloud." Sister Agatha says. In her hands she's got a willow switch, where she got it from, I don't know. Probably had it hidden under her dress.

"*Oh sinful nation,*" I read on. I don't know all the words and have to read slowly on some of them. "*A people laden with* ini—*iniquity, a seed of evil...doers, children that are* cor —*corrupters. They have* forsack—*forsaken the Lord.*" I stop and look up. "How long do I have to read?"

The willow switch comes down on the little stand. I'll read forever, then. I take a deep breath and keep going. Even when my stomach rumbles, she doesn't tell me to stop. My mouth goes dry. I think she must surely be hungry too, but she doesn't leave the room. My head starts to feel heavy, my knees and hips and back ache. The room is too hot and too dark. My eyes blur and my tongue gets thick. I start to tip, and Sister Agatha brings her switch down on my knuckles. By chapter twenty-six, I think my throat will crumble.

At chapter fifty, I can barely read a word without licking my lips and I start to cough on the dry spot in my throat. I cough so hard I can't stop and at last she says, "Enough." I fall over onto the floor and curl up with my arms around my knees, trying to stop the coughing. Sister Agatha says nothing.

She opens the door and leaves me on the floor. It's Mama who comes in with a cup of water. I hate her and I don't want her water, but I'm so thirsty I take it and drink it in one go, throw the cup across the room and curl back up on the floor. She doesn't even look a bit sorry.

"Isaiah, you've got to get up," she says. "There are things to be done." I curl away from her reaching fingers. She grabs me anyway and pulls me into sitting. I pull my arm away. "You've done this to yourself, you know, the way you've behaved." She sucks air. She is Jezebel and Judas and all the evil people in between. She reaches out to me again. "Come, we'll get you dressed and—"

I slap her hands away and stand on my own. My knees creak and my legs shake. She tries to reach out again and steady me. I don't want her to touch me. And I want her to hold me and tell me she's sorry and this was all a mistake, and she'll take us back to the ranch and things will go back to like they were before. I can feel the tears coming. But I don't want Mama to see, I don't want any of them to see. Mama watches me but doesn't follow.

I have to hold on to the walls as I walk. Reuben's sitting on my bed in the empty dormitory, digging his fingers into the flesh of his arm, making long red scrapes. He jumps up when he hears me shuffling in, my legs still wobbly and hurting. He's got blood under his fingernails.

"I knew it, I knew they would—here," he helps me sit down. "I tried to warn you. Maybe you do have the Devil in you—why would you say that to her?" He's talking fast, twisting his shirt sleeve tight on his arm.

"Why did she hit me?" I take a deep breath. "Why do they all hate me so much?" And then I cry and I can't stop. Reuben sits down next to me and puts his arm around my shoulders.

"I don't hate you."

"Sometimes you act like it," I say. "Sometimes you're really mean to me." Just two days ago he twisted my arm until the skin burned like a rash, and he'd laughed about it. Sometimes he yells at me for no reason because I've asked him a question or suggested doing something.

"I don't mean to be," he says. "Sometimes I can't help it."

I wipe my snot with the back of my hand. "Sometimes I can't help it, either. I just get so angry and they're unfair. When Little Mary peed her bed last week, all they did was slap the back of her hand. It wasn't even my fault the bible fell...maybe I am like those people with the demons inside them."

He pats me on the back. "Maybe you've just gotta try harder to overcome them. Maybe that's why your Mama brought you here, so we can help you get the demons out." I decide I'm done crying and wipe my nose one last time. "Hey, my sister, she can make your knees feel a little better. She sort of rubs them and then ties cloth around them. She doesn't hate you, she'll help."

At supper I don't say a word to Mama. Genesis looks tired. So tired. She doesn't even try to argue with Mama about why we're here. Mama eats like normal. She pauses for a second and presses her napkin to her lips and gives a little hiccup. She puts her fork down. "Isaiah," she says. I stare at my plate. "You really must remember you're not on the ranch anymore. I'm mortified by what you said to Sister Agatha, and you deserved your punishment. You must also apologize to her, and to all the other children and Sisters." Genesis seems to wake up a bit. Her forehead wrinkles and she pulls her mouth tight.

"We are dwelling with God now," Mama says. "And such behavior will not be tolerated. Humility, obedience. No belligerence, no cursing. I hope you will take the pain you're feeling and turn to God, ask for his forgiveness and salvation."

Mama looks like she's going to keep talking but Genesis just says, "Mama" and she goes quiet. At last, the church bell rings. Genesis and I start to stand up, but Mama puts her hands on ours.

"I just want what's best for you girls, for your salvation. It won't come easy, but this is for your own good."

Genesis pulls her hand back. "Mama, you know nothing about us." She takes my hand and pulls me away. In the hall, she holds me tight. "We're going home, just remember that. We're not meant for this place. We're not here forever." She lets me go and disappears around the corner.

I wake up late in the night. Everyone is asleep. I can hear them breathing. I'm wide awake. It happens a lot. Ever since we got to the Community, I've just stayed in bed until I fell asleep again. But I'm too riled up. I sit up. There's no windows, but there's a small lamp always kept on at the end of the room, in case the little kids get scared of the dark or has to pee in the night. One of the old ladies usually sits outside the door for a while until they're sure everyone is asleep.

I move as quiet as I can across the room and open the door real slow. It barely creaks. No one's in the hall. The lights are always on out here. I know the way to Genesis's room. Her room is dark, but there are cracks in the corners of the ceiling and night light peeks through. I can find her.

"Isaiah?" she whispers. She's been lying awake too. She shifts and I lay beside her. She pulls me close and we barely fit in the bed together. She's warm and smells like soap and onions.

"I hate it here."

"I know." She presses her face into my hair.

"Do you think I've got the Devil in me? Reuben said that might be why Mama brought us here."

"Hush," she says. "That's all nonsense. There's nothing wrong with you. They're all crazy here." She squeezes me.

"Don't you let them break you. They've got nothing on us. Don't you try and become one of them. You never will be; you weren't meant to be."

We lay quiet for a minute. Then she asks, "What did you do that got you into trouble?"

"I told Sister Agatha to go to hell. She slapped me for dropping the bible."

I can hear her smiling. "You give 'em hell. Gramma would be proud."

"I miss you." She says she misses me too. We fall asleep like we used to. In the morning Sister Agatha and Sister Philippa are staring down at us.

"Sneaking around in the night?" says Sister Agatha. And then both of us are kneeling over broomsticks again.

GENESIS

Judith was the favored daughter. Leader let her roam around the Community. She had keys to every lock, and had more freedom than any other women, including her own mother. Her mother was meant to be a beacon of perfect obedience, expected to look the other way at the women her husband made eyes at. She often took to bed with migraines leaving Judith to keep the house in order. Judith generally did what was asked of her and rarely questioned it. I could not understand why, though, because, when alone, she would divulge her displeasures.

She mumbled about how her father just assumed she'd do his bidding, "Like a lap dog," she said, even as she did the things he asked of her. "He disregards my mother," she'd say, though not particularly fond of her mother to begin with. "She's a coward, she lets him..." she waved her hand dismissively "—do what he will, and we all have to listen to her complain about it when he's not around."

Her mother took her displeasure out on the children. "We're not good enough, we're never good enough," she said.

"We slouch, or we're too skinny, too fat, too grimacing." To her father, his children were emblems of his virility and prestige; though some of them were plain, none of them were ugly or sickly, but all were well-fed, and well-kept; even those who were not openly claimed by him, as if to say *Look at me, look how well I can provide.*

I asked Judith why she didn't leave. She gave a short, derisive laugh. "I don't know anything about out there. I've never even read a book that wasn't approved by Mother." She lowered her sewing to her lap. "My oldest brother Adam left. He's just about as far as you can get in this country. Mother and Father don't speak about him anymore. Mother burns all his letters without opening them. If I go, it will be the same. I wouldn't even know where to go or how to get there. So I'll stay here with Mother and Father."

She stayed because she was certain she had more freedoms granted her as the favored daughter than she would have as a single woman without financial support anywhere else. She had been convinced she could not make it in the world alone. Here, she didn't need money; she only had to ask her father for something (which was never much), and he gave it as long as she kept it secreted in her room.

There were, though, things he would not grant. She indicated her sisters across the room. "They assume we'll all be married off and get our own cabins here in the Community. But that will never happen. Father won't ever allow any of us to get married or leave home—not with his blessing anyway." She continued her sewing. "It's just as well though, we're related to most of the marriageable men around here anyway, brothers, cousins. Either Father would have to bring in converts or allow us to marry outside. But no man will ever win Father's approval. He's practically said so himself." She deepened her voice in imitation of her father. "'When the right man comes along, I will know.' But when one came along I thought he'd willingly hand me off to, Father convinced him to marry Sarah Guthrie, now Carter."

Sarah Carter was about Judith's age, a sallow girl with flighty eyes, and had three babies with her husband William. He was a fine-looking young man with a kind face. He seemed a quiet, but devout, man. Judith had not been in love with him; she had believed they could be content, though. She had, after all, been raised to believe she was meant to be married and bring up children in the Lord under the tutelage of the Community.

Only later would I learn the real reason Leader could not marry off his daughters; it was too risky to let a man into his family who could reveal his secrets. Leader did not trust men. Women, on the other hand, he could charm with small secrets and frippery. He'd whisper slyly and say not to tell anyone else and offer them small sips of hidden gin, a set of ribbons, favoritism for their children. And the women held these secrets, fluffed up with the trust he'd placed in them, and they'd give him things in return, all their gossip, their wealth, their children.

"Maybe he'll marry off Jerusha," Judith continued. "If only to appease Mother." Judith's face set, her gaze to nowhere. She sat stone still for a moment, as though deliberating within herself over the next words on her tongue. "She's not Mother's daughter."

"But she lives in your house," I said. I thought perhaps she meant Jerusha had been a foundling of sorts. But in my gut, I knew what she was implying. It was only then that I realized nearly half of Leader's ten children—four daughters and six sons including the one who left—were roughly within three or four years of my age. I had assumed they had been born in rapid succession. I hadn't considered the sheer number of them would have been impossible even for the most fertile of women. "None of your brothers are twins, are they?"

Judith shook her head. "Some of them could very well be, but no. Mother's only borne five children: Adam, me, Matthias, Ruth, and Reuben. The others were left on our doorsteps by other women. And every time a new one showed up, we left town." Judith explained. Her expression became thoughtful. "Benjamin's mother wasn't much older than you when she showed up at the door with him. She had an angry older woman with her, some lady who was keeping her, I can't remember if she was a relative or not. I think the girl was an orphan."

My face must have fallen into a look of horror. "Oh, she certainly looked older than her age. I suppose Father wasn't aware of her real age. She was very obviously young, but looked old enough. There's never been another so young show up at our door with a baby." Her words offered me little comfort. What she was telling me sounded like town gossip, things the old biddies say to each other on their porches in the heat of the summer. But she was his own daughter, if anyone knew truths about the man, surely it would be his own daughter, a daughter discontent, yet not willing to give up the comfort of her family.

"Your mother..." was all I could manage to say.

"She's a godly woman. All of them who leave a child on our doorstep, she takes without question. Maybe she has words with Father about it, but never in front of us. Those boys look so much like Father, there'd be no chance in denying them, anyway. Except for Reuben, don't know where that little tow-headed bastard came from. I love that child, you know, but he's one little son of a bitch."

"Do you mean your mother...?"

"Mother? Heavens no! I told you she's a godly woman. Reuben is definitely Father's son, he's just the only one who took after Mother. She lost one between Ruth and him, and it was so bad she thought she'd never have another. Now she favors him. Like he's her gift from God for caring for all the bastard children she's taken in over the years. She lets Father have his say over all of us but Reuben. He's never been punished a day in his life. Hardly even reprimanded. And it shows. He's got...*oddities* about him."

Isaiah seemed to get along with him well enough, but I had noticed that other children tended to keep their distance from him. He was the youngest of the Leader's legitimate children, but there was another younger, a girl about eight. "Elizabeth," I said. "Was she the last?" I felt hope and dread in asking that question. Hope that Leader's wife had finally managed to rein him.

"She's the last one we took in," said Judith. "She wasn't even a baby. She was already walking and talking. Her mother was part of our last congregation. Her husband realized Elizabeth couldn't have been his, since he was out at sea for a season a year before her birth. It took nearly three years for him to recognize the likeness between Elizabeth and us girls."

"Maybe he didn't want to believe it." I said, my stomach sinking. "That must have been just before you came here."

"Father fled and we followed, carrying Elizabeth with us," she said. "And who knows how long it will last. Although, all those times before, we didn't have property like this, isolated, where people leave you alone if you keep quiet and out of their hair."

"You don't think he's taken heed?"

Judith's face darkened. "Lucy McDonnell had a baby girl three years ago. She hasn't had a husband for four." She was watching her sisters. The church bell rang, calling for Benediction. "Who knows how many more are out there."

A few days later, Mama announced that Leader would like to meet with us. "Why?" we replied.

"He is the father of a community and should know all his children," said Mama.

"We're not his children," I said with as much disdain as I could muster. "We have a father."

Mama sighed. "You know what I mean, Genesis."

"We've been here for months, why does he want to see us now?"

"We believed it would be best you settle in before he opened his wings toward you."

"'We'?" I repeated.

"I'm not settled," said Isaiah. She smashed her fork into her potatoes, creating crisscross patterns. "I'll never be settled."

"Tomorrow after supper you will be excused from your night duties and we will go to his study," Mama said with finality.

I told Isaiah to stop playing with her potatoes and sit up straight. Mama carried on eating. Isaiah glared at me, said the potatoes were watery. Mama laid down her fork and took a deep breath, holding her napkin to her lips. "Girls, please."

"I'd thought you'd be more concerned with her table etiquette," I said. Mama's face was paling, her hairline started to glisten. She pressed her napkin to her mouth.

"I think we're done," she said.

"The bell hasn't rung," said Isaiah.

"Please go," Mama said, her voice quivering. I started to gather the half-eaten plates. She grabbed my hand. "Just go, I'll take them." She stood and gripped the table. "Out."

Isaiah and I exited the room. I heard Mama shuffling quickly behind us. The sound of her vomiting muffled as I pulled the door closed.

"Is she sick?" Isaiah whispered.

"Looks like." I said. I wanted to believe she was only sick, but the nagging in my gut told me it was more.

We joined Mama once we'd cleaned up from supper the next night and brushed our hair again. Mama was just redoing her hair when we came to her room. She had recovered quickly from her bout of illness the night before. She hadn't appeared at breakfast in the morning, but she'd been around at lunch looking as healthy as ever.

Had her face plumped since we'd arrived? Mama had been attractive as a young woman. Perhaps not striking, not one to leave men breathless, but pretty enough with a quiet, trust-worthy beauty. She still had traces of that hidden behind her stoic and stolid face. But I'd seen mothers of eight or nine children with softer features than my mother now displayed.

Mama smoothed her skirt and asked if we were ready. She took our hands as if we were still small children. I took my hand back. I was no child; I was nearly as tall as her, I'd run a house-hold. Isaiah, though, kept her hand in Mama's as we left the women and children's house. She moved her fingers under the hem of Mama's sleeve, pressing the pads of her fingers against Mama's wrist. "Stop that, Isaiah, what are you doing?" Mama said, shaking Isaiah's hand off.

I knew what she was doing. But she seemed unperturbed, so I knew Mama's life was to continue for the time being. It was dark outside, early nightfall, the air cool. It was fall. On the ranch they'd be taking inventory of the herds, getting them ready to ship to buyers. We followed Mama around the back of the church. A small room was built off the back of the chapel, Leader's study. Mama knocked on the door. We waited as we heard shuffling and voices moving. The door opened, revealing Leader and Sister Agatha, no doubt discussing the godly welfare of the children, particularly of Isaiah the Demon Child.

"Addie," Sister Agatha nodded to Mama.

"Agatha," Mama replied. Sister Agatha said nothing as she sidestepped us, her lips tight and narrow, her eyes hard on us, on Mama.

"Addie," Leader said, guiding us in and shutting the door.

"I've brought the girls."

"I see," he said. "How do?" He hadn't changed much from his arrival. He still wore that soft-brimmed hat, though I suspect he'd had it replaced at least once or twice, for it looked hardly more worn than at our first encounter.

"Hello," Isaiah mumbled.

I had nothing worth saying to the man. He'd taken our mother. He'd taken us from our home. I'd hate him until the end of my days. He was a charlatan, a hypocrite in Gomorrah, preaching godliness and purity in Christ while he took it upon himself to single-handedly multiply and replenish the earth, regardless of marriage vows.

"Genesis," Mama said warningly.

"I was fine," I replied. "Now I'm here."

Mama gasped my name and Leader smiled, but it was not a smile of warmth, mirth, or comfort. "Yes, well, it does take some adjustment moving from the corrupt world to our haven," he said. He and Mama smiled at each other. I could have spit. I could have pointed my rifle straight between his eyes. If he ever came for me, I'd drive a blade right between his bones.

"Genesis, stop scowling," Mama said.

"I can't."

Leader laughed his laugh, that curdling laugh. His office was sparse, a desk with a lamp and a leather ledger with a bible splayed open. A set of bookshelves stood mostly bare except for a couple rows of religious discourse and hymnals, old ledgers filled with his past sermons. Only one extra chair was in the room, across from his desk. And there was a window with hand-sewn drapes. "What do you want?" Leader asked.

"My gun," I said.

Leader chuckled. "No, my dear, I mean for your salvation?" Mama was glaring at me. I didn't answer. "Surely you intend to have a good husband, a godly man, and bring up children in righteousness, prepared for the last days when Revelation is brought to light?"

I shrugged.

"No," Isaiah whispered.

"What's that?" Leader's eyes glinted, his smile as threatening as ever.

Isaiah straightened and looked him straight in the eye. "I don't want to get married. I'll never get married."

Leader moved toward her, bent to her level. "What *do* you want, then?"

"I don't know," Isaiah answered. "But I won't get married." Leader patted the top of her head, ran his hand over her braid so it passed through his fingers like a snake.

"Isaiah," he said her name with deference. "A grand name for a little girl," he said. I wanted to break his wrist. "But you're no ordinary child, are you?"

"Oh," said Mama dismissively. "Tales of the town-folk. They've always said weird things about my family. As you know, Leader, of my parents—" Leader paid no attention to her, but she kept talking as though he was, "—big stories about ordinary people. We're no different than—"

"You're not one of us anymore," I said. I couldn't stand by and let her speak as though she had never left us, as if she *knew* us. She hadn't seen what Isaiah had seen; she hadn't witnessed the times Isaiah's intuitions came true. I hadn't personally known my grandfather, but I knew him through my grandmother and my father, and the stories they told. Mama had set us all aside, and now here she was, presenting us like she had any right to weigh in on our legacy.

Mama looked as though she could have burst; her lips tightened, her cheeks turned red. But Leader's presence halted her. The energy between us caught his attention and he finally let go of Isaiah's hair—she'd stood stone still—and turned his attention to me. "Your mother is very happy here. And she's given her heart to God. She's a gentle woman, and has struggled with her departure from you, what she's given up for you. What more she could have offered—" His eyes flashed with a bit of annoyance. "But she held you in consideration with every step." He put his hand on my shoulder. It was warm, too heavy. I brushed it away and stepped back.

"I'm sure she did."

"Judith enjoys your company," he said. "She's given to bouts of loneliness here, unfortunately. She tells me you're a hard worker, never shirking your duties." Mama's anger melted and she almost beamed at the praise.

"I do what's got to be done," I said. I did not admit that I found no use in fighting. What was to be gained from fighting every little thing but bruised knees and rasped knuckles? All I wanted was out, and every day I hoped Mama would realize her mistake and take us back or Daddy would come for us.

"You'll find your place here," he said. "And Little Miss Isaiah will too, I'm sure."

"What does Mama do for you?" Isaiah asked.

Another smile bristled his beard. "She transcribes my dictations. She arranges the hymns. She's indispensable to me." Mama's blushing made my stomach churn, and I could say nothing. I knew right then that my mother was one of his women, that she was carrying his child. She had come for us to complete her family and prove something to Leader. If my father, a sweet and gentle and handsome man still in his prime could lose my mother, what then had Leader offered her? What honeyed things had he whispered to her? And what had she offered him in return? Other than the fidelity she'd once given Daddy, what else did she have to offer? Us. Our legacy.

I glared at Leader, and he smirked at me, the corner of his bristled mouth twitching. "I'm really very tired," I said, shaking my head. "And I've got to be up early to get breakfast going." I swallowed against the bile in my throat as Leader nodded and agreed. He ran his hand over Isaiah's hair again, pressed his hand against the small of Mama's back.

And when we'd left, gone around the church, Mama turned to me. "Can't you even try to be content here?" She seemed both angry and near tears.

"We were happy where we were," I said, and her emotion took the edge from my voice. Was she really so blinded by her devotion? "Mama, they hate us here. And you don't see it."

"Leader said Judith..."

"She's the only one. The others..." Mama looked at me as though she was seeing through me. She gathered her reserve. The emotion left her.

"Well, you're here now." She turned on her heel and left us in her dust.

ISAIAH

Sometimes—but not very often—we are free to play, when the adults run out of stuff for us to do. We get our coats and mittens and we go outside, running around the houses and through the barn. We go squealing and chasing after each other. There are always three tagging because there are so many of us and we have a lot of space to run around. The little kids really aren't good at tagging or running, and that's why us older girls help them. It's always the boys who start it—Aaron Fisher and Jacob and Billy White and Boaz Smith.

There are only two other girls my age: Martha and Lizzy, and we each take a younger girl by the hand to help them run away from the boys. I've got Little Mary, who's only five. I've got her hand and I'm pushing her up a stack of hay in one of the empty stalls and Aaron Fisher is chasing after us, trying to get to Mary. We're laughing and screaming in good fun. I know eventually Aaron will just tag me, but he acts like he just wants Mary and I act like I have to protect her.

And then we hear someone cry really loud and one of the other girls starts yelling. We stop playing and leave the stall to see what's going on. Aaron's little brother Caleb is on the ground, crying. Reuben's standing over him. He's been chasing for some time, and I think he just got tired of it. Aaron goes to his brother.

"You can't just go pushing little kids down!" Lizzy is yelling at Reuben.

"I didn't push him that hard," Reuben says. "He's just being a baby."

"Yes, you did!" says Martha. "We saw you. We all saw you!"

"I didn't!" Reuben says, and he looks at me. But I don't back him up. He picks on the little kids all the time, always calls them stupid, pushes them down, makes them cry. Aaron gets up and pushes Reuben so hard he falls just like Caleb did. And like that the playing is over. Reuben screams and jumps up, then head butts Aaron right in the stomach and they both fall over. They roll around, slapping and pulling at each other.

Now all of us are screaming for both of them to stop. Next to me, Martha says, "Reuben's mother is going to be mad. We're all gonna get in trouble."

"Why would we get in trouble? They're the ones fighting."

Martha shakes her head and her eyes are big watching the boys. "We *all* get in trouble every time Reuben fights."

"Well that's not fair," I say. "It's not our job to keep Reuben in line."

"Aaron stop!" Lizzy is shouting. Aaron's got Reuben pinned down. "His mama will kill us, stop!"

But no one steps forward to stop them. Reuben is slapping at Aaron, and Aaron hocks spit in the back of his throat, and just before he spits, I run over and push him off. Aaron just lays on the ground and Reuben jumps up and runs away. "He's gonna tell," Aaron says. "I should have punched him, since he's going to tell anyway."

"I'll tell him not to tell," I say.

Martha shakes her head. "He's already telling."

"I'll stop him," I say, and I run out after Reuben. He's already on his porch when I catch him. He's got two long scratches down his face.

"What?" he says.

"Don't tell on Aaron."

"He tried to beat me up. He sat on me."

"You pushed down his little brother."

"Caleb was being a baby because I tagged him. It's not my fault he wasn't fast enough."

"He practically *is* a baby."

"Well, I don't want to play with babies."

"Well, you hit Aaron first," I say. "So you're the one who started it. I'll tell that you started it. If he gets in trouble, you should too."

He scowls. "He's bigger than me."

"Everyone's bigger than you," I say. "Everyone's going to be mad at you if you get them into trouble."

"Will you be?"

"Maybe," I say. "Yes."

"Okay," he says. "I won't tell."

"He said he won't tell," I tell the others, and they all nod. But when we get back to the children's room to get ready for the night, Reuben isn't there. Leader's wife stands at the door with Sister Agatha, who's holding a ruler. Sister Agatha calls to Aaron, and he slouches when he walks to her, not trying to defend himself or anything.

"Hey!" I say, stepping in front of the two old ladies. "It's not his fault. Reuben started it!"

We're not supposed to speak unless one of the adults speaks to us first, and the other kids go quiet. Reuben's mama glares at me. "Reuben pushed Caleb down and then Aaron pushed him back, but then Reuben head butted him."

Leader's wife shakes her head. "If you saw the whole thing, why didn't you stop him?"

"She did stop them," Lizzy says. Sister Agatha glares at her and she shrinks back.

Leader's wife nods to Sister Agatha. "Hands out," Sister Agatha says. Aaron sticks his hands out with his knuckles up and I put mine out with my palms up. Leader's wife grabs my hands and turns them over, jerking my arms. Sister Agatha brings the ruler down on Aaron's knuckles and the *smack* makes us all jump. She does it until his knuckles turn red. And then she comes for me, and I pull my hands back just as I see the ruler come down.

"Hands *up*," Sister Agatha says, smacking my elbow. I put my hands back out, but I pull them back again without meaning to and she hits me on the shoulder with the ruler. Reuben's mama pulls my hands out again and holds them. Her fingers pinch mine. I wince as the wood hits my knuckles, one, two, four times. When she's done, I yank my hands back. I want to take that ruler out of Sister Agatha's hand and smack her with it from head to foot, until she's even redder than our knuckles. But the old ladies leave and shut the door behind them.

"I'm gonna punch Reuben myself as soon as my knuckles stop hurting," I say.

Aaron shrugs and puts his hands in his pockets and skulks to his bed.

"You *said* you wouldn't tell!" I say to Reuben in the morning. I show him my knuckles, they're a little purple, but they don't hurt anymore.

"I didn't!" he says. "Well, I didn't want to. But then she saw my scratches and said if I didn't tell her who did it, she'd just go in and wallop everyone."

"You ought to say sorry to Aaron," I say.

"Why?" He says. "He beat me up. He spit on me."

"You told! And he got in trouble. And me too!" I say. "And you're the one who started it. *I* got in trouble and I'm the one who stopped him beating you up!"

He sighs and turns away from me. He never says sorry, but when we are all given parts in the Christmas play, he gets chosen as Joseph but says Aaron should get it instead.

"You're being Joseph," his mama says.

"But Aaron's bigger than me, and he looks older," Reuben whines. All the rest of us are quiet.

"It's already decided," she says.

Reuben screams. It makes us all jump. He screams that he always has to be Joseph. His mama breathes fast and she keeps saying "You're being Joseph, Reuben," until she's shouting it over him.

And then he just stops yelling and crosses his arms and says, "Gabriel's better. He's an angel and lives with God. Joseph's just a smelly carpenter. He's a *mortal*. He's not even Jesus's real father."

His mama tilts her head and sucks in her lips. "Fine," she says. "Aaron, you're Joseph this year." And Aaron sits up straighter and smiles.

Sister Agatha chooses me to be a sheep, and when I tell Mama, she shakes her head and makes an angry "hmm..." in the back of her throat.

"I like sheep," I say, catching peas that roll off my fork. "They're soft and fuzzy. I said that Little Mary should be Mary because they have the same name, but they said she's too little to carry a baby."

"Whose baby are they using?" Genesis asks.

"Mary's little brother."

Mama goes "humph," again. "A *sheep*," she says, and turns to Genesis. "Can't they see how beautiful she is? *She* should be playing Mary." Mama called me beautiful and it makes me feel weird. All the peas roll off my fork, bounce on the table and onto the floor. Genesis is looking at Mama with her eyebrows together and her mouth slightly open. "Well, she is," Mama says. "A *sheep*. Sheep is what they give the small children."

Then she stands up, bumping the table. She opens the door and leaves. Genesis and I look at each other and then jump up to follow her. Mama pounds on Sister Agatha's door, and as soon as it opens she says, "Why is my daughter playing a sheep? My daughter is *not* a sheep."

Sister Agatha is surprised at first but then she laughs. "What would you have her be? She's definitely no angel."

The other doors are cracking open and eyes peek out. "She's prettier than any of the girls you've got to play Mary," Mama says.

Sister Agatha laughs again, "God didn't choose Mary for her looks, Addie."

"Certainly some men on earth don't either," Mama says. I hear someone gasp from behind a door crack and Sister Agatha glares at Mama.

"Your daughter's a sheep so she can maybe learn how to behave like one," Sister Agatha says, "So she can learn her place. It's that or the ass, she won't even need a costume for that!" and she slams the door.

"Even the ass was less of one than you are!" Mama shouts at the door. She huffs, turns and sees me. I try to shrink away. She softens and sighs and shoos us back into her room to finish dinner without another word about it all.

She makes my sheep's costume black. It matches my hair. Sister Agatha glares at me in it on Christmas Eve, but she says nothing and just grunts. I *baa* too loud as Leader's wife is reading the Christmas story because I can and it makes some of the grownups watching laugh. When we join Mama again in the congregation, she pats my head. We stay up late to sing Christmas hymns and listen to passages of Jesus' life and miracles. And right before we're sent off to bed, we all get cups of warm, sweetened milk with cinnamon.

There are no presents in the morning—Mama says it's because presents are distracting from the real purpose of Christmas—but we each get an orange. And we all have supper in the big dining hall and there are thirteen turkeys and ten hams and bowls and bowls of potatoes and bread and pies—I can tell which ones Mama and Genesis made because they look the best and taste the best.

We aren't supposed to get presents, but Reuben comes down from his family's table to hand me a handmade doll that looks like me with black hair and black button eyes. "I made it," he says, "Well, Judith really made it, but I sewed on the eyes. But don't tell Father that or he'll whip me." He tucks his hands into his pockets and his cheeks turn red.

I haven't played with dolls in years, but I smile and tell him thank you anyway. He hasn't given anything to anyone else. "It's a great present," I say. He turns even redder and hurries back to his mama's side. I turn to show the doll to Mama. She smiles and nods. She's wearing earrings that dangle and sparkle. She touches them whenever Leader looks our way.

GENESIS

Leader was gone a couple weeks. No one else was allowed to lead sermons or Benedictions, so we did not have to attend them. But Leader's wife lurked and hovered around everyone. She kept eyes on us young ladies as we worked, she hovered over the other woman at their work, smacked at the knuckles of any child that got in her way or twisted their face the wrong way. Mama was pulled from her duties in the church, and Leader's wife especially hovered over her, saying nothing as Mama sewed or ladled out stew or kneaded bread. Mama behaved as if Leader's wife was not there, breathing down her neck. Once, Mama had to stop what she was doing and rush away to vomit in a waste basket, and even then, she was careful not to step on the other woman's toes. Leader's wife made a noise of disgust and walked away.

I, however, was not so accommodating. I had enough of the woman's breath on my neck, her condescending words about my handiwork. At the laundry, where I was already hot and tired and sore, she hovered over me, saying nothing, so close that when I stumbled back, I stepped on her toes. "Do you need something, ma'am?" I snapped at her. "I'm rather busy, if you can't see, and it's much too warm for you to be breathing down my neck."

Her mouth fell open in mock surprise. She tutted and said, "Now, Miss Genesis, a quick temper is unbecoming of a young lady." She waited for me to reply, but I bit my tongue. And she left. It was almost a relief when Leader returned because his wife went back to hiding in her house while the rest of us worked.

And when he returned, he requested that I be the one to deliver his lunch to his study each day. It had been Sister Lucy McDonnell's assignment. "I'd rather not," I told Leader's wife, who relayed the message laced with contempt.

"He's requested you himself. I suggest you heed your calling." The pain of the broomstick still a vivid memory in my bones, I consented. Sister Lucy turned her nose up at me whenever she saw or passed me by. We hadn't had any sort of camaraderie before; I could barely contain my own disgust for her after what Judith told me.

Judith came the first time I delivered to Leader. "Why would my father request you?" she'd said when she'd found out. She bit her lip and wouldn't look at me. "You be careful with him. Don't—don't say anything that might...don't act like you want to do it."

"But I *don't* want to do it."

She let herself glance at me briefly, her eyes sharp, before they fluttered away again. "Have you...?"

"Have I what?"

"Been with a boy."

"I've never even kissed one," I said. "And I'm fourteen. I haven't been to school in over a year, when would I even have had the time?"

She cut me off with a sharp laugh that made my hair stand.

"You lived in a world full of men. You had plenty of time. No one was around to watch you."

"I watched myself."

She sighed and finally looked at me, her eyes softened. "You're a good girl," she said. "And strong." She knocked on the door, her father looked at her quizzically and said it wasn't necessary for her to accompany on a job one young woman could do perfectly well on her own.

"Be kind to her, Father," Judith warned. Leader sighed her name with a weariness only parents carry for a difficult child.

"Nevertheless," she said later, after complaining about her father's absurd preference. "You'd better go alone next time. He doesn't take well to being challenged too much. I know my limits."

Subsequently, the deliveries were short and direct, with hardly more than a few words exchanged. Then one day he told me to wait before going back to the kitchen. My heart stopped, sank like a rock in my gut. "You read very well, I've heard," he said. "You liked to read, before you came here."

"Yes sir."

He handed me the bible from his desk. I did my best not to touch him—the thought of touching him sickened me—like touching something rotten. He pointed to a verse down the page. "Start here," he said. He sat at his desk and ripped his bread, sopping up gravy.

Numbers, chapter five. I cleared my throat, already eyeing the words ahead. "*And every offering of all the holy things of the children of Israel, which they bring unto the priest shall be his. And every man's hallowed things shall be his: whatsoever any man giveth the priest, it shall be his.*" I stopped, looked up, at him slopping gravy down his beard.

"Continue," he said around a lump of food.

"*...If any man's wife go aside, and commit a trespass against* him, *and a man lie with her carnally, and it be hid from the eyes of her husband and be kept close and she be defiled, and there be no witness against her neither she be taken with the manner...*" I continued to read to the end of the chapter. My face grew hot, my stomach in knots. "*And if the woman be not defiled, but be clean, then she shall be free and shall conceive seed...then shall the man be guiltless from iniquity, and this woman shall bear her iniquity.*" I finished and shut the book, placing it back on his desk. "If you're done, I'll take your tray back now," I said, my hand out to grab his plate.

"You do read well," he said, sitting back with his hands clasped over his belly. "Just food for thought, Sister Genesis. Scripture to consider as you settle in here."

I left quickly, and, outside, ran into Leader's son Benjamin. He was tall, eighteen, the same sandy-brown hair as all the others. "Whoa there, little sister," he said, catching the tray.

"I'm not your sister."

"*The elder women as mothers; the younger as sisters, all with purity,*" he quoted. "Until that changes, of course." He winked and laughed, the same laugh of his father. "Careful now." He ran his hand up my arm, cupped my elbow. I slid away from him and carried on. That night I unearthed Isaiah's knife from below the wardrobe and strapped it to my leg.

Mama's shape was slowly growing more noticeable. I saw her smooth her skirt, the gentle curve of her belly beneath the cloth, and I knew the other women noticed, too. Still, I wanted to deny it even then. The dresses were wide and not the most flattering cut, puffing out at the waist every now and then. And Mama was getting to the age where women start to grow paunchy. But I could not deny it forever. We could all turn away, ignore, but in a few months, it would be obvious to even the most oblivious. No one mentioned it, no one spoke about it all. Mama herself carried on as if all was normal, she never made any mention at all. I could hardly breathe in her presence. *It shall be his. It shall be his. She be not defiled. He be not defiled. They shall be put to death.*

I wasn't sure if Isaiah had figured it out yet. She didn't have much experience with grown women. We'd seen pregnant ladies in town, and she knew how it happened, but I wasn't sure she noticed Mama; I doubted she knew the early symptoms. That was a conversation Gramma had meant to have with us later, when we were older. I didn't know how to tell Isaiah or whether I should. I didn't know what it would mean to her. To me it meant my mother was a whore and a hypocrite. I knew she and my father were still legally married. I knew she'd brought us to the Community to show she was a good mother, that she was worthy to carry Leader's child; that she wouldn't abandon it on his doorstep like all those other women.

At Benediction, I watched her at the front of the congregation, her arms up in praise as she led them all in hymns that grew more passionate as Leader prayed ever louder over them. Isaiah had slipped out with Reuben. In front of me, Brenda Peters was wailing, her face wet with spirit. She kept peeking through her closed eyelids, looking to Benjamin, who in turn snuck looks back and she'd grow more passionate.

Mama in front with her rounding belly, Leader at his pulpit calling down Heaven. Everyone else with their eyes closed, arms thrust to the ceiling. I left. I went outside. In the height of the hysterics, it was easy to slip out unnoticed, everyone focused instead on displaying the intensity of their own devotion. I stepped around the side of the church and looked up at the stars, drawing the constellations in my mind. The bears, the hunter.

When we were very young, Mama used to tell us the stories

of the stars. Mama buried a baby, and the stars stopped telling stories. Mama carried another baby and came for us.

"It's chilly out here." Benjamin. Alone and moving toward me.

"It's not."

He leaned beside me, his elbow knocking mine. "Are you waiting for me?" I said nothing. I pulled my hands behind my back. "We have yet met face-to-face."

"You know who I am, I know who you are," I said.

He chuckled. "Come on, little sister, we can make a little pleasant small talk." He moved closer, his whole arm against mine.

"I'm not your sister."

"Don't I know it," and then his arm was around my waist, his chest against mine. I pushed against him as he pressed me to the wall. I couldn't move. I stiffened as he brought his lips to my ear, his one hand grasping my back, the other on my hip. "Oh the things I've heard of you. The little harlots, the devil's daughters," he whispered, his breath sticky on my neck. "Temptress raised to the pleasure of men." His lips were on my neck, hot and wet. His grip too tight for me to struggle.

So I stiffened, brought up my leg slow—only enough to get my fingers on the hilt of Isaiah's knife. I put my own arm around Benjamin's waist, holding tight. He took my movements as my own hunger meeting his and grew more fervent the tighter I clutched at him. Only when he felt the point of the blade at his ribs did he realize I was entrapping him, one leg wrapped around his, my arm clasped around him. He stiffened as I pressed the blade. "What do you think you're doing?" he tried a dismissive laugh, but it tremored. I pushed and he tried to pull away, but I clung to him. "You won't really cut me." I pushed until I felt the fabric of his shirts release, until the skin broke enough to release blood, enough for a scar.

"I will," I said. I'd never cut anyone before. I'd never shot anyone before. I'd never drawn someone else's blood; I'd never been sure I could. But I did then.

He tried to pull away, gasping "You crazy bitch." But I gripped him like he had me, moving the knife beneath his chin.

"If you ever touch me again, I'll slice you from gut to gullet," I nicked his chin with the point and released him, pushed him away. When he could no longer see me, I took deep breaths and trembled, his string of obscenities trailing me.

I told Judith.

"Did you entice him?" she replied, her eyes steady on me.

"No, he repulses me!" I said. I told her how I'd cut him.

"Oh," she said. "He told us he'd cut himself shaving." She spread flour over the countertop and pulled dough from a mixing bowl. "He doesn't like being bested," she said, punching down the dough with floury knuckles.

"Does anyone?"

"He's not used to being turned down," said Judith. She plucked chunks from the dough, turning them over in her hands until they were perfect little spheres. Each of her rolls were perfect, while mine were lumpy before they rose and baked. "Keep it on you," she said, "the knife. But…" she paused, dusted more flour onto her hands. "Father favors him, and he always finds a way to get what he wants."

ISAIAH

Little Mary is sick. I hear her crying in the night, so I go to her bed to check on her. I think maybe she's wet the bed again. "No," she says, "My throat hurts." I sit on her bed and scoop her into my lap. Her skin is hot. She's sweating.

I pull her close and rock a bit. "You've got a fever." And then I feel it, that thing—the *thump*—under her skin. I've felt it a dozen times, and I've never been wrong. I want to be though, especially this time. It's not so strong this time, right now. Little Mary's sweet and good, always kind to the other children. She's got red hair and freckles and never causes problems except for the bedwetting.

She calms down and stops crying and falls asleep with her face in my neck. I lay her down and go to the door. "What's going on?" one of the little boys asks, "Why is Mary crying?"

"It's nothing, just a little fever, go back to sleep." I open the door. It's old Sister Margaret standing guard tonight. She's the oldest lady in the Community. She's asleep in the chair, her head tilted back against the wall, her mouth wide open. "Sister

Margaret," I whisper as loud as I can. She snorts but stays asleep. I poke her shoulder. "Sister Margaret."

She jolts awake. "You!" She says. "You! Always a problem you!" When her eyes focus, she tries to swat at me, but I'm too far away. Sister Agatha's door opens and she comes out, tying a robe over her nightgown—her room's the closest to the children's room.

"Sister Margaret, what's the problem?"

The old lady's got hold of my collar now. "It's her, I caught her sneaking."

"I'm not sneaking!" I say. "I woke you up on purpose, I promise! It's Little Mary."

Sister Agatha rolls her eyes. "The bedwetter again...you can release the girl, Margaret."

"She hasn't wet the bed," I say, straightening my nightgown once Sister Margaret lets go. "She's got a fever."

"What's that? Speak up, girl," says Sister Margaret.

I raise my voice so the old lady can hear. "Little Mary's sick!" The other sisters' doors are opening now, and I can hear some of the kids whispering to each other.

Sister Agatha finally follows me into the room. "Hush, all of you," she says to all the kids chattering, and she goes to Mary's bed and feels her forehead.

"She's been crying. She's sick," I tell Sister Agatha. "She needs a doctor."

"Doctors are charlatans, claiming the powers of God for themselves," says Sister Agatha. "It's just a fever. All children get fevers."

Reuben's up now and comes over, rubbing his eyes. Sister Agatha tells him to run to Mary's parents and tell them to come get her. Little Mary's whimpering. Sister Agatha sits on her bed and says, "Hush, child, your father's coming for you." She looks at me standing at the end of the bed. "What are you still doing up?"

I want to tell her again that Mary needs a doctor, but I know she'll only yell at me. "Will she be alright?"

"Children get fevers all the time," she says again. "Go back to bed."

I do as she says but I lay awake. Reuben comes back with Mary's daddy who carries her out. Reuben comes back to bed and Sister Agatha leaves and closes the door. "She needs a doctor," I whisper to Reuben.

"We've never had doctors. Mother says they deny the power of God."

The doctor couldn't help Gramma. But he's helped me and Genesis with fevers before. Mary's got a fever, that's all. I want to tell Reuben about the thing I feel on people sometimes, about the dream I once had about the sheriff's brother hanging in a tree. But I think he might call me a witch, or a demon, and try to stone me like all those people in the bible. "I think Mary's really sick," I say instead.

"Lord will have her or He won't," he says.

At supper the next day with Mama and Genesis, I tell them Little Mary was taken sick with fever. "God bless the child's soul," Mama says. "Remember to pray for her."

"Will it help her get better?" I ask. "If I pray, does it work?"

Mama smiles at me. She doesn't smile often, and she hardly ever smiles at me. "It can," she says.

I look at Genesis. I want to tell her about the thump too, but I don' think Mama would like to hear it. I started feeling the thump when we were *outside*, and she doesn't like us talking about outside. "She's real sick."

I think Genesis understands. She pauses her fork. "Did you touch her?" She asks me.

"Yes."

"I'm sure Isaiah is fine," Mama says. "The both of you hardly ever brought home fevers from other children."

"Sister Agatha says no doctors," I'm talking mostly to Genesis, though Mama thinks I'm talking to her too. Genesis puts her hands in her lap.

"Well sometimes the best thing is to just let it run its course," Mama says. "What are doctors anyway but snake oil salesmen and atheists?"

"Mama..." Genesis starts to say and I'm afraid they're going to start arguing again like always, but Genesis just takes a big breath and says, "Well I guess prayers are all Little Mary and her family have got now."

Mama's smiling again. She pats her belly, then she takes both our hands and says, "Why don't we pray for her right now?" She leads the prayer, asking God to take care of Little Mary and help her body overcome the sickness plaguing her. I hope it cures Mary, because she's sweet and good.

But Little Mary's still sick the next day and the day after and the next. I stop by their little house and asked her mama if she's feeling any better. Mary's mama is young and pretty with glass-blue eyes and the sweetest, softest voice. She looks real tired and is bouncing one of her two little babies on her hip. "She's still sick."

"I've been praying for her like my mama said to," I tell her.

She smiles a little. The baby inside begins to cry. "I'll let Mary know you're thinking of her." Her voice gets tight like she's trying not to cry. The baby in her arms starts crying so I tell her I better go.

Genesis and Judith help me make a doll out of cloth scraps for Mary and Mama and I take it over after supper. Mary's mama looks even more tired, but she lets us in. Mary's laying on a small cot, her hair's all wet, her face is redder than her hair.

"We've tried everything," I hear her mama say. My mama

says something real calm, but Mary's mama starts crying anyway.

I kneel next to Mary's cot. She's asleep, so I just tuck the doll in beside her. I brush her cheek with my hand. The thump is there. It's so strong now, like a thump against my hand, it surprises me, and I let out a little shout like I've been burned. The mamas stop talking and ask what's wrong. I can't say anything and I start to cry. Mary's the youngest person I've ever felt with it. The only other kid I've ever felt it in was Rudy Baker and he was almost twelve and even the doctor said he was gonna die because he was always a sickly child.

Mary's mama cries harder and Mama goes stiff. "I think it's time we go. It's obvious Mary needs her rest." Outside, Mama grabs me by the shoulders and bends so her face is level to mine. "What was that all about?"

"Nothing."

She shakes me a little. "Don't lie to me, Isaiah, I'm your mother. I know when you're lying. What was all that in there?"

"You'll say I'm lying! You don't understand, you won't!" I say. Mama's only ever pleased with me when I'm asking about praying or when I can recite a whole verse by heart. They don't believe in doctors here, they don't believe in witchcraft and people who feel things beneath the skin unless they're silly old men with gray beards or women who make babies when they're too old or haven't got husbands.

"There's something wrong with you, Isaiah." Mama's voice is high, not like when she's angry, but like she's scared. Like I may have hit my head too hard like the Pattersons' slow son, or like I'm the one who's sick and is going to die soon.

I start to cry again because I'm not Genesis and I'm too young still to be able to stop myself from crying. "She's going to die! They didn't get a doctor and now she's going to die. I know she'll die. They always do. Like Gramma." And then Mama's pulling me close and hugging me tight, whispering "hush, hush" and I can feel her plumped breasts against my check and her firm, rounding belly against my chest.

In the night, we all hear the wailing. I hear it first because I never went to sleep. Or maybe we don't actually hear it, but we're soon all awake asking what's going on before any of the old ladies are up and scrambling in the hallway. Reuben and I get out of bed and go to the door, cracking it open enough to see the old ladies, including Mama, leaving their own bedrooms and putting on their robes and heading outside. Reuben and I follow behind them.

The night puts goose bumps on our skin. There's the sound of a woman wailing, the saddest noise I've ever heard. Maybe it's her that makes our skin prickle. "Little Mary's dead," I tell Reuben. We've got our hands together, standing in the dark while the old ladies are trying to comfort Mary's mama, who's outside on her knees with her arms around herself, rocking back and forth and carrying on. Reuben's hand is warm and alive and nothing is moving beneath his skin. I feel another hand soft on my shoulder. It's Genesis. None of us is crying because we're too busy watching Mary's mama cry for the whole world.

Mary's the first person they've ever buried here. Leader gives a funeral sermon in the chapel about heaven's arms being opened to all the dear little children and God calling back the souls of his most precious. "Sweet Little Mary is now free from all the pains of mortality, she'll never have to experience the heartaches and temptations that come with temporal life," he says.

All the while, Mary's mama has stopped wailing. She's stopped crying altogether. Her face is gray and her eyes are red. I let Mama hold my hand at the burial and I lay the little doll I made on the coffin. Mary's mama watches me with her frozen, sad eyes and my skin prickles, but her husband takes her by the shoulders and leads her home.

I sneak out of bed in the night and crawl into Genesis' bed. She says if I get caught sneaking to come see her, they'll make sure I can't do it anymore. But I'm careful. I always wait until everyone is asleep. And when it's Sister Margaret at the door, it's easy to sneak past. "Who's the baby's daddy?" I ask Genesis. I'm talking about Mama. I'm sure she's known about the baby longer than I have.

"If you think about it real hard, I'm sure you can figure it out," she says. Some nights she's so dead asleep when I come, I can't wake her enough to whisper with me so I wander around the Community instead, but tonight she's as awake as I am.

"When are we going home?"

"I don't know," she says. "Soon, I hope. But if we try to leave too soon, they'll just come after us."

"How do you know?"

"I just do," she says, and I know she won't say any more about it.

"Are you going to get married if we stay here?"

"No."

"Reuben says his Daddy might give you to Benjamin," I tell her.

"How does he know?"

"He heard his daddy and Benjamin talking about you."

She grunts. "And he heard them say they're going to marry me off?"

"Reuben just said they were talking about you is all. I don't know anything more," I say. "Reuben says Benjamin wants you." If Genesis is married, she'll move into her own house, and I'll never see her. If she's married, she could have babies who will get sick and no one will call a doctor for her. I don't like Benjamin, he likes to nap on the hay bales when we're supposed to be mucking stalls and makes the rest of us work. He says mean things to Reuben and practices his sling-shots on us kids; he pushes the older girls up against walls and puts his hands up their skirts.

"I won't be marrying Benjamin," she whispers, like that's the end of it. But Benjamin never stops when we ask him to.

"Reuben says girls have to be at least fifteen before they're married."

"We'll be gone before that then. People are starting to whisper."

"About me?"

She sighs. "About you, about me."

"Because of Mary?"

"Yes," she says. "Her mama has been telling all the other ladies about how you touched Mary and cried."

"Am I going to be in trouble?"

She doesn't answer right away. "I don't know."

Genesis is asleep the next night. I try to get into bed with her, but she just rolls and faces the wall. I get up and creep back down the halls instead. Sister Margaret's asleep in her chair. Outside it's dark. Sometimes I think about walking out the Community gate and walking all the way back to the ranch, but Genesis says I won't make it halfway before they catch me.

GENESIS

Mama grew rounder and Isaiah inched beyond the edge of redemption. She'd never seen a child die before; and she lashed out. She stopped trying at all to be good. She seemed to relish antagonizing the "old ladies" as she called them. She slipped curse words into her conversation with the sisters, she'd counter their scripture with others, emphasize the *damns* and *asses* and *whores* when they appeared. Isaiah found herself in constant companion with smacks across the knuckles and her knees on the broomstick.

"Your sister seems to have become some sort of a whirl-wind," Leader mentioned over lunch one day. "I can't go a day without one of the women mentioning her to me."

"She always has been," I said.

"Hot blood in your family," he said. I shrugged in response. We'd fallen into a rhythm more or less. He kept his distance, attempted to strike up casual conversation and I complied, always aware of the knife strapped to my leg. But I hadn't needed to pull it out since my altercation with Benjamin. He hadn't tried to approach me again though he'd send me snide smirks and glances when he could.

"I suspect all that's needed is a firm hand," Leader was saying.

"I think the firm hand is what's released Isaiah's impishness," I replied. "She's doing it on purpose now."

"And not even you can rein her in?"

I shrugged again. Isaiah was a force unto herself, but she would behave for me if I asked her to because I was never against her. I didn't care to rein her in. Let her terrorize them. I almost envied her. I couldn't bring myself to release control and become primal and vindictive. I continued begrudgingly through the tasks I was assigned. I dreaded the pain that might come if I didn't—the aching knees, the growling stomach, the welts. I could take the pain, but I hated it. Isaiah, it seemed, used the pain as energy, storing it in preparation for the next round. She blanked at pain, sent herself to another world.

"A patriarchal hand," Leader said. "I think that's what's missing." He dug into his food. "You know," he continued between bites. "When you get married, you'll have your own home here. And if you wanted, you'd be granted guardianship of your sister. I could arrange that for you."

"Why such special privilege for us?" I said, more curious than I wanted to admit.

"You're not ordinary girls," he said. "And we wouldn't have you marry just anyone. You've got an established history in this area. And your sister has whatever it is she has. The women here are no match for her."

"What about my mother?"

"She could live in your home, too, if both of you were so inclined."

"And her child too, I assume."

His lip twitched behind his gravy-speckled whiskers. "Yes, yes."

"No."

"No?" he repeated.

"No, I don't want anything of yours," I said. "'*Everything shall be his.*' I *have* a home. This isn't it." I left without his dismissal.

There were girls older than me still unmarried, but Leader had not yet seen fit to marry them off. As Judith said, he would never allow his daughters to be married so I knew why Jerusha, who was nearly seventeen, and Ruth, hardly a year younger, remained. But there was also Brenda Peters, and she was itching to be married, or at least be bedded. I saw the way she ogled after the men. After Benjamin set her aside—no doubt by his father's orders in effort to "woo" me—Isaiah said she'd spied her necking Marcus Culper. Yet Brenda still seemed set on Benjamin and was against me with vehemence.

"I turn fifteen in May," I told Judith. It was getting closer. Already the snow on the peaks was receding.

"I heard," Judith said. She scrubbed against the washboard, something gray-white. A shirt, maybe long underwear.

"I expect my mother's baby will be coming sometime between now and then too," I said, wiping perspiration from my forehead.

"She looks it." She wrung out the garment she'd been scrubbing and handed it to me. I fed it through the wringer, water gushing out, and threw it in the basket with all the other damp clothes ready for the line. Judith's hands were pink and wrinkled. I offered to switch and we shuffled around the washtub. The water in the tub was hot, slick with detergent.

"Benjamin's meant to court you. Like a gentleman," Judith said. "I overheard him and father discussing it." She paused and

110

considered me a moment when I finished. "We've had to send girls away with pockets of cash because of him."

"I was in this town first," I said. "And my father would kill him before Leader got me past the hills." She smiled weakly at me. There was another matter on my mind, though. The night before, I had come into the room to find Brenda and Judith's sisters standing suspiciously close to my bed. "Do you have a place you can hide things?" I asked Judith. I figured she must, because we all did. "I feel the other girls are gunning for me."

"They always are."

"Brenda's sweet on Benjamin," I said. "More than sweet. She sees him watch me. She's going to find a way to terrorize me. They'll tear everything apart, I know they will."

"I've got a place."

The next chance I got alone in the room, I exhumed my books and handed them over to Judith's care in a stack of clean linens. "Read them, if you want." I told her. She ran her fingers along the spines. She took them and I never saw them again, but I could not have bequeathed them a moment too soon.

I returned from dinner a couple nights later to find Sister Phillipa and Leader's wife standing smugly by my bed, the sheets haphazard, my wardrobe akimbo and my garments spread about. I clenched my fists against an outburst.

"We were informed you may have some unapproved items," Sister Phillipa said.

"Did you find anything?" It took all my nerve to remain calm.

The older women's faces set hard. "It appears everything is in order," said Leader's wife.

"Or perhaps we haven't found it yet," said Sister Phillipa. "But rest assured, we'll be watching for it. Straighten your things out." The two of them left me to the mess they'd created.

Brenda made no attempt to mask her smirk when she saw me pushing my wardrobe back.

They had been eyeing me before, and now I knew they would double their sentry. Sister Phillipa often made me do things twice, my seams, my ironing, the sheets on my bed. They all lay in wait for me to make a mistake, or do something they could skew to their advantage.

One afternoon as I was left alone to iron bed sheets, Marcus Culper came rushing into the room with his hand bleeding, frantic. "Bandages!" He gasped. I rushed to the cupboard of scrap linens, and pulled vinegar from the detergent shelf. He opened his bleeding hand, a gash in the meat of his thumb. He bit his lip against the splash of vinegar. I pressed the clump of rags to the wound.

"What happened?"

"Hoof pick," he said. "Damn horse spooked and my hand slipped." He took a few deep breaths, settling. "Sorry to scare you, I didn't mean to shout."

He was a nice enough boy, on the cusp of nineteen, the son of quiet, pious, older parents. But I'd seen him eye me with the rest of them, and I knew of his less-than-pious dalliance with Brenda.

I wrapped his wound for him. "I've heard worse." I said. "Best luck with the horse. Watch that pick a little better."

He thanked me with a tip of his hat and left. I went back to my ironing and didn't think much of the incident until I returned to the room and, once again, found Sister Phillipa awaiting me, this time with Brenda at her side.

"So," began Sister Phillipa, "You were alone with a young man today. You know we don't condone that."

"He'd hurt himself, I helped him bandage it," I felt myself saying, but I knew the words were falling on deaf ears. They'd already reached their conclusion. I highly doubt Marcus had any part in it. More likely Brenda or one of her cohorts had been passing by and saw us through the open door and knew how to twist the image. Sister Phillipa carried on as if I hadn't spoken and as I watched her mouth move, I was already resolving to do whatever she had in store for me without argument.

"You know the rules, we've told you time and again. We can't watch you all the time. Lord knows how many of the young men you've probably already tempted when our heads were turned." She carried on for several minutes. I considered escorting myself to the broomstick. But I let her finish her self-righteous diatribe. I wondered if she, too, had been bedded by Leader. She was older than Agatha and my mother—probably close to Leader's wife's age. I could not imagine her sneaking into Leader's study with her skirt lifted over her waist. Phillipa was dry as burnt toast in the summer desert. She was plain, tall and thick-framed with wispy hair. Her passion was Jesus and making us young ladies as miserable as her. Even Jerusha and Brenda often took to mocking Phillipa.

When she finished her lecture, she bid me to follow her, Brenda trailing along. Phillipa closed the door to the familiar broomstick room and said "Undress."

"What?"

"To your under things."

I could not believe she was serious, but Sister Phillipa was not the type to jest. Brenda's face held sullen, but her eyes danced with evil mirth. Sister Phillipa remained unmoved. She held out her arm for the dress as I undid the buttons and stepped out of it. I refused to be humiliated, and I stood with my shoulders back, my hands on my hips. I couldn't hide the knife, I knew there was no sense in trying. Phillipa's eyes flared, "What is the meaning of this?!" She gripped my arm, twisting my skin. "You're going to kill us all in our sleep!" She cried and held my arms while she motioned for Brenda to unstrap the knife. They released me once I was unarmed, and I was directed to read the destruction of Sodom and Gomorrah. Brenda was excused with my dress in hand. The candle burned down and Phillipa lit another before leaving as well. I understood I was to remain there until they returned for me.

The candle burned down and I was left in the dark. I had long since moved away from the bible and the broomstick. The next morning it was Judith sent to retrieve me. Me, nearly naked and curled on the floor. She wrapped a blanket around me and helped me hobble to my room for new clothes.

"They took the knife," I said. "It's Isaiah's knife. It wasn't mine to have stolen."

"They made you strip," Judith said with tight lips. "To humiliate your flesh."

"I'm not humiliated in isolation," I said, trying to jest. "You can't be humiliated by yourself, and in the dark."

Her smile was disappointed. "If they'd made you walk through the whole town stark naked, I'm sure you'd have done it with your head held high." She massaged my knees while I smoldered and winced.

"I don't see how forcing you to expose your flesh is punishment for possibly exposing your flesh."

"I suppose you fight fire with fire." My kneecaps creaked beneath her fingers. "Complaints about you and your sister fall on deaf ears when it comes to my father. He seems to find the two of you entertaining." She pinched my knee, held it, tightening her grasp. She looked at me with her face stony. I winced as her grip tightened, my knee throbbed. I tried to pull away, but she clutched harder. "Why?" she said coldly. "Why is that? Why is he so accommodating of you?"

"I don't know!" I gasped, throwing my hands on hers, trying to pull them off.

"Genesis, you can tell me," she clasped my hands, locking them in that vice of hers. My knuckles ached, pressed tight against each other. "Tell me, why is my father so enraptured by you? So favoring? What have you been talking about—what have you been *doing* in there at his lunch times? He's already set plans to build you a house, a house for you and your sister and mother and that bastard she's carrying!"

I pulled myself away from her. "I swear to you Judith, I don't understand your father's interest in me. I haven't done anything to encourage it. I hate your father with every fiber of my being. Rest assured I'd cut his throat if he ever made a threatening move toward me."

She bit her lip, turned her face away from me. She took a few deep breaths, sniffled. "Don't—don't you let him...." she whispered, her voice shaking. She's worried for me, afraid I'd been had; afraid her father had seduced me—or worse. I took her hand in mine, she squeezed it gently. She swiped the back of her free hand across her nose, finally turned to me again. "Well," she said, sliding her hand into her pocket pulling out a wad of white.

"A bonnet," I said.

"They've requested you cover your hair altogether now."

"Ah yes, my hair, my ultimate weapon of temptation." The absurdity of it set us to laughing while she pinned it on me.

"Our little Quaker lady," she said.

"A wolf in sheep's clothing."

"The thorn in our sides."

I hobbled to deliver Leader's lunch. "You've been dealt with harshly," he said once I placed the tray on his desk. "I've heard tell that you were found in a state rather distressing to Sister Phillipa and Miss Brenda."

"If helping someone clean a wound is 'distressing' then I suppose so."

He opened a drawer beside him. "The ladies do get a bit overzealous at times and become rather passionate in their duties unto the Lord."

"Passionate," I repeated, watching his movements as he reached into the drawer and stood and moved toward me. He held Isaiah's knife up.

"You mean to do harm with this, Sister Genesis?"

"It's for my own protection," I said.

"And what could you possibly need protecting from? Kitchen mice?" he said, he held the dagger away from himself, as if daring me to take it. A smirk twitched on his lips. The hair on my neck quivered. He did not blink, did not shift his gaze at all. If I tried to take it, what would he do? Would he twist it on me, hold it against my throat? What would he expect in return? I dared not take it. I wrapped my arms across my chest. He cleared his throat, pulled the knife back. "You have no need to take matters of protection into your own hand," he said, "No one here is out to harm you. So I think I will hold onto this." And he placed the knife back in his desk. I was dismissed.

Part of me was kicking myself. Why hadn't I taken the knife back? I looked up as I passed his house; Mama was coming out the front door. We locked eyes for a moment. She looked caught, sheepish. The curtains in the window lifted, Leader's wife's face appearing, sneering. There was no love lost between the two of them, so to see Mama exiting the other woman's home was startling. What had gone on in there? What had been said? Threatened? Mama swallowed, wiped her hands on her skirts. She lifted her chin and quickly made her way back to the church.

A cradle appeared in Mama's room soon after. I noticed it at dinner and pointedly ignored it. But it stood there in the corner, drawing my eyes like Lot's wife to Sodom. I said nothing, Mama said nothing, her belly bumping against the table. I couldn't eat, Mama barely ate. She had missed Benediction claiming faintness. Leader's wife took her place, glaring down at me the whole while. And even from where I was standing, I could see the red bruise rising on her cheek. It was not a mark my mother could have made, not in her current state of frailty. Mama's hands were narrow, the mark on Leader's wife was not.

I regarded my mother, looking for any signs of what had passed between the two women. Then I noticed it, the faint swell of the bottom lip. Leader's wife had slapped her hard, wearing a studded wedding ring. Luckily, Leader's wife was frail, too, and the damage was hardly noticeable. But I noticed it, and I felt something for my mother I had never once felt for her before: compassion. Mama's belly had grown rounder while the rest of her seemed to wane, her cheeks hollow, her skin sallow. And now, with her swollen lip, she was almost beautiful in a haunting way. She was not my mother anymore; she was not the woman who tossed my books into the fire, who dragged us away from home in rapture. She was someone else entirely, someone small and timid and tormented.

"You're looking pale, Mama." I said, an olive branch.

"I just need more meat is all," she sighed. "But I so often see it and I can't bring myself to eat it. The smell." It was the closest we ever came to discussing her pregnancy.

"Denney makes good steak," Isaiah offered. I expected Mama to tell her off for mentioning our life outside, but her eyes misted and she smiled.

"He does," she said. We fell back into silence, but I felt us all beginning to breathe again. Mama tucked a flyaway behind my ear. "At least they didn't cut it off." Her palm was warm on my chin.

ISAIAH

At night, I can wander and no one can tell me to do anything. I don't need that much sleep and when I do sleep, I sometimes have dreams about Gramma and Mary and the man in the tree and the wailing. At night, the coyotes howl, and there's owls hooting. The cows all sleep, and the dogs and horses and sheep. It's mostly quiet and the moon comes out bright and white and all the stars, but they're brighter when there's no moon.

I walk around the church, touch the outside of it. Our house back on the ranch is painted white, but the church is just rough grayish wood. When I'm almost around back, I hear voices in Leader's study. I freeze. The door opens and feet move. I peek around the corner. It's Sister Agatha. Her hair's all down and tangled. She straightens her robe and nightgown. She stops and looks around. I hide back around the corner until I hear her walking away. I move quiet as I can toward the study. The door is cracked open, enough for me to peek in. Leader's got his undershirt on and nothing else. His desk is crooked, and he pushes it back in place. His bottom is almost just as hairy and gray as his beard.

My stomach churns and I look away just as Leader starts to bend over to pick up his pants. I run away because I feel sick and giggly at the same time. I just want to laugh and vomit. Sister Agatha is a harlot! I know what that means now. Sister Agatha's a liar and a sneak, too. Leader is an adulterer. And it's the funniest thing in the whole world.

I tell Reuben his daddy's an adulterer. We're mucking horse stalls.

"He ain't. He's a man of God!" Reuben says, smacking his shovel against a pile of horse dung.

"Well I saw him. Him and Sister Agatha."

"No you didn't."

"I almost did."

"You're lying."

"I'm not," I say. "Are you going to shovel or not? I've done almost twice as much as you."

"My hands are getting sore and it smells in here," he says.

"It's just horseshit. It doesn't smell that bad." He scowls at me and I smile.

"I'm gonna tell Sister Agatha you cussed."

"Go ahead," I tell him. "She's nothing more than a whore for your daddy."

"Shut up." He throws down his shovel and clenches his hands.

"Why? It's true!" I say. He's getting mad and I want to laugh at him. He's always teasing me about my Gramma, and saying I was brought up a heathen. "Where do you think all these extra babies come from? The ones without daddies?"

"You don't have a father."

"Yes I do," I throw down my shovel too. I'm started to get riled up. "And we're going back to him. My daddy's a good, honest hardworking man and yours is a lying, lazy old man with a hairy ass who ruts with other men's wives!"

"Well your mother's one of them. She's a temptress like the rest of them!"

I topple him to the ground and punch him smack in the jaw. He tries to push me off, but I'm too heavy. He tries to slap me back, scratches at my arms. I spit on him and he starts to scream. He screams like a little girl and screams that I'm a demon whore. I shout that he's a son of a bitch. He gets his hand around the end of my braid and pulls real hard. My head jerks up. I scratch at his arm and scream just as loud as him.

Some of the older boys hear us and come in to laugh and whistle until Reuben's brother Matthias pulls us apart. Reuben's gotten me pretty good, scratches all over my arms, and my scalp hurts. But he looks worse. His lip is split and bleeding and his eye is getting puffy. He looks at me and starts to cry. Matthias laughs, "A little girl bested you!"

"Shut up!" Reuben shouts and blood spit bubbles out his mouth. Matthias only laughs harder and I feel bad. He's still holding us apart. I'm done being angry. I'm about to say sorry when Leader and his wife show up. Leader's looking at Reuben like he's a pile of muck, and his wife is looking at me with wild eyes, her face getting redder by the second. She grabs me and I know I'm in trouble. At first I try to struggle, but she's got me too tight. I hear Reuben and Matthias say, "Mother, no," and then she slaps me straight across the face, so hard the smack makes everyone silent. She grabs a switch from one of the other boys' hands and spins me around, hitting me willy-nilly. My back, my bottom, the backs of my legs. Each hit cracks like a whip and I almost cry out but I'm mad again and I bite my lip.

I'm thinking of ways to keep myself from crying, and all I can think is how much I hate her and some stupid scripture. *To everything there is a season, and a time to every purpose under the heaven.* Everyone in the barn just stands by watching. *A time to be born, and a time to die; a time to plant and a time to pluck up that which is planted.* She's gone crazy, hitting me as hard as she can over and over. My eyes tear up because the burning's started. *A time to kill...*I bite into my lip so hard it bleeds. *A time to love and a time to hate. A time to kill.*

At last, she's worn herself out. She drops me and the switch and nearly tumbles over herself. She's breathing hard, wheezing. She puts her hand to her head and sways a little. She steadies herself against the stall. I wipe the blood from my lip and I glare at her. "Someday I'll feel your death." I don't know why I say it. Everyone is quiet.

Leader's wife grabs Reuben's hand and pulls him out of the stall, half dragging him, half leaning on him. "I suggest you all get back to work," Leader says. The others all leave the stall. I'm lying on the floor. He reaches out to help me up but I smack his hand away and grab my shovel, pushing myself back up. I want to hit him, just take my shovel and beat him right across the face with it, but I'm tired and sore, and I know he could do much worse to me than his wife did, so I just grip tight to the shovel.

"I'll feel her death, I swear I will," I say, gripping on my shovel and looking him straight in the eye.

"You could be the death of us all," he says with a laugh and tips his hat and leaves.

When he's gone, I run my fingers over the back of my leg. Welts run along my skin like fat worms. I go back to shoveling the muck alone.

They make Genesis stay busy all through dinner, so it's just me and Mama at the table. She's looking ill and hardly eats. I can hardly sit or lean back in my chair. I don't feel much like eating either. "Are you going to vomit?" I say. She doesn't answer. "Can I go?" She nods and I take my plate. "Do you want me to take yours?" She nods again.

Before I get to the door she says, "Are you still hurting?" She's got her eyes closed, gripping the table.

"I'll be fine," I say.

"Answer the question."

"Yes," I say. "I still hurt."

"She hit you too hard then." She takes a deep breath.

"I split Reuben's lip and gave him a black eye."

"She hit you too hard," she says again. She's looking sicker by the second and I leave.

Reuben stays in his mama's house. I'm too sore to lie on my back, but I can't fall asleep on my stomach. I want to tell Reuben I'm sorry, but I don't know when he'll be back. I don't really hate him. I get up and go outside when everyone's asleep. It's late enough that even Sister Flora, who was sitting at the door, has gone to bed.

I go to Leader's house and look in all the windows until I find where Reuben's sleeping. I knock on the window until he wakes up. I've got to stand on my tip toes to see just over the edge. He gets out of bed and opens the window. "I'm sorry for punching you in the face," I say as soon as he gets the window up. "I don't know why I told you all those things, even if they're true."

"It's not true."

"Anyway, I'm sorry."

His lip is puffy and his eye is dark. "I'm sorry too."

I shrug. I beat him better than he beat me. "How long are you gonna have to stay here?"

"Forever, I guess," he says. "Mother says I shouldn't be around you anymore."

"Just because I punched you in the face doesn't mean I hate you. I'll try not to do it again. You hurt me sometimes too."

"I know," he says. "But Mother says you're bad for me. She had to lay in bed all day after—you know."

"Serves her right," I say. "I've got welts the size of snakes."

Reuben sighs. "Why do you have to make her so mad?"

"Why does she hate me so much? She's hated me from the beginning."

"You're my only friend," he says.

"That's not true," I try to lie. "The other boys..."

"They aren't really my friends. They only let me play with them because they're afraid Mother will whip them."

"They tell you that?"

"I heard them talking once."

"Your mama whips people even when they are your friend," I say. "Just because I punched you doesn't mean we're not friends."

"You're still going to be my friend?"

"If you want me to be." He smiles and I smile back. "Come outside with me."

"If Mother finds out, we'll both be in trouble again."

"Has your mama ever even hit you before?"

"No," he says. "But she'll hit you again."

"That's nothing. I don't care if she hits me a hundred times. She'll kill herself before she breaks me."

He scratches at his arm. I know he's been doing it all night. "Mother..."

"She doesn't want you to have any friends. I'm your only friend," I say. "And now we'll probably never get to see each other."

"Alright." He pulls on his boots and climbs out the window.

"Where should we go?" I say.

"Have you ever seen how far the land goes?" he asks. "We could go to the edge of the fence."

"Alright," I say. The moon's only half full, so we have to go slow. We walk and walk but still don't get to the fence. "I bet it goes all the way to the hills," I say.

"I didn't think they were so far," he says. "They look closer. I thought we'd be there by now." We stare at the hills. They are the western hills, and they are smaller than the mountains to the east—the ones my ranch touches—they are rounder, too, not as sharp and jagged, but both east and west are black in the night. But then I see lights blinking off in the distance, bright and round—they are not on the hills, they are in the field.

"Hey, I think someone's out there," I say, pointing to the lights.

"M-maybe we should just go back," he says, but I tug on his arm.

"Come on, we'll be sneaky so they don't see us," and I pull him along. We stumble over rocks and sage bushes and gopher holes. We get closer to the lights and start hearing voices and car engines. "Headlights," I whisper, and we crouch down, running from bush to bush to stay hidden as we move closer. Men are walking in front of the lights, pulling crates from the back of trucks and carrying them to a little cabin, they rattle like glass. It seems much too small to hold them all.

I hear Leader's voice, but I don't know what he's saying because Reuben hears him too. He pulls on my arm, and his voice is scared. "Ok, let's go back now. Or try to find the other end. Let's just go away from here, please?" I nod and I take his hand and we sneak back into the dark, leaving the men and the trucks and the cabin and Leader behind.

GENESIS

I'd gotten used to entering Leader's study before I finished knocking. I'd knock once, wedging the tray against my waist, and immediately enter, eager to get in so I could get back out. It startled me to walk in and see two other men, normal men in charcoal-gray suits, slicked chair, and shined black shoes, sitting across from him.

"I wasn't told you had someone," I said. All of us regarded each other with surprise, one of the men's mouth hanging open, frozen on a word I'd interrupted. Leader's mouth puckered, his eyebrows knit in irritation pointed in my direction. It was the first time he'd ever looked at me in anger. Usually, it was amusement in his eyes, or challenge. But this time, his mood was dark and his displeasure bored into me. "I—I can only carry one lunch at a time...no one said anything about bringing a second," I stuttered, unsure what to do. The suited men regarded my bonnet, one smiled, one puffed air out his nose, a chortle.

"Just bring it here," Leader said, scowling. His voice was different, too. Gone was the voice of the charismatic, self-righteous man and in its place one hard and cold like steel. There was no "Sister Genesis," no big, blood-curdling grin. They watched me shuffle to the desk, drop the tray in front of Leader, the plate and silverware rattling, the gravy jiggling. I glanced at them men, they smiled at me like zoo-gazers. "I don't belong here!" I wanted to scream at them, "I'm not one of them!" But all I did was avert my gaze, wiped my palms on my hands. They were too clean, too neat, too *metropolitan*. I'd never seen anyone like them before. "Go on," Leader said in his non-Leader voice.

Behind me, as I exited, I felt the men's attention turn back to each other. "Like we said," one of those city slickers began to say as I reached the door, "If you won't, we'll find someone who will..."

That night, I was summoned back to Leader's study. He sent his youngest daughter, Little Elizabeth, into the kitchen to tell me while I was up to my elbows in soap suds washing supper dishes. Brenda Peters was meant to be helping me, but she'd conveniently developed a migraine and "the heat of the water was just too much" for her. I was left with Nattie Smith; just turned thirteen and moved up to the young women's dorm. She was small and quiet, and a little afraid of me, so she kept her distance. Two of the older single women were scraping and drying.

Little Elizabeth came in with her pink tongue sticking through her missing teeth. "When you're done, Father wants to see you," she said. The two Sisters glanced up and back down again, pretending like they didn't hear or care, and Nattie kept right on scrubbing.

"It's gonna be a while," I said; we were only halfway through. Elizabeth shrugged and turned on her heel, her loose brown curls bouncing on her shoulders. The Sisters *tsk-tsked* quietly, but not quiet enough I couldn't hear.

When I finished, it was dark, I was tired, and I did not want to go to Leader. But I had sent Nattie on ahead, and she'd surely already told the other girls I was heading to Leader's study. So I went, biting my lip and wringing my hand. The Leader I'd seen just hours before was a different Leader. And while the Preacher Leader might keep me at arm's length, I was not sure what Steely Leader might do.

I knocked on the door. "Enter," came his voice; back to Preacher Leader. I entered, once again, to find him not alone, only this time it was Benjamin seated across from him. I was not comforted by this; my anxiety only heightened. I froze just over the threshold. My throat clenched and my heart beat inside me like a trapped bird. I remembered something Gramma had once said to me, "Some men are like wolves—they prey on weakness—don't ever let them know you're scared." So I stood tall and tried to breathe around my heart.

"Come on in, Sister Genesis," Leader said, beckoning me away from the door. Neither he nor Benjamin stood when I entered.

"What's all this about?" I said, not moving. Father and son glanced at each other. Benjamin rocked a glass on his knee, amber-yellow liquid sloshed about inside. Then I noticed the bottle on the desk between them, another filled glass.

"Word is your birthday's coming soon, just a couple of weeks," Leader said. He reached into his drawer and pulled out a third, empty glass. He un-stoppered the bottle and tipped it, the glass clinking, the slosh of liquid. "Fifteen, isn't it?"

I said nothing. I watched the booze rise in the glass. There wasn't much when Leader quit pouring, not even half full. His ring clinked on the glass when he lifted it. He stood, bringing it to me. I let him stand there with his arm outstretched, offering me a glass I did not want to take. "It's illegal," I said.

"Men's laws can't touch us here," Leader said. Behind him,

Benjamin drained his drink in one go. Almost all my life, booze had been illegal. Gramma had had some stashed away "for medicinal purposes," she'd said. She'd used it on our teething gums, sloshed it down ranch hands who'd needed broken fingers and noses reset. Mama barely approved of its use even on those times. Daddy wouldn't allow it; he'd grown up with a father who drank too much.

"My mother wouldn't like it," was all I could think to say.

Leader's eyebrows twitched. "Is that so?" He held his arm out, still and steady as ever.

Benjamin scoffed from his seat and poured himself more. "That there brought those pretty earrings your Mama's got," he said. "And that cradle. I brought that in myself. Did she like it?"

I took the glass, if only so I could clench something. It smelled like cleaner. I did not drink. Leader returned to his seat; the two of them faced me. So this is not about God at all, I thought. At least for Leader it wasn't. "You're a charlatan," I said, my anger rising.

"I've been called worse," Leader said. He tapped his ring against his own glass. "You're beginning to understand." He took a drink. "There's no money in cattle. There's no money in anything these days."

"Except for this," Benjamin said, lifting his own glass.

"Why are you telling me this?" I said. "When I can leave— when I can leave and go straight to the police?"

"You could," said Benjamin. "But they won't bother us. Not if they want to keep buying their wives all their pretty dresses, keep those shining shoes on their kids' feet."

I squeezed hard, wanting to shatter the glass in my hand. "Why are you telling me this?" I repeated.

"You ought to understand the duty you'll bear in this family," said Leader. "That land of your grandfather's, it's got all sorts of nooks and crannies just a stone's throw up the canyon.

How much do you suppose he'd stashed up there in his day?" He turned to Benjamin.

"Thousands," Benjamin answered. "As legend tells it."

"There's nothing there now," I said. "He put it all in the ranch."

Leader swayed his head thoughtfully. "It's not treasure we need, girl."

"Your grandpa was able to hide up there for weeks at time," Benjamin said. "And was not once found by the authorities."

"And someday," Leader said, "That land will fall to you... and your husband."

My palms sweated against the glass. So this was it. "Is this some sort of proposal?" The two of them shared a smile.

"No," said Leader, in a way that I can only describe as the sly tongue of the Devil—a voice that sent a chill up your spine. Gone was Preacher Leader, replaced with that other man. "This is an examination."

My gut sank, I stopped breathing. "A what?"

"We need to see all we're getting," Benjamin said. "Need to see if you're worthy." He brought his glass to his lips. "Take off your dress."

My skin went cold, like I'd stepped into an icy stream. I'd take off my dress and then what? All I could think in that moment was that if Mama had left us on the ranch, this wouldn't have happened. The men there, though dirty and poor and uneducated had more manners and respect for a girl than this, than these men claiming to be for God, who bribed officials with black market money. "No," I said. The word came out as icy and hard as I felt.

"We'll get your sister to do it then," Benjamin smirked. I threw the glass. He ducked and it shattered on the bookcase, the contents spraying him. He jumped, wiping whiskey from his ear. "You stupid bitch!" he shouted and made to move toward me. I stepped back. Leader cleared his throat heavily, and Benjamin backed down, flopped into his chair.

"Isaiah's a *child*," I said.

"She's almost twelve," Leader said. "And from what I know seeing my own daughters grow up, that's close enough to womanhood. And, given your relation, I'd say we could deduce as much from her what we need to see from you."

I knew he wasn't lying, from the way the words came slithering out of his mouth, I knew he'd pull Isaiah in and have her stripped down in front of me. Judith had said he wasn't interested in young girls, just young *women*. But he wasn't beyond using children to get what he wanted. And he did have a fascination with Isaiah. I'd seen it the day we met him outside Feaney's store five years before. "She's just a kid..." I said. My voice wavered, though, and they heard it. They heard the pleading; they smelled the fear, and they smiled.

Leader leaned back, lacing his fingers behind his head. "I suggest you start with the bonnet."

So I did. I unclipped the bonnet, unpinned my hair. It had grown nearly three inches since we'd arrived and it fell past my collar bone. I unbuttoned my dress, slipped out of it and let it fall around my feet. Hoping this would be enough, I paused, but they only raised their eyebrows, waiting and expecting. Goosebumps rose on my skin. "There's nothing to be shamed of," I heard Gramma tell me. I inhaled, lifted my chin, eyes to the ceiling, glaring at God.

Then there I stood, naked as a bird. I was still hardly more than a girl myself then, still short and thin and straight-hipped, not much of a bosom to speak of, but I stood there with my chest puffed, my chin up, my fingers curled into fists at my side. I would not look at the two of them, but I knew they were looking at me. Though they stayed seated, they might as well have crossed to me and touched me, for I felt their eyes on me like fingers, trailing all the edges and hollows of my body. I made one turn before I brought myself to look at them, seething with rage I was too afraid to act on. Benjamin I had handled, but it was him alone then, and I'd had my knife.

Benjamin raised his glass to me in a crude salute, and Leader nodded. I scrambled back into my dress, not worrying about the underthings. I had to get out. I was so angry, so mortified, that I couldn't speak. I was full of too many words and not enough of them. I wanted to strangle someone and I wanted to cry. I wrenched open the door and ran. I ran to my mother.

By the time I threw open the door, I was crying, heaving for air I could not breathe. "Mama!" I cried out, startling her at her prayers. I stumbled to her, fell beside her. "We have to go! We can't stay here!" I came to her trembling, and she herself quivered. I wanted her to wrap her arms around me, pull me into her, but she did not. She shrank away from me like a wounded animal, her eyes big and worried. She was not at all the woman I had feared as a girl. She was a shell, hollowed by a mania I didn't yet understand. But right then, seeing her like this, it angered me further. Who the hell is this woman? I screamed inside. I grabbed her hands, pulled them to me. "Do you know what they just made me do?!"

"You don't know, you don't know..." Mama started crying. "I wish it wasn't Benjamin," she said. "I tried to suggest Matthias, he's a sweet boy, but she won't let—"

"Mama, don't you understand? It won't matter who I marry. Benjamin will come for me no matter what. You weren't there, you didn't see the way he..." I shuddered at the memory of his gaze on my flesh. "I'm not marrying him." I said. I stood. "I'm getting out of here. I'm getting out of here—"

"No," Mama begged, grabbing my arm. "Not yet. Please." She was so frail, that instead of pulling me back, she lifted from the bed when I tried to pull away from her. "Please don't leave me yet...I can't—" She was so pitiful I could not say no. "Just wait," she said. "Wait, and then you can go." Wait for the baby to come, she was saying, she did not want to birth her baby alone. She'd always had Gramma before, and now she had a bunch of women who vied for the attentions of the same man.

I sat beside her, my hands in my lap. She stopped crying and said nothing. We did not touch. "I will not marry Benjamin," I said. "I'll never marry him. I'll never marry *anyone. Ever.*"

Mama laid her head against my shoulder, put her hand on mine. "No," she whispered. The next morning, Isaiah and Reuben were missing.

ISAIAH

I wait for Reuben outside his window while he pulls on his boots and overshirt. He climbs out real quiet. We stay quiet as we walk past all the little houses, and then we are out beyond them and we can talk normal. "It's a little cold tonight," he says, hugging his arms.

"It's not so bad," I say. "You'll get used to it." The moon is bright enough that we can see well enough to go farther than we normally do, all the way to the edge of the fence. The cows at pasture are standing still and black and don't pay any attention to us. They're sleeping. Every now and then one of them wakes up and moos, or maybe she's sleep-mooing. There's a big old juniper tree right at the fence and we sit beneath it. We lean back against the rough trunk. Reuben closes one eye and points up at the sky. He's tracing the three stars in the hunter's belt.

He'd never even heard of such a thing as the star-shapes until I told him. I don't remember all the stories Gramma used to tell us about them, so I make them up a bit for Reuben, but he doesn't know the difference. "There's not really a hunter," Reuben says. "It's just a tale."

"So what?" I say. "Just because it's a story doesn't mean it can't be interesting. Doesn't mean it's bad either. Wasn't Jesus always telling stories?"

"I guess," he says. He drops his hand and scratches his back against the tree. "Maybe the star-tales are like parables."

"Yeah, a parable." We sit quiet a minute just looking up at the stars and listening to the coyotes far away and the cows nearby.

"Do you think the coyotes can smell us from here?"

"Nah," I say. "They're pretty far. Even if they do, the cows'll go crazy and they'll warn us." So far the cows are just lazy, sleepy fat cows. I get thinking about Mama and the cradle in her room. I've never thought about having a little baby brother or sister before. Reuben's got a little sister, but he probably doesn't remember when she was born, he was only three then. "My mama's having a baby."

"I figured. She's getting real big."

"She's got a cradle in her room now and everything."

"My mother doesn't like yours much." He's frowning.

I know why. Genesis said if I thought about it, I would figure out who the daddy is. Mama's always blushing around Leader, always acts different when he's talking to her. I figured it out after I saw Sister Agatha come out of Leader's study with her skirts twisted. "Do you know how babies are made?"

He's quiet for a second or two before he says. "Yes," and I know he's lying.

"You don't. All this time you've gone on about whores and harlots and you don't even know what they do."

"Well then just tell me," he says, so I do. I tell him everything Gramma told me when Genesis started bleeding. "I knew it was...something," he says. "Something that had to do with being too close together."

"Haven't you ever seen the cows rutting?"

"It can't be the same as that! It looks so silly when they do it."

"Maybe people look silly doing it too," I say.

"Then why do they care so much about it?"

"I dunno, it all seems silly to me," I say. It's getting a little colder now, so we scoot closer together so our legs and shoulders are touching.

"So you'll have a little brother or sister."

"Only thing is, we don't have the same daddy," I say. "And there aren't any unmarried old men here." I know he'll get angry if I say what's next, so I don't know why I do it anyway. I just whisper, "It'll be your brother or sister too." I feel a little disgusting saying it. I think maybe he's going to shout at me or twist my arm, but he says nothing.

He sits still and quiet. And then I hear him start to cry. At first it makes me angry. "Aw, what are you crying for?" Then he buries his face in his elbow and keeps crying. Real crying, crying from a sad deep inside him. I'm confused and a little sad for him and I don't know what to do except put my arms around him and hold him tight. He hugs me back and cries. We stay out beneath the tree too long and forget to go back before we fall asleep.

GENESIS

They locked me down once they realized Reuben and Isaiah were gone. I was already up, already in the kitchen pulling out cooking sheets and mixing bowls for breakfast biscuits. I was already up to my elbows in flour with the other single women when Leader's wife came storming in, her own apron tied on her waist. "Where's your sister?" Her eyes burned and she clutched at my arm.

"What?"

She pressed her fingernails into my flesh. "Your sister! She's taken my boy. She's gotten him killed! I know it. Where is she?"

"Isaiah's missing?" My heart thrummed. I knew Isaiah wouldn't have left without telling me. She might have been hiding somewhere. Or Leader was hiding her somewhere, I thought. Hadn't I done what he'd wanted last night? Was he holding her hostage until I agreed to marry Benjamin? But then why would he hide Reuben as well?

"She's possessed Reuben, convinced him to follow in her devilish footsteps, disobeying me!" Leader's wife dragged me from the kitchen, across the yard, back to the house.

Oh Isaiah, what have you done? "They probably just fell asleep somewhere after sneaking out," I tried to tell her, but the woman was beyond words. It was early light out, the western sky still deep blue. The Community was waking, coming alive, moving about behind their doors. We stopped in the yard, she shook me, shouting, calling everyone's attention to us. The people stepped over their thresholds to witness.

Leader appeared on his porch, placing his hat on his head. "What's this?" Behind him followed all his daughters and sons, except for Reuben, who was missing.

"The little one! She's taken Reuben!" Leader's wife released me and threw her hands to her face. "She's led him to the Devil."

It was a whir then. I saw Mama, still in her nightdress and robe, looking gaunt in the face as ever, eyeing me with a hollow gaze. We looked at each other and understood; if Leader's wife found Isaiah before anyone else, it would be fire and brimstone for my sister. Sister Phillipa dragged me away, back to my room.

Judith reached me, took my hand. "I'll find her. I'll get to her before Mother does." I was locked in my room, left to stare at my hands with my heart in my throat and a stone in my gut. *This will be it. This will be the end,* I thought.

ISAIAH

They find us asleep with our arms around each other. It's Judith, Benjamin and Matthias that find us. "Oh, sweet Jesus," Judith says, and I know we're going to be in trouble. All of us are silent as we go back. We get to their house and our mamas are standing in the door.

"Oh God in heaven they've been found!" Mama cries, and tries to come out, but Leader's wife pushes her back.

"Judith, take Reuben inside," Leader's wife says as she makes straight for me, her eyes crazy.

"Mother!" Reuben starts to say and grabs my hand, but it doesn't matter. Judith is pulling him away and he's trying to hold on, but she pulls hard, hides her face from me. Just as Reuben's hand slips from mine, his mama's on me.

She holds me by the collar and slaps me, I hear Mama saying "Sister, no!" and Leader's wife slaps me again. She grabs my hair and pulls my head back so I'm looking straight into her crazy eyes. She's spitting angry. "You could have killed him!" she's screaming. "You could have killed him!" She starts dragging me across the yard, toward the women and children's house. Mama's escaped, trying to talk Leader's wife down, but the old woman is crazy and pushes Mama away so hard she falls right on her big belly. She stands and stumbles, holding her stomach like it hurts.

Leader's wife wraps my braid tighter around her hand, twisting my head so I can hardly see anything. We're in Sister Agatha's room, and Leader's wife is knocking things over on Sister Agatha's desk. Agatha is there suddenly, "I'll get them," she's saying, and Leader's wife pulls me along, down the hall to the broomstick room.

"I'll teach you, I'll teach you!" Leader's wife keeps saying. I feel the switch come down on me before the door is even closed. She's just as wild as last time, maybe even more, and I realize that this time she'll kill me. She'll kill me even if she'll kill herself to do it. I've lost count of the smacks, they're coming so fast and hard I can't breathe. Just when everything on me is hurting, she throws down the switch and reaches toward Sister Agatha who hands her something shining. I hear metal blades slide across each other. Scissors.

I didn't cry all while she was smacking me, I didn't even make a sound. But I'm screaming now. I try to pull away, but she just grips tighter on my hair. I shake my head, trying to get her to let go. I scratch and slap her hand. I try to stamp on her feet, hurt her more than she's hurt me. "Agatha!" she yells over me, "Hold her!" She pushes me to my knees.

Then Sister Agatha's in front of me. She grabs my arms and holds me by the wrists with one hand and holds my chin with the other. I keep screaming and wiggling. "You'll end up with shears through your skull if you don't stop, girl!" Leader's wife shouts.

I scream so hard my throat rattles. Leader's wife pulls tight on my braid and I start to cry. I feel my hair tearing. She's rough with the scissors, chomping them through my hair. And then it's done. The scissors snap shut, and my head pops forward. I hear my braid drop to the floor. Leader's wife throws the scissors down and Sister Agatha lets me go. I fall. The old ladies start to leave and I crawl after them, I get Sister Agatha's skirt in my hands and I pull it as hard as I can, screaming as loud as I can. The dress rips, but she pushes me back just as they get to the door and slam it shut. The lock clinks.

I bang and bang on the door and I scream and scream every curse I know. I kick and bang and scream until I can't hold my head up and I just curl up on the floor and cry. I touch my hair and I cry.

GENESIS

I hardly breathed until I heard Isaiah's screams. I ran to the door then, tried to pull it open. I shouted for my sister, demanded the door be opened. In a frenzy I took scissors to the door, pocking the wood with useless gouges. I knew it would do nothing. I was locked away the rest of the day, and Isaiah was locked away for three days with only bread and water delivered morning and night.

I contemplated how I'd kill Leader while I drew long, pale gashes in the door with the scissors. I'd scalp him, skin his beard, leave him as naked as he'd left me. I'd gut him, cut him open like a butchered cow. I'd take his wife down for good measure, too, but her I'd strangle; I'd do it with Isaiah's hair. When I'd exhausted my violent visions on the lot of Leader's family, I turned to Mama. It was her fault we were here to begin with. She ought to be punished, too, I thought. Until I saw her.

Her hair was frayed, her eyes empty. She looked like a madwoman and I knew she never intended this. She was punishing herself. She wouldn't eat, and, when she did, she'd throw it all back up. Her hair turned white, her skin turned gray. She prayed a string of unintelligible mumbling, rocking back and forth.

When Isaiah was released, Mama wept into her jagged hair. Judith tried to straighten out the severe cut, resulting in a short bob, the shortest Isaiah's hair had been since her infancy. If she'd have been younger, she'd have looked like a boy.

Reuben was kept at his mother's side, excused from any duties the other children were assigned. Isaiah, her hair shorn like Samson, stopped fighting. She was bruised and sore, her black eyes hollow. She did not talk back; she didn't speak at all. When the Sisters asked her questions, she stared at them without blinking, still as a statue. Rather than infuriate them though, it seemed to scare them, and they let her alone. She would not eat; she would not do chores. Instead, she got up, made her bed, and sat all day on top of it until it was time to go to bed.

I refused to deliver Leader's lunch. I told them if they made me, I'd gut him body and soul. They gave the job back at to Lucy McDonnell. I never saw Leader's wife, with the exception of Sunday sermon, Reuben fast at her side, bruise on her eye. I'd have gutted her too, given the chance. I'd just look at Isaiah and the fury would rise; if I'd had a gun, I'd have taken them all down. But I didn't know where they kept them. Leader did not apologize, nor did he mention the incident. He carried on as if it was all standard. He instructed the men to break ground for a new cabin.

And Mama sickened, grew even more manic. She'd looked at us like we were ghosts tormenting her with our appearance. She took to her bed, covered in sweat. Sister Phillipa woke me in the middle of the night, her voice anxious, "It's your mother."

"Is it..." I could not say "the baby." I could only make do with, "Is it time?" My gut flittered and sunk. The zero hour. We could deny it no longer. Guilt welled in me as I rose from my bed. An infant didn't deserve this, didn't deserve to be despised by his blood, even if the blood we shared would only be half. *I'll never love him.* But I could accept it. I'd accept it.

Sister Phillipa didn't answer, just bid me to come. So I followed her to Mama's room, where she lay on her bed surrounded by the other women. To my anger and surprise, Leader's wife was among them. I wanted to strangle her then and there, but my mother's condition quelled me. She was an awful sight, soaked with sweat, so pale she was almost translucent, her stomach distended while the rest of her was frail.

"We heard her cry out," one of the women said.

"We thought it was the baby, but she's saying there's no pains."

"She asked for you."

So I was there. Mama looked at me, her eyes focusing. She smiled and reached out for me. I let her take my hand. She was slick, cold. She smelled sour. I was numbed with an overwhelming flood of regret and resentment beyond my comprehension. "Get Isaiah," I said.

No one argued. I held my mother's hand, sat beside her bed. Isaiah was delivered and took her position beside me. Mama said her name and reached for her as well. Isaiah pulled back stiffly, just out of Mama's reach. Disappointed, Mama dropped her hand. Isaiah leaned forward and extended her arm over Mama, her hand hovered over her chest. She bit her lip and pressed her palm against Mama's skin. Mama laid her hand on top of Isaiah's and they paused, Mama's chest moving up and down beneath their hands. Mama's eyes closed. I touched my fingers to Isaiah's arm. She looked at me with her tunnel-black eyes.

She shook her head.

Mama saw. She opened her mouth to speak, squeezed my

hand with little strength. "Genesis..." She tried to say, imploring me.

"We'll bury you beside Gramma," I said. She nodded and closed her eyes again.

She took three days to die. The child was already dead, had probably been dead since she fell on it. This we would not find out until later, until we got her body back and a doctor examined her. Isaiah and I stayed at Mama's bedside nearly the whole time it took her to die. They let us. Neither of us cried. I would blame Leader forever for her death, but whether she'd left us or not, I doubt we would have made it through the rest of our lives unstrained. We were too different, too much out of her view of perfection, too far from what she had envisioned for us. But perhaps if Leader had not seduced her, we would have learned to live together just as she and Gramma had.

The other sisters came in and out, prayed over her, told us to sleep. Mama's would be their second death. "Mother prays night and day," Judith told me. "She's looking ill herself."

Your sins will find you out.

"We're getting out," I said to Judith. She teared up, but nodded. She squeezed me and left for the night. Or so I thought. She returned hours later holding Isaiah's knife.

She took my hand. "I wasn't here," she said, "and I never broke into my father's office."

It was getting late, the candles burned low, when Isaiah gasped, pulling me from my reverie. It wasn't so much a gasp as one long, drawn out inhale. "Genesis," I heard her say in a low voice, and Mama was gone.

Not knowing what else to do, we stood hand in hand and stared down at Mama's body. With Mama now gone, there was nothing to keep us. I grasped Isaiah's hand, seized with burning intention. "We're going."

I gripped the knife. I pulled her away from our mother's

bedside. "Are we just gonna leave her?" she asked. For now, I thought, my mind whirring. Our interlude of melancholy was suspended and in me rose a frantic desire to leave, to get out. We spoke in raised voices, and the others heard, they came into the hall. I pointed the knife at them as I dragged Isaiah along.

"She's dead and we're leaving!" I exclaimed. I had become the madwoman. Sister Phillipa tried to talk me down, and I saw Sister Agatha run out the door, headed for Leader's. Someone wailed from Mama's room, confirming her death.

Sister Phillipa stood before us, blocking the exit with her stature. "Is this wise?" She said, "You're behaving like a crazy woman. Surely this is your grief and it would be best--"

I was nose to nose with her in an instant, pulling on her collar to bring her face down to mine, the point of the blade beneath her jaw. "You move out of my way or I swear to God I will cut your neck open right here in front of everyone." She swallowed and stepped aside.

I pulled Isaiah over the threshold, picking up speed as we got outside. Sister Agatha had raised alarm: *Addie's died, her daughters are crazed!* They were coming out, and we ran, the knife raised. Isaiah suddenly screamed my name and I felt her tug, her hand slipped from mine. I fell. Leader's wife had grabbed her. The woman was waifish by nature, but fervor turned her in another being altogether. She had wanted to be rid of us since we'd arrived and now that we were leaving, she couldn't release us.

Leader was coming toward us, walking at his self-assured leisure. I pounced. I took Leader's wife by the front of her dress and drew the blade across her cheek in a smooth sweep, blood beaded from the slit. She cried out and released Isaiah, held her hand to her cheek. I grabbed her hair then, pulling her close to me, the knife at her throat. Isaiah took hold of her wrist, her eyes glistening.

"You stop right there, Leader!" I said. "All of you stop, or I will cut her again."

"Genesis," Leader pleaded, he continued speaking but his wife screamed over him. The other adults moved toward us, and I pressed the blade tighter to the woman's neck. Leader motioned for everyone to halt. He held his palms up to me. "I know you won't hurt her," he said.

"No?" I said. "She killed my mother, I could do it." The knife vibrated in my hand, the tip bit into her skin, a small bead of blood appeared.

"You will burn in hell, girl," Leader's wife spat. "You and your witch sister!" She attempted to shake Isaiah off.

"My sister and I are leaving, you follow us, and I will make sure this whole place goes to hell with us." Leader and I eyed each other, each of us weighing out our options. He could try to keep me there, force me to stay, force me to marry Benjamin, but I could kill his wife in the process, then I would probably kill Benjamin if given the chance. I could kill Leader's wife, and they would all have a reason to pounce, to hold us there. I just wanted to go home. I just wanted to go home and forget about the Community. I pushed Leader's wife to the ground and took up Isaiah's hand again.

"I told you I'd feel your death," Isaiah said, glaring down at the older woman. Leader's wife looked up at her with wide, terrified eyes.

We ran. I heard some shuffling, someone asking if they should go after us, and Leader saying no, just let us go. We ran in the dark, climbed over the gate, tripped on sagebrush, scraped our knees on the dry soil. We ran until we thought we'd die. Miller's ranch was two miles away—we ran for maybe a mile and a half, and trudged the rest. We fell on the Millers' door with all the energy we had left. Mr. Miller opened his door, catching us as we tipped in. He called back to his wife,

"It's Levi's girls!" She came running down in her nightgown and gray-streaked hair. They scooped us inside, let us sleep while Miller sat on his porch with a shotgun, took us home in the morning.

Daddy came out to the porch as we drove up. Isaiah and I leapt from the truck as soon as Miller stopped and we ran to our father. The three of us stood on the porch, staring at each other for a brief moment of relief and surprise. He looked older and gray, and changed. He had always been a tall, lean, clean-shaven man, but he'd grown a mustache and stubble and his body had thinned in our absence. "It was so much worse there," I said with a cracking voice. Daddy pulled us in tight, into a violent and desperate hug while the dam broke.

PART III

SUMMER 1933- SUMMER 1935

GENESIS

I hadn't expected my mother's death to sting me as it had. I had been so angry with her in the time leading up to her death, angry at her for abandoning us, then for dragging us to the Community. She had ruined everything, including herself. But your mother is still your mother. The day after we came back, Daddy drove us back out to the Community with the Sheriff Burnhamto get Mama's body. "She's still my wife," Daddy had said when the sheriff asked why. "And she should lay with her family." Leader was nowhere to be seen, and the others were apprehensive at first about giving her up—they'd already gotten her in a coffin, nearly put her in the ground. Isaiah and I stayed in the truck while everyone's eyes stayed on us. Judith came to the window, holding my books wrapped in a sheet of linen.

"Mother's taken ill," she said. "She's been in bed since the moment you got out. We patched her up..." she eyed Isaiah.

"I'm sorry about the cut," I said, but I wasn't.

"It's nothing, really. It hardly needed bandaging. It was

clean," Judith said. "She's always been prone to frailty, and..." She shrugged and tried to hand my books to me.

And she killed my mother, I wanted to add, I wanted to spit the words at her. I didn't need to; Judith seemed to read my thoughts and dropped her eyes. But it wasn't fair to Judith, it was not her fault. She had been my friend.

"Keep them," I told her, tapping the books. She smiled and patted my hand.

They loaded Mama's coffin into the truck and we left. The doctor and sheriff came, they opened the coffin, looked inside to rule out any foul play. Doctor said it was most certainly the death of the baby that had caused Mama's subsequent death, the rotting infant making her sick. I didn't ask if he could have saved her. From his utterance of "Unfortunate," I gathered that he could have. I could not read Daddy's face as he looked on our mother's misshapen body. He'd lost Mama before we did. I wondered why he never just divorced her. She couldn't request the divorce herself, but Daddy could have done it, and I didn't think they'd loved each other anymore. I wasn't sure they'd ever loved each other, but he did not set her aside. I thought it would be improper to ask right then.

We buried Mama beside Gramma like we said we would. We did not mention the Community; we did not mention her ever leaving us. Two weeks later, a note was delivered from Judith that her mother died. *She died believing your mother was haunting her,* the note said. I hoped my mother was haunting them all. I didn't tell Isaiah. She already knew.

I never told Daddy all the details about living in the Community. I hadn't wanted Daddy feeling guilty that he let us go, believing Mama when she'd said we'd be safer with her. I told him Leader was a bootlegger; but I did not tell him about Benjamin, or that he and his father had coerced me into stripping before them. I told Daddy about Isaiah's hair being cut as punishment—how else could I explain it? But I did not tell him about the broomsticks, or the whippings, or that Mama had become a ghost. I didn't tell anybody about any of these things. I didn't want to talk about the Community at all; I wanted to forget about it altogether, but the town wanted to talk.

Everyone was polite enough not to ask us directly, but I knew they whispered to each other. *Did you hear their mother took them out to that whack ranch?* I imagined they'd said. *Their mother died giving birth to that charlatan's baby.*

"Sorry to hear about your mother," they said to us. "Does he really keep all the women for himself?"

I'd shrug and reply with something snide, vague, like "There's more children than all the married couples can account for."

"Ridiculous," they'd say, though obviously intrigued.

Even though the season had already opened by the time we'd returned, Daddy took it upon himself to give the season-opening speech to the hands as Mama once had. He wasn't quite as articulate as Mama and was much crasser. "These are my girls, any of you much as throw a wandering eye on them in a way I don't like, I'll shoot your balls off," he'd say. "And that's if neither of them cut you open first." He'd laugh then, and those that knew us would laugh too. It was jest and gravity in one.

The temporary hands came in greater numbers than they had in years before—many of them too thin, too desperate. Sometimes whole families came through, stayed a night or two with us, bunkered down in tents on the land or huddled together in Gramma's room—Isaiah and I were still haunted by the room and continued to share the same bed, making up for all the months the Community had kept us apart. Each person passing through looked rougher than the last, the men thin and haggard, the women gaunt and looking twenty years older than they were, their children dirty and ragged. We hardly had enough to keep them all, but Daddy took on as many as he could. Some just needed a week or two of work as they passed through, a hot meal. We still had plenty of clothes from our childhood that we gave up willingly to the children.

We had to cut into our own stock to keep everyone fed. Our pantry was perpetually low, the potatoes and corn and bottled beans gone in a matter of days. The mothers who stayed with us ate sheepishly, their men with guilt. I looked at them all and thought—*Is this what it means to be a proper wife? To follow your husband through the dirt and grime of the world? To follow him through hunger?* We fared better than most—we never went hungry at least—a few ranches around us were given up, the Millers' among them. But we felt the strain as well. A cow or two a month would go missing; sometimes we found pieces of them on remnants of old fires along the very edges of our land.

We had to let many repairs on the house go undone, the paint flaked and curled, the porch rails cracked. We had to make do with taking out and adding stitches and strips of cloth to my dresses as I got taller and my body filled into womanhood. I patched Daddy's pants, and hemmed Gramma's old things for Isaiah.

Daddy taught me how things ran on the ranch because someday it would be ours, mine and Isaiah's. I didn't know then that it already was, that Mama had signed her ownership over to us when she took us to the Community. Daddy must have known, but did not tell us, and I never got the chance to ask him why. He told me how we traded, how to keep the herds balanced, how to check the fences, keep the men in line. Still, he never showed me the ledgers, never showed me how much was coming in and how much was going out. I thought that meant we were doing just fine.

And despite the rough patches, it felt like we *were* doing just fine. It felt like we could put the whole fiasco of the Community behind us because we had our father and our home back.

By our second summer back, I was sixteen, liquor was legal again, and I noticed a difference in the way some of the younger hands looked at me. There was one, Arlo Shepherd, who arrived that summer with a fresh face and soft hands; he'd never worked a hard day in his life, but acted like a hotshot around the ranch. He wasn't bad, just arrogant and cocksure, and I did my best to ignore him.

But one night, I'd stayed out a bit too late in the barn fawning over a new colt with Isaiah, and I crossed paths with Arlo as I made my way back to the house. He was fresh from the newly-reopened bar and stumbling over himself. Liquor may have been legal again, but Daddy still expected the hands to stay respectable and able to get up for work the next morning. I could already tell Arlo would not be waking up in the morning by the way he approached me, slanted like he was trying to walk uphill. I could not avoid him, he was directly between me and the house, so when he called out to me I stood still and let him come to me.

Arlo babbled and slurred to me, telling me the night was fine, that my hair looked nice in the moonlight, and that I ought to be kissed in said moonlight. Then he reached for me, took hold of my wrist. He was not aggressive or rough, but I panicked, remembering Benjamin's hands pinching that same wrist behind my back, and I swung out and broke Arlo's nose. When his head popped back, and his hand came off me, I gut-punched him and ran away. I sat on my bed, hugging myself until Isaiah came in much later. When she asked what was wrong, I said "Nothing," and when she got into bed beside me, I fell right to sleep and nearly forgot about Arlo.

In the morning as I was making breakfast, Daddy came marching back into the house, jaw set and eyes blazing. His footfalls were hard and heavy on the porch, and when he entered, he stared at me from across the kitchen. "Are you hurt?" he said. He spoke low, but I heard the fury in him; it rumbled deep like an earthquake.

"No," I said, shaking my head. I wasn't sure if it was me he was angry with. He grunted and turned hard, reaching for his shotgun. Then he pulled open the door and went marching back out. It hit me then that he was going after Arlo; someone had seen or heard from a distance and told Daddy that Arlo had done something to me. I went after Daddy. I'd never seen him so angry before and it scared me what he might do. My voice was frozen in my throat and I couldn't call out after him, I couldn't explain. So I just followed him into the bunkhouse, paying no mind to the groggy, half-dressed men.

Daddy went straight to Arlo's cot, lifting his shotgun. He ripped Arlo's blanket off him and jabbed him hard in his side. Arlo woke abruptly, his eyes wide and confused. "Get up, get dressed, get gone," Daddy said.

Arlo's nose was big and purple, bleeding into his eyes. I felt guilty but still could not bring myself to speak. The smell of his boozing wafted from him. He opened his mouth to protest, but Daddy only pointed the gun between his eyes. "I thought I was clear about touching my daughters," he looked over Arlo's bruised face. "You're lucky she got to you first. Now get up and get gone."

Arlo didn't try to argue and gathered his things, all the while Daddy's gun pointing at him, and the rest of us watching, frozen. Arlo stomped out with his boot laces flapping, Daddy followed close behind, and I came after. We trailed along to the front of the house, but Arlo kept going down the drive. Halfway, he turned around and shouted obscenities back to my father, who in turn shot at the air above him, we all flinched, and Arlo hurried on. We watched him go, and right then I decided I would never tell Daddy about Benjamin and Leader. Daddy had never asked, but I knew I couldn't ever let him know. I knew right then that Daddy would kill for me, and I was sure Leader was not above killing either. I wouldn't even tell Isaiah, afraid she'd let it slip and we'd end up with a war on our hands.

The seasons bloomed and waned, and both Isaiah and I were children no longer. I was asked on dates, but I was afraid of the attention. What if they were like Benjamin? Would I watch my father kill someone then? What if they wanted to kiss? What if I was forever haunted by Benjamin, and anytime someone tried to touch me I reacted like I had with Arlo? So I grew to fear men that looked at me.

Isaiah, on the other hand, smirked at and joked with the younger hands in ways that made them fall over themselves; they went red and flustered around her. She was growing more striking each year. The hands were afraid of her and enchanted by her, but they'd do nothing out of fear and respect for my father. I knew she didn't really think of them as anything more than the boys on the ranch; she thought she was one of them. She didn't, or couldn't, think of herself as being capable of enticing them. But at fourteen, she blossomed into more of a woman than I had been at her age. Her eyes turned dark, poignant, like staring into an abyss that cut through souls when she was upset. Her hair grew back fuller than before, the fine hair of her girlhood gone.

ISAIAH

Genesis asks me if I want to go into town with her. "Might as well," I say. By midmorning, she's got breakfast cleaned up and we're in the truck, the key already in the ignition. "Daddy doesn't need the truck today?"

"Wouldn't be taking it if he did." She grinds the truck into gear and we bump and sway over the gravel.

"Where are we off to?"

"I want a watermelon," she says. "And we might as well check the post and see if there's any material marked down. I could use a new dress, you could use a new shirt or two as well. And we need more buttons and thread."

"Feaney's and the post office then."

Genesis shrugs and pulls onto the tarred road leading to town. "You've got somewhere else in mind?"

The old church is still empty. The diner is the only new building, and, though the storefront has been standing since forever, there's a new soda fountain. It used to be where the newspaper was printed until we just got lumped in with the county paper. The in-town kids go there after school and all through the summer, but us ranch and farm kids don't make it to town that much. "Daddy says we can go," Genesis says, "The soda fountain. If we want."

"It's a bit early for ice cream." And I don't want to see any other kids. I haven't been to school in nearly four years. I haven't even spoken to most of the others since then. More often than not, the in-town kids attend the high school in the big town over the pass. I would have started last year, had I finished at the town school here.

Like she's reading my mind, Genesis says "You can go to school this year if you want. There's still time to register. I'll even drive you." If she had gone like she was supposed to, she'd be finishing this year.

I shake my head. If either of us was the schooling type, it was her. "Don't know what I'd do with all that education," I tell her. I have no plans to be a nurse or a teacher or really anything other than what I already am.

"We've got the ranch anyway," Genesis says. Yeah, we've got the ranch. We pull into Feaney's first, on the south end of town. The doors on the truck squeal when we open them. A woman nods at us as we pass her in the door. She's familiar but I don't remember who she is. She's at least as old as Gramma was. Maybe she was part of the old church congregation.

Inside the shop is dim but several people mill about. Mr. Feaney's at his counter chatting with Mrs. Garrett, the banker's wife. She wears too much make up, trying to cover up her wrinkles but it just makes her face look chalky. She's a nice lady, if a little over-the-top. "Hello girls," she says. Her voice is too high to be natural. She has a habit of trying to speak like some high society lady from back East—like the doctor's wife.

"Morning, Mrs. Garrett," Genesis and I both say.

"How's that lovely father of yours?"

"He's fine," Genesis says. "I see your toothache's cleared. You got to the dentist after all."

"Oh yes, dear," says Mrs. Garrett. "Though it took me nearly half a bottle of gin to get there!" She starts to laugh and then seems to remember that we're just girls and not her luncheon ladies and chokes on her laugh. "Well, I suppose you've got some business to conduct with Mr. Feaney here." She thanks the old man and wishes us a good day.

Feaney seems relieved to see the back of her. "Biggest gossip in town if there ever was one," he tells us. "Now what can I do for you ladies?"

Genesis hands him a slip of paper. "Daddy's made a request for these."

Feaney calls back to his grandson Keith, a boy of about twenty with a square face and broad shoulders. He looks out of place in here, where everything's stacked tight. I imagine he knocks over more than his fair share of goods each day. He smiles shyly at Genesis who hardly gives him any notice in return. Feaney and Keith make themselves busy gathering Daddy's things while Genesis and I go to the back of the store where Mrs. Feaney leans over her fabric counter, flipping through the pages of a catalog.

She looks like everyone's grandma—even more than our Gramma ever did—with hair all silver and plump hips. "You can buy a whole house and have it delivered by train, did you know?" she says as we step up to the counter.

"They've been doing it a while," Genesis says.

"How do they get it from the train to here?" I ask. We're quite a ways from the nearest train station.

Mrs. Feaney sets aside her catalog and is clearly disappointed by our unimpressed reactions. "By truck, I suppose," she says.

"It comes in pieces, not as a whole house," says Genesis.

"That'd be a thing to see though, wouldn't it?" I have to say, imagining an entire house like ours making its way through the pass, just trucking along down the road.

"We're in need of some buttons and thread and any marked-down fabric if you've got it."

"Got a few new patterns in, too, if you're interested."

The Feaneys send us off with a stick of candy each, like we're children who've behaved well. We try to act like we're too old for candy, but we take them anyway and pop them in our mouths as soon as we're outside and walking down the street to the post office. We pass by the soda fountain and I can see a couple girls I recognize through the window.

None of the kids in there are really any better off than we are; in fact, we probably have more money than a lot of them, but something about them still makes me feel grimy and uncultured. The girls I spot are all within a year or two of my age, girls I attended school with. Betty, Melissa, and Samantha. They see us pass by and recognize us as well, and we all wave politely. We've all known each other since we were little girls and we'll always share those days in the school yard when we got our braids pulled by the same boys.

I can bet at least one of them will be married in the next two years with a kid coming soon after. It's already happened to a couple of girls Genesis's age. I watch the three of them as we pass, see them chatting, noticing how grown up they seem now. Betty used to run around in bibs like me when we were girls, hand-me-downs from her brother. But now she looks pretty in a simple hand-sewn, but stylish, dress. In my reflection, I look just like an older version of myself from those school-girl days, still wearing worn-out bibs and my hair pulled back into a single braid.

A couple more women stop us on the street and ask after

Daddy, promise to stop by with a casserole sometime. "Daddy's popular, isn't he?" I say to Genesis.

"He's an eligible bachelor," she says.

"Those ladies are all married."

"Doesn't stop them wanting to take care of him," she opens the post office door. "They all brought him food while we were gone." Whenever she talks about being in the Community, she always says "when we were *gone*" like we'd just disappeared for the better part of a year. She never talks about the Community if she doesn't have to.

There's generally not much in the post and anything that comes is for Daddy: letters from livestock traders and bills and notices from this place or that, once in a while a letter from someone looking for work or from his sister, our Aunt Celia, in North Dakota. We've only met her once, right before she got married and brought her man to get Daddy's approval since their own father's been out of their lives for decades.

Mr. Eckhart, the postmaster, hands us over our stack, peering over his thin glasses balancing on the end of his long nose. He's an impossibly thin man the color of old paper. "Looks like the ranch is picking back up again," he says. "Your stacks have been getting bigger lately."

"It's been hard for everyone," Genesis answers. I've lost count how many times I've heard that over the last few years. "Daddy's had his work cut out finding new traders after so many of the old ones went under."

Mr. Eckhart nods. "One more," he says, sliding another envelope across the counter. "Not addressed to your daddy."

Confused, Genesis takes the envelope and I strain to see it. Sure enough, scrawled across the front is her name. "Thank you, Mr. Eckhart," she says, her eyes still on the letter, and she turns to head out the door. He's disappointed she doesn't open it and read it right there. Nosy bastard, Gramma used to call him. She was convinced he reads the mail before giving it over to the rightful owners. But Genesis's letter is unbroken.

We're back in the truck before Genesis opens the letter. She pulls out a sheet of paper and another sealed envelope. She reads through the letter. "It's for Judith," she says, tapping the envelope. "From her brother Adam. Judith somehow got a hold of one of his letters and wrote him back, telling him to send his letters to me and I can get them to her." She hands me the envelope and the letter and starts up the truck. "I wonder how she got a letter out."

"Matthias, I bet. When he was sent out to find his bride." I read through the letter addressed to Genesis. *I would be much obliged to you for this... It's been so many years since my sister and I have been able to speak to each other...I haven't forgotten them since I left even though my mother and father all but disowned me...* "I wonder what hers says." I wish I could open it and read it myself.

"Don't you dare, Isaiah," Genesis says. "Judith deserves some things in her life that are untampered with."

"I know." She still treats me like a child sometimes, doesn't trust me to be responsible and respectful of other people. I set the letters in my lap and pop the end of my candy stick in my mouth. "'Untampered'. You and your fancy book-learning words."

"You and your damned ranch-learned ones." I stick my tongue at her. She smiles and flicks my ear quickly between shifting gears.

Genesis was driving the truck by the time she was my age, but I haven't gotten the hang of it, all the pedals and the gears. The thing's dead and it's not like an animal you can just talk and push into doing what you want it to do. There's a horse that was born the summer we came back from the Community. I asked Daddy if it could be mine and he said sure, so he and I raised the colt up just for me, and I take him at nights to see Reuben. Even if I could drive the truck, I couldn't take it out to the Community. Besides, I like the feel of the horse moving beneath me and the smell of the night rising dry from the warm earth and the millions of stars free and unframed above me.

I don't go every night. Not even every other night. I just go when I feel like going. Reuben tells me to come back every night, but I tell him no. It's too far, and I've spent enough time there. I didn't go for a long time, not until my horse was big enough to break. I keep my knife on my ankle like Genesis did. She figured out I was going back to the Community and said, "At least just take the knife. Just keep it on you." So I do. I haven't ever had to take it out though.

When we get home, Genesis heads straight to the kitchen to start on supper. I sit on the porch and listen to the chopping, the sizzling sounds coming from the kitchen. Some women hum or sing while they work, but Genesis is silent. She used to, before we went to the Community. I think maybe she's just lonely in there, but when I offer to help, she's just as silent and extra frustrated. I can't chop things right, or stir the gravy fast enough, or I'm too slow and in the way. She always pushes me out of the way and takes over. And if I just sit there and try to chat with her, it's all "mhmms" and "yeahs" and "I dunno, Isaiahs." It's hard to laugh and joke with her anymore.

I can laugh and joke with the hands. But they're usually too busy for much more than a few minutes chat and won't talk frank with a girl around. These days, there's only one person who really talks to me anymore, and that's Reuben.

And at night, when everyone's gone to bed, I tuck Judith's letter into my overalls, saddle up and head down the valley, walk my horse through the Community to Reuben's window. He's sitting up on the edge of his bed and when I knock on the glass, he jumps a little. He's tall now, tall and skinny, still blonder than all his brothers. His hair's still fine like baby hair, fine and blond.

"I wasn't sure you were coming tonight. It's late," his voice is deeper now, though he still hits a spot now and again where it breaks like he's choking on his Adam's apple.

"Only decided tonight to come," I say. He grabs a lamp, pulls on his boots. He still comes out the window, though I'm sure they all know he's sneaking out. They just don't care. His mama was the only one who cared before and she's been dead three years.

He pats my horse, strokes his neck. "Still ain't got a real name for this one yet?"

"He's fine being called Boy."

"That's not a name for a horse," he says and we go to the barn, Boy following the reins in my hand. "He's a big, strong stallion, should be given a name to go along with that."

"Hephzibah."

"That's a woman's name."

"Lucifer then."

"You can't name a thing after the devil!"

"Why not?" I say.

"It invokes evil."

I roll my eyes. "Then just let him be with Boy."

Reuben sighs and gets a bucket of oats for Boy. We settle into the hay stable, Boy munching on the oats. The other horses stir and snort, annoyed we're there with the light. We lay on the stack of bales.

"I saw there's a new cabin going up," I say.

"There's two," says Reuben. "Matthias and David are due back soon."

"So they found themselves wives then?" I'm trying not to laugh because the whole thing is bizarre. There aren't enough young women for all the young men coming up in the Community. The only ones marriageable are Reuben's sisters and even if their daddy let them marry, they're related to all the men still unmarried, so Leader sent his two remaining unmarried sons out "gathering" as though they're picking candy out of jars. I can only think of what those girls have in store for them, converting to such a place.

"It's not funny, Isaiah. They need wives—and wives who will uphold the beliefs."

"Thank God I'm not one of them."

"One of them's already got a couple of kids, so she'll help build up the Community."

"The other one's fifteen?"

He scowls and mumbles something like "seventeen."

"Poor girl."

"What's it to you?" His feathers are ruffled now, and I'm smiling.

"Nothing, just feel bad she's got to marry your brother. All of them are enough to make anyone miserable!" And I start laughing. He stops scowling. "So when is it your turn to go out 'gathering?'"

He turns red and pushes me off the hay. "Ah, shut up."

"Go and find her at a well. Work seven years for her. Work fourteen and get two!"

"You're blasphemous," he says, but he's all smiles now as he helps me back up on the hay. "I've still got a while yet before they make me take a wife. I don't have an interest in sneaking into town like my brothers do to...to be with the girls there." He blushes.

"You don't have to, I sneak in."

"Yeah, but you're not—you know," his face is blooming red. His eyes start to glaze over as he looks at me. I can see his mind's turning; he gets ideas in his head that he doesn't like and he lets them grow until it takes over his whole mind and body.

It always happens so fast, there's never a chance to talk him down, instead he just explodes. He's been this way since we were kids, but it's gotten worse since his mama died.

I know what's coming next and I try to move away, shift out of his reach, but he's fast as a striking snake and his hand is around my elbow. He's stronger than me now. I haven't given his growth much thought, he just sort of got bigger than me without my realizing it. And his daddy doesn't let him laze around like his mama did, and I can feel the strength of his hand gripping me. "You aren't are you?" He pulls me close, his grasp tightening, his nose an inch from mine. I can smell the onions of his dinner on his breath. "You're not like those girls, you're still whole aren't you? You've got all those men around you. Who knows what you all get up to out there." His eyes blaze like his mama's. "You've been with them, haven't you? You and your whore sister!"

I pull away from him. I'm ready to go for my knife if I have to. "What's it to you if I did!" I jump down from the bales, grab Boy's reins.

His face falls. "Hey wait!" He jumps down after me, reaches for me again, his fingers gentle, apologetic. I pull away. "I'm sorry. You know I don't like the idea of you—I worry about —you're my friend after all. We've been such close friends for so long." He grabs hold of Boy's reins with one hand and takes my hand with the other, pulls me to him. Kisses me too hard. And all I hear is my own blood. My neck twinges, bent under his desperation. His lips are hot, hard, chapped. My gut swoops and then all I feel is anger.

I push him away. I look at him and my anger turns sad and back again. "You're too lonely here," I say. "And it's your own fault."

"Please don't go."

"Let go my horse."

He drops his hands. "When are you coming back?"

I pull myself into the saddle, stick my heel in Boy's side. "Maybe tomorrow. Maybe never."

Reuben grabs my ankle, still gentle. "None of them know you like I do."

I kick free of him. "You just shut up." He trots after me, pleading. My head's swimming, my lips burn with the taint of his. I leave him behind in the barn and trot Boy past the house.

"You're out late." It's Judith, sitting on her porch, clutching at a shawl over her shoulders. I hadn't realized I'd led Boy so close to the house.

I halt the horse. "So are you."

We watch each other. Boy shifts beneath me. We hold our breath. Judith speaks first. "I just couldn't sleep. There's not enough air in that house." She looks me over. "Has he scared you off already? It's barely been half an hour."

So she listens. Or she hears at least. She probably hears everything. "I'm not afraid of him," I say.

"He isn't getting any nicer."

I don't want to talk about Reuben right now. "So you're getting new sisters."

"The brothers are forced to marry and us sisters are left free. Alone and free."

"Come stay with us." It's words, a joke maybe. I decide it's a joke. "I'm sure we could find you a husband if you want one. There's plenty to choose from at our place."

If she smiles, it's too small and too dark for me to see. "It's not far enough," she sighs. "Someone's got to keep everything in line."

"Why not your sisters? It doesn't have to be you."

"You should go home." The conversation is over. I nod goodnight and prod Boy forward.

But then I remember the letter in my bibs and backtrack.

"Oh, by the way," I say, pulling the letter out. Her face gleams as she takes it. Even in the dark, I can tell she's crying. She puts her hand to her mouth and stares at her name on the face of the envelope.

"He got it."

"We'll send your reply out for you."

"I'll have to steal some paper from Father's study."

"It's not like I won't be back."

She nods, a couple loose tears fall on her cheeks. "Thank you." She stands to take the letter inside, already pulling it open. I leave the desperate boy and the sad sister behind their fences. When I get home, I take Boy to the barn, remove his saddle, press my nose into his neck. Musky, grassy. But even this cannot erase Reuben's kiss.

I slide into bed beside Genesis. She wakes. "Welcome home," she's annoyed.

"Sometimes I sleep," I say. "I saw Judith, sitting all alone in the dark."

"She's still around then."

"I don't see why she doesn't leave."

"I suppose it's her home," says Genesis. "Where else would she go?" She pauses. "Where would you go?"

"I don't want to go anywhere. I don't need to." I'm perfectly happy on the ranch with my horse and the cattle and Daddy and Genesis. "Why? Do you want to go somewhere?"

"I'd go see the ocean," she says without hesitation.

"You want to leave here?"

She sighs and rolls to her back, puts her hands under her head. "No, it's not like that. I'm content here. I don't need the world, the whole world—that's what I've got books for. But if I could, I'd like to see the ocean, just once. Just to see if it's really like how they write about it."

"I can take care of myself," I tell her. Someday she might

169

get married, move on from here. I don't want her to become Judith, to stay because she thinks I can't handle myself. She thinks I'm still a kid. At my age she started running the house and then was under threat of marriage. She could go on and leave me and see her ocean and I'd be fine.

"People like us don't see the world," she whispers so low I'm not sure she's speaking to me. She rolls to her side, turning her back to me. And in the morning she's awake before me, up and placing pancakes on the table before I'm even dressed.

"Morning," Daddy and Denney say as I take my seat. Genesis hands me a plate with a small stack and points her spatula at the bacon in the middle of the table, butter and syrup beside it. I'm halfway through my pancakes before Genesis brings her own plate to the table and sits. Just as she's got her fork ready to dig in, Daddy tips his coffee mug and it's empty. Genesis moves to stand up again.

"I'll get you more coffee, Daddy," I say.

Genesis relaxes and eats. The kettle's on the stove, still warm to touch. I bring it over and Daddy holds his cup to me. I take his plate to the kitchen sink and place the kettle back on the stove.

"We're taking inventory today, you gonna come join?" Daddy asks me.

"Maybe after I help Genesis clean up a bit first." Everyone's eyebrows rise. It's not usually like me to stay in and do domestic stuff without being asked. We finish up breakfast and Daddy and Denney head out.

Genesis washes the dishes in the soapy sink and hands them to me to rinse and dry and put away. She doesn't say much, doesn't mention my staying to help. It isn't laundry day, but I'm already thinking that maybe I should do better to help when it comes around next week. Seeing Judith stuck and always fixing her family, she looks tired and forlorn with no one to talk to and no future to look forward on. I don't want Genesis to feel like she's stuck because of me. She's too handsome, too smart to stay somewhere she doesn't want to be.

"Fair's only a few weeks away now," she says.

"How many ribbons will you bring home this year?"

"I've won just about all the ladies" she says. "Maybe this year I'll go for all the men's as well."

"Think you could take on Daddy?"

"Oh, I don't know. He hasn't got an outlaw grandfather, does he?"

"Nor our Gramma," I add. "Do you think she ever won ribbons?"

Genesis shrugs. "I never saw her shoot, even though she always watched. I never saw her pick up a gun. That picture hanging up in the sitting room is the only time I've seen her with one." Genesis washes, pulls soap suds around, her gaze out the window, following one of the new hands across the yard.

GENESIS

They called him the Indian. But it wasn't until you were up close that you'd even think he was half of a half—and even then, you might not have known unless someone told you. He wore his dark hair long, so it fell into his eyes and brushed his shoulders. His name was Jax, he came to us the first time that summer just after I turned seventeen, and I watched him whenever I had view of him.

He didn't arrive in the spring with the first wave of hands. He just appeared one day it seemed. I saw him walking across the yard to the bunkhouse. "Who's that?" I asked Isaiah, since she knew more of the hands than I did.

"They call him Indian," was all she knew then. "Quiet type."

Many of the other hands buddied up in the summer—they always did—but Jax did not. He got on well enough with everyone from what I saw. He laughed with them, but he didn't offer his own jokes. He worked alongside them, joined them when they went out or came to chat at the porch. But he rarely spoke first, and while he was friendly with the others, it was obvious he did not quite fit; that there was something that stood him apart, that he was alone unto himself.

"That Indian kid really knows his stuff," Daddy said to Denney over dinner one evening. I hid the racing in my heart behind forkfuls of food.

"He's good then?" I asked, feeling myself grow hot.

Daddy shrugged, paused, considered me. "He went to a year of college."

"He went somewhere out East," Denney added. Going East was stepping up in the world. Back East might as well have been Europe to us. Why on earth would he come back this way? I thought. Why would he come back this way where the men were dirty and rough; where the work was hard and covered your hands in thick calluses?

At first, I was only intrigued by him. In all the years of hired help, all the men that came through the range, there had always been attractive young lads that would make me blush with any notice girlish reactions to older males. And then there had been Benjamin and I wanted nothing to do with men in that way. But Jax drew me. He was quiet and somber, polite and respectful. He was unobtrusive without seeming timid. He didn't look at me like the other hands—neither like a sister nor a potential lover. He was smart and carried himself steadily.

At nights, after dinner was done, I took myself out to the porch into the cool air of the evening to watch the last of the day draw to a close. The hands hanging about the yard, Daddy and Denney talking, leaning against fence posts, Isaiah playing cards with the gaming hands. The cows and the horses black and brown spots amidst the wild grasses and brush, the mountains on the fringes of turning purple-black against the dying sun.

Mid-June, summer well underway, but the evenings still cool. I heard a few of the hands coming around the house, just returned from town, no doubt. Warren Beaufort and Skinny Joe (called so to distinguish him from the other, broader, Joe) came around the porch, Jax between them. They nodded to me, "Evening, Miss Genesis."

"How's the town?"

"Same as ever," said Warren.

"Took in a little radio listening," Skinny Joe added.

"Don't you have a radio out there in the bunkhouse?"

"Can't hardly hear anything," Warren said. "Everyone's always yammering."

Jax's eyes moved between the three of us as we spoke, still yet to contribute. I went hot when his eyes landed on me and I gave my full attention to the two men flanking him. "Anything interesting on that radio?"

"Louis and Schmeling," said Skinny Joe with a whistle. "What a match."

"Boxing," Jax said, for my benefit.

"I know," I said. Warren and Skinny Joe chuckled. They'd been coming to our ranch since they were my age—nearly seven years. They knew me, I knew them. I knew their affinity for boxing, and I'd learned from them.

Jax blanched, smiled weakly in his shame. "Sorry," he said. "I didn't think you'd have been interested in..."

"And who was the victor?" I cut in.

"Schmeling," Warren answered with glee.

"I suppose one of you owes the other something," I said.

"A letter and photo from my sister," Skinny Joe grumbled.

"That's not so bad—"

"And two bucks," he scowled.

"You can pay it back little by little, you know like, what's that word?" Warren looked at me.

"Installments," I said.

"Yeah, that," Warren said and he laughed.

"Well don't let Daddy hear—he'll want to pay it off himself," I said. They nodded and laughed and wished me goodnight. Jax, though, stayed behind, sheepish and staring. "I'm not that interested in boxing," I said to him. "But they are, and I've known them since I was a kid."

"I'm sorry about that, again," he said. "I just usually see you reading, so I figured you—" he let his words trail, at a loss for how to finish his thought before changing the subject. "So what's that you've got now?" I held up *A Farewell to Arms*. He moved closer to read the title. "Quite a book for a young lady's leisure."

"I read an Agatha Christie book last week," I said, not intending to sound as snide as I did, but I couldn't help it. He had misjudged me twice, and this was the first time we'd spoken. "And I'm not a little girl."

He swore at himself under his breath. "I did it again. I didn't mean..." He sighed and I had to bite back a smile. "I know...I suppose you've read a lot."

"As long as it isn't in the bible, I'll read it," I said. "Though I don't even think I need to read that anymore, I've got enough of it embedded in my memory without my wanting it there."

"My name's written beneath the cover of one somewhere, but I've never read a word of it." He sat on the steps, mere feet from me, close enough I could have reached forward and run my hand through his hair.

"You never met my mother," I said. "In the days she was around, she was sure to make you remember at least one verse word for word."

"*Consider the lilies...*'"

"That's one of them," I said, "Well, not even one. Only a few thousand more to go."

"Have you counted them?"

"I'd have killed Jesus myself if my mother'd made me do that."

"No doubt," he said. "I've seen you shoot."

I blushed to think of his watching me. Could he have been watching me the way I'd been watching him? His eyes were large, amber, set deep beneath a sturdy brow. The night sky was deepening quickly, and, as he turned to watch it fall, I saw in his profile the regal silhouette of his ancestry.

"I heard you went back East."

"For a while," he said flatly.

"You didn't enjoy it?" I'd hardly been farther than the surrounding towns, barely crossed the border to the next state, but I knew there was more, and I wondered about it.

"It's different there," he said. "The schooling was alright. But there isn't this." He looked out at the mountains, black now against the deep purple of the evening.

With the exception of Benjamin, I'd never been kissed before. And after him, I couldn't even think of being kissed. But I was thinking about it then. I was judging the shape of Jax's lips, wondering how they'd feel on mine. I suppose, when I was younger, there were times when I thought fleetingly of love, brief daydreams in passing. But now I never thought of the ranch hands in that manner, that was a world for the books I read.

But sitting there in my chair on the porch with handsome, regal, quiet Jax, for the first time I wanted to be seen by a man, to be looked at as more than just a girl. He was only a few years older than me, four or five at the most, but those years seemed a chasm. I felt like a child, a giddy, silly little girl who knew nothing about intimacy and romance.

The two of us were seated there innocently, him looking at the stars, me looking at him. Nevertheless, when my father and sister came up, I was abashed, my head warm as I tried to keep a cool demeanor. Jax stood as Daddy approached. "Evening, sir," he said. "Miss Isaiah."

"Jax," Daddy said and nodded warmly, fatherly like he was with all the hands. He and Isaiah looked at Jax, then me, and back again. Isaiah's black eyes twinkled while Daddy seemed confused; he knew something was going but he couldn't quite pin it—or maybe believe it. We were, after all, not even sitting next to each other.

"She reading to you?" Isaiah said. "There's usually a crowd when she reads."

"Not tonight, no," he said. "Maybe next time, though." He nodded goodnight to us all and made his way to the bunkhouse. Daddy kissed me goodnight, and Isaiah smiled at me like a buffoon. I turned away from her, hiding my own smile in the falling dark.

ISAIAH

I've decided to let Kenny Bowles kiss me. He's sixteen, the youngest of the hands. I haven't been out to the Community in over a month. Maybe I won't ever go back. But at night I sit up thinking about Reuben, wondering if he's lonely—knowing he's lonely. I think about his kiss and the way it set my skin to tingling.

So I'll let Kenny kiss me and forget about the whole damn thing. He's gangly with red hair and freckles and stumbles over his words, but he's the closest to my own age and I figure he's got little experience in kissing so he won't know I haven't got any either. I'll kiss him and forget about Reuben.

So I seek him out in the horse barn. He likes to go in and brush down the pregnant mares. He's in the farthest stall with the big roan mare Trixie, one hand on her belly, the other brushing her long neck. "Hey, Kenny," I greet him.

He looks up, tips his chin to me, "Evening, Isaiah."

"It's Miss Isaiah to you," I tease. "I'm a lady after all."

"Only lady here I see is this mare." He smiles, and his big

front teeth only add to his goofy look. He's like a little boy grown up too fast without taking time to fill out.

"You suppose you're an expert on ladies, are you?" I say and a blush rises from his neck and rushes to the tips of his ears. I almost feel the blush myself. "How's the old girl?" I say quickly, letting myself into the stall.

He pats her round belly. "She's fit."

I place my hand near his. The fur is soft and the skin ripples beneath my touch. Beneath the taut roundness the foal is knocking against her mother's sides. "Did you have your own horse back home?"

"Yeah," he says. "Well no. It wasn't my horse. The man we rented from, it's his horse—was. I used to help out on his farm until...well he had to sell the farm. Then my brothers and I all had to spread out and find new work."

"A lot of people had to sell their property the last few years."

"Y'all have made it through," he says and I shrug, patting Trixie's side. "Maybe there is treasure buried here after all."

"If there was, I wouldn't tell you."

His goof-smile is back, crinkling his sunburned nose. He's had a sunburn since day one that just peels off only to burn again. "Oh, you're saying your gran'pa wouldn't have let me into his gang?"

"He had a no-freckles policy."

"He had to have had one guy with freckles."

"He's buried with the treasure."

"So there is treasure!"

"Sure there is," I say. And then I think, heck here goes nothing and just like that, I get on my tiptoes and plant my lips against his. He's warm, his thin lips chapped by the sun. He's not ready for the kiss of course, and it's awkward with his lips still pulled taut into a smile. So I pull back. He's stunned and the red rises so fast on his face I'm afraid he'll faint. He drops the horse brush and gives a jittery little laugh. It was a bad kiss, but it was a surprise.

He puts his hands on my waist and pulls me in for another go. His lips are softer, we're both ready this time. It's not so bad, but there's nothing more than that. There's no warmth rising in me, no fire. It's not the same. He's too goofy, he's too boyish and not at all like Reuben. He's too timid. So I pull back and give him an apologetic smile.

"Gee," he says, his mouth a stupid grin.

"I'm sorry."

"It's nothing. I mean, it's nice." I can tell he's about to lean in again and I step back.

"No, I mean I'm sorry, but I think I'm just not ready to be kissing boys yet. I thought I was," I say. I just want to get out now. His glee is melting to embarrassment. "Don't let Daddy or Genesis find out. Goodnight." I all but run out of that barn, leaving him shamed in the smell of horse manure.

Maybe Kenny wasn't the right one to break me of Reuben. I start to think of other possibilities, but then I know I will go back to Reuben. I'll let him sweat a few more days though. Tonight, I spend hours walking the perimeter of the ranch, along the barbed wire and cracking wood posts. And when the moon rises high in her bright sliver I crawl into bed beside Genesis. She's asleep on her belly, her hair falling across her face. She looks a bit like Mama, except softer. Maybe she doesn't look like Mama at all. I'm not sure I really remember Mama all that well. There are photos of her somewhere, hanging in the sitting room maybe, or squared away in either Daddy or Gramma's room. I don't know, I never go any of those places.

Genesis's eyes open and, at first I can see the fear—the kind you get when you wake up and see another pair of eyes staring at you when you were expecting none. She relaxes, coming to her senses. "What are you looking at?" she says.

I want to ask her if she's ever really kissed anybody, but she rolls over and goes back to sleep. I see her and Jax eyeing each other. A lot of nights now they sit on porch talking. They talk about books, about Daddy and Gramma and I'm sure they talk about me. And when Genesis reads to the hands, he's the only one fixed on her. The others look at her, but their minds wander after her words. I see Genesis watch him too, the way her eyes move after him. Jax and Genesis. They are both soft and gentle to each other. Not like Reuben and me. I move close enough to my sister to smell the clean scent of her fresh-washed hair and fall asleep.

I stay away from Kenny all the next day. I stay away from the horse barn and the horse pastures and corrals. Instead, I stay by the castrating corral where the bull calves are being banded. The little calves squawk and whine but everyone is efficient and doing their job, so it's over quick and the babies are released one-by-one to their bellowing mothers.

Genesis has a pie cooling in the window when the day is done and the table set with a chicken and peas. And after we've eaten I help her clean up before she goes out on the porch to enjoy the last of the evening in Jax's company. I sit there on the porch with them as night falls. When Daddy's bathed, he comes out and joins us, taking his chair beside Genesis and I lean against his knee as he makes himself a part of the conversation. He throws out numbers—the heads of cattle, the horses and colts, his own years on the ranch when Grampop was still around.

"He was a no-nonsense man," Daddy says, "Even as an old man. 'Course, I only ever really knew him as an old man. Every now and then he'd tell a story from his rough-riding days and he'd laugh. And whenever he laughed, it was with his whole gut, a big booming laugh like every funny thing he heard or recalled was about the funniest thing he'd ever known. He never chuckled. Either he laughed all the way or not at all. And when he really wasn't laughing, you worried you'd all end up gutted any minute."

"He didn't shout though," Genesis adds.

Daddy scratches at the stubble under his chin. "Not ever in anger. Sure, he'd yip out an order when things needed to be done or when they were going awry, but he wasn't a yelling man. When he was angry, he was measured and tempered. When he was real angry, he spoke with the chastising voice of God. His voice was big and gruff and carried—his anger could silence a battlefield, and he wouldn't raise his voice much more than I am now." He rubs at his chin, his mustache. "He died just after Addie and I married—which, son, let me tell you was a bit of a relief. Who knows how times the old man might have considered skinning me alive just be for being the roustabout who married his only daughter."

"Gramma always said he liked you," Genesis says, shaking her head at his tall tale.

Daddy grins. "Truth be told, your Gramma was just as worrisome as your grandfather. She was a formidable woman," he says to Jax. "She once chased a pack of coyotes away from a lame calf." He strokes his chin, his eyes twinkling. "There's something about the women in this family that make you feel like they could chew you up and spit you out." He laughs and lays his hand on my head, gives Genesis's hand a squeeze.

"Fair warning," Jax smiles politely. His eyes catch my sister's.

Daddy's hand rests warm on my head like a blanket warmed before a fire on a cold night. He lets Genesis go, gives a little tug on my braid and says, "Well I suppose it's time I call it a night."

Jax stands as well, "Goodnight, sir." Daddy nods and heads inside. Jax slides his hand through his thick black hair then slides it into his pocket, turns to the sky. "I guess I'll say good-night to you ladies as well." Genesis's "goodnight" comes soft. She folds her arms around herself and Jax slips down the steps and moves across the yard into the dark.

"Look at you fawning," I can't help but say. She's like a girl from her books, breathless at the sight of her lover.

"Oh, hush up you." She stands and stretches. "I'm off to bed." She runs her hand over my hair as she walks around me. "Try to be back before breakfast at least."

"Genesis?"

She pauses at the door. "Yeah?"

"He's a nice one." I know this because I've watched him. I've watched him watch her, I've watched him when she's not around. I've seen how he acts around the other men, and even with me. He's polite and sturdy and thoughtful, just like her.

She smiles, nods, and disappears inside. I sit and watch the stars, the house creaking and settling, the smell of night rising in the hush of everyone's sleep. I lose time like this, staring at the stars, and long after I'm sure everyone is steady asleep, I stand to go saddle my horse.

Boy's shoes clink on the stones. The feel of him beneath me, that gentle rocking, soothes me. The night is full with the sounds of cricket chirps, coyote howls, and cattle lows. When I get there, I notice the Community has a new entrance. They've taken down the gate and replaced it with a nice log arch. It makes the place look almost welcoming. No doubt they did it for Reuben's new sisters-in-law, to make it look just as normal as all the other ranches around. I bet the gate will go back up though.

I dismount and walk Boy through the entrance and into the center of the Community. Boy and I take a minute to watch through Reuben's window. The room's dark and I can't quite make out his shape in bed. I lean against the window, my forehead against the cool glass, trying to get a good look but it's too dark. I knock. No movement. I knock again. He still doesn't stir. I could just go home, but I came all the way out here and don't feel like turning back quite yet.

I put my hands in my pockets with the loop on Boy's reins and lead him around the house. He swings his head as he follows after me, his ears moving and listening. There's the women and children's quarters, the dining hall, Benjamin's cabin, Little Mary's family. Her mama's had two more babies—both boys—and nearly died from the last one. Of course they didn't call a doctor, or even me, but she came through it alright, Reuben told me.

The church is still there, tall and gray in the night. For old time's sake I decide to walk around it, touch the wood. They've given it a new coat of paint. It's gritty with dust both under and over the paint. I notice dim light at the end of the church. Leader's study. I slow down and move along the wall. I hear muffled knocking and scuffling. So the old man's at it again? Sister Agatha still?

The thought of it disgusts me, but I'm curious anyway. I'm tall enough now that if I stand up on my toes and hold on to the lip of the window, I can just see over the ledge. My blood flushes and I go warm as I peer into the window. The curtains are drawn, but there's a good-size triangle at the bottom I can see through and my heart's in my throat. It isn't Leader.

It's Benjamin and whoever the girl is, she's not his wife. Her back is toward me and I can't quite make her out, but I know Brenda hasn't got long auburn hair. I know this girl he's got is no one I've ever seen. She's on the desk, her dress bunched up around her hips, Benjamin between her high knees, clutching her bottom. The desk shifts beneath them, scratching and knocking on the floor. The two of them are making a good deal of noise too, him huffing and puffing, and her making something like a squeak and a moan at once.

I'm frozen watching them and my blood's pounding so hard it's a wonder they can't hear it as well. I want to look away —I know I should. But I can't, even though my fingers are sweaty on the ledge and my toes are trembling. I can't even breathe.

"It's Matthias's wife."

My heart just about shoots out my throat. I jolt so hard I thump against the wall and scrape my chin and elbows on the wood. Reuben's suddenly beside me, puts his hand over my mouth and pulls me close with the other arm, half-dragging me away from the window while the girl inside screams in surprise. "What was that!" I hear her say.

Reuben takes me and Boy around the side of the church in a hurry. We stand still and listen to the door slam and quick footsteps I'm sure are coming for us, but they fade. Probably they don't want to be caught. Reuben lets me go. "They used to do it during Benediction, but they can only disappear at the same time before people start to notice."

"We slipped out all the time."

"We were kids," he says. "She's doing your mother's job now."

"My mother wasn't knocking knees with your brother." My blood's still rushing and my voice is harsh and fiery.

He grunts in disgust. "Gosh no. I mean helping out with the hymns and stuff for sermon, leading them at Benediction. She transcribes for Father. He says she's got lovely handwriting."

"He probably thinks she's got other lovely things about her too." He glares at me, but I shrug it off. "Is she the one with the two kids?"

"No, *she's* uptight and prudent." He pauses. "She reminds me a bit of Mother."

I almost make another snide joke about his mother, but I remember I came back to make up with him. "So I guess she's not sneaking off with Benjamin as well."

"She isn't pretty like Amelia." He takes Boy's reins and we walk to the barn.

"So you think she's pretty?"

He shrugs and I can't help but wonder how many times he's watched them, and wonder if he likes to watch them. I've heard the hands make jokes about touching themselves, and I wonder if Reuben's done it. I can't really imagine him doing it. But then again, I never imagined he'd kiss me so passionately. Thinking about it makes my guts go warm again.

"I think she only pretended to be God-fearing to get a husband so she could get off the street," Reuben is saying. "Matthias doesn't care much. He didn't want to get married to begin with, but Father made him." I follow him into the barn. Now he's talking about God again, I can forget about the naughty stuff.

Matthias isn't so bad, he's better than the rest of Reuben's brothers. I think maybe he'd like to leave if he could but he knows his father won't let him and he hasn't got any money or connections to go out on his own.

"I thought you were in bed," I say to Reuben as we enter the barn. The other horses raise their noses and ears, nudging over their stalls to sniff out Boy.

"I've gotten used to being awake a few nights a week." I know that's my doing. He gets a bucket of sweet oats for Boy, who munches on them like a starved child.

"He acts like he never gets them at home."

Reuben strokes Boy's neck. "It's been a while since you came last."

"I had things on my mind."

"Look, I'm sorry about last time, alright?" he says. I'm not sure what to say back so I just stare hard at Boy, stroke him with determination. "I thought you'd like it."

"Why?" Suddenly, I'm irritated. I *did* enjoy, but I didn't mean to, and who was he to think I would? "Because I'm some demon harlot that comes from out *there*?"

"No," he growls. "Because we've been friends a long time. I thought—you're like a special sort of friend to me."

"I'm your only friend."

"You don't have to be such an ass all the damn time, you know!"

It's the first time he's cussed at me. It's the first time I've ever heard him cuss at all, and it shocks me like a slap to the face. I could snap at him again, but he's scowling something fierce, sad in his eyes, and my anger turns to furious shame. "Look, I am your friend, alright? I'm your damn friend and I came back to see you because I missed you." He perks up. "But we aren't *that* kind of friends!"

His neck flushes red all the way up over his ears and across his cheeks. "Oh." We're both focused hard on Boy now. Boy's eyeing us, wary of all the attention he's getting. "Are you even interested in boys?" Reuben says. "I mean, are you fond of men at all? I've heard girls like you are often—well, you wear boys pants all the time and all!"

"You asking if I'm into ladies?"

"It's an abomination if you are."

If I'm not interested in men at all, it means he's got no chance at all in my liking him that way. "No," I sigh. "I'm not interested in women. Not interested much in men either." I take a deep breath, remembering the rush I felt at his kissing me. I add quietly, "At least not yet anyway."

My heart's beating softly now and I'm replaying his kiss

and Kenny's kiss over and over again. I try to shake them away, tell myself no. I don't want him to kiss me again. I like us as the friends we are.

"So we're back to being friends then?" he asks. I look at his stupid, teasing smile and say yes.

GENESIS

July Fourth was always a big day on the ranch. It was the only holiday that fell during the high season when all the hands were there. It was one of the only two times Daddy butchered one of our cattle. He'd dig a hole and fill it with hot coals and stones and lay the skinned and quartered beef inside, and it would roast all night and all the next day. For days before, I busied myself in the kitchen on my free time making pies.

We'd go into town and fill the truck with baskets of corn, watermelons, tins of beans, bags of cornmeal and potatoes. Every pot and pan we had was put to work. We turned the back porch into a makeshift prep-kitchen, Daddy and the hands lined up with paring knives for the potatoes, and their bare hands for corn shucking. Most of them could peel potatoes and cut onions well enough. I showed them what to do, and they did it. We built up small fires and let them burn down to coals to cook peppery, buttered potatoes and crisp, tart cobblers in the deep, heavy iron Dutch ovens. We'd boil beans in milk cans, cook cornbread in sheets. Even Isaiah didn't have to be coerced to help.

We had a couple of old ice cream makers, and everyone took turns churning and cranking through the heat of the day. Work on the ranch is never done, but there can be one day or two when the most basic of chores can suffice. Some of the men pooled their pennies together and traded them for small fireworks—bottle rockets and firecrackers and the like. It was a day full of banter and powder-smoke and summer heat.

During the lean years, the spread wasn't so full, the number of firecrackers diminished, but we still always had the cow and the raucousness, Daddy always made sure of that, sometimes even paying for fireworks out of his own pocket.

Everyone rotated between helping with the cooking, the ranch chores, and playing "dodge the firecracker" until the cow was pulled up, the last cob of corn boiled, and the last pot of potatoes was pulled out. Daddy called us all together and gave his yearly mid-summer speech. He stood on the top step, Isaiah and me on either side of him, Denney just off the bottom step.

In the past, Mama stood beside Daddy and Gramma had us girls off to the side. Everyone could see us and know it was our family feeding them. "That's how Grampop did it," Gramma had once told us. "Your daddy had to be coaxed to take his place. He hated the idea of filling your Grampop's shoes when he was gone." They were big shoes to fill after all.

But now Daddy did it as natural as if he'd built up the ranch himself or been Grampop's own blood son. "I want to thank you all for your help," he'd say. Inevitably, someone would call back "Well, you're paying us!" and everyone would chuckle, including Daddy, then he'd continue. "I just wanna thank you all for all you do here, for the good, hard work you've provided me and my family." In the last few years he'd started to add, "And for showing respect to my daughters."

Then he'd say, "Let's dig in!" and they'd all let out a great whoop.

Isaiah and I were ushered through the buffet first, the rest following behind. The lot of us piled our plates with sweet, tender roast beef and cornbread and all the fixings. We'd gather and disperse around the immediate yard on stumps and mismatched chairs. And for a few moments it would only be the sound of eating, the slop of lips and fingers being licked and the small moans of pleasure.

The food stayed out, the flies constantly swatted away, everyone going back for seconds or thirds, picking at what was left to snack on through the afternoon and into the early evening while the ranch shooting contest commenced. When I was a kid, when Mama was still around, the shooting would start in the afternoon, before dinner, but now it was held later, after the food was done cooking and everyone got at least one plate or two, so I could be a part of it. It was hours of gun smoke and banter, everyone fed and still eating.

Daddy always began the contest by lining up five cans and bottles on the fence and stood back fifteen paces. With the same rifle, anyone who got at least three of the five stayed in. Then the line moved back another five paces, and we could all use whatever gun we wanted from then on as long as it wasn't a shotgun. I used my revolver the first thirty paces and took up my rifle after that. Isaiah took part, but usually was out by the fourth or fifth round. I knew she was a better shot than she let on, but she just preferred watching.

At fifty paces, there were only about seven of us left, including Daddy, me, and Jax. Denney was out at 30, same as Isaiah, the two of them sat by with watermelon slices, the juice running down their arms. By the next ten paces, we were down to four. Jax knocked three, and I came directly after.

All eyes were on me, including his, and it was his gaze I felt more than anyone's. I missed the first bottle. I missed the second can and heard a collective hold of breath. If I missed another I was out. Daddy had gotten four, and Robby Burton had gotten three. I'd been getting in at least the top three since I was twelve. In the last two years, it came down to me and Daddy. The only time I ever slid back was the year we came back from the Community and I'd gone a good nine months without even touching a gun. I had a reputation to keep. Especially since all the guys had told Jax about my shooting skills. Why I thought a man would be impressed by my ability to kill him quick and clean from fifty paces is beyond me, but I believed I needed to beat Jax to win favor in his eyes. Maybe I thought if he saw I could take care of myself, he wouldn't worry about me becoming clinging or dependent, that I wouldn't be as much work as the other girls.

I slowed my breathing. I could hear Gramma's voice in my head: Don't be silly, girl, he's just a man, he's just a fancy. I took a deep breath, readjusted my rifle and took the next three shots one right after the other, quick and clean, getting them all, only pausing to pump a new shot into the chamber between each. Everyone let out a sigh, a few whistles, hollers of "That's our girl!"

We moved back another five paces. Daddy got three, Robby got three. Jax got one, missed, and missed again only getting one more shot before he missed again. I was both disappointed and relieved, bolstered and giddy in my own confidence. I got four. A roar of excitement from my crowd. I beamed so much so I didn't pay attention to the numbers in the next round, but I know Robby was out and it was down to me and Daddy as usual.

The sun was setting, the sky bright, hazy orange and pink. Daddy missed, hit, missed, hit, and missed again. I hit all but the middle one. They cheered again, hollered something fierce, calling me their little Annie Oakley. Daddy hugged me too tight in his pride, kissed the top of my head. "Now even I know not to cross you," he said, his laugh booming over everyone's. Jax stood by, clapping along with the rest of them, not hollering, but watching, his face calm and unreadable. Was he impressed? Scared? Did he suddenly love me? I couldn't tell then. But he smiled and nodded, and I buried my face in my father's shoulder.

A big fire was built up just as the sun dipped low. The flames went up and up and the hands spent the rest of their fireworks as night fell. Isaiah and I flanked Daddy, he on a chair, we on the ground. We lounged around, watching the town's fireworks appear bright and sparkling miles away. All around the valley, other ranches and farms let off their own small ones, like fireflies popping up in the dark. We didn't note the hours growing later and later, too energized by the excitement of the day. Someone started singing around the fire—someone always started singing. There was always a guitar, and sometimes there was a fiddle.

"*Who's gonna shoe your pretty little foot?*" one of the Collins twins sang, and Michael Bennett started to pluck away on his guitar. "*Who's gonna glove your hands?*" The second Collins twin had joined his brother. Daddy grinned, bobbing his knee along. He knew this song, we knew this song. Gramma taught it to us. Daddy gives us girls a squeeze on either side of him. "*Who's gonna kiss your red ruby lips? Who's gonna be your man?*" The brothers' voices were raspy and twangy. I eyed Jax across the fire, the red light glowing on his skin, glimmering in the dark of his eyes.

"*Papa will shoe my pretty little foot,*" I sang along in my head. Isaiah sang out loud. Still young, her voice was gritty, amateur, but smoky. Her singing voice wasn't moving by any means, but it was comfortable and home-grown and it had been a while since the men had heard a lady sing. *"Mama will glove my hand."* Jax caught my eye, my own heat rose with the flames. *"Sister will kiss my red ruby lips. I don't need no man, I don't need no man..."*

I needed this one. Heart throbbing, I froze as the Collinses picked the song back up and Michael Bennett plucked away, Jax and I staring at each other across the fire. Daddy released me, using his hand to tap in rhythm on his knee, focused only on the musicians. I stood, smiled absently at Daddy, who smiled warmly back and turned back to the music.

In brisk, wide steps I went around the mares' barn, my mind a flaming fog. The night air cooled my fire-hot skin but it couldn't touch the heat pulsing inside me. *Thrum.* I heard him behind me, felt the heat of him as he caught up and caught me by the elbow, pressed me up against the side of the barn, his body against mine and I welcomed it.

"You're just a kid," he whispered, his forehead against mine, our breasts pressed together. Was that my heart or his beating so fierce?

My voice came in a breathy whisper, my throat too tight for anything more. "I'm not," I said. Then he pressed hard against me, pulling me into him, body and lips, clutching me as I clung to him. Lord, I thought, I could swallow him whole. He smelled of smoke and sweat and something else, something burning and raw. His mouth was hot on mine, grasping. I thought my heart would burst from my chest. It lasted an eternity. It lasted a second.

He pulled back, growled, slapped his palm against the barn in frustration. "You're just a kid," he repeated heavily into my ear. But he still clutched me, the both of us pulsing. Back at the fire, the song was done, everyone clapping. Many girls my age were married and mothers already; how could he think me too young? Five years was not so great a difference, I wanted to say, but I my throat felt thick, my tongue too hot.

Jax released me slowly, gentle, kissed me warmly on the cheek. I thought he'd chuck me under the chin like I was a kid, and I thought I'll kill him, riled up as I was. But he didn't stoop to patronize me. Instead he pulled away with a sad, apologetic smile and shoved his hands into his pockets before walking off into the dark.

I stayed against the barn, cooling down, listening to the music from a distance. A few clouds moved across the sky, the brilliant stars milky in the black heavens around the thin, silver sliver of moon. The regular sounds of the night—the owls and coyotes and crickets—were replaced with the sounds of crackling and popping, the smell of smoke and sulfur on the air, sparks dazzling across the black valley. And me there against the barn with my knees too week and trembling to take a single step, determined to make one single man mine.

ISAIAH

Jax hasn't been to the porch in a little while. It's been a couple weeks. For the past week, Genesis herself hasn't been on the porch. She's been spending evenings on target practice, getting ready for the fair contest in another few weeks. But I still see them watching each other, her eye on him from across the yard, his eye on her as she hits target after target every evening. We can all see it, all of us on the ranch, like waiting for a storm to break.

"Did she make you mad?" I confront him one afternoon. He's splashing water over his head from the pump spigot behind the bunkhouse. He shakes his hair out like a dog. He says nothing.

Mama used to yell at us to stay away from being back here. The hands' bath and toilets were out here. It used to just be the spigot and a couple outhouses until Mama and Gramma convinced Grampop to spend the money on a real bathroom with a flushing toilet and running water for the main house. Grampop had said if his men couldn't have such luxuries, they couldn't either. Gramma and Mama said "Fine, we'll pay for it." They set up a food booth at the fair and raised prized chickens and sold quilts and jams and all sorts of little things for a year until they came up with half the money. Then Grampop gave in and paid the other half and it was all built, the bathroom in the house and the bath house for the hands. It was the last he'd built on the ranch before he died.

The men often walk from their bath house back to the bunks in nothing but a towel or sheet wrapped around their lower halves. I guess that's why Mama didn't want us back here. But she's gone now, and most of them don't bathe but on Saturdays, and only at night. The rest of the time, they strip off their shirts and splash themselves with the spigot to cool down or rinse off. It's a hot day today, and five of them are taking their afternoon break to wet themselves down.

"More like he pissed her off, probably," Michael Bennett says and laughs, using his shirt to rub water off his face.

"Nah," says Robby Burton. "He'd be shot clean through the heart if he'd made her mad." He and the other three men laugh. Jax just sighs and pulls his shirt off to run it under the water stream.

Sweet Jesus, I think when I see what he's got underneath there—he's smooth-chested and muscular—more muscular than I thought. I thought he was just skinny, but he isn't. He's tanned and got one long scar that cuts across his left breast and to his belly button. It makes my heart race a little. I try not to stare, try not to show any reaction. Sweet Jesus, Genesis is smart to go for him.

I shouldn't be that surprised, ranching's tough work, and many of the hands have good physique—even if some are a little underfed before they get to us. All of them have got small scars and scrapes puckering their bodies, but Jax is like something else and I'm suddenly aware of the other half-naked men around me. It's been hot since the sun came up but now I'm starting to sweat. I feel strange in my own body, notice the tightness of my bib-fronts over my chest—already my bosoms are the same size as Genesis's. I didn't have them a year ago, and now I do. I shift, hunch my shoulders, pull my hat down to my eyebrows. "So which is it?"

Jax wrings out his shirt, flaps it out and pulls it back over his head. "She didn't upset me." He starts to walk away.

"Then what is it?" I have to skip a little to keep up with him. He pulls a saddle from a hitching post and swings it over his shoulder, heads for the breaking corral. "I know you two have something going on. All of us see it."

He stops, looks at the sky, sighs. "You're just a girl, you don't understand. The both of you are just girls," he finally says. "She's too smart, and too young to be getting wrapped up in men."

"She's been running our house since she was fourteen, fifteen. And even did most of it alone before then. She's almost been married off to a real son of a bitch," I say. I'm sure my sister won't like me telling her secrets, but I do anyway. "She's been more my mother than ours ever really was."

"I'm going away at the end of the season."

"You can always come back," I say.

He turns and goes back about his work. I head back up to the house where Genesis is hanging linens out to dry. They're already getting warm in the sun, flapping in the hot breeze.

"Need some help?" I push at the billowing sheets.

"Your fingernails dirty?"

I drop my hand. There's not much left in her basket anyway. "I saw Jax without a shirt on just now."

"Yeah?" she says, raising her eyebrows. She's pretending not to care.

"It's a pleasant view. He's got a great big scar."

"Don't they all?" She chuckles, pulls a clothes pin from the hem of her apron. "Looks like you're a woman after all, sneaking around to get glimpses of shirtless men at work." She pulls a towel from the basket and flicks it out at me.

"Hey!" The snap on my thigh stings even through the denim. "I wasn't sneaking. And I thought maybe you'd like to know." I throw her the last towel in the basket. "Unless maybe you've already seen?"

"It's none of your business if I have or haven't." Her cheeks glow.

"The two of you did disappear a quick minute apart from the bonfire."

"Oh, that was nothing," she says, not looking at me.

"Don't worry, Daddy didn't notice." I'd spotted Jax skulking back to the bunkhouse not five minutes later, and Genesis returned to the fire right after.

"I think maybe...." she starts to say. She picks up her basket, props it against her hip. "I haven't got time for men."

I'm still thinking about the men and their bare chests. It gets me thinking about my own body and the kiss, and I start to think that maybe I'm ready to try it again. I won't try it with one of the hands, though; that turned out a disaster last time. I know who it has to be.

But when I get out to the Community, Reuben isn't in his room, and he isn't the barn. I mount Boy again and we trot out to the tree at the edge of the property. He isn't there either. Did he go away? I don't recall him saying so. He hasn't stepped outside the Community since they built it up. Did Leader send him out gathering already? By the Community's standards, we were both nearly old enough to get married, but usually they let boys wait a while. What kind of girl would he bring home? Would she be someone like me, someone dark and rough? Or maybe he'd go more pious, someone tender and pale that wouldn't challenge him and would know the bible inside and out. Maybe she'd bruise under his touch. Would he stop wanting to see me if he got married?

Just when I'm asking myself all these questions and starting to get jealous of a girl that might not even exist, I come around the church and see a light coming from the porch of the big house—Leader's house. Thinking it might be Reuben, I head over.

It's Judith. She's standing on the top step holding out a lantern. "Good, you're still here," she says. "I thought I heard you going by."

"Where's Reuben?" I say.

"Mother never punished Reuben, but Father does," she says, reaching into her pocket. She pulls out a letter. I take it, thinking it might be for me, but it isn't. It's for her brother Adam.

I stick it in my pocket. "So you got into your father's study," I say, trying to hide my disappointment.

"It isn't hard," Judith says. "Well, it wasn't. I've done it before. But this time Reuben went in and he...well he found something he shouldn't have and then he decided to confront Father about it." She pulls her lips tight. "Father locks the study now. So I don't know how many letters I'll get out of the paper I've got."

"Where is Reuben?" I ask again.

"He's locked up."

"In jail?" I say. "What the hell did he do?"

"No," Judith says as if that's a silly notion, which I guess it is; why would finding something in Leader's study put him in jail? "In the room," she says. She doesn't say which room; I already know he isn't in his room.

"For how long?" I say.

"Until he agrees to comply with Father, I suppose," Judith says. "Until he understands."

"Comply with what? Understand what?"

"I don't know," Judith shrugs. "He never got a chance to tell me what he found. I just heard Father yelling that at him." She shifts nervously and I know she wants me to go.

I go back four nights in a row, but Reuben is still not freed. I start to wonder if maybe Leader's killed him. I say it jokingly to myself, but part of me believes it. The fifth night I go back, Judith is waiting again. "He isn't here," she says. Maybe Leader *has* killed him! I think. Or maybe he sent Reuben away because he wouldn't comply.

"Where?" I ask, my heart thumping with worry. Reuben might not be the greatest of friends, but he's still my friend.

"Father took the boys with him on business. Well, he left Benjamin," Judith says, and this time I understand why she's looking nervously around the dark. "So I suggest you'd better go. It won't be a while yet until they're back. A week at least."

"But Reuben's alive and well?"

"Why wouldn't he be?"

"And he's coming back?"

"Of course he's coming back," Judith says. Then she laughs. "You really think Father would let one of us go? Come back in a week or two, and Reuben will be free to you, I'm sure." She glances across the commune at Benjamin's house. "You'd better go."

I don't make her tell me again. I leave and head back home, all the while wondering what Reuben's got himself into.

GENESIS

Daddy attended the fair for business. He took part in auctions, met other livestock traders. He made plans for bull swaps and herd sales, buying more or selling some, attempting to get a contract or two. For us girls it was leisure. It was time for candy and ice cream and the chance to see our peers. When we were in school, it was the only time we saw our classmates during the summer. Now it was the only time we saw them at all.

When I got old enough—twelve—I started participating in the shooting contests. There weren't many girls to begin with, but by my third year—the year we returned from the Community—I had beaten everyone in the girls' division and was moved into the women's division a year early. When I was sixteen I came in second. The next year, I was determined to be first, and it quickly became apparent I would accomplish it.

There weren't many women to compete with, a good number of them were past child-bearing age, done raising babies. Some were young like me, and only a few were mothers and wives with young children. One woman by the name of

Carice McGrath, I remembered from years past, came from deep in the mountains to register with a big belly swelling out from her skinny frame. They tried to discourage her from participating, afraid the baby would be shaken loose during the tournament.

"Sirs, I just look bigger than I am," she tried to tell them, and when that didn't sway them she said, "I'm a pregnant woman with a gun, I don't think you want to be upsetting me. I've taken down a mountain lion without blinking and I won't flinch to take you too."

The seasoned mothers standing nearby laughed. Gramma had liked Carice. Carice who'd had a baby at fifteen and another one a year later with one of the Johnson's hands, and was now having a baby with who even knew, but Gramma had called her spunky, because she didn't even let her babies wane her feistiness.

She was the one who beat me the year before. The registrars let her carry on, and her baby stayed put. She came in close second behind me at the rifle range, but she shook my hand and we smiled for a photograph together at the end. Two of her teeth were brown with rot and at least two or three were missing. "They think we're made of glass or something," she said with my hand in hers. "As if their own mothers and grandmothers and even some of their own wives haven't scraped to their bones to survive out here raised their own children that way."

"Congratulations," was all I said to her in return.

"She's a little crazy, isn't she?" Isaiah said beside me as we watched her waddle away.

We're all a little crazy out here, I thought. "It happens when you live in near-isolation," I said.

I won a little money with each ribbon, some of which I shared with Isaiah on fair treats. The vendors wouldn't let me play any of the shooting games. But they let Isaiah go ahead, not knowing that at that distance, she could hit them all, but she always missed one or two on purpose. We milled about with a few other young people, anyone we knew from our grammar school days, and for a few nights a year we all felt socialized, gossiping back and forth about those we all knew.

Sometimes I still braced for the questions and low whispers about us and the Community even two years later, but new scandals had risen to fill the space in the collective conscience. *Maggie Bernshaw's knocked up, some boy from a county up north getting married in October. Just saw Michael Spurrs heading off to the bushes with an east-county girl.*

I believed the Community to be behind me, to be nothing more than part of my legend. But it was there. Leader was there. I felt his eyes on me the day of the pistol range, just as I was calculating my third target. I looked at the place where Daddy, Isaiah, Denney and the others leaned against the spectator fence, the lot of them clapping me on. Sliding my gaze along the crowd, I spied the bastards. Leader in his stupid hat. Leader with his sons beside him—Reuben included. My gut bottomed out. I felt naked all over again and wanted to curl into myself. My gun hand ached with the desire to point it at them and send bullets straight through their skulls, so I could be rid of them once and for all.

I looked back at my family. Jax and Skinny Joe were sliding in with them. Daddy needs a few hands to help with the "display cattle" as he calls them, the ones on show as a sample of our herds. He traded out the hands each day of the fair so they each got equal chance to go. And Jax was there that day, the day Benjamin and Leader had ventured in to take part in the business of trading cattle.

Jax and I hadn't spoken since Independence Day, but he was there to watch my final tournament rather than going off somewhere else. "That's my girl!" Daddy shouted above everyone else, and, seeing them all standing there beaming, I recalled Daddy sending Arlo away at the point of his gun, and my world felt safe and there was nothing Leader could do from beyond that fence.

I got the ribbon, I got the trophy, I got the money pot. Leader and his boys dissolved into the crowd for the time being. My family gathered around once the photo was taken, passed around the trophy. It was Isaiah who saw the Community bastards re-appear. "What's he doing here?" she said.

We paused, held our breath as the four of them halted before us. Daddy's hand tightened on my shoulder. "Miss Genesis," said Leader in his slippery drawl. "We were aware of your knife-handling skills," Benjamin rubbed his chin, "but what a revelation you are behind the trigger." He laughed; it twisted around my guts.

"She can well hold her own," Daddy said, cutting through Leader's laugh. As much as I wanted Daddy to kill the man, I also abhorred the thought of Daddy killing a man.

Matthias stood back, eyes apologetic and afraid. Reuben looked worried; the last time I'd seen him, he was still a little boy, but now he was taller than both Isaiah and me—tall and skinny with fuzz on his upper lip. He seemed bewildered by the whole thing, by the fair and the confrontation, by our father standing beside Isaiah. His eyes shot wildly between us all. Benjamin leered indiscreetly at me, rubbing at the scar on his chin. I was waiting for him to lick his lips. My insides quivered.

Daddy clutched us girls. Denney and the hands stepped up close. "Well it's been a pleasure to see you girls again." Leader tipped his hat to us, winked at Isaiah. Benjamin tipped his chin, eyes still locked on me. I felt Jax's arm brush against mine, my hair tingled, reaching for him. I stood a little taller.

They were gone, Reuben tripping along behind, and we

turned back to ourselves, though our celebrations were dampened. Daddy announced he had to get back to the auctions and slipped a few dollars to Isaiah, Denney went with him. She shoved her money into her pocket saying, "There's kettle corn with my name on it," and she was off with two of the hands close behind her like her own guards.

"Who were they?" Jax asked, referring to Leader and his boys.

Skinny Joe and Robby Burton were left with Jax and me. They shifted with their hands in their pockets, looked to me wondering if they should be the ones to say or not.

"The ones who took my mother," I said.

"Right bunch of bastards they are," Robby Burton added. "Hanging about the auctions and doing business as if they aren't a bunch of women-thieving nut-cases out there."

"'Bout near broke Mr. Levi when your ma took you girls out there," nodded Skinny Joe. "We'd all have killed the lot for you if he'd told us to."

"Which one were you going to be married off to?" Jax said.

Robby and Skinny Joe did not hide their confusion and shock well. *Isaiah*. How much had she told him? I couldn't look at any of them.

"The worst one," I said. "But he's got a scar to remind him I don't come quietly."

I tried to play it off, smiled at Skinny Joe and Robby, who returned it uncomfortably. "We best go help your pa," they said, tenderly tilting their chins to me before they left.

"I'm sorry, I didn't realize they didn't know. When Isaiah told me, I thought..." Jax sighed, handed me my trophy. "I expect they wouldn't have given you much choice in the matter of marrying him?"

"He's married to someone else now, has a couple kids." I was still trying to play it down, like I hadn't been coerced into baring myself for the safety of my sister—like it had just been a business negotiation that fell through. "Seems the type that a wife wouldn't stop him from pursuing others."

"Like father, like son," I said. I didn't want to talk about Benjamin anymore. My skin crawled at the very thought of him, and my stomach was still churning.

But Jax didn't press the conversation, instead, he brought his hand to my chin, brushed his thumb along my jaw. At first, I flinched, but his rough palm was warm and gentle. The churning in my stomach turned to a swoop, and an explosion of butterflies; the crawling in my skin turned to a tingle. Then I burned, a heat that rose up from the depths of my gut and pulsed in my blood.

My sister and her sentinels returned and Jax stepped away. All the rest of the night we didn't touch, we didn't go off alone, always accompanied by Isaiah and the other hands. When Daddy gathered us, we piled into the truck, Isaiah and I in the cab with Daddy, Denney and the hands bumping along in the bed. I could see Jax from the side mirror. He smiled and laughed with the others, every now and then his eye catching mine watching in the mirror.

My trophy grew warm in my lap, my palms left misty prints on the surface. It was already late when we left the fairgrounds, and it was a good hour between there and home. I smoldered. When we pulled up to the house, I was the first out of the truck, everyone else leisurely climbing out and making their way to bed. I went straight for my room, discarding my trophy on the kitchen table.

Half the buttons on my dress were undone before I made it to the top of the stairs. I was too warm, my head buzzed. I tugged off the dress as soon as I passed through the bedroom door and let it fall, nearly tearing off my bra immediately after.

I pulled my nightgown over my head as Isaiah entered. "You're eager to get to bed," she said.

"It's too hot."

She shrugged, tugged on her own nightshirt. We went to bed, laying atop the covers. She babbled, saying something about Reuben looking like he'd made a decision, but I wasn't listening. She asked me questions and I grunted responses until the night grew later and she stopped talking. I turned away from her. I flamed, a heat that radiated like the sun inside me. I rolled over and again. I listened to Isaiah's breath slow and deepen. I sat up, my body on fire. I touched my fingers to her forehead, it was warm but not like mine. I wasn't ill; it was something else. I gave her the lightest of taps. Her face twitched but she did not wake.

I slid from the bed, keeping my eye on her, went to the window. I saw him out there, a shadow in the heated darkness. He could not see me any more than I could make out his face, but I knew his eyes were on the window and he knew I was there.

I moved from the room like a ghost, silently down the stairs in the dead of night, glided out the back door and across the porch. The earth was warm and hard beneath my bare feet, I took no notice of the stones and twigs. My blood hummed louder than the crickets.

I found him waiting between the barns, radiating much as I was. We melted together. Lips found lips, chest to chest, fingers found flesh. He grasped at me and I clung to him, lost my fingers in his thick, soft hair. We gasped for air and the taste of each other. We blazed to our very bones. *Your father's going to kill me*, he breathed into my mouth. *Only if I tell him to.* Into the barn, up to the hayloft. Hands fumbled and fluttered in the dark. His bare chest was hot and solid as we lay on loose hay.

The scents of hay and the musk of horses, sweat and skin burnished by summer sun.

I held my breath as his hands pushed my nightgown up, over my hips, my stomach, my chest. But his touch was soft, inquiring. And when looked at me, it was more than that, he *saw* me; he marveled and his fingers brushed my skin like he was running his hands over mink or fine silk, his lips explorative and worshipping as he lay me back in the hay.

Jax paused above me, awaiting my permission. I answered with my hips. He held me close and tight and I bit my lip against the pressure, the pain of it ebbing away with his kisses and melting under the heat between us. He was gentle but unwavering, and I was sure he'd done it before. More than once. But I didn't ask, and I didn't care; I didn't care if there were other women, I only cared that I was the one right then. Breaths in steaming bursts, bones grinding on wood. Flesh and hot, sleek skin. I felt unlocked and unburdened, something in me set free. I was unbroken. I was everything I wanted to be, and I was safe. I was living and not alone.

The horses stamped and huffed below us. An owl sounded from the far end of the roof. We lay in the cadence of our cooling breath, my fingers trailed his scar. He took my hand in his and kissed the tips of my fingers. We did not speak, tranquil in the moment.

We couldn't stay there all night. I'd said my father wouldn't kill him, but in truth, part of me wasn't so sure. What father would condone his daughter being caught up with one of the hired, temporary help? My mother had insisted we go away with her for this very reason. Daddy probably would have sent him packing at the point of a gun. The respect they had for each other was too great for me to cause its destruction. So I straightened my nightgown and slipped from the steaming heat of the barn to the open night, feeling freed, like coming up for air after drowning.

I snuck back into my bedroom. I stood in the doorway and watched Isaiah sleeping in our bed. She looked innocent in the moonlight. I knew she wasn't a little girl anymore, even if I felt like she didn't know a thing about the world, that she didn't understand the threats in store for her as she grew older and more beautiful. But she wasn't me. She'd come out of the Community bruised and battered, too, and she'd been alright. She even kept going back. She was no longer a child, and I wasn't either.

I sat on the bed and brushed her hair from her face. She woke. "Hey," she said groggily. "You're up late," she added with mischief in her voice.

I smiled at her in the dark. "I don't think..." I said, halting. "I don't think we can—that we *need* to share a bed anymore."

She placed her hand on mine and replied, "We've been too old for a while now."

Outside was the owl, crickets chirping wildly. "But maybe," I said, "Maybe one more night?"

She moved over and I laid beside her. "Well?" she said.

"Well," I said, smiling. Then I cried. "I thought I was broken." Then I told her everything. I told her about Benjamin pushing me up against the church, about Leader and Benjamin making me undress for them, about them threatening to hurt her if I didn't agree.

"And now there's Jax," she said.

"And now there's Jax," I said.

"And you don't need me anymore," she said, "To keep the dreams of Benjamin away." We locked fingers and smiled and laughed and slept.

ISAIAH

I've been sleeping out on the porch for the last week or so, it's been so hot. Genesis convinced Daddy and some of the hands to rig up some screening around half the posts and railing to keep the bugs and critters out, and even added a screen door with a simple latch to keep it from slamming in the wind. It's a room without walls, and I preferred a hammock to a cot, and Genesis strung me up one. I suppose when winter hits, I'll move back into the house, but for now I prefer to stay out here. I can hear all the crickets and the sounds of night and feel the air and come and go without disturbing anyone.

It makes it easier for me to go wandering out at night, though I haven't been out to the Community since before the fair. It was strange to see Reuben out. Judith had said something about Leader taking him along on business. I didn't think it mean he'd be taking him everywhere. I wondered what Leader had been doing at the fair, maybe the same thing as Daddy, looking for dealers. After what Genesis told me about her and Benjamin and Leader, I don't I wondered what else they could get up to. And I'm itching to ask Reuben, but I just haven't felt like going back out there.

Even though I knew Leader left the Community on business and sent the boys off gathering, it was the first time I've seen them outside, and it's strange to think of them being out and able to enter *our* world. None of them had really done anything to me, though Genesis had said they'd threatened they'd use me to get what they wanted from her. And I remember how Leader slid my hair through his fingers... Maybe I could get Reuben to come out here now.

Just when I'm thinking maybe I'll go out there, to at least ask Reuben if he'd risk coming out here, the doctor comes around the corner. He comes straight to the back porch without having to knock the front door until someone wakes. Someone must have told him about my new screened-in porch room.

"Miss Isaiah?" he says through the door.

I've already been lying awake. "Doc," I say, sitting up. "It's been a while."

"Thank God for that, I think," he says. "I haven't had too many inconclusive cases lately."

Inside, the kitchen light comes on and Genesis opens the door in her nightdress, her eyes bleary with sleep. "Evening, Doc," she says. "I heard you pull up."

I'm already pulling on my boots.

"Should I pack her something for breakfast?"

"I'm not sure there's time for that Miss Genesis," says the doctor. My door squeaks when I open it. "I'll bring her back promptly when we've finished. It's the Johnsons. They've got a baby coming and it's been a rather hard go of it. They've asked for Isaiah directly. I couldn't give them a definitive answer..."

"A baby?" I stop. Sometimes I wonder why people call on me, why they need to know right then if someone's gonna make it out of whatever situation. When I say I don't feel death, they're relieved and keep on with whatever they've been doing. And when I say "Yes, I feel it, it's coming soon," even though they're sad, they still seem relieved and then they also keep on going with whatever they've been doing—spooning broth, or cold cloths, or praying. In the end they all thank me for letting them know, even if I haven't changed a thing.

I like giving them the comfort, I like that they call for me, but I hate feeling the death. I especially hate feeling it on babies and mothers. It's sad when old people and men die, but when it's babies and mamas, the loss seems double. And I always think of Mama. I always think of her swollen and dying, feeling the heavy thrum beneath her skin, the hollow darkness of the already dead baby. I don't want to go with the doctor. I want to tell him No, he'll just have to wait and see if this death happens or not just like everyone else.

Genesis stands at the door, waiting to see what I'll do. "They asked directly for you," the doctor says again.

I can't disappoint people who are already fearing the worst. And it's not like I have to do much, just touch them and say yes or no. I nod. "Alright."

"I'll save you some breakfast," Genesis says.

I follow the doc around to his car. He opens the door for me. He drives fast and the car rattles and jolts over potholes. He's focused on the road, his bushy gray eyebrows pulled together.

"Can you tell if the baby's dead already?" I watch him closely but he says nothing. "And what if it is?"

"That's not for you to worry about now."

We hit a jackrabbit, hardly more than a bump. The doctor doesn't even notice.

"I didn't even know they were having another," I say, clutching at the edge of my seat.

"It's Maggie," he says.

"Oh." She's their oldest daughter, just a year older than Genesis.

"The baby's head is too large," he says. "Can't get him through the canal."

"So what will you do?"

"She'll have to go the hospital over the hill. I just didn't want to move her and make her suffer the journey if she was also on the verge of death herself."

The Johnson's place is just on the outskirts of town. Doc stops so fast we slide in the gravel, and all but leaps from the car. The Johnson place is really three houses, one for the old man and old lady and one set of their children and grandchildren, and two more houses for the other two children and their families. We're going to the far one, the one for their older son and his family. They've got a bunch of kids, eight or nine.

Doc pounds on the door before walking straight in. "I've got the girl," he announces. All the littler kids and all the Misters Johnson are sitting in the front room.

"Bring her up, Doc," comes one of the Mrs. Johnsons from upstairs, worried voice and all. I hesitate to go. What will I see when I get up there? Will it be Mama all over again, body too frail, belly too big? Doc rests his hand on my back, urging me up the stairs. I'm going. It's Gramma Johnson who leads us in.

It's not as bad as Mama. The room is nice with pretty yellow curtains and an open music box on a dressing table. Maggie's on the bed, face round and red. She's plump like a pregnant lady should be. Her mother sits on the bed, holding her hand and her sister Katie and her aunts and her oldest girl cousins are all there in the room.

"Hello," I start to say, but Doc rushes right on ahead. Mrs. Mama Johnson moves over to make room for me.

Maggie's in pain, but she smiles when it passes. "Oh no, if you're here that means it's time to say my goodbyes, isn't it?"

She's the only one who smiles at her little joke. She's just trying not to cry.

"It's been almost two whole days," her mama says. Everyone's exhausted, Maggie especially. They're scared of what I might have to tell them.

"Well it looks like you're in a bit of a mess," I say, trying to match Maggie's lightness.

Again, she smiles. "Well, get on with it," she says.

I nod, start to reach for her. Mama Johnson grabs my other hand, her palms are wet and hot and I can feel her blood pulsing. They all stop breathing as I reach for Maggie's chest. I feel her heart beating fast and strong and her skin is hot and slick, but I don't feel the dark thump. I give her a real smile and everyone relaxes. If only for a moment.

"And the baby?" Maggie asks. I stare at her big swollen belly, a little afraid of it, in truth. It's strange to think there is a human in there beneath the tight skin. A pain comes over Maggie and her mother holds her hand and soothes her. When it passes, they lift Maggie's night shirt so the stretched skin of her stomach is exposed for me. I clench and unclench my fingers before I reach for her again. It's tight, hard, hot, and at first there is nothing else.

And then it's there, deep and so strong it makes my gut wrench, the pulse of death, and I know the baby's already dead and gone. I pull my hand back; sweat's growing at the back of my neck, my stomach swirls. "I'm sorry," is all I get to say before Maggie and her mother and all her family let out a sob. Doc leads me out of the room; we stand on the landing outside the door. My head is light, my skin prickling.

"So Maggie can be saved?" Doc asks.

"I didn't feel anything...but the baby..."

"I figured it might be too late."

"But she's strong," I say.

The doctor sighs. "It won't be a pleasant drive. If I had the anesthetic and the right implements, I would do the procedure myself, but as it is... Would you mind coming along, just to keep an eye on her?"

I say I will. He returns to Maggie's room, there are words—the doctor says the baby will have to be cut out—and a few moments later, Maggie comes out gripping the arms of her mother and the doctor, wearing a robe over her night clothes. I follow them slowly down the stairs. The men scramble to help get the doors and ease Maggie into the back of Doc's car. I sit on one side of her and her mother on the other. I feel her skin now and then between her pains. Just as we come over the rise and start to drop into the next town, I feel the thump, faintly, barely. A brush of death. I know this doesn't always mean they will die. It means it might be coming if we don't do something about it. It means death's lurking, waiting for his chance. She's so tired and hurting and she's trying not to cry, but the tears come anyway.

"Doc..." my voice is rough. "We best hurry."

The doctor's car whirs as he speeds up and we finally squeal into the hospital. I help get Maggie to the door, where some nurses take hold of her. Doc takes me back to his car. "I'd stay," he says, "But I suppose I ought to get you home."

"Will she be alright?"

"She's in good hands," says Doc. "You didn't feel it on her did you?"

I shake my head, but then I admit, "It was starting. But I think we got here in time."

He nods. The engine groans. "Thank you for your help tonight, Miss Isaiah, I know it's not so easy for you."

He's tired, and so am I. I lean back against the seat. "Maybe next time she should choose a man with a smaller head." The both of us laugh, and it's the last thing before I drift off to sleep.

The sun is just peeking over the east hills when Doc nudges me awake. Genesis is standing in the front door, flicks the porch light on as we pull up. "Would you like some warm cornbread, Doc?" She calls out as soon as we open the doors. He says why not and Genesis sits us down at the table with cornbread and jam and glasses of milk.

"How was it?" she asks me once the doctor's left.

"Maggie Johnson. Baby was too big. It died before they could get it out."

"And Maggie?"

"Took her to the hospital. I think she'll be alright."

"Not like—" she never finishes, but I know what she means. She urges me back to bed. "Sleep as long as you need."

I have nightmares about Maggie Johnson, only it's Genesis writhing in the bed. When I wake up, it's past lunch, there's a covered plate of fried chicken and corn on the table for me. Genesis is reading on the sofa, her legs draped over the arm. We aren't churchy people, Lord knows we've had enough of that. We don't care about sins of the flesh because we don't care about hell. Our own Gramma spoke often about her free-wheeling. Plenty of girls around here go unwed to roll around in the hay, Maggie Johnson among them. Folks here turn a blind eye to their frolicking daughters until their belly swells— it's only then that the shame is real and everyone scurries to cover it up.

"Jax is leaving at the end of the season," I say. My tone comes out flat, dreadful. Genesis plugs her thumb in her book, looks at me with fire in her eyes. "I'm not saying it to taunt you..." I try to explain myself but I don't know what I'm trying to say. She softens, sits up, tucks her book into her lap.

"I've told you I'm not going anywhere," she says. "I know he's going, they all do every year. I'm not so besotted that I've forgotten."

I think of Maggie there in her bed, the man who put the baby in her gone. She at least had her mother and sisters and aunts and grandmother. Genesis has only me and I know nothing. I've always been out of the room by the time Doc gets the babies out. Part of me wants to tell her to be careful, to stop before she ends up like that, but I'm the younger sister, the girl who's still a girl.

"Jax will go when the season ends, and I will stay. And I stay from this season to the next and the next and forever," she says and opens her book again.

A couple days later, the doctor visits again, carrying a jar of jam. "From the Johnsons," he says. "Maggie is home and healing, the family is mourning the baby, but they're very thankful for Maggie's health."

"Glad to hear she's doing well," I say.

"Have you ever considered going into nursing?" he asks.

"No," I say. I don't add that I could never make it through all the days of feeling the death on people, one after the other. It makes me sick enough as it is. The doctor tips his hat and is on his way. I give the jam to Genesis.

GENESIS

I didn't go to Jax every night. Not even every other night. Alone with me in the barn, I'd lay naked against him, the lantern in the corner casting shadows over the hay bales and us. "How did you get the scar?" I'd gathered the courage to ask him after the second or third time we were together.

"I told you things in the East are different," was his answer.

"Tell me about out East."

"The cities are big, sprawling. The buildings rise stories high, so high you can see them from almost anywhere. And there are people everywhere," he told me. I asked him often to tell me of this or that about the city. I couldn't imagine the miles of streets and buildings that seemed to match the height of the mountains.

"What does it smell like?"

"Oil and rot and hot metal. And the air is heavy like right before a thunderstorm."

"All the time?"

"More or less." To me it sounded terrifying and mystical,

and I could understand his aversion to it, he being somber and open-spirited as he was.

As the summer days shortened we spoke of many things, of books, Isaiah, my mother. I'd told him of my experiences in the Community, of Gramma and the stories she told of Grampop.

He told me he had a sister and a brother, that their names were Sarah and River, both younger than him. His sister was my age, he spoke of her as if she was still a child, the way all of us older children do. "She's not so young," I told him.

"She's not," he said, "But she's not...like you." I did not tell him she probably wasn't so innocent and oblivious as he thought she was, I smirked at myself because I felt the same way about Isaiah.

During the day, we carried on as though nothing had changed between us. He sat on my porch when I read, he stood beside me and challenged me at my target practice. We acted, but everyone could tell something had changed between us. We were not so bashful around each other. Even Daddy noticed it—or maybe Denney and mentioned it to Daddy. And Daddy invited Jax in for dinner one night.

It was rare any of the hands were invited in. Daddy wanted it clear that the family house was the family house and he never wanted to appear to show any favoritism to any of the hands. It had only happened a handful of times in my growing up years. But Daddy brought Jax right in. I worried Daddy would grill him about his intentions; that it would scare Jax away, that it would make him think I expected something to come out of this summer.

Isaiah grinned something stupid and mischievous the whole time, finding the entire situation funny. I flamed with embarrassment, now knowing my father was aware of my infatuation. I wondered if Daddy knew about the intimacy between us, and I wondered if he would be accepting of it, I unwed and only seventeen. Plenty of his contemporaries' daughters were much the same. But I also was sure Daddy would find me disappointing—that I was just another one of those girls. He always told me I was smart and had a good head. And little girls want to stay little girls for their fathers and at the same time want to be seen as grown women. It is an awkward transition from one stage to the next, especially when there is no mother around to navigate and buffer the way.

If Jax had been a rougher hand, less refined and respectful, I'm sure my father would not have humored us the way he did. I'd seen Daddy drive out hands who broke his rules and respect at the end of a barrel and stern admonishment. But Jax was down to earth and humble and gracious, and the evening passed well despite my own discomfort. Daddy would grin at me, and I'd grin back. Jax sat across from me and I wouldn't look him in the eye, and when our feet knocked together under the table, we immediately shifted them apart. Daddy and Denney asked questions about back East, about Jax's life beyond the ranch, and Jax answered all their questions gracefully, without seeming overblown or reticent.

Afterward, Jax tipped his hat to us and wished us good-night. We barely even exchanged smiles. "He's a good kid," Daddy said once Jax was out of ear shot. "And smart, like you." When I said nothing, Daddy stretched, scratched at his belly and said with a yawn, "You know, I think I might miss him when he goes."

"I don't think you'll be the only one, Daddy," Isaiah said.

And I said nothing.

At the end of each summer, Daddy took the hands and the sold cattle over the hill to the trains. They'd be gone a couple weeks, and Daddy would come back with three or four hands he'd keep on through the winter. Jax would not be among them. The ones that stayed either had no other family, needed extra cash, or had knocked up a girl in town and were obligated to stay. Those that left for the season gave us their goodbyes and their thanks. Sometimes they returned and sometimes they didn't.

Jax and I had never talked about his leaving. Or his returning. Maybe we worried the other might not feel as strongly, or we didn't want to burden each other with promises. Feelings can wane over a season apart, we both knew that. So we never talked about love, or building a life together. We talked about anything else.

And on our last night together, he told me that his given name was not Jax.

"What do you mean that's not your name?" I said. "Don't tell me it's something like Archibald or something like that."

"It's nearly as bad as that."

"Reginald. Or Hamlet."

"Orliss," he said.

"It isn't."

"It is," he assured me. "After my grandfather. It's a name all of us have always hated, my grandfather included. I've been told he begged my mother not to give me his name-- 'Then for the love of God, give him something subtler as a second name!'"

"And she went with Jax?"

"Well, no." He fell quiet. "It's short for...an Indian name." He ran his fingers over his scar.

"What is it?"

He sighed and told me, some name that was long and unpronounceable to my tongue, but I got how Jax could be derived from it. He explained that it roughly translated to Son Who Walks with the Night.

"Who was it that was Indian?"

"My grandmother is Lakota," he said. "We never actually learned to speak the language, but we grew up with her and my grandfather just off a reservation in South Dakota. My father died in a mine when I was eleven and Ma went to New York to work in a factory and sent us back whatever money she could."

When Jax went out east for school, he got to see her through her last year of life. "She was already sick when I got there. I took the train up to her once or twice a month. She died and I came home." She never saw her younger two children again.

I lay there with my head rising and falling on his chest thinking, *Lord what a sad pair we are.* Not knowing how else to respond, I said, "Gramma always claimed her own grandmother was Navajo. And they said my grandfather had a little Apache in him, and that's what made him so fearsome."

"Everyone out here will claim some Indian blood."

"Gramma did also say not to believe all the legends they told of Grampop," I said. "They do also say he sold his soul to the devil in Montana, and that he fathered a child in every town he passed through—more than a hundred."

Jax smiled at that. "None of them ever showed up at the doorstep demanding a cut of the gold?"

I thought of Gramma saying, "Maybe he's got a bastard or two running around out there, but they aren't here now so what's it to me?" I relayed this to Jax and he laughed.

"What a woman."

"She had sins of her own."

He kissed me and whispered in my ear, "And now so do you." We did not say goodbye. At least not with words. We made sure to remember every bit of each other, the scars and the hard places and the soft, hidden places. We'd stayed tangled together until the horses stirred and we could hear the rooster, until the tips of the eastern mountains were rosy pink.

And when the time came, he tipped his hat to me and got on his horse and went away with others in a cloud of dust and a torrent of discontented cattle bellows.

Isaiah and Denney and I watched them go from the porch.

Denney held his hat to his heart as though it was a funeral, and Isaiah tapped her elbow against mine. And when we could all no longer see them, I went inside and tied my apron on, getting to work on scrubbing down the house before we settled in for winter. It was September, when mornings and nights were cool and the day hot.

By the time Daddy would be back with Skinny Joe, Robby Burton and Silas Abbott, it would be October and the hills would be orange. I—with the forced help of Isaiah—completed the thorough cleaning of the house. And we formally rearranged our sleeping quarters. We had agreed we didn't need to share a room anymore, and with Isaiah deciding to sleep on the porch, I'd just stayed in the room. We cleared out Gramma's room, put into trunks and chests what we couldn't be parted from and gave away or burned what we could. I moved in there, leaving Isaiah our girlhood bedroom.

In separating our things, I noted our stack of menstrual rags and immediately tried to think back to the last time I'd laundered them. My gut sank. Isaiah had been irregular since the day she started the year before. But I had always been regular, as far as I could keep track. I never paid much attention to the course of my monthlies; I dealt with them when they came and gave no other thought to it. But I'd never missed any.

"Shit," I said to myself, suddenly angry. I jammed the rags into the drawer and forced it shut. We went to the bathroom and undressed, stood on the toilet across from the sink to look at myself in the mirror. My stomach was still as flat as ever. Maybe it was a little softer? I cupped my breasts. Definitely firmer. "Shit."

Gramma had told us about babies and how they came about, but she had not told us how to keep one from coming on. That was knowledge reserved for whores and discontented wives. In the heat of things, I hadn't given it any thought, the possibility that I might get pregnant. I sat on the toilet, my fingers to my lips, my mind buzzing and numb to coherent thought. Isaiah's knocking made me jump. "Daddy's back!"

Now? Shit *shit*. "I'll be out in a minute!" My voice was shaky, strained, enough that she could hear it.

"You alright in there?"

"I'm fine!" I snapped, my tongue thick. I breathed, willed myself to calm. "Just..." scrambling for a lie. And I settled on, "Monthlies, you know."

"Alright," she paused. "Well Daddy's not quite back yet. We only just spotted him coming out of the gorge."

I composed myself with a splash of cold water, willed my hands to still as I buttoned my dress. I was there on the porch to greet Daddy with a hug, conscious of the shape of my body, though I knew he'd tell no difference. He smelled of the wild, pine and rancid sweat and mud and horse hair. I had to pull away from him.

"I'll get you a new bar of soap," I said, trying to make a joke of it. Daddy laughed and kissed my head, tugged on Isaiah's braid and made his way to his chair at the table to pull off his boots. He talked enough of the journey that I had no place to tell him—I couldn't think how to—so I resolved not to.

I went to see the doctor at his office in town—which was really just the converted parlor of his house. "I've got to go into town today," I told my father in the morning.

"I'll come," Isaiah offered.

"No," I said, "I haven't got too much to pick up."

"But—"

"You stay and help Daddy," I said, grimacing at the mothering tone in my own voice.

"See if you can swing by Feaney's and pick up some tobacco for Denney, will you?" Daddy said. I told him I would.

I hurried into town, parked outside the bank and walked to the doctor's, worried anyone might recognize our truck and see it at his place. I wasn't even sure he was in and I paced along the side of his house for a few moments before he stuck his head out the window and said, "Is something wrong, Miss Genesis? My wife says you've been out there a fair while."

"Well, I suppose I could...I just have a question...that you could..." I couldn't find my words.

"Come on through the door then."

Stepping inside made me start sweating, I ran my palms over my skirt. He motioned me to the reclining bed, put his glasses on his nose, looked at me with a kind, inquisitive gaze. "What can I do for you? You can trust that what you tell me won't leave this room."

"I..." My hand went to my stomach.

He folded his hands together. "When was the last time you had your monthly?"

"I don't know," I admitted.

The doctor nodded. "I suppose there's a young man involved." I could only nod. His face was soft, grandfatherly, full of understanding. "Well I can just check to confirm, see how everything's moving along." Again, I nodded. He instructed me to lay back. He pressed gently over my stomach, "Hmm," he said. "How have you been feeling? Any dizziness or vomiting?"

"No. Doc, I really only thought to come in because I couldn't remember the last time I bled. I don't ever really think about them until they come on."

He nodded, moved to the sink to wash his hands, and asked

me to pull off my underwear while his back was turned. I laid back down, closed my eyes against the feel of his cold fingers, the slight pain as he pulled and pressed and pushed.

His examination completed, he told me I could sit up and straighten myself out again while he re-washed his hands. "Well," he said. "I wouldn't say you're quite three months along yet, but definitely more than two."

He sat on his stool, his hands folded neatly again, his eyes full of concern. "I suppose the young man isn't present?"

I wanted to explain that Jax had only just left. I wanted to tell him that Jax didn't know. But all I said was "No."

"I'll leave you to tell your father—and your sister. If you wish. Some girls prefer I tell." I shook my head. "Well, I'll leave that to you then. But, please, if you have any concerns, any *apprehensions*, you come to me, understand?" His tone was firm and compassionate. "Don't you go doing anything stupid. No gin baths, no rue tea, no 'tripping' down the stairs. You'll likely harm yourself more than anything. You're a smart girl with a good head, and I don't want to see you ruin it, alright?"

"Yes sir."

"I know I'm not a woman, but I know about women's things. If there's anything you worry about, you come to me. If you aren't comfortable consulting me, you can speak to my wife." I nodded, gathered myself, pulled out cash. "Oh no, my dear. I've used your sister's services enough to cover your cost." I tucked the money back away, composed myself to leave. "Your daddy's a good man," he said as I made it to the door. "And he's got much to be proud of in you."

My throat tightened, my eyes welled. "Thank you," I said and left. I drove too fast on the way home, chewing my lip with worry. I'd never really given motherhood much thought. I was already keeping a house, and I hadn't spent much time around babies and children since we were children ourselves. On the ranch, cattle and horses birthed and mothered and I saw them with their young, and it was all well and natural to them. But I didn't have much of a notion how it went with people. I'd seen Mama grow sicker and weaker all through a pregnancy, I'd seen girls in town growing round, and cooing at their fat, rosy-cheeked babies. I was suddenly both relieved and despaired that Mama was gone; she hadn't lived to see me become the basest of sinners in her eyes, fallen to the ways of all those other lowly ranch girls who could barely spell their own names. But she couldn't be here to tell me what I was supposed to do. I didn't even have Gramma to tell me it was all going to be okay. When I got home, I still did not tell Daddy. I did not tell Isaiah. I still couldn't really say it to myself.

ISAIAH

The days get cooler and Genesis mopes around, missing Jax. Daddy always pats her on the shoulder when he walks by her. We all do kind of miss the hands when they leave. It's quiet on the ranch without the lot of them. But I find Genesis chewing her nails and staring off at nothing.

At the end of October, we get a cold snap. We wake up to thick white frost over everything. Genesis keeps the oven warm with baking bread and cookies and pie. Daddy clears out the fireplace in the parlor and starts a fire roaring but it still doesn't warm us all the way upstairs where we sleep.

I crawl into bed with Genesis at night, both of us wearing two pairs of the thickest socks we own, and mittens and sweaters over our nightgowns and long-johns underneath. We huddle together and pull the blankets up over our heads.

"Where do you suppose Jax is now?" she whispers.

"Out somewhere pining for you probably," I giggle. "Kicking himself for ever leaving you. Maybe he's writing bad poems just for you: *Genesis, my moon, my* luna, *too far away.*" That makes her laugh. "Is his butt hairy?"

"Isaiah!" she gasps and laughs. "No."

"I saw Leader's once, it was like staring at the back of a mangy dog."

"Ick, I don't want to be thinking of Leader's nether parts," she says. "What about Reuben, have you seen his?"

"I bet it's skinny and white as the full moon," I say.

"So you haven't seen it?" Her voice shifts.

"Nah," I say. She's quiet. It's pitch black beneath the blankets and I can't read her face. I start to feel hot because I know she's thinking and it's about me. Her quiet makes me feel guilty. "He kissed me," I say quickly. There's no air and I have to pop my head out. The air in the room is cold, fresh. Genesis's head comes out too.

"How?" she says.

"What?"

"How did he kiss you?"

"I dunno. Hard, I guess. Too hard." She's quiet again but her eyes are on me. I still can't see them more than just hollow spaces in the dark, but I know they're on me. "And then I kissed Kenny."

"You kissed Kenny?"

"Yeah. Yeah, I did and it wasn't...it wasn't bad but it wasn't...I just... I don't think I care much for it. I'm off kissing for a while. I told Reuben if he tries it again, I'll slice his throat."

She's still quiet and I'm too hot. "So you've kissed two boys."

"Yeah."

"On the mouth?"

"That's the only kissing that counts, isn't it?"

She says nothing.

We wake up to a fine skiff of snow. Cold gray-white fog hangs in the air, hiding the mountains and the edges of our land. We can barely make out the bunkhouse and the nearest barns. Genesis and I stand at the back door and just stare out at it. Daddy's gotten a fire going, but we still have quilts wrapped around us.

Daddy comes through the fog and snow carrying a pail of steaming milk, his footsteps are black behind him. He taps his boots on the porch steps to get the snow off. He hands Genesis the milk pail. "You haven't gotten breakfast started yet, have you?"

"No, not yet."

"Good, I was thinking I'd have the men come in, if you're up for it."

"I can do an apple cake and some ham steaks." She holds up the pail. "And hot sweet milk for everyone?"

"Sounds good, thank you darling." Daddy kisses her fore-head. The cold comes off him and makes me shiver as he leans to kiss me too. He reaches for the door again, ready to go back out and work until breakfast. "Isaiah, that horse of yours needs his stall mucked."

I almost wish he'd just tell one of the leftover hands to do it —I'm not thrilled about going out in the cold—but I know he won't. It's my horse. "I'll be out there," I say. Genesis is already scooping flour into a bowl. I get bundled with my long johns and thick socks and gloves and head out to the barn.

I'm just about done mucking Boy's stall when I hear the hands walk by, heading up to the house. I toss down new bedding straw and give Boy a pat, promising to come back and groom him later.

Genesis hands me an empty plate as soon as I get in the door and shuck off my coat. Everyone is around the table and it's warm and smells like cinnamon and fried ham. Genesis stays in the kitchen and eats leaning against the counter. I pull the step stool next to her after I've filled my plate. We can see the whole table from here, hear all the banter and chatting. Everyone compliments and thanks Genesis between bites.

"It's almost like January weather out there," someone says.

"It'll clear up," Daddy says. "Every few years there's an untimely hard cold snap comes through like this and it clears up."

"What's it mean for winter?" Robby Burton asks. This is the first time he's stayed on through the winter. He used to go home to Texas to his mama and sisters, but the last of his sisters got married last year and his mama went off to live with an aunt.

"Some would probably say it dooms us for a hard winter, but that's all poppycock," Daddy answers. "It likely just means we're getting a cold snap right now."

Genesis is eating fast, one bite following right after another. "Hungry?" I ask her.

"Must be the cold," she says. She cuts herself another piece of apple cake and eats it slower.

It's so cold out, I'd rather stay inside with Genesis than go out. We spend most of the day sat in front of the fireplace, playing cards or her mending and patching clothes or reading to me. By mid-afternoon, the snow's turned to gray sludge and the fog lifts, but the sky's still white and the mountains are too, even the dark triangles of trees on the north slopes are dusted white.

Daddy's right and the cold breaks two days later. The sun comes back out and the snow on the valley floor disappears. All the snow left is just on the mountaintops. I go back to my own room at night. I'm a little sad of it, sharing with Genesis those few days was almost like being little girls again.

But talking about kissing boys has made me think of Reuben again. It's so many months now, I can't think why I haven't been out to see him. With the weather back to normal, there's nothing holding me back. So I mount up and head out to see Reuben.

"Sister Margaret died," he says first thing as he climbs out his window.

"About time."

"I don't even know how old she was, I don't think anyone did," he says. "Judith said she's been old since Father was a young man." He's trying not to laugh because it'd be disrespectful, but I can see he wants to. "No one even noticed for two whole days. Someone just finally realized they hadn't seen her for two days."

"That's awful," I say, trying to be serious too. "But it kind of serves her right." She was a right old hag that was mean to all the children, not even just to me like all the other sisters.

"At least her passing was peaceful. She was asleep in bed."

"I wouldn't care if she'd gone hacking and trembling. She wasn't a nice old lady," I say. He shakes his head. "So you all made it through the cold snap alright otherwise?"

"I was a bit glad you didn't come because I didn't want to leave the house," he says. "But we were all cooped up together, me and the girls and I could just about stand it. And Father kept going on and on about this and that nonsense." We enter the barn and he scoops oats for Boy. "But why haven't you been coming?" he asks.

"I did come, but Judith said your father had you locked up, and then took you away with him," I say. "I didn't know you were back until I saw you at the fair."

"That was four months ago."

"It got cold," I say with a shrug. "Well...?" I say as we settle into the hay.

"Well what?" Reuben grunts, not looking at me.

"Well what's been going on with you?"

"You first," he says, digging a pebble out of the packed dirt.

I sigh. "You know it's all the same for me. Ranch life," I say.

"Now you. Why did your father lock you up? What was it you found? Why is he taking you outside now?"

Reuben plucks the stone and tosses it across the stall. It skitters across the grown. "You remember the cabin out at the edge? The one we saw all the men at that one night?"

"Yeah."

He gets to working on another stone. "My father is not a man of God," he says.

"Well I could have told you that," I say. "We already knew he was an adulterer."

"No," Reuben says. "I mean he really isn't a man of God. He doesn't care about God at all. All of this—" he waves his arm through the air. "All of this is a lie." He gets the next stone out; it's bigger. This time he throws it. It whacks against the wall and shoots back into the ground with a *thunk*.

"I know," I say. He looks at me with his eyebrows together. "Genesis told me. Leader showed her."

He scowls and turns his face away from me again, and starts plucking at loose hay. "My father is a man of money. And secrets." he says, shredding a piece of hay with his fingernails. "Dark secrets and dirty money."

"Then why were you out with him?"

"I found the ledgers," Reuben says. "And I threw them at my father and told him he was a charlatan and a swindler. And he and Benjamin and Daniel just laughed. They sat me down and told me everything. They're all so thrilled by their cunning. And once I started speaking their sins against them, my brother started hitting me. Every time I said I'd turn them all in, they'd hit me. They said I'm part of this family and that's more impor-tant than anything—God, the law, everything. And now that I know, I'm expected to live up to the family and do my part— and the police will only see that we're family and I'll hang with the lot of them if I say anything."

"Jesus," I say, and a chill curls up my spine. I didn't think Leader would go so far to threaten even his own son. When I was a kid, Leader and the Community had just seemed like a silly place full of mean old ladies and strict rules. It's not a silly place at all. It's ruthless. The air grows thick and dark, and my heart races a little, and I start to think maybe I shouldn't have come out here. "And what..." I say, my tongue feeling thick. "What does your father make you do?"

He shakes his head. "Not so much so far," he says. "But I've seen..." He stops, tears at the hay, and shakes his head again. "Matthias told me it's better to just go along with Father, then it's not so bad. He said we can be the good ones, the ones that keep everyone in line, because if we don't, no one will. But..." he pauses. His cheeks start to turn red, and he digs into the dirt with a twig. "You know when father took me and my brothers out, we went to a...a house of women."

"A brothel?" I say. I almost laugh, thinking of Reuben, who'd cried when he'd found out his father was an adulterer, who'd only seen women in plain faces and drab dresses. He couldn't even *say* the word brothel. Reuben groans. "And did you...?"

He's scowling so hard—I know it's a crisis for him—but I can barely keep in my amusement. "No," he says, disgusted. "They bought me one to...*teach* me...But she was so old and saggy—she could have been my mother." He squeezes his eyes closed. "I had to slap her to get her off me. Then we just sat in that room until I thought it was long enough to convince the brothers. I ended up having to wait outside for all of them. Even Matthias."

"Well there's no love lost between him and his wife; he might as well get it somewhere," I say, grinning silly. Reuben finally turns to me, his blue eyes sharp and dangerous as icicles. He clenches his fists. I stop grinning.

"Maybe..." I say quickly, knowing what might be coming next. "Maybe just give it sometime, and maybe you can save up some money—take a little at a time. Until you can get enough to leave."

"Father won't let me out of his sight," Reuben says, relaxing his fists. "He locks the study and won't let me in there without him. Not until he trusts me not to run off and turn them—us—all in."

"You're out of his sight now."

Reuben scoffs. "If he found me gone in the morning, believe me, he'd find me by nightfall." He picks at the hay again. I dig my heels into the dirt, scooping bowls into the ground. I dig my fingers into the hay. "If Father's allowed to get away with all of this for so long, it makes me think maybe there's no God at all."

I don't know why it makes me so sad to hear him say that. He's always loved God and the bible and hearing him say that is like listening to his childhood die. I sigh, let my legs fall flat. "Look, just because your father's a fraud doesn't mean that God is. Maybe it just means He doesn't care as much about what goes on down here as everyone thinks He does. At least not anymore, not like in the bible."

Reuben looks at me again and smiles a little. At least he's not scowling. "You've never cared about God."

"No, but..." I say, tapping my toes together. "Maybe there's something."

"You really think so?"

I shrug. "Well I..." In all the years we've known each other, I've never told him about feeling death. As a kid, I worried he'd call me a witch and try to stone me. And then it just never really came up. I'd never even mentioned going out with the doctor because I just didn't want to get into the argument about doctors again. But I figure with him questioning God, maybe now's as good a time as any to tell him.

"You what?"

I don't really know how to say it. I've never really had to say it before; everyone just knows. "Well...I know people are going to die."

He waits, expecting there to be more. Then he says, "We all know that."

"No—I mean, yes, but I know *when* people are going to die," I say. "Well not exactly when, but I can tell—I can feel it creeping up on them."

"What do you mean?"

"I just..." I say, pulling my braid over my shoulder. I twist at the fray at the end and stare at my knees. "Sometimes when I touch people, I can feel something—like a thump or a swirling, something that feels dark and threatening. Or...One time I dreamed about a man hanging in a tree and we went off and found him."

Reuben's quiet a moment. "How long has this been going on?"

"Since I was a girl."

I look up and he's staring at me, not angry or scowling or even with an eyebrow raised. He's just staring. "Little Mary?" he says.

"Yeah."

He doesn't blink or break his gaze. "Mother, at the end, was saying you sent your mother to haunt her, that you put Death in her."

"I didn't," I say. "I don't curse people. I just—"

"But Mother said—"

"Your mother was crazy!"

"So was yours."

"But your ma—" I stop myself. "I didn't bring it up to argue about whose mother was crazier. I felt your mother's death coming. But I promise I didn't kill your mother."

"Even though she killed yours?"

"Reuben," I say, thinking he just wants to keep arguing about it. I look back down at my knees.

"I would have wanted to kill your mother if she'd killed mine," he says.

I look up again. "Well I'm not in the business of killing people."

He grunts. He sits back against the hay, crosses his ankles over each other. "So what does it mean, you feeling death?"

"Nothing," I say. "I don't know. Sometimes I can tell they can be saved, like by a doctor or medicine or something. Sometimes people just like to know if it really is the end."

He nods and lays his head back, eyes closed. "So maybe there's something out there..." he says, mostly to himself. We both go to being quiet again. And after all of that, the quiet feels too big.

"So..." I say to fill the empty space. "So you got a whore and all you did was slap her in the face?"

"Shut up," he says, and pushes me over. I fall into the hay, laughing. And then he smiles too. And the next thing I know, he's holding me down, his hands on my shoulders, sitting on my stomach; and then we're kissing and I'm afraid the heat coming off us might set fire to the hay.

When I get home, the light in Genesis' room is on. Curious, I lean close to the door and hear her sobbing, muffled but still I can hear it. Didn't know she was really so shook up about Jax's leaving. I tap on the door before I open it, thinking to make a bit of a sisterly joke about her mooning.

But I open the door and there's nothing to tease about.

She's curled on the floor, holding one hand to her mouth to quiet her crying while her body shudders, blood blotchy on her nightgown. "Genesis?" I hurry to her, kneel beside her. My heart is racing. She turns her head away from me. I touch her skin, hold her, feel for the thump. It's both there and it isn't. Like it's ebbing away now. "What's happened?" I start to ask, but then I catch the bed and the mess on it, black-red blood puddled on the sheets and something small, slick and I know what it is. Sometimes the cows drop unformed calves in the field that come out pink and melted-looking and dead.

"I didn't do it, I didn't do it," Genesis is whispering.

"Oh, Genesis," I stroke her hair until she calms down.

She grabs my hand, her eyes are glassing, looking far away. "Don't tell Daddy."

I sit there with her head in my lap, stroking her warm, matted hair. I can't look away from the bed. My sister was going to have a baby and I didn't even know. She didn't even tell me. I can't be mad at her because I just imagine her in here all alone and in pain, losing a baby she was keeping secret.

"We best get you cleaned up," I say like I'm talking to a sick child. She lets me help her up and down the stairs to the bathroom. We go as quiet as we can so we don't wake Daddy, but his room is on the far end of the landing and he sleeps through just about anything. I get Genesis settled in a bath and go up and get her bed cleaned. Not knowing what else to do, I wad up the sheets and pile them in the corner, the sleek little baby inside. The mattress is stained but I'm too tired to clean it now. I decide to take Genesis back to bed with me. By the time I lay beside her and wrap her crying self in my arms, the night sky's already turning. We fall asleep exhausted to the bone.

It isn't long before I wake up to Daddy tromping down the stairs, ready to start his day. He's always up just after the sun and spends a couple hours working—milking or checking his logs—before he comes back in for breakfast. Genesis always has breakfast ready. I look at her still sleeping, her face puffy from the night of crying. I get up. I put on her apron and do my best in the kitchen without her.

"Where's Genesis?" Daddy asks when he comes back in, his eyebrows raised at seeing me covered in flour and spattered bacon grease.

"In bed," I say, putting a plate of bacon before him. "I burned the bacon a bit. And the biscuits too." The bacon is almost black and the biscuits are a solid brown, though the one I tested was still doughy in the middle.

"I'm sure it's fine, darling," he says, but his face says different. Still, he tucks in like a man going on an adventure, slathers his biscuits in butter and honey. I can hear the bacon crunching from where I'm standing in the kitchen. He follows each bite with a big swig of milk. "She come down with something serious? Should we call for the doctor?" His eyes flash as he looks at me, suddenly remembering I am the angel of death.

"Just woman's troubles," I say. She's not dying, that much I know, but I'm not sure about whether or not to call the doctor.

Daddy looks relieved, but he clears his throat and coughs. "I see." He won't pry too much more, since he's got nothing to offer on women's business.

"She'll be better in a day or two," I tell him.

Bacon crunches in his mouth, another gulp of milk. "Here's hoping," he tries to laugh, to make me laugh. I can only smile a little, try to show it's all okay. After all, I agree with him.

The next day, Genesis is back at it.

GENESIS

I hadn't known you could mourn something that had never really been, that you could mourn something you hadn't grown to care for yet. My problem had solved itself; I never had to tell Daddy. I didn't have to become another one of those lonesome ranch girls with an unfathered bastard. And yet I grieved. My no longer having it made me want it all the more.

But I couldn't just lay in bed and weep. I took a day, smelling the smoke from Isaiah's dismal cooking and then I got up and we burned the bed sheets once Daddy was off and busy, telling him it was just garbage and scraps I'd felt needed to go. In quiet times, I found myself wondering how long I could have hid it, regretting my not telling Daddy. I wondered how it would have felt later on, what it would have been like to hold my own baby. I pictured Isaiah and Daddy bouncing a fat baby on their knees and cooing until it laughed. Daddy would have forgiven me almost as soon as he'd known, I'm sure of it now.

I didn't know my milk would still come, as if confused about the sudden expulsion of the baby it was preparing for. I didn't know what else to do but return to the doctor and tell

241

him what had happened. He told me the milk would dry up on its own, and it was not nearly as much as I would have made had the baby been born like it was supposed to. I told him how I'd felt achy and out-of-sorts all that day, how in the night I'd woken up in pain that lasted a few hours before the thing slipped out in a rush of blood.

I wept the whole time I spoke and apologized. He comforted me and patted my shoulder and said it was perfectly acceptable and expected. "You'll be alright," he said. "It's not uncommon." Mama and Gramma had each lost at least one or two, some later than mine. "Take some rest, take care of yourself," the doctor said, "And when the time comes, I'm sure you'll be a lovely mother."

It was months before I could go a day without feeling a stab of melancholy over my baby that never was. Isaiah tried to speak to me about it, "How long did you know?" she asked.

"A few weeks," I told her.

"Why didn't you say something?"

"I didn't know how."

In the days directly after, she kept touching me, feeling my skin, shaken by the sight of me smeared in my own blood. I told her if she didn't stop checking for my death, I'd break her fingers, and she stopped. I thought of Jax in those days. I wished he had been there. I wondered what he would have felt, knowing he'd created a child. Maybe he already had one out there somewhere. Maybe that's where he returned.

I asked Daddy what'd made him stay all those years ago. "All of it," he said. He had not been from anywhere nearby. He'd come as a hand in the summers, married my mother after several years, that much I knew, but I was ignorant to much of the rest of it.

"Tell me the story," I said.

He brushed his hand over his gray-streaked hair and over

his scratchy jaw. "I came out here at sixteen," he began. From North Dakota, moving his way south toward Mexico, hopping from farm to ranch for a day or a week of shelter and food and a few bucks. "Then I got here and stuck it out," he said. "Your grandfather was a man larger than life—I'd heard stories of him when I was kid. Of course, he wasn't all he was built up to be in the tales. Just a down-to-earth old man with some wild stories from his youth."

"And Mama?"

Daddy scratched his stubble. "She really wasn't much different than you. She had her girlfriends—"

"I don't really have any of those." My mother had been well-regarded in town, I knew that, though she let many of her tics fall by the wayside in time.

"But she read and baked—sweet girl, loved Jesus."

"And what about you? You and her."

"There wasn't really any courting going on between us, not for a while," he paused. "I thought I had a girl back home the first few years."

"You did?" This I never knew.

Daddy nodded, "Always figured it would be Anna I'd marry. We'd known each other all our lives. Her ma and mine were the best of friends, our pas grew up together. I think everyone expected us to just grow up and marry each other," he explained. "Then one summer she decided she couldn't marry me..." He trailed off. "No, that's not quite right." He stared into the fire. "Turned out my pa and her ma had been having a love affair for who knows how long—years, I'm guessing." He smoothed his mustache. "Anyway, my ma ran them both off and scorned their whole family."

From there, he told me, he was so ashamed, he couldn't go back home; he and Anna could barely look at each other. He stayed on at the ranch year-round. "Well," he said, "Well, I guess

I was still smarting from the hurt of that and I turned to your mama. To tell the truth, she didn't have many men for her and I think she tolerated my attentions because she had them." He sighed. "I don't mean to make Mama sound like a marm. She wasn't by any means. I think it was a combination of men's fear of her daddy and her own quiet and pious ways that kept them away. She was pretty enough to cause a glance once or twice. She didn't care much for the low-brow grime of the ranching life."

"But you still got married," I said. My heart sank a little, wondering if Mama had gotten knocked up and they'd both felt obligated. I wanted to believe they'd loved each other once, but if an unwanted baby had been the case, I wouldn't have been surprised if that's how my parents ended up in the end. But I'd known my mother was righteous and proper.

"Listen," Daddy said softly, apologetically. "We liked each other well enough. We got along, and there was nothing stopping us from marrying. Your Grampop was getting old, worn out. He wanted a son who'd keep his place going. He didn't say so much, but we all knew it. The man and I grew close enough —I may have even replaced my own father with him. And your mama wanted a settled-down life with a husband and babies. Though I think she would have preferred more of a scholar, I asked her to marry me and she agreed."

"Was it ever...did you ever love each other?" I felt out of place asking it, but I wanted to know.

"It was good for a while. It wasn't always like it was at the end," he said. "There were some tough times at the beginning that were out of our control, what with the first baby stillborn, and then her daddy's dying. For all she held against him, she loved that man. But we stuck it out. And then you girls came along and everything was good. We loved you both enough that I think, at times, it overflowed to each other. When you were young, it was easy. And then we lost a couple more." Here, he paused again for some time, surely remembering the ache of the losses.

"She lost three babies?" I said. *Four,* I silently counted the one we buried with her. I had known she'd lost some, but I hadn't known it was that many. There were six little headstones out in the little cemetery. I'd always thought most of them were Gramma's.

"She took it hard. And then she worried. She worried all the time that she couldn't raise you right. That you'd end up stuck and poor and uneducated, that you'd end up in hell. And as the both of you got older...well, you know how it ended."

"You don't worry about us, Daddy?"

"I'm the only one left to do so." He took my hand. I wanted to ask why he didn't divorce her, she'd left him for another man after all. I thought that was a good an excuse as any, but again, it seemed insensitive to bring up after talking about his dead babies, and his defending Mama's coldness toward us as girls. "All I've ever wanted for you girls is to be happy and know that you can take care of yourselves. And I think you've done pretty well."

"We're still just girls, Daddy," I said.

"Yeah, but I think just about everyone's afraid of you two, what with our little Angel of Death back there and you Miss Annie Oakley."

The weather turned cold as the holidays came, when we gathered around like a family warm and cozy in our home with the hands. And as the New Year passed, my grieving ebbed away and the sun came back around, lighting each day a little longer and eating away at the snow on the hills.

Isaiah and I continued to collect Judith's letters to her brother and she and I traded notes as well. I told her of Jax and the loss of the baby, and she sent her condolences and informed me of her own family's dealings. She and her sisters were still unmarried with no prospects, while her brothers were all married with the exception of Reuben. *Even Jerusha's all but accepted her lot to remain a spinster forever.* Her sister-in-law had a child that everyone was certain was Benjamin's though she was Matthias's wife. They all went on behaving as though it was all as it should be—even Matthias.

She told me her father favored a new woman, a single mother from over the mountain not much older than Judith herself. *Father talked her into joining when he met her at the fair. I expect we'll have another little bastard running around here soon.* She told me of her brother Adam, his wife and two children, that he'd invited her to stay with them if she ever wanted. *Like a maiden aunt in all those books!* I sent her books with Isaiah, and she returned what she read. I'd tell her she was still plenty young enough to find her own man out there if she doesn't want to play the part of Maiden Aunt. *If men here, claiming to be of God can behave as they do, what must men be like on the outside?* She wrote in response. *Is it better to be brazen or secretive about bad behavior?* I wanted to write back, *There are plenty of upstanding men out here.* But I didn't. There were plenty of bad men outside the Community, too, worse ones even. At least, within the realm of the Community, she was left much to her own devices, running her father's house and his other daughters. *Someone's got to stay and make sure they don't do anything stupid.* So she stayed.

The snow on the peaks dissolved, turning the fields nearest the gorge to swamps, signaling the return of the seasonal hands. Daddy and Denney went off to get them and brought them back in truckloads, just in time for the calves to start dropping. Jax was not among them. I watched and waited, hopeful when I saw the Daddy's truck or figures coming up the drive with packs on their shoulders. By the end of spring, I stopped watching and knew he wasn't coming. What could I say to him anyway?

Without him, summer passed for me uneventfully, though I turned eighteen, Isaiah fifteen. She drew eyes that followed her much longer than acceptable, and I ignored the advances of boys and men altogether. The end of the summer was strange and wet. Storms rose up hot and sudden, with crashing thunder and sheets of rain and flashes of lightning so bright they blinded. The house would shake, the horses would scream, and the cows would bellow. Then, just as quick as they began, the storms would clear and the day or evening or night would be calm as a Sunday afternoon, the sun emerged, drying everything hot as it was before.

ISAIAH

I feel it on Daddy.

It's so gentle I can almost convince myself it isn't there, that it's just the thump of his own blood. But I know I'm lying to myself. I know, because it makes my stomach sink like all the other times, makes my own heart stop for a moment. It's there, underneath his skin. I feel it one day when we're gathered on the porch enjoying the cool September evening and I bend over the back of his chair to kiss him on the cheek. The air is too heavy to be inside, we can tell there's another storm brewing even though the clouds are fluffy and white and lazy.

I press against his cheek and feel it, like a cat's tail teasing. I don't know when it will happen until it happens. I hold there for longer than usual, my stomach hollow and all the air drawing tight in my chest. *No*, I try to tell it, but I know I've got no power over it. I do not tell Genesis.

I pretend it isn't there. I pretend I can't feel the death brushing against my father's soul. But when I'm alone in my room at night, I cry and, even though I know I can't stop it, I tell myself I have to try. I follow him around. I don't even go wander at night. I watch Daddy in the corrals, worry when he's on an unbroken horse, whenever the cattle crowd around him, whenever he's on a ladder.

He's not sick, he doesn't cough, doesn't even sweat. There's no signs of his dying, and after two weeks I almost forget. *Maybe there is no Death*, I tell myself. I go back out to see Reuben.

In the last year, Reuben's grown tall and handsome with his ice blue eyes and blonde hair; he might be the most handsome of all his brothers someday if he stops scowling so much. His father doesn't take him out often, but when he does, he's gone for weeks at a time, and he's told me he should be back by now.

"How was the trip?" I ask him when we get to the barn. He answers by kissing me. We kiss all the time now. That's as much as we do, though. Sometimes we rub our clothed bodies tight together, or let hands wander and feel, but we have never gone farther. Maybe he still thinks it's a sin. Maybe I'm afraid we will go there and never come back.

But tonight, we are each feeling too full of something, too full of dread and fire and whatever else lurks in his secrets. Reuben practically falls on me, his lips sucking at mine and it's like lightning in my body that drives me to kiss him back. I can't help but slide my hands from behind my head and around his, my fingers in his greasy hair. His hand moves on my hip, tugs under my shirt. His hand on my skin is like a brand, trailing hot as he works up my stomach, rubbing my skin a little too roughly. And when he squeezes my tit for a moment I forget about Daddy and Death lurking beneath his skin. All I want is Reuben to touch my skin and press me into the earth.

We moan into each other's mouths and before I know it, I've got my leg thrown over his hip and I'm clinging to him. But then I feel him pressing against my thigh, his hands at the clasps of my overalls. I think of my sister covered in the blood of her lost baby, and Mama and the baby that killed her, and of Daddy and the shadow that's following him. I can't breathe and I have to stop it. I push Reuben off so hard he thumps against the dirt.

He's stunned and confused. And even though I know he doesn't understand, I can't explain it to him. I glare at him and he glares at me. He grabs at me, pulls me to him, jams his lips against mine, yanks and tugs and my clothes. I pull away from him, try to push him away. "Stop," I say.

"Why?" he says, heated. "Don't you think this has gone on long enough, why don't we just do it?" He grips hard at me, holds me fast.

"Because," I choke. I feel a dark sob welling in my gut. All I can think about is Daddy, but I don't want to tell Reuben. I don't want to talk about it at all. I need to get away from him. I need to get home. I need to find a place to cry alone, and scream for Death to leave us alone. Reuben tugs hard on my bibs so one of the straps breaks and I knock my head against his. Our skulls crack, his head flies back, and pain shoots through my own. I pull myself away from him, and stumble as the room spins. In the corners, a dark shadow swirls. I can already feel the tears coming, and I run. I run from Reuben and the barn, from the shadows in the corner. I stumble and sob and I get halfway to the main road before I realize I've left my horse.

I don't care to go back. Miller's was the only other place between the Community and town, but the Millers are gone now and their place is empty. So I just keep walking. I get to town in a couple hours, my arms tight around my cold self. Shivering, I make it to the doctor's place. I don't expect anyone to be up, but there's a light on somewhere in one of the back rooms so I knock. It's the doctor himself who answers and brings me inside, asks if something is wrong.

"No," I tell him, "Just lost track of my horse and it's still a long way home."

He throws a blanket around me and tells me to warm up. His wife comes out to check on who it is in her front room, lets me know she'll get me warmed right up and hands me a mug of warm sweetened milk moments later.

As Doc's getting his jacket on, a younger man also comes down the stairs. "Isaiah, do you remember my son?" Doc says.

I remember the doctor has a son, but he's at least ten years older than me so I don't know much about him. I don't remember ever seeing him, though I must have when I was a child, coming here with Mama. "Hello," I say.

"Robert, you remember Isaiah, don't you?" says Doc.

"Sure," Robert says, but I think he's just being polite. On the ride home, Doc tells me his son is also studying to be a doctor, and he's brought his new fiancée home to meet them. I've just about dozed off by the time we pull up to my house. I thank the doctor and go to bed.

Daddy's still alive in the morning. I feel a little sick to my stomach, a nagging nausea that stays with me all day. Once Daddy's out the door, I turn to Genesis. "I need you to take me out to the Community. I left my horse and I need to get him back before they keep him."

"What do you mean you left your horse there?"

I bite my lip, judging whether I should tell her about Daddy or not. "I ran away without thinking."

She freezes. "Was it Reuben? Did he *do* something? Or did you see Benjamin? Leader?"

"No," I say. "Nothing like that. Reuben and I just got a little riled up and I left without thinking. I didn't feel like fighting." Let her think we'd argued, I figure.

"Alright," she sighs. She grabs her revolver and hands me a sheathed dagger. I try to tell her it's nothing, but she insists.

She stops the truck at the Community gate and I walk the rest of the way. I strap the dagger to my ankle, hide it under the cuff of my pants. I've never come during the day before, but I worry about my horse. I walk right to the barn. It's still morning and everyone's busy doing something.

The boys are mucking in the barn. They stop when they hear me come in. There are more of them than there were when I was there. They don't have any girls out here to help them now. Most of them were hardly more than babies when we were here, now they're four years older. I recognize them even if I can't remember all their names.

"Little Mikey Carter is that you?" I say, leaning against one of the stalls where three boys work. Mikey was only about four the last time I saw him, not even old enough to be in the children's dormitory.

"Yeah?" he says. He doesn't recognize me.

"Don't you remember me? You used to sit on my lap in Sunday school." He just shrugs and the other boys snicker. They used to do the same thing, too, but I don't push it. "There's a chestnut horse," I say, "With a black mane. Would have been new in here this morning."

"Stall on the end," Mickey says. "Saddle there too."

"Well, what's this here?" Someone says from behind me. It's Aaron Fisher. "Been a while since we've seen you around. You missed us?" He looks me up and down. He's tall and weedy, grown too tall too fast.

"Just here for my horse," I say. "Left him for Reuben to look after for a bit." Then I see Leader and Reuben appear at the doorway at the far end of the barn. I'm embarrassed to see Reuben, embarrassed I didn't explain myself. The knife on my leg itches as I see Leader. Thinking of what he's done to Genesis, and hearing Reuben speak so darkly of him, I've started to fear Leader and what he could do to me, too.

I push past Aaron, head for the stall with my horse, knowing Leader's closing in. My saddle's on the wall. Reuben must have unsaddled Boy last night after I ran off. I pull the bridle off a hook just as Leader and Reuben enter. Reuben's sheepish next to his daddy. Leader's older, his stupid hat still there, still the creepy son of a bitch he ever was.

"This is a nice surprise," Leader says. "I was wondering when you'd pay a visit to the rest of us." His eyes linger on my face, but I know he is getting a good look at the rest of me too.

"Just here for my horse."

"I assumed you'd return, still I thought we'd have to house him for an entire day before you came for him. We'd have taken care of him in your absence," he says. He steps up to me and the horse and I step back, my hand on Boy's side. Boy sniffs at my hair and I slip the bridle into his mouth, tug the straps over his nose with trembling hands.

"Stay for lunch? I can have it delivered to my study."

"My sister's waiting for me outside."

"Just a few minutes is all."

"Father," Reuben says.

"You can let the boys ready your horse while we chat," Leader says and pats Boy. "Beautiful horse for an equally striking girl. I bet your daddy has his hands full fighting off the marriage proposals." His other hand clenches and unclenches.

"I'm fifteen," I can only manage a whisper as he reaches for me. His hand slides over my braid. I shiver on the inside, but I'm frozen like stone, gazing into Boy's side.

"It's grown back even lovelier than before."

A scraping, a knocking. Reuben's yanked down my saddle. He hurries over and throws it on Boy's back, pulls the strap around and hooks it in almost one motion. It's the smoothest I've ever seen him move. "She's got to go," he says, his voice low and gruff.

Leader drops my braid. My chest releases and I scramble onto Boy. Reuben hands me up the reins and pats Boy's rump, his scowl's the deepest I've ever seen, his eyebrows hard together and his brow wrinkled. I open my mouth to say something about last night, and he looks ready to whisper something too, but then Leader starts to speak again and I spur Boy forward, not caring if Leader gets out of the way or not.

People are milling about now and watch me trot through, confused to see me, looking at me like I'm a ghost. Genesis is leaning against the truck, her revolver hanging at her side, ready if she'd needed it. She nods when she sees me coming and gets back in the truck, starts it up and we go home. When I get back, Daddy's saddling his own horse.

My gut sinks. He's got an overnight pack. "Where are you going?" I ask. He doesn't ask where I've been. He never does.

"One of the bulls got out," he says. "Up the gorge sometime last night I think."

"Daddy, you can't," I say, but I know it won't make a difference. I'm not sure he really believes I can feel death coming on someone. He jokes about it, but I think he thinks it's all just coincidence, since most of the people the doctor brings me to are in already in bad shape.

"We need that bull," he says. "Wasn't ours. It's McAllister's and he was a pricey trade."

"Why don't you send one of the hands?"

"We need the stock inventoried and I'm the only one who knows the gorge well enough to get this done quick."

"Well then let me come with," I try to argue.

"Haven't got time to wait for you to gather your things," he says. "That bull might already be halfway up the gorge by now. I might be back tonight, tomorrow afternoon at the latest."

I jump down from Boy. "Daddy..." I start, but I know there's nothing more to be said. "Be careful."

He smiles. "Of course, baby." He kisses me, his breath warm on my hair, and he climbs up in his saddle.

"We'll be waiting for you."

"But don't wait up too long. Go on doing whatever you girls get up to when I'm out." He winks and spurs his horse. I watch him until my eyes cross.

I put Boy out to pasture and go up to the house, sit in Daddy's chair on the porch, watch clouds rise over the mountains that just engulfed my father. I watch and watch, my heart thudding in my chest, my gut stone-laden. I sit there all day, don't even touch the sandwich Genesis makes me.

"You okay?" she says and sits as well, staring at me with concern.

"Storm's brewing." The clouds over the hills are turning dark and more have gathered over the valley, growing darker by the minute.

"Daddy's..." she starts to say, but she looks at me and sighs. "He's been out in storms before." But she isn't soothed by her own words. Her mouth twitches. I know she wants to ask me if I felt it, felt death on Daddy. "We'll wait it out," she whispers.

Within the hour, the sky's dark and the rain is falling. Then it's slashing. Genesis brings out blankets. Lightning crackles above us and thunder rolls. It lasts well into the night, Genesis and I just sitting, staring out at it, wrapped in quilts. The hands slosh around, trying to get somewhere dry to watch the storm as well.

In the flashes of light I see my father soaking wet, lying in watery mud that rises all around him, I see him stumble and slip, hear his horse scream; I see the cliff they both go over. My crying's covered up by the storm, and Genesis can't see me between the lightning flashes. We fall asleep in our chairs to the roar of the storm.

And in the morning the sky is clear and blue. Genesis

brings me milk. "He isn't coming back," I croak. She nods, her jaw tight, her eyes glassy and focused hard on the mountains ringed with morning.

We disappear inside, cling to each other through the day. And as soon as night falls, and Genesis is asleep on the sofa, I saddle Boy back up and run him hard to Reuben's. I pull Reuben from his window, drag him to the barn, bury my face in his neck. "My father's dead," I say, and I sob. He holds me close to him while I cry, my mind foggy. I grow hot and desperate and I kiss him. *Kiss him until the hurt goes away.*

Then we're tugging and scrabbling at each other's clothes, clawing. He pins me against the wall, lifts me, presses into me, my pants like hobbles around my ankles, our tops are crooked. We're too quick, too eager and desperate and fumbling, but then he's in me and it hurts. It hurts but I don't care. We aren't gentle or romantic and I don't care; I find relief in it and cry out. And just when the pain starts going away, it's over with a little moan and hot breath on my neck. We collapse against each other and I go on crying again, and he's the only thing that holds me together.

PART IV

FALL 1935 – SPRING 1937

GENESIS

We sent search parties out to find him. We knew he was dead, Isaiah and I, but we didn't tell anyone that all they'd find was a body; we let everyone reach that conclusion themselves. Groups went into the gorge each morning and camped for the night and came back with nothing. Even Isaiah and I went on a couple excursions, since we knew the gorge just as well as anyone. But we did not find Daddy. The townsfolk couldn't give up any more of their time and two weeks had passed. Sheriff Burnham came to tell us they'd keep searching, but we couldn't be too hopeful. We sat him down and Isaiah told him she'd seen Daddy was dead. "There's no point searching for a man past rescue," I said.

"I really am awful sorry, girls," he said. "Your daddy was a good man," they all said.

We, again, became the subject of whisperings in town: our father missing, his death seen by his youngest daughter, a successful cattle ranch left in the hands of two young women. *Our own Annie Oakley and the little dark-haired witch.* The women stopped by, bearing baskets of food and condolences.

They came for weeks, and I expect half the reason was to see if we'd descended into madness, become feral, isolated girls of the frontier. Life had to go on for us and I wondered how.

Our hands had to be paid and our livestock shipped out. Denney took care of all that; Daddy had already had the buyers arranged for the season, but what would come next? I considered it might be worth selling the place. When I asked Denney, he said to do what I thought best, but I knew he'd be sorry to see it go. Chances were he'd be out of a job; we were the only family he really had. "You could get a lot for it, just considering its history," he said, and I think it broke his heart to say so. My grandfather had built it up with his own hands, had fought lawmen who had tried to take it from him, left his legacy on it.

I wasn't sure we could sell it anyway, given there was no body and therefore no proof of my father's death. But I took Isaiah, the two of us dressed in our best—I managed to coax her into a dress by saying we need to make an impression that we were grown women—and went down to the bank.

Mr. Garrett the banker also served as the town's solicitor. He took us into his office with the big, bulky dark wooden furniture. I held myself straight, steadied my gaze. "What can I do for you ladies today?"

"I think you already know why we're here," I said. "Daddy's gone and I want to make sure things are in order. You know, for us."

"Yes, well, see law says we can't declare a missing person dead until seven years—"

"Mr. Garrett, you know my sister," I said.

Mr. Garrett sighed. "One moment," he said and stood, went to the door and called out to one of his assistants to bring the dossier for our ranch. He resumed his seat and the assistant handed him a thick file. Mr. Garrett rifled through the pages. I was eager to ask what was all in there, but I felt it best to say nothing. I assumed it was bills of sales and trade papers. He stopped at one page and held it up. "Well, it seems the ranch is already legally yours," he said.

"What?"

He passed the page across the desk for Isaiah and I to see, his finger pointing out the neat signature of our mother. "Seems about four years ago your Mama came in and relinquished her ownership to you girls."

Seems. He knew of this, of course. His signature was right there next to Mama's, and he was nowhere near old enough to be forgetful. I had to stay myself from rolling my eyes.

"Mama left it to us?" Isaiah said.

"I'd have thought it would have gone to Daddy when she died," I said.

"Well, traditionally speaking, it would have gone to him once they married. But your grandfather had made it explicitly clear that ownership was to be hers alone when he passed, not to be altered by marriage as is usually the case." He shuffled the papers back into place.

"Well how is it then, the ranch?" I said. "What have we inherited? Is it still doing as well as they've always led us to believe?"

"I'll be honest with you, Miss Genesis, it does owe some. Now, it's not as bad off as many of the others. Lord knows how it's been for all of us lately. The money your daddy borrowed was mainly to pay wages. It's nothing a few good seasons can't fix; cut back on the hires, get yourself a good head rancher."

"We've got one."

"Yes, Mr. Denney's an alright man, a little *peculiar*..." he said, pausing. When we did not react, he carried on. "Not nearly as suave as your daddy, but he's got a head for running ranch hands at least." He laced his fingers on the desktop. "Now, if you were to sell, I'm sure the price would be plenty more than ample to cover the debts and set you girls up good for life. It's a hard life, ranching."

"Oh, I dunno, Mr. Garrett," I said. "It's all we know." Though I had been considering it, hearing the prospect come from someone else filled me with a desire to cling to it. It was our home, our blood was in the ground. It was our livelihood, our legacy.

"There has been an offer..." he said, dangling his words like a carrot.

"My father's been...gone... hardly more than two weeks," I said. "How can there already have been an offer?"

"A man and his sons came in just yesterday inquiring about the property." Mr. Garrett said, ignoring my question. "They seemed quite eager, in fact..." He blathered on, but my mind latched only to *a man and his sons... A man and his sons... A man and his sons* eager for our land, and Daddy hardly cold, wherever he was.

"Mr. Garrett," I said, cutting him off. "Who was this man?"

Mr. Garrett coughed nervously. "Well, I'm not quite at liberty to say, Miss Genesis."

"I think we have a right to know who wants to buy our home," I said. He gave a shaky laugh. "I mean, Mr. Garrett, is he local? Do we know him? Or is he from out of town?" Isaiah had been looking at me with her head tilted, questioning. She understood in a moment and turned her eyes to the banker.

He shifted under her gaze and pulled at his collar. "Well," he jittered. "I suppose you've met in the past...he's been a part of the community for some time and—"

"The Community?" Isaiah and I both said. I was well aware of the semantics at play.

Mr. Garrett realized his slip, pulled at his collar, exposed the red flush of his fat neck. "*Our* community—the *town*..." He stumbled on his tongue. His flustering confirmed what I feared.

Leader had come offering for the land. My blood ran cold and determination bloomed fiery in my chest.

"We're not selling," I said.

"Well, if not him, there will probably be many more." The banker went on, wiping his brow, "It's prime real estate with a legendary history. The longer you hold out on selling, the more you'll drive up the price..."

"We're not selling," I said again. "We're keeping it." I sat tall, looked him right in the eye. "We'll run it, we've got Denney. And my Daddy taught me how to keep things going. You'll see, Mr. Garrett, we don't need no 'man and his sons' to save us—to *relieve* us of our heavy burden. It's ours and it's always going to be ours."

He nodded, smiled tightly, coughed, and closed our file. "Well then, I do hope you'll continue to keep me as accountant and solicitor."

"Why of course, Mr. Garrett," I said sweetly, mockingly. "Who else but you." In truth, there was no one else in town. He held all our finances in his hands. "Just remember sir, I'm the blue ribbon sharp shooter in this whole county, so all the numbers better match up as they should, or you'll find out just how good I am."

He laughed until he saw I was not joking and he swallowed nervously. "Yes, well, I suppose we shall see much of each other in the years to come."

He was not wrong about the offers. As word spread about my father's disappearance and our inheritance, offers for the land came regularly, but we held our ground and I found myself in a new realm of responsibility. Denney helped me, he showed me the log books my father kept. I tried to hide my shock at the numbers. I told him I was determined to get the debt paid off, so we sold more than we usually did, and didn't take any new hires.

Isaiah often slept late. Denney and I ate without her and he left to deliver a bull calf across the state. He'd be gone over night at least. "You can take Butter this time," I told him. "It'll be a lonely drive."

"I'd rather she stay with you girls," he said.

"Next time then," I said and wished him a safe journey. "We'll see you in a day or two." I dressed in pants and boots and Daddy's old coat and took his rifle out to do perimeter checks. I saddled up one of the young mares and headed out for the far fields. It was cold and quiet, everything covered in a skein of furry frost that crunched beneath boot heels and horseshoes. An icy gray fog rolled out of the gorge in a cloudy river. The sun glowed white and dull in the overcast sky.

Butter trotted along beside me. I scanned the huddled cattle, their heat hung above them. The numbers seemed right, they seemed content and unthreatened. Sometimes, in the spring, right after the calves have come, the little ones manage to get outside the fence and mama and baby bellow and cry to each other across the barbed wire until one of us humans can get the calf back through, then we spend the rest of the day trying to figure out how the damn thing got out. Sometimes the adult cows follow their stomachs and get their heads stuck in the fence trying to reach for the brush on the other side, even though it's all the same damn stuff. Sometimes there are coyotes or wolves lurking nearby that agitate the cattle and I've had to shoot a few rounds to scare them away. These are the things that filled my days, barbed wire and brainless beasts.

Butter ran off ahead, ears perked up to something ahead in a juniper thicket. She growled and yipped. I dismounted, rifle in hand. It could have just been a young cow that wandered off from the rest of the herd; it could have been dead and devoured by a pack of coyotes. Or it could have just been a hare. I followed after her anyway.

It was a dead calf, chunks of its flesh missing, what was left furry with frost, though it couldn't be more than a night old. The kill was off, the tears too neat, too clean. My skin twitched and I gripped my rifle, my eyes scanning the thicket. Charred logs, a black spot on the ground, a pat of earth left unfrosted, the perfect outline of a curled body. Butter chased footprints that led behind a tree. I called for the dog, but before she came bounding back, I heard frost cracking behind me and my heart hit my throat. I turned, raising my rifle, only to meet the force of a padded fist. The gun thudded one way and I the other.

He was tall, gaunt, unfamiliar, too thin, even beneath his layers of shirts and jackets. He was crazed, his patchy hair standing on end. He held a knife, fell on me, held me down, a knee in my stomach, a hand on my shoulder. I struggled and fought, used all my strength to hold back his knife hand. Butter barked, running back. The man's attention turned to the dog and Butter leapt on him with a growl, sinking her teeth into the layers of the man's arm. I clawed my way out from beneath him, reached for the gun, and he brought the knife down, but in his struggle to shake off the dog, the knife caught only my coat and tangled. The man threw Butter off, the dog landed a few feet away with a little yelp but didn't seem too badly hurt and stood again. I grabbed the gun, cocked the lever. The man was after me again.

And I shot him. Through the bridge of his nose. The blast echoed on the frost, cracked against the trees. The man's head kicked back, and he froze for a single moment, suspended in time. All I heard then was my own breath, the blood pulsing in my ears. Smoke curled blue-gray from the end of the rifle. The air was so cold. There was no sound. Then he crumpled. The frozen ground crunched beneath him. I stared as Butter sniffed at the body, blood oozed black into the frozen ground. I thought maybe I should be feeling *something,* shock or nausea or relief, but I felt only cold. Frozen.

Only when Butter pressed against me, checking to see if I was alright, did I move. I knelt and examined the dog. Denney would be heartbroken if something had happened to his dog. There was no blood on Butter except her paws where she'd stepped in the dead man's puddle. I poked and prodded, and Butter was unperturbed, so I knew nothing was broken. "Good girl," I said, and vowed to give her a mountain of bacon when we returned home.

The horse was still standing at the edge of the thicket, head down, chewing wild grass. I ran her back to the house and leapt up the porch steps, shouting for Isaiah as soon as I had the door open.

"Genesis!" She called for me from the parlor. She sounded worried, and I found her standing at the window. Leader was walking up our driveway from a brand-new truck. Behind him followed Judith and some other woman I didn't know.

"Oh God, not now."

"Not now?" Isaiah said. "How about not *ever*?"

We watched them walk all the way to the door, let Leader knock a few times. Judith looked cold and still, holding a small box in her bare hands. For Judith's sake, I opened the door. "Sister Genesis!" Leader boomed.

"I'm not part of your congregation anymore."

"Doesn't mean we can't be neighborly. I never had the chance to give my condolences for your father."

"Daddy's been gone for months."

"All the more reason to see how ya'll are doing."

"We're doing fine," I said and let them stand there.

Judith cleared her throat, her request to speak, and Leader nodded. "We brought you some molasses cookies," she said, holding the box out to me.

I smiled at her, took the box and relented. "How about you come in and get warmed up for a moment." Isaiah grunted beside me. "Just a moment, though."

"Of course, of course," Leader said, stepping in. "We're well aware of the time it takes to keep up a ranch." The three of them sat on the sofa, Judith a little apart, the other woman nearly in Leader's lap. She was about thirty, fair-faced though obviously had lived a tough life before the Community. She happened to glance at Isaiah's glare and quickly dropped her gaze. Judith examined the room, straining to read the spines of my books, bewildered by the collage of photographs on the walls.

Leader was the same, exactly the same. The same hat, the same black clothes, the same poisonous grin. The same eyes that slid over you without moving. I fought the instinct to curl away, to hide my body from him. "You mean to shoot us, Sister Genesis?" he said. I'd forgotten I still carried the rifle.

"I was out checking fences," I said. "Isaiah, would you mind?" I handed her the cookies and the gun, and she took both to the kitchen. "What do you want, Leader? I know you didn't just come out here to bring us dessert, and you didn't come to pay your respects."

"You think so low of me?"

"I think nothing of you."

Judith hid her smirk, and Leader gave his wicked smile. "I am, in truth, here to offer some relief. A solution, if you will." Isaiah returned and leaned against the entryway. Leader became distracted by her and I had to clear my throat to call back his attention. "Now I know you girls are smart and hard-working, but it can't be easy for you out here all alone—"

"We're not alone," Isaiah said.

"Well—"

"We're not selling," I said. "Not to you, not to anyone else.

This is *our* house and *our* ranch, and we aim to keep it that way."

"Yes, however—"

"We're not selling," I said again. The air went still between us, hummed with animosity, each of us weighing out our options.

Finally, Leader clapped his hands on his knees and said, "Then I suppose there's nothing more to discuss," and he stood, the woman right behind him, though Judith was reluctant. I opened the door for them. "Good day, young sisters. Ya'll take care of yourselves out here." He grinned with a tip of his hat and escorted his lady out the door.

I grasped Judith just before she exited. We said nothing, but Isaiah hurried over and slipped her the latest letter from Adam. "Sorry I didn't bring it sooner," Isaiah whispered, and then they were gone. But I knew that would not be the last time Leader would attempt to cajole us.

"You didn't happen to mention to Reuben about Denney being gone did you?" I asked my sister as we watched the truck drive way. She turned red, opened her mouth to speak, but I cut her off. "It's nothing to argue about right now. Right now I need you to grab a shovel."

"Sweet Jesus, Genesis," were the first words from Isaiah's mouth when she saw the scene. "Who is he?"

"A poacher, a rustler, a lunatic. I don't know!" I said. "He came after me, nearly got me with that knife. Now help me bury him." We speared the earth with our shovels, but the ground was nearly solid and it took us almost three hours of sweating and swearing to get eight inches down. We hit a layer of large rocks too frozen to wedge free.

"I can't dig anymore," Isaiah heaved.

"We can't just leave him," I said, the panic setting in. "The coyote's will get him. They'll shred his corpse across the land."

We paused and considered allowing just that to happen. But if the wolves came for him, they might turn toward the cattle. We sat, biting our lips, deciding what to do.

"You got a good, clean shot at least," Isaiah said.

"I *am* the blue ribbon sharp shooter in this county," I said. And we burst into anxious laughter. The panic overwhelmed us, and I knew we shouldn't be laughing. I'd just killed a man who was slowly turning to ice before our eyes. The dog was off licking at the dead cow, knowing she shouldn't eat it—because the cows were off limits—but her instincts told him to, and we just laughed.

"So what do we do? Do we keep him until spring?"

"Oh, he'd thaw out in the barn and make the place stink more than it already does."

"Maybe Denney will know what to do."

My heart clenched. "We can't tell Denney."

"Why not?"

Truth was, I didn't know. I didn't know why I was so set on hiding it from Denney. I'd had all the right to shoot the man, but Denney would never have forgiven himself for not being there. And Daddy had never killed a man. For all the times he'd shot *at* vagrants, they'd all left alive. What if the whole town knew I'd killed a man? Would they send someone out? Would the excuse be made that we couldn't handle the strain of running a ranch? Would they say I was crazy and cart me off to an asylum? "We've got to get rid of him before Denney gets home."

We watched Butter gnawing at the calf's foot, knowing we should stop her, but we did not. "We could..." Isaiah hesitated.

"What?"

"We could make him fit," she said. "We could get him to fit in what we've got dug."

Oh God, forgive us.

I will never forget the sound of crunching bones, of boot soles and shovels on solid flesh. I'll never forget the way a face looks when the skull is caved in, the ache in my own live bones and muscles caused by the effort of breaking a body, crushing it to nothing.

And when we were done, and the corpse covered in icy earth; when we'd burned his clothes, we took the rest of the frozen calf back home and butchered it. We washed our bodies and our hands and our feet and our clothes. We washed soot and blood from our hands, and as I watched the water run brown along the porcelain edges, I groaned.

"We could have just burned him," I said. Then we'd only have had to worry about burying bones and ash. Isaiah looked at me, horrified with the same realization. We were sent into another fit of laughter, shaking with gut-wrenching mirth. We did not go back out and dig him up. There would be no time now. Denney returned the next day and we smiled, though we worried what the thaw would bring.

The thaw came on the early spring sun, signaling the new season. The body did not come back up, and we prepared and waited eagerly for the return of the hands. Denney brought us home a golden collie puppy we named Honey and she followed us around as we prepped the ranch for the new season.

I was afraid no one would return, but they did, ready to work for me and Isaiah. I took my father's place in opening the season. I could barely make it through without tearing up, seeing the familiar faces like Big Joe and Robby Burton and the Collins twins. I couldn't thank them enough for returning, despite the lower wages and the lack of my father's guidance. "Just remember," I told them at the end, "If you cross me or my sister, I'm the best sharpshooter in this county and we've got acres and acres where no one will ever find you." Though it kept them in line for the most part, it wouldn't stop Isaiah eating them up in the years to come.

Though I still had my domestic duties, I made my rounds on the ranch. I inspected perimeter fences, I took inventory of the calves and foals and oversaw the branding, I personally handed out the wages. I was determined for life on the ranch to carry on as it always had, saw to it that the hands respected and trusted me and that I respected them for their willingness to return.

Again, Jax did not come back. I had expected the sting to be less, given I hadn't seen or heard from him for the better part of two years. I tried to think of other men, let one or two from town take me to see a movie in the next town, Keith Feaney was one of them. But my interest never settled on any of them. I couldn't even let any of them kiss me and I started to make excuses that I was too focused on the ranch and had no time for romance. When I went out, Denney and one or two of the hands would be waiting up for me on the front porch, and they'd see me safely inside with a pleasant, "Good evening, Miss Genesis, he better have been a gentleman." I'd assure them I was unscathed and uninterested, and we'd all be awkwardly relieved.

And then one day, as Big Joe and I stood watching the yearlings being broken, he mentioned how he, "Ran into the Indian some time ago."

"Did you now?" I said, eyes steady on Johnny Collins on a roan filly.

"Up in Washington at a logging camp."

"Small world then."

"Said he was headed up to the Yukon," he said. I didn't ask if they spoke of me, if Jax mentioned me at all or even asked after me. I got the feeling Joe was itching to tell me something along those lines, but I was embarrassed to continue the conversation. I didn't want to ask and be seen as an eager, yearning schoolgirl. So I didn't. I acted as though the ranch was all that occupied my heart. Thankfully Big Joe left the conversation where it was.

I tried not to think about Jax, but I couldn't for all the loneliness I felt. I was so engrossed in running the ranch just right, and keeping up with the domestic side of things, so that when the town ladies came over they saw I was capable and have nothing more to gossip about. They already gossiped about us, and they gossiped about Isaiah. I knew she had started bedding Reuben, I always knew it was inevitable. I knew it'd happened because she carried herself differently afterward, like she knew what power she had, like she had been destined to become as she was.

ISAIAH

W e don't always do it when I go out there, although it happens more often than not. It's always quick and hard, like starved wolves going for a wounded hare, fingernails clawing and teeth sinking into flesh. I've come home with bruises inside my thighs and along my spine and the imprint of Reuben's bite. I've come home with flakes of his skin trapped in the crescents of my fingernails, with hay knotted into my hair, reeking of him.

"You'll tear each other to pieces," Genesis says with a sigh. And she says nothing more about it. But I know she wants to.

We can't stop ourselves. Sometimes it's in the barn, sometimes it's against the church, sometimes it's out among the sagebrush beneath the stars. He digs his nails into my skin and growls "Damn you, Isaiah" before he rolls off or pulls back and we breathe with slick, heaving chests.

He beats his fist against the ground just beside my head, bites me too hard this time. He bites the flesh of my shoulder so sharp the pain surprises me and I throw him off. "What the hell, Reuben?" I press my fingers into the place he's bitten, check for blood, but there's none. "What is *wrong* with you?"

"You!" he says. He lies on his back, his arm draped over his eyes, his bare chest heaving up and down. He's still skinny, but his muscles have toned.

"I'm not the one biting."

"You're a succubus," he growls.

I don't even know what that word means, but the way he says it, I know it can't be a compliment. "And you're a son of a bitch."

He props himself up on his elbows, scowls. "Can't you see, I don't want to be like them!"

"Then don't be!" I say, but I don't really know what he's going on about. He doesn't tell me all that goes on, other than the whoring and the fact that he hates everything he has to do.

"They take me out there, make me do things. And then they take me to these whore houses. It's like one sin stacked on top of another and another," he says. He's not even looking at me, he's glowering at the sky.

"You still care about sin?" I say. "You sure don't hesitate to come at me—" He's not listening to me though. He's still talking.

"Then they take me to these whore houses and I've given in to everything else, so it's sometimes just so hard to refrain. All these empty women with their sagging breasts and their worn out—" he turns to me again. "And then I get back after all that, after all that saying 'No' and I see you, and I can't stop myself."

The words may have been flattering had they come from someone else, said in some other tone. If I had not been compared to prostitutes. If he had not said those words with disgust. "Fine," I say, standing, pulling my shirt over my head. "Fine. If you don't want me..." I nearly tip over in anger as I yank my overalls on. "If you don't want me, I'll leave. I'll leave and I'll find someone who does want me!"

"Isaiah." He reaches for me. "That's not...I..." But I'm already on my horse. "Isaiah!" He shouts as he falls behind me. "You do that—you go out and find other men—then you'll be just a whore as well! You'll go to hell for it!"

"Then I'll take all of Babylon with me!" I shout back. I kick Boy into gear and the rush of night wind tangles my loose and wild hair.

"I need you to come with me," Genesis says from my bedroom door the next morning. "I need you to pick up some stuff from Feaney's while Denney and I meet with Mr. Garrett."

I grunt into my pillow, but I'm ready to go in twenty minutes, shifting in my overalls because the strap rubs where Reuben's bitten. There's a plate of cold sausage links and boiled eggs in the kitchen.

"You weren't up," Genesis says. "So I didn't do much by way of breakfast." She pins up her hair while I scarf down two links and start cracking an egg. She puts on a nice hat and picks up Daddy's ledgers from the table. I follow her outside, biting half the egg in one go. Denney's leaning against the truck, tossing bits of ham to his dog. He sees us, whistles, and Butter jumps into the bed of the truck. Denney opens the door for us and I pat Butter's head before I get in.

Denney drives and I sit between him and Genesis. She's all dressed up. The hat and the dress even match, they both used to be Mama's. Genesis has done something to the dress, though, made it seem new. But sitting right next to her, I can tell it's worn, the pale blue is almost white in some spots. "When did you get this dress done?" I ask.

"Last week," she says. She picks at the ledgers in her lap.

Denney notices this too. "We had a good year," he says. "I think Garrett will be impressed."

"Let's just hope our numbers and his match up."

"Garrett's always been fair," says Denney. "Don't see any reason for it to change just 'cause your daddy's gone. You've done as well as you can."

"And what about next year?" she says.

In all the years I've known Denney—my whole life—I've never heard him and Genesis say so many words to each other. Denney was never a man who said much. I look at Denney, his stubbly round face, the wrinkles at his eyes. His face is familiar and kind and calming and I can't help but think how good he's been to us, how I've taken him for granted until now. I'm suddenly glad he's here, that's he's always been here.

Denney looks over at me and smiles, winks playfully, starts whistling. "Things'll work out, they always do," he says and goes back to whistling.

When we get into town, Genesis hands me a list for Feaney and a wad of dollar bills. She straightens her hat and dress and she and Denney head for the bank. Inside the store, Keith's at the counter, weighing out a bag of nails for Owen Johnson, Maggie's daddy.

"How's the baby?" I ask Mr. Johnson. Maggie's married one of the Petersons and had a healthy little girl.

"Getting big," he says. "Hey Keith, how about a stick of candy for Miss Isaiah here? Put it on my account." I start to say he doesn't have to do that, but he waves away my response and Keith pulls me out a cherry flavored one. "We can't ever really thank you enough for helping us out with Maggie." Mr. Johnson takes his sack of nails and tips his hat to me on his way out.

"My favorite," I say to Keith, tapping my candy stick on the counter.

"I remember the regulars," he says.

"Aren't we all regulars?"

"You always get the cherry one."

"What if I decided I hate cherry now?"

"I can switch it out if you want."

"No," I laugh and pop the end into my mouth and hand him the list. "Where's your grandpa?"

"Broke his foot," says Keith.

"Doing what?"

"Fell on the stairs."

"Well old folks break easy, I guess."

He laughs. He's got a nice smile, it makes him look a little less oafish. He reads over the list. He knows it's Genesis's handwriting. "How's your sister?"

"Old," I say without thinking. "She's aged a hundred years." As soon as I say it, the urge to cry comes sudden and I have to blink fast to keep the tears back.

He speaks softly. "Let me get these rounded up for you and help you get them out to the truck."

Butter leaps around, excited for attention, as we walk back and forth and Keith finally pats her head when we're done. "How about a Coke?" he says, "Might be a while before your sister's done."

"Yeah, alright," I say and wait for him on the front step. He comes back out with two open bottles, hands me one and joins me. I'm tiny compared to him. The cola's cold and sweet. His leg knocks against mine and his arm is warm beside me. I can't help but wonder what it'd be like getting wrapped in his arms, feeling the muscles in his chest on mine. I swallow down a fourth of my bottle in one gulp.

"Thirsty?" he says. "I carried twice as much as you, what do you have to be thirsty for?"

I wipe the back of my hand across my lips. "It's good," I say. "You're a good boy," I blurt.

"Glad someone other than my grandma thinks so."

"I mean," I say, "I'm sorry it didn't work out with Genesis."

"Ah well, I never intended to get too serious with her. I just thought I'd show her a good time as long as she let me. I know how hard and lonely it can be to be without...to be an orphan."

I'm burning inside, and it's not from the Coke bubbles. I knock back the rest like it will quench the fire kindling inside me. The bubbles make me cough.

"Maybe you ought to slow down," he says, half joking, half concerned.

I see Genesis and Denney coming from the bank. "I guess it's time to go," I say, handing him the empty bottle. "Thanks for the Coke. Maybe I'll let you treat me to another sometime."

Genesis and Denney and Keith all wave politely to each other. I climb into the truck between the two of them again. "How did it go?" I ask.

"We'll make it another year," says Genesis. "But we can't keep any winter hands on if we want to keep the debt down and pay it off by next season."

"You're staying though, right?" I ask Denney.

"Of course he is," Genesis says, like I'm dumb for even asking.

"Course I am!" he says, much more cheerful than Genesis.

"Glad for that," I say and pull the rest of my stick of candy out of my pocket. Genesis eyes it. "Owen Johnson paid for it. And Keith treated me to the Coke." Her mouth is tight, but she nods and faces the window, already thinking and worrying about something else. I suck my candy and think *I'm gonna let Keith Feaney kiss me.*

I wait for the bruise on my shoulder to fade first, and it goes just in time for the town's Fall dance. Genesis and I never usually go, and she's a little old for it now, but I decide I'm going this year. "I wanna go to the town dance," I tell Genesis. I'm sitting on the toilet with my toothbrush in my hand while she washes her face in the sink.

"Denney's got the truck," she says. He's taken the rest of the hands home.

"I can take Boy," I say.

"Are you asking my permission?" She dries her face. "Since when have you ever needed my permission to go off and do something?"

"Well I was hoping you'd help me," I wet my toothbrush, "with a dress. And hair."

"What's wrong with your hair?" she says. "There's nothing wrong with you wearing it the way you always do. But I can give you a dress for the night."

"You're really not going to help me do anything with my hair?"

"We can try something," she sighs.

And a few nights later, she tries to coif my hair but it's too thick and long and it just doesn't look right on me. We both look in the mirror and laugh. It looks ridiculous. So she unpins it and brushes it out and braids it down my back again. Neither of us know a thing about makeup, and we've decided it's not a nice enough event to try it out now. "I doubt any of the other girls will really be gussied up," Genesis says. "Besides, you don't need it."

She lets me borrow her light blue dress. It's tighter on my chest than hers. "You're built like Gramma," she says. She's thin these days, thin like Mama always was. She looks me over. "Well I guess you're ready as you'll ever be." She hands me a jacket before I go out the door.

"Sure you'll be alright here all by yourself?"

"It'll be me and the ghosts," she shrugs. "I can bring Honey inside if I get too lonely."

"A dog inside? Mama'd kill you."

"Then I'll have two companions—Mama's whining ghost and dumb old Honey."

I slip on my jacket and climb into the saddle. I have to hike the skirt up my thighs in order to sit right. The air comes in cold between my legs, and the leather of the saddle rubs against my bare skin. Even I know I'm showing more skin than acceptable, and I dismount just before I get into town and pull the skirt back down to my knees, walking the rest of the way. I hobble Boy outside the town hall so he can munch on the brown lawn. I can hear the music inside, a hometown band trying to play Bing Crosby. Mrs. Garrett's at the door welcoming everyone in. "Isaiah, I wasn't expecting you to come tonight. Is your sister here too?"

"Just me," I say.

"Well, look at you in a dress and everything, just a doll," she says. "Go ahead and hand your jacket over to old Feaney over there and come on in."

When I walk into the hall, I immediately wish I hadn't come. The lights are too bright, and almost everyone from town is here. I can't see Keith right away, but they all see me come in, the boys give me their look-overs, eyes lingering a little too long on my bare legs, on the buttons straining on my bosom. It's like the fair but without the cotton candy and games. Some girls I know wave politely at me and I wave back, but I don't join any of them. They have blushed cheeks and their hair is all twisted up like crowns with little flowers. It makes them look like little girls. I run my hand over my own hair, feeling flyways let loose by the breeze. *Look, look,* they whisper to each other, *It's the Death girl done up in a dress.*

I stand there and try to make up my mind about leaving

when Mr. Alvin Coburn approaches me. He's the oldest man in town, a widower who's at least 90 years old with one milky eye and skin like leather, but he doesn't let it stop him from cutting a rug with the young folk. "So have you come to take me away finally?" he jokes.

"I think you'll outlive us all, Mr. Coburn."

He asks me to dance with him, and I really don't want to because I hate touching old people. Death follows them around like a stray cat, ready to sneak up and claim them at any moment.

But I take up Mr. Coburn's offer because I don't know what else to do and I let him push, pull and swing me around the dance floor to a fiery fiddle-stomper. He's surprisingly lively for such an old, half-blind man and Death stays away from him for the time being. He bows to me as the song ends. "You're the prettiest one here," he says and winks at me. I have a feeling he says that to all the girls. Already he's making his way to the next one.

They're cutting pieces of sheet cake on tables along the wall. I go to grab myself a piece and hear a snippet of some girls' conversation about a boy I don't know, someone they go to high school with. Katie Johnson, Maggie's sister, smiles at me. "I saw Mr. Coburn got you," she says. "We all have to have our twirl with him. Same every year."

I don't respond right away because I'm shoveling cake into my mouth. Beside her, LaRae Kitchens' mouth is pinched. "So what finally brought you out of those overalls and dragged you out among the living?" she says.

"Prowling," I answer.

"Well," Katie says before LaRae can say anything back. "Well you look nice," she says. I know she's being sincere. She pulls LaRae's elbow and leads her to the other side of the hall to a group of boys, all of them glancing up at me between their conversations. Keith Feaney comes off the dance floor, leaving one of the Johnson cousins—either Mabel or Georgia—in the hands of one of the Baker boys.

"It's a surprise to see you out," says Keith.

"Thought I'd try something new."

"I'd say it suits you, but it is a little strange to see you in a skirt."

"It's Genesis's."

"How are you liking it?"

I look around the room, see all these faces I've known all my life. I've been in many of their homes, felt the death on their parents and grandparents and brothers and sisters and babies. I know them all and I don't. "I'm not sure I do," I say.

"Well let me show you how to have a good time," he says, holding his hand out to lead me to the floor. The band's playing their own country version of "Pennies from Heaven."

"Oh, alright," I say and put my hand in his. We don't stand too close because the chaperones would tut. As we sway, I notice a new group of young men come in—they're from the Community. Aaron Fisher is one of them. Reuben is not. "Do they come often?" I ask Keith.

"Every year some of them come. I see them in town some nights too," he says. Aaron sees me, and I smile at Keith. I will let those Community boys see how much fun I'm having. I'll bat my eyes and dance with all the other town boys, and maybe even Aaron and he can go back and tell Reuben I'm getting on just fine without him.

When the song's done, I go right up to Luke Baker and ask him to dance with me, and from there on I've got a partner for each song without my having to ask. I dance the whole night, not letting up except to get a drink or two of lemonade with one boy or another. And toward the end of the night, I corner Aaron, tell him he ought to dance with me for old time's sake.

"You escaped," I say.

"Just for tonight," he says with a wicked little grin, and I know he's thinking the same thing as me: the look on Reuben's face when Aaron tells him about this, about my dancing with him, about my ease with all the other boys, boys I've known my whole life. "You clean up nice," he says.

"You're not too bad yourself," I tell him. "Now dance with me like the Devil's got a hold of you."

When the adults call for the last dance, it's 11 o'clock and Keith seeks me out, tells me this last one's his. He offers me a ride home afterward as we're all filing out. "I brought my horse," I say.

"It's a bit late to ride him home now," says Keith.

I don't tell him that I've taken Boy out much later than this. "I can't just leave him hobbling around town all night."

"I'll keep him at ours."

I agree and we get Boy settled in the Feaney's back yard, where he can munch on Mrs. Feaney's dormant lawn and shrubs. "Grandma can get more," Keith says when I say I feel bad about Boy eating their yard. I wait outside while he goes in to get the key for his grandpa's car. We push the car out of the driveway and down the road a bit so we don't wake his grandparents. Then we drive out of town, onto the dark road toward home.

We are alone and quiet, just the rattle and pop of the car around us. "Thank you," I say after some time.

"It was good to see you come out tonight," he says. "Being out here alone trying to run things, it's got to be lonely for the two of you. Especially since your daddy..."

"We're not so alone," I say. I'm growing warm. "And we aren't little girls. We can handle it." I watch his hands on the steering wheel, sturdy, strong hands. I unbutton my top two buttons, release some of the tightness on my chest. I know

Keith notices, but he pretends not to. We pull up to the house and sit for a moment. He stares out the windshield at the dark house, his hands still on the steering wheel, and I'm staring at him. I hear his breath getting deeper. "Keith?" I say, "You can go on and kiss me."

He drops his hands from the steering wheel. "I'm not expecting--"

I slide toward him an inch, two inches. He faces me. "I know you want to."

When he does kiss me, it's hungry and eager, but not rough. It is different than Reuben; different and exciting. He smells different, the slide of his tongue more timid, the taste of his mouth, sweeter. He pulls me in gently and I cling to him, pressing into his thick chest. His hands are warm as they slide along my spine, over my hips. I'm pulling him into me, pulling him down until he is top of me, growing hotter and more feverish by the second and the car steams up, skin squeaking on the seat and shoe heels and knuckles knocking against glass. I'm tugging down his pants and he's pulling at my underwear. One of the buttons is popped off my sister's dress.

And though we're devouring each other, though he takes me like a river breaking through a dam, there's gentleness to him, like he's trying not to hurt me and he's enjoying every moment of it. And though it's cramped, I find only pleasure in it. He doesn't push me away when it's done, but collapses into me and I feel his heart thumping against me. He holds me, pulls me in close and tight before he groans and peels himself back.

He catches his breath. "I didn't mean..."

"It was me," I say. We sit there and breathe, straighten our collars.

"I'll walk you to the door," he says. He gets out of the car first, walks to my side and opens my door, takes my hand, escorts me to the house.

We get to the bottom step when we hear Genesis, her voice cool, "Is that Keith Feaney?" She's pulled a chair around from the back. Butter's lying at her feet. I let my hands fall from Keith's arm.

"What are you still doing up?" I say.

"Couldn't sleep in the emptiness." She turns to Keith, who's standing like a startled deer. "Thank you for bringing my sister home. I think it's best you go home now."

He nods, turns stiffly, and goes back to his car. We watch him until the headlights are swallowed in the dark.

"I suppose that was you thanking him?"

"What do you care?" I snap. "You didn't want him."

"So you're just going to take up my dregs then?" She says, jaw set and arms folded tight. "Do you even like him?"

A growl rises up in me. Who is she to scorn me? "I like him well enough, obviously," I say, moving for the door.

"And what if he falls in love with you, Isaiah? He can't handle you and you'd be bored by him!"

I stop with my hand on the doorknob. "Maybe you bored him and that's why he came to me."

"He didn't come to you, you took him."

"I'll take whoever I damn well please!" I say. "At least I won't turn into some old hag like you, pining away for someone who's never coming back because he doesn't give a damn about you!"

I have struck too low. I know it as soon as the words have left my mouth and ring in the cold air between us. She is blazing when she stands, her arms crossed hard over her chest. I feel the heat coming off her and I step back. She whistles for Honey, who jumps up and comes to her side.

"He's the marrying type, and you're just a whore," she says.

"You'll break his heart. You'll go on screwing everyone else! You'd probably fuck the whole town!" She turns sharp and she rushes inside before I can think of something to yell back, Honey following behind her. I fall in her seat, wrap my arms around myself, let the cold seep into my bones. Maybe they're right after all, maybe I *am* just a good for nothing whore.

In the morning, Genesis is already up and out. I take another horse into town when I know all the Feaneys will be at the shop. I leave them a note saying *Thank you and sorry, it won't be happening again.*

GENESIS

The winter came on cold and we matched it. We spent weeks speaking little. I deliberated with myself why I should be perturbed by her actions. Was it jealousy? She had been right, I didn't much care for Keith Feaney beyond anything more than friendship. I didn't want him, and it was a small place, and Isaiah and I weren't that far in age, the trading of men between us was inevitable. I didn't want it to bother me, but it bothered me still. There I was worrying about our livelihood, keeping it out of Leader's hands and there she was traipsing about, taking up with whomever.

I held my pride like a prize. The cold kept us inside, too close to breathe away from each other. She often stood at the threshold of the kitchen, hovering with words on her tongue, but I'd turn my back to her and ignore her until she left me alone.

It was the quietest winter we'd ever had, just us two and Denney, made even quieter by the silence Isaiah and I traded. Christmas passed under forced cordiality—an unspoken truce —Denney did most of the talking and sighed when he ran out of things to say. He spent New Year's Eve at the bar. Isaiah went out as well, and I was left home alone with the dogs, staring into the fireplace, thinking about making up with Isaiah. But what could I say? She had called me a hag and I had called her a whore. When Denney returned, he said he'd seen her in town, but she didn't come home that night or the next.

I was starting to worry, and considering heading into town for her myself when a car with shining chrome came chugging down our drive. Denney was out checking fences. It was Mr. Garrett who stepped out of the car. I groaned, but I let him in.

"Mr. Garrett," I said, stepping aside for him.

"Miss Genesis," he greeted. He unbuttoned his coat, but I did not offer to take it, so he kept it on. I directed him to the sofa and put another log on the fire.

"What brings you all the way out here, Mr. Garrett?" I did not sit with him, nor did I offer him coffee or water.

He pulled out a kerchief and wiped his brow. "Well," he coughed and leaned back, resting his heel on his knee. "Is your sister here?"

"No."

"And Mr. Denney?"

"He's out *working*," I said, crossing my arms. "I know you didn't come here to check on the whereabouts of everyone, Mr. Garrett, so now why is it you're here?"

He laced his stubby fingers together over his knee. "Well, I know you girls work hard, Miss Genesis, I know you do, but you see, I've got obligations—and you see—well, you see, your accounts have a deficit—"

"You say that as if we're the only ones around here that do," I said, spitefully adding, "Mr. Garrett."

"Well, it's true, you're not the *only* ones—" he said, looking around the room, no doubt searching for the gun. I had half a mind to go fetch it. "But, you see, I've got—there's higher-ups in my line of work, you know. There's always higher-ups, and, well, truth is, I've had an offer on your debt—"

My heart stopped. "And," I breathed to keep calm, "Did you take it?"

"Well no, not as of yet," said Mr. Garrett. "But it's a mighty thing to consider. After all I've—we've—the bank's got our own creditors, and they're always itching for us little guys, you know—"

"Mr. Garrett," I said through my tightening throat. I was losing my resolve. "Mr. Garrett, you've known us all our lives. You've known my mother and father and grandmother. You've seen we're trying, we're *trying*, Mr. Garrett. You see there's no one else here but me and my sister and Denney. We've got no one on the payroll, just us. You even said yourself if we keep tight the way we have, we'll be back to zero in just a couple more years." I sounded like a little girl trying to sound big, my voice was breaking. I was begging. He sensed the change, and looked away from me, sheepish, his red cheeks going redder, the sweat beading on his brow.

"You know we've always come good. And we're not so far behind as some, you've said so yourself," I continued. "One more season, please, Mr. Garrett. I really have appreciated all you've done for us so far, and for holding out on us this long. But I implore you, please, just hold out a little longer. We'll come good, I promise. Please, please hold out for me—a girl you've known all her life—and don't go giving in to some sleazy man you don't know from Adam. You know we have nowhere to go."

Mr. Garrett shifted and cleared his throat, picked at a thread on his knee. He ran the kerchief around his face, pulled on his collar. The fire crackled, but I felt cold, my breathing short. He cleared his throat again, embarrassed. "Well," he said, "Well, Miss Genesis, I suppose we can look into the accounts again and crunch the numbers. I'm sure we can come to some agreement." He stood, pushing his kerchief into his pocket. "I know you're a good girl, a smart girl." At last, he put his hat back on and made for the door. "I shall leave you to the rest of the day and get something drafted for us to look over together."

"Thank you, Mr. Garrett," I said, guiding him through the door. He paused at the threshold and offered me the only sincere smile he'd ever given.

And then he said, "You know, Miss Genesis, it might not be such a bad idea to get yourself married and settled down."

The brief peace I'd felt between us was quickly replaced with the perpetual irritation I felt for him. But I bit my tongue, not wanting to give reason for him to renege. "Thank you, Mr. Garrett, I'll think about it."

The next day, Denney and I went down to sign the new payment agreement at the bank, stating we'd have such a percentage paid off by the end of each season for the next three years. I was wary—no one trusted banks in those days—but I put my faith in Garrett. Though he was a weasely little man, he was a man who stood by the law and held to his contracts.

That night, Isaiah returned. We all three at dinner together. Isaiah was bedraggled and smelled like tobacco and hay. "Where the hell have you been?" I said.

"Out," she responded.

Before I could begin a diatribe on her, Denney coughed loudly, clanking his fork hard against his plate, not wanting to be a part of this conversation. So we said nothing more to each other and went to bed. Not long after, Reuben came to Isaiah, driven through the cold by his heat for her. She didn't know that I didn't sleep. I spent the nights dozing fitfully, dreaming wakefully. Anything woke me, the smallest creak of the house, the hoot of an owl, the gleam of moonlight through the curtains.

I heard Isaiah sneak down the stairs, open the door, let him in. I heard him whisper desperately, begging and apologizing. *Groveling*. And all she could say in return was "How the hell did you get here?" The shock was evident in her voice. As far as I knew, Reuben hadn't set foot outside the Community since they'd settled; it *was* a surprise. It was Isaiah. Isaiah drew him out.

I went to my door, cracked it open, sat and tilted my ear. He brought up the rumors he'd heard. She'd been with someone else, dancing, necking outside the bar. "I told you," she said, "I told you I'd find someone else who wanted me if you didn't. You're just another one."

"I'm not," he said, the edge on his voice made my hair stand. I grabbed the door, ready to go in there if he so much as moved to harm her.

"What do you want?" Isaiah said, and there was silence between them. I imagine in that silence she let her nightgown fall. "Is this what you want?"

"I don't," he choked, but it was not convincing.

There was movement and a groan and the sound of wet lips on skin. I shut the door, though it did not drown out the sounds of their raucous lovemaking, the groans and the gasps and the knocking. I curled back in bed and clutched a pillow over my head, wishing to be anywhere else, chastening myself for not going down, breaking it up, chasing him away.

Eventually, I fell asleep, only to be woken at dawn by Denney pounding frantically on my door. I leapt from the bed, every bad scenario running through my mind; fire in the barn, Reuben'd strangled Isaiah.

"Somebody's cut the fence," Denney said the moment I opened the door. "Half the herd's missing."

All the air in me rushed out. "No." We needed that cattle. We'd rented two extra bulls and kept them longer to breed the maximum we could, in hopes we'd have more calves than ever to sell the next season. We had more pregnant heifers than we ever had. Those missing cattle meant more than just missing heifers, it meant the loss of potential profit as well. We couldn't hope to pay off our debts in time without those cattle. I dressed quickly.

I knocked loudly on Isaiah's door before thrusting it open. There was no evidence of Reuben's ever being there. Isaiah, naked, woke and rubbed the sleep from her eyes. "Get up," I said, "We've got a problem."

"What's going on?" she was asking, but I was already rushing down the stairs. She met me in the barn just as I'd finished saddling horses. "What is it?" she asked again as we mounted.

I opened my mouth but was too distressed to speak, so I just spurred the horse and she followed. Denney was waiting for us. It was more than just a cut in the wire. Posts had been uprooted and thrown aside, the barbed wire twisted. The frozen earth had been churned up by hundreds of hoofprints—a stampede's worth—leading through the break, scattering around the foothills. A few cows had stayed close, happy enough with the brush just outside the fence, but many had wandered way beyond our dim morning vision.

We dismounted, mouths open at the damage. "There's horseshoe marks here," Isaiah said, pointing at her feet, just beyond our fence. I looked at Denney, hoping it had been him who'd ridden there. He shook his head. I glared at Isaiah, seething. Her jaw slackened as it dawned on her too. Reuben had been sent to her, to keep her occupied and inside. She bit her lip, pulled at her braids.

My fury erupted "GODDAMMIT!" I screamed. I tore off my hat and threw it, kicked at the loosened earth. Anger roiled inside me and burst in a cry of indignation that echoed over the frozen hills and frosted pastures. "I'll kill him!" I shouted. "I'll kill the son of a bitch!" The horses jolted, and the dogs whimpered. Isaiah's eyes widened in shock as every obscenity I'd ever heard poured from me. Denney stood by with his hat in his hands, twisting the brim.

I picked up rocks and clods of frozen dirt, their cold burned my palms. I hurled them haphazardly, any way my arms swung, until I lost my balance and fell on my backside on the hard ground. My temper blew out then and I dropped my head in my hands. Would that man never leave us alone?

The dogs paced and whimpered around me, licking at my elbows and knees, trembling with concern. Denney and Isaiah stood by, silent. The horses huffed, clouds of breath billowing from their nostrils. As my blood cooled, the sun rose. Distantly, cattle lowed at the rising light. We were too far from the house, but I knew the rooster would be up causing a ruckus. The horses in the barn would be twitching, whinnying for breakfast. The milking cows would be bellowing over their swollen udders. There was laundry to be done, a fireplace to be cleaned, clothes to be patched; an endless list of dos.

I pushed the dogs away and stood, brushed myself off. Isaiah dusted off my hat and handed it to me. "How many do you think are out?" I asked Denney, repositioning my hat.

"A couple hundred," he said, putting on his own hat.

I sighed, and pulled myself onto my horse, whistled for Honey to heel. "Isaiah, go back and milk the cows, hay the horses. And when that's done, we've got two hundred scattered cattle to wrangle." She nodded without retort and clambered onto her own horse.

We split up to cover more ground, but with only three of us it was slow-going. It took all day—dawn to well after dusk— riding all over the foothills, chasing after groups of threes and fours, back and forth, back and forth. We only had the two dogs, so Denney had to go it alone, as well as fix the fence. The dogs helped, but they had their downfalls. Honey was still young and timid around the cows; I often had to repeat commands two or three times in rising levels of frustration to get her to listen. Isaiah had Butter, who was more seasoned, but Isaiah hadn't worked much with the dogs and her mixed commands left Butter confused.

We paused only to water the horses, the dogs, and ourselves and by the end of the day, we still had forty head missing. We slumped around the dinner table with cold biscuits and ham. I was lightheaded with hunger, but I couldn't eat, my stomach churned. "Some probably got into the gorge," Denney suggested. It was dangerous in the daylight; there was no way I'd allow any of us to up there on the breadth of dark.

"Some might have been stolen," Isaiah said flatly. She picked at her cold ham.

More than likely they were both right. Regardless, we knew we'd never see those forty head again. I crushed a biscuit with the tines of my fork. "I'll think of something," I assured them. Exhausted and grimy, I climbed up the stairs and fell, fully dressed, onto my bed.

The crisis broke the stalemate between Isaiah and I. "Jax is stupid for leaving you," she said.

"I shouldn't have called you a whore," I said.

She burst into tears. "I'm sorry, I'm sorry about Reuben," she said. "I should have known something was up when he showed up." She pulled her braid around her eyes and sobbed into it. "Maybe I *am* just a whore." She cried like a little girl. I wanted to tell her to stop, to compose herself. Sometimes I forgot how young we still were. I wasn't even twenty; she was only sixteen.

I sighed. "Hey," I said, pulling her hair down. "You know Leader, he probably threatened Reuben. I'm sure Reuben didn't want to double cross you." For all his faults, Reuben had always—for some reason—been faithful to my sister.

Isaiah looked at me with her red-rimmed eyes. She'd been beating herself up over the past few months. She'd been letting men take her to bed—or rather just pushing her up against the wall at the bar. She'd been getting drunk and sleeping in the barn, not wanting me to see her after her nights of debauchery.

Harlot. Whore. She'd been told for so long that was the way she was heading, she'd just gone ahead and done it. But our mother had been an adulteress, and our grandmother a loose woman for a time before her. One of us two was bound to be.

I put my arms around Isaiah and holding her close. "Gramma once told me, 'Take as many men as you want to bed, but do it because you want to, not because you think it's all you're good for.'"

Isaiah just slumped against me, "But you haven't been with anyone but Jax, have you?"

I ran my hand over her hair; it was warm and sleek under my palm. "No," I said. "I haven't." Isaiah groaned against me. "But Gramma was a straight up whore," I told her.

"Genesis!" she gasped, sitting up.

"Well she was," I said, smiling for no reason. "How else do you think she kept her family fed after her daddy died?"

"Did she tell you?" She was smirking now, too.

"I worked it out," I said. "All the little quips and sly remarks over the years. Oh, I think she took plenty of men for free because she liked the way they looked or whatever else. But she took plenty for money as well."

Isaiah laughed and fell back again, sighing "Oh, Gramma." We sat silently for a moment, lost in our own worries, replaying the last day in our minds. "Genesis, what are we gonna do?"

I stroked her hair. "I'll think of something," I sighed.

In the end, it was decided we'd breed both Butter and

Honey with another full-blood collie belonging to the Johnsons. We sold two mares—my favorite included. Then I sold a parcel of land.

It was small, and awkward-shaped edge of no consequence at the front corner of our property. It went to a nice couple from a town not too far away; they were expecting a baby and planned to build up their own little homestead. They were nice enough. Nevertheless, I cried myself to sleep over it. The money helped, but I silently vowed not to sell another plot so long as my sweat went into that earth. We had more than enough to cover our loss and to hire all the help we'd need for the upcoming season. We even put out advertisements in the newspapers.

As the weather warmed, we looked forward to the opening of the season. We opened the bunkhouse and aired it out, shook out the blankets and starched the pillows. We re-ticked the mattresses, swept out the cobwebs. Denney repaired broken beds and floor boards and roof leaks. We repainted and dusted and reassembled. I was determined for the season to start afresh for everyone.

And just before they were all due to return—before Denney was to start carting truckloads from over the mountains —Isaiah called out to me from the front porch, where I'd sent her to beat the rugs. Worried it was Leader or Mr. Garrett come to call again, I left the basket of wet clothes on the back porch and hurried forward. Isaiah was smiling, watching down the drive where a lone figure came walking, a rucksack over his shoulder. Tall and lean; long, black hair.

It was Jax.

He hadn't known my father had died. He'd been in the Yukon just as he'd told Big Joe and didn't return to South Dakota until the next year. He bumped into Robby Burton there, who'd told him of Daddy's demise. "I saw your advertisement," he said.

And when autumn came, I stood before him as he came to say goodbye and I asked him to stay. "Unless you want to go," I said. "Unless you've got somewhere to be." Some other woman. Some other home.

He responded by throwing his stuff at my feet. It was then, after he'd agreed to stay and moved into the house, that I'd told him about the baby I didn't have. He told me he was sorry he hadn't been there, sorry I hadn't told him, that I'd had to go through it alone. "I would have come right back," he said. "I would have come, and I would have stayed."

ISAIAH

SUMMER 1940 – SPRING 1941

"We've got names picked out," Genesis announces over supper, her hand on her round stomach. She and Jax glance at each other and smile. "Name it after Daddy if it's a boy. After Gramma if it's a girl."

"Don't you think it's best to wait until after it gets here?" I say. I was, for Genesis's sake, glad when Jax returned and when he stayed. And I was just as pleased as they were to hear they were having a baby. It's taken nearly two years to get this one, but not for their lack of trying, I know. They aren't as quiet as they think they are. And, though I approve of their naming decisions, something nags at me.

"There's no harming in deciding beforehand, is there?" my sister says. "And we aren't that far off, just a few more months."

I shake the nagging feeling away, put my own hand on her stomach, feel the tightness, the roundness of it. Thunder rumbles outside and rain falls on the roof and splashes on the windows. Lightning flashes closer and closer as we finish up dinner and Jax and I wash up while Genesis sits in the parlor with her feet up.

I wash and Jax dries. He doesn't say much, he never does, but when we are blinded by light and a crash that shakes the house, we both jump and he says, "That one was close."

We hear Genesis groan. "Are you alright in there?" I shout to her.

"I pissed myself!" she calls back. "A lot. I may have ruined the sofa." Jax sets down his drying towel and goes to her. I hear him soothe her, and she snaps that she's fine. She moves upstairs to change and Jax comes back in the kitchen for baking soda.

Movement outside the window catches my eye. The night is blue. If it wasn't storming the sun would just be setting. Instead, everything glows deep blue. The hands are running, shouting and waving at each other in the rain and thunder. "Jax," I say. Something's wrong out there. Jax sees and hurries out the back door. I hear him shout; he has a way of shouting that doesn't sound like shouting. The sky crackles purple and white and soon he's running out there.

There's two men carrying a body between them. I stop breathing. It's one of the new hands, a kid named Tommy Curtis. He's hardly more than a boy. I open the door as they bring him in. "He's been struck by lightning," Jax says. "Lay him on the table," he tells the hands.

Tommy's clothes are steaming and torn. The dining room fills with the hands wet and dripping with rain. "Tear open his shirt," I say, pulling my own sleeve up.

"He's still alive," says one of the hands.

"He's got a pulse," says another.

"Just knocked out."

But they open his shirt and we all make some small noise, a gasp, a whistle, a nervous laugh. Tommy's skin is covered in a lightning bruise like a purple tree stretching over his torso and up his neck. I place my hand on his bare chest. His heart is thumping, jittery, but Death is not here.

"What's going on?" Genesis comes down stairs, sees us all crowding in the dining room, Tommy's body on the table. "Go for the doctor," she says calmly, and she sits at Tommy's head. I grab the key for the truck, pull on a hat and go.

The old doctor has stopped doing house calls, he stays in his house clinic, taking patients there for minor problems. His son Robert is here now, living just next door; it's him I go to. He answers and I can see his wife sitting at their table, trying to feed their baby something from a spoon.

"It's one of our hands," I say. "He's been struck by lightning."

Doc Jr. nods, grabs his bag from the sideboard. His wife waves distractedly at us. He jumps into our truck with me. "You won't kill us, will you?" he says when I grind the gears.

"I don't drive that much, but I'll try not to." I get the truck moving and I drive a little too fast. The rain is letting up, but Doc Jr holds the door handle with white knuckles.

I have to pee. I drive faster. When we make it back to the house, everyone's still stuffed into the dining room and Tommy is sitting up on the table, shirtless, his hair standing. He's drinking a glass of water and looks a bit bewildered but seems to be alright. When he speaks, he shouts. "Doc, you made it!"

Doc Jr smiles, sets his bag on the table. "Battered eardrums, I think," he says. Genesis takes Tommy's glass and shoos the hands out the door.

I slip into the bathroom. Only a little comes out even though I felt like I was going to wet my pants and it stings. It's been like this all day. When I come back out, Doc, Jr's examining Tommy, lifting his arms, poking his fingertips, turning his neck.

"What's that?" Tommy yells.

"I think you'll be fine," Doc, Jr shouts back. "He'll probably be a little sore," he says to Genesis and Jax, "And a little hard of hearing for a while. But he should make a full recovery otherwise. I don't think he was hit directly, must have been pretty close to wherever it hit though."

"You're gonna have to speak up, Doc," Tommy yells.

"You'll be fine, son!" He helps Tommy up onto his wobbly legs.

Genesis excuses herself to the toilet. Jax helps with Tommy. "I'll walk him out to the bunk, and I'll take you home, Doc," Jax says. They get Tommy's shirt back on and then it's just me and the doctor.

"Hey, Doc Jr?" I say as he's putting his bag together. He looks at me expectantly. "It's probably not a big deal or nothing, but I was wondering, since you're here, if you could take a look...down there...for me."

"Have you been experiencing something out of the ordinary?" I'm afraid to answer, afraid my sister will hear. "Is there a room more private?" he asks, and I lead him up to my room.

"It stings when I piss—pee," I say as soon as the door shuts.

"Well, if you'd kindly remove your clothing, I'll see what's going on," he says. He turns his back to me and pulls gloves out of his bag. I take off my pants and underwear, lay on the bed knees up. Of all the times I've been in this position, don't know why it should make me so uncomfortable now. I clear my throat to let him know I'm ready and he turns, pulls the chair over and positions himself.

"Have you got some concern about what it might be?" he asks from between my knees.

"Well," I say, "There was a man a few nights ago—a passer-through," I remember to breathe as I feel Doc Jr's fingers on me. I don't even talk to Genesis about things like this. I don't even talk to the men about it; we just get it over with and go our separate ways. I feel my cheeks burning, and I feel awkward saying nothing, so I just keep going "I met the guy at the bar. I wasn't drinking though. Just cola. I went with the hands. They didn't see. Well, they saw me dancing, but we went outside, me and the man—but nobody saw us. We weren't *outside*, really, we were around back, where no one goes except to piss and throw up and..." I know my cheeks are flaming. I must sound like a ten-cent whore.

Doc Jr. just nods, sits back, peels off his gloves. "It's just a minor infection," he says. "It's common enough. Just drink lots of water and urinate when you feel the need to. Keep clean. It will go away on its own in a day or two." He stands, moves to the other side of the room, turns his back. I dress quickly. "And I suggest sticking with men you know." I'm just about to tell him to mind his own business when he turns around and adds, "I'm not saying this as judgment, Miss Isaiah. I'm saying it as a matter of precaution, for your own sake."

"Oh."

"Strange men can bring strange things with them," he says.

"You said it will go away on its own?"

"If it doesn't clear up in a couple days, come see me. Or my father, if you'd rather, since you've known him longer." He snaps his bag closed. He turns his back as I dress again.

Since the old doctor doesn't do house calls anymore, he also doesn't call on me anymore. I didn't do anything other than let him know whether or not someone was worth sending to the hospital, but seeing Tommy on the brink of life got me thinking. What good was it just knowing people were going to die? Even if I couldn't save them, I was tired of just feeling the life slipping away from people. I have this odd gift, isn't there more I could be doing with it?

"You know," I say, pulling overalls over my feet. "I used to help your pop sometimes when I was a girl."

"I remember," he says. "He said something about you brought comfort to people." He glances over his shoulder to see if I'm dressed and quickly turns back when he sees that I am not.

"Oh," I say. I get my straps done up and I tug at them as I stumble on. "Well I was thinking—if you needed help—I mean, I don't have much to do here, and with Genesis's baby coming and all, it'd be nice to, you know, be able to help."

He turns around to face me. "Do you have a mind to go to nursing school?"

"I never finished school," I say, and my hopes fall. "Is that the only way you'd take me on?"

He smiles. It's a nice smile. "People around here don't need certified nurses. They just need someone who understands they won't take the time to convalesce but will tell them that catalog tonic can't cure a thing." I don't know if he's saying yes or no so I just stare at him. He chuckles and says, "I'd be glad to take you on as my assistant, Miss Isaiah."

"Well gee," I say, a little embarrassed now. "Thanks, Doc."

"Call me Robert," he says. "I grew up hearing everyone here call my father Doc and it feels wrong taking the title while he's still living. All the old people still call me Robbie."

"Robert," I repeat, and something about calling him by name makes me blush.

Genesis is surprised to see us come down the stairs and narrows her eyes at me, but she says nothing. "How's that baby doing Miss Genesis?"

"Getting heavy," she says. She hands him a dollar and some change. "Thanks for coming out, Doc. Jax should be around front now." He wishes us good evening and Genesis closes the door behind him. She presses her fist into her back, stretches.

"You alright?"

"Baby's just wiggling," she says.

"That's good isn't it?"

She shrugs. Neither of us know much about babies. I feel the urge to piss again but I wait for Genesis to go back into the kitchen and finish up the dishes Jax and I left in the excitement over Tommy. Afterward, the two of us sit on the porch. Well, she sits and I swing in my hammock. The storm's long past now and the sky is spotted with black clouds that pass over the stars. We can breathe again.

Jax returns home, kisses Genesis on the head and says he's going to bed. He's the man of the ranch now, and he's up at dawn just like Daddy was. Genesis still takes charge of the books and meets with Mr. Garrett, taking both Denney and Jax with her. These days, she's so content, I can't help but feel the same. She rests her eyes and hums. I don't tell her she's humming a hymn.

The doctor doesn't sit me down and teach me so much as he lets me accompany him on house calls. He tells me about this pill and that pill, about what this rash means and what that bump means. He shows me how to inoculate the school children, dress open wounds. There's a lot to learn, more than I thought, and we're starting with the simple stuff.

But it's only a couple weeks later I'm awakened in the middle of the night.

"Isaiah?" It's a voice of a man that sounds familiar but I can't place it in my grogginess. I turn over to see who it is. It's Leader's son Matthias. When he sees I'm awake, he takes off his hat.

My first thought is to shout for Jax and Genesis. I haven't seen Reuben for over two years. He tried to come see me again, but I went straight to Genesis and told him he was outside. She sent Jax out to chase him off. I heard Reuben crying out that he'd just come to apologize, saying he would have told me, but he was too scared of his father. He was blubbering and begging, calling out my name. It was embarrassing for both of us. He must have told his father about Jax, because Leader had left us well enough alone since he'd come back.

Now Matthias was standing on our doorstep. I sat up, reaching for the knife in my boot. Matthias raised his hand and stepped cautiously toward my door. "Judith begged for you," he said.

"What's the matter with Judith?" I say.

Suddenly, the light flips on and the kitchen door bangs open and Genesis is standing there in her nightgown, her hair loose, her belly stretched out in front of her, shotgun tucked and aimed at Matthias. Jax is behind her. He tugs on her shoulder and she pulls away, cocks the gun. "What the hell do you want?" Pregnancy has made her terrifying, and Matthias stumbles back, nearly falling off the top step. I jump up, unlatch my door and stand between them.

"It's not Judith," Matthias says behind me; I hear him swallow hard. "She just sent me to get you."

Genesis lowers the gun, "What is it, then?"

"It's Reuben," Matthias says, and my heart sinks. I've been so angry at Reuben for years, but to think of him dying hurts. "He's been ill for days. Hasn't been able to get out of bed."

Genesis sets her jaw and shakes her head at me, begging me to forget about it. But I can't. I can't just let Reuben die. "Fine," Genesis says. "You," she points at Matthias, "You wait out front. I'll send her out in a minute." Matthias nods and makes his way around the house. Genesis pulls me inside. She takes her pistol from the cabinet and thrusts it in my hand. "Take this with you."

"I'm not taking a gun, Genesis, I'll take my knife." But she pushes it into me. I sigh and take it, stuff it down the front of my bibs. She follows me out the front door.

"As soon as he's getting better—or not—you come right home," she says, loud enough for Matthias to hear.

Matthias and I don't talk the whole way. He parks outside the gate—they've got a full gate now, and a solid plank wall, so no one can see in. The gate opens, and it's Judith and Jerusha, they hurry us in and rush to close the gate behind them. The three of them sneak me into the big house.

Reuben is red, his blond hair so wet it's dark. He is thin and his heart beats in the cavern of his throat. His mouth is open and his eyelids twitch. I lay my head on his slick chest and hear the rattling in the cage of his ribs. His skin is so hot it's like touching an iron. He wheezes.

"We've done all we know to do," Judith says. She blinks quickly, her eyes shining with tears she's holding back. "He's been this way for days," she says. "Just tell us...tell us what to prepare for."

I do not feel Death on him. I treat him. I lie beside him, my head on his chest. I dream of Death, of his pale, hollow face breaking into a grin that gleams like stars in the night sky. He opens his mouth and breathes me in, swallows me whole until I am left alone in darkness.

When I wake, it is to the true darkness of night, and I'm not sure I am awake. The door is open, a dark figure stands in the gap. I watch it and it watches me, the face a big black blank across the room. I think maybe it is Death and I close my eyes tight, try to shake him away, but when I open them again, the figure is still there, breathing low. The hair on my neck stands up and I think about reaching for the gun I put in Reuben's nightstand. But is it a man or a shadow?

I watch without blinking until the shadow moves away, I

close my eyes, curl into Reuben's body; thinking that I've never seen Leader without his hat. The heat of Reuben washes over me and draws me back to sleep. A rush of wind wakes me again, a creak in the night.

I am suddenly too awake in this dark. I wonder if I've actually been asleep at all. Footsteps shuffle in the hallway. Someone is wandering the house. I crawl over Reuben, tiptoe to the door. It moans when I crack it open. The footfalls pause and I do too. When they carry on and I hear the faint *click* of the front door, I sneak to the living room, hoping to see who it is sneaking out.

It is Judith, in her nightdress and loose hair flowing as she walks. She almost glides, slipping through the night. Genesis has gone into the night in nothing but nightgown and loose hair before; I remember watching her then, too. Judith disappears around the church. If it is not Leader using his study for night time secrets, it is one of his children.

I go back to Reuben's bed. "Isaiah," he says, and my name sounds like a draft through an open window. I hold my hand above his open lips to catch the hot, moist breath in my hand. I touch his skin to clear it of death. His fingers brush my skin weakly. We sleep.

The birds call the break of morning, not many hours later. I turn my face to Reuben's. He has gone from red to pink; the rattling in his breath has calmed.

When Judith enters, she is dressed properly, her hair tied back, awake and alert as if she was not out only mere hours before. "How is he?" She says.

"Better," I say. "Still hot, but his fever broke last night."

She brings me food; we eat and watch Reuben stir. His eyes open and focus. He licks his lips and Judith smiles, holds a cup to him. He drains her water, then does the same to mine. He falls back into his pillow, catching his breath. I take his hand in mine.

"He would have let me die," he croaks, scowling something mean, a new anger dark in his eyes. He's talking about his father. Neither Judith or me says any different. Little Elizabeth (who isn't so little anymore) opens the door, checking to see if Reuben was any better. Leader passes behind her in the hall without a pause, like a shadow. He's not yet wearing his hat; my breath catches. It was not Death watching me in the night. It was Leader.

"Is there no food for the man who owns this house?" Leader yells from downstairs. Elizabeth and Judith exchange worried glances.

"Father's been...cantankerous..." Elizabeth explains to me, and Reuben grunts. "Since his...accident." We hear pots and pans being bashed around and cabinet doors slammed. Leader's calling fire and brimstone on the heads of his slothful daughters. Elizabeth sighs. "I'll go," she says.

"Bastard," Reuben growls. He closes his eyes, lays back, holds my hand. He's asleep again.

"It wasn't an accident," Judith says, her eyes on Reuben. "Father went off for a couple weeks—business, he said. And when he came back, his whole leg was swollen like a watermelon, the bones were all shattered. Then he made us all build that wall, and put up guards and no one's been sent out converting since." Leader starts shouting again downstairs. Judith looks exhausted, deep bags under her eyes. "I had to beg him to send Matthias for you. You don't know how many scriptures I had to toss at him to get him to allow it, to convince him that it was his duty as a father to do his best by his son." She scowls. "His own son..." Leader's voice rises. She sighs in frustration. She strokes Reuben's hair, presses her lips to his hot crown. "Thank you for coming," she says to me before she goes.

"I know you don't...trust us." She leaves me alone with Reuben. I hear her shouting back to her father until things calm down and the smell of bacon rises.

Reuben wakes several times, a little longer every time, and I soothe him and feed him broth. When it is nearly evening, he holds my hand against his skin, strokes my hair. "You came to me," he says.

"Of course."

He kisses me, and for the first time, he is tender. It makes me want to cry. And then we are naked and moving silently beneath his sheets, his skin so hot it burns me. He is still weak and it exhausts him. "I have to go home," I whisper to him as he fades to sleep. I slide away from him and dress. When I go downstairs to find Judith, I find only Leader, standing before the door, leaning on a gnarled cane.

He waves for me to follow him. "I'll pay you for your time."

"It's really no bother," I say. I really just don't want to spend a moment longer with him.

"No, no, I insist. Then I'll have Daniel take you home."

I follow after him, down the porch, across the yard, to his study. He pulls keys from his pocket. He fumbles the keys, slips as he tries to insert the right one in the lock. "I really don't need the money," I say again.

Leader's voice is low and hard. "I must pay you for your services, Isaiah!"

My heart races and I know I should leave, but just as I make my decision to run, he opens the door, grabs me by the wrist and pulls me inside, locking the door behind us. He drags me across the dark room, stomping to the lamp. The study goes from dark to dim. He fumbles with his keys again, uses another to unlock a drawer in his desk and pulls out a metal lockbox. From that, he grabs a fistful of bills and stuffs them down the front of my bibs.

"Take it, take them," he says, his breath is hot and smells like meat gravy. He twists my arm around my back and jams his hand further down my overalls. He pushes me up against the wall and squeezes hard on my tit. He still wears that stupid hat. He tugs my braid from behind my back and wraps it around my neck and laughs. I try not to breathe too heavy, thinking maybe he'll strangle me with my own hair, but he doesn't. Instead, he buries his nose in my neck, the hair-noose, and takes deep breaths.

He presses against me, yanking at the button on my bib strap. My shoulder is pinched and my blood buzzes in my ears like angry bees. His hat flops off. The top of his head is bald; only a few long hairs combed over the dome. As his grip tightens on my wrist, and his free hand tugs and the button pops off the strap, I can think only in phrases and snippets chasing each other, like tuning a radio dial. *Trials, troubles, tribulations such as never...for every Thing there is a season... every time it rains, it rains... "There's something* wrong *with you, Isaiah...thou shalt not steal, thou shalt not... get thee hence, Satan...* I shouldn't have left the gun in Reuben's night-stand. I knew I would forget it. Then I remember...I remember...

I hear myself scream, a war cry, and Leader suddenly growls and staggers, and I am pulled back into the study. My hand is wrapped around the hilt of my knife, the blade sunk deep in Leader's shoulder. Blood blooms and trails down his chest. I let go of the knife, leave it in him. We are both shocked, but it doesn't last long. It's not a fatal wound, too high up and all it's done is anger him.

He backhands me hard across the face. He wears a big silver ring and I feel it cut into my cheek. I fall away from him, crawl toward the door. He reaches out for me, the knife wobbling in him, and I kick, aiming for his groin but my heel meets his gut. He doubles over in pain. It's enough for me to get to the door and unlock it. I slam it on him as I run.

I hear Leader shout, growling like a bear. His sons are on the porch. Benjamin leaps down, grabs me by the shoulders. "What have you done, you little bitch?" I break one arm free and break his nose. His head flies back and he stumbles, releasing me. I run without looking back, I trip over rocks and sage brush, slip on the gravel on the road. I wipe the blood away from my cheek. I'm gasping, the air burning my lungs, but I can't slow down, I can't stop.

I'm so tired when I get to town, and I veer onto the doctors' street. By the time I get to Robert's house, the cut on my cheek has crusted over. His wife answers, and her mouth falls open in surprise. I know I look bad, dry blood on my face, one side of my bibs lopping loosely, my hair in disarray. I am haggard and exhausted.

"My goodness, Isaiah," Robert says. "Bring her inside, Anna."

"I'm sorry," I say as they set me on the sofa. Their little boy starts crying upstairs.

"He was already awake," Anna says. "I'll go to him."

Robert turns my face to look at the cut. "Who did it?"

"It doesn't matter," I say. "I'll kill him next time."

He shakes his head in frustration. "There shouldn't *be* a next time," he says. He dabs at my cut, scrubs at the dry blood. "You really ought to keep better company."

I push his hands away. "Thanks, Doc, but your advice isn't necessary. You're preaching to the choir."

"If it wasn't necessary, I wouldn't need to be saying it." I bite my lip because I feel tears coming and he sighs. "Did this person hurt you in any other way?" I shake my head. "Alright," he says, and finishes cleaning me up. "You're already bruising, but you'll be okay. Do you want me to take you home?"

"No," I say. "Genesis really will kill him if she sees me like this. And I'm so tired. I'm just so tired and I can't explain to her right now."

"Alright," he says again. And I curl up and fall asleep before he even brings me a blanket.

GENESIS

"I'll kill him," I was saying for the umpteenth time when the young doctor brought Isaiah back to us. "I knew you shouldn't have gone," I said, tilting her chin this way and that to inspect the bruises.

"Genesis, I'm *fine*," she said, pulling my fingers from her face "I got him worse than he got me." I dropped my hands and Isaiah smirked at me. I placed my hand on my belly and smiled back. Motherhood was getting to me. Isaiah patted my belly and disappeared up the stairs.

"Thanks for bringing her home, Doc," I said.

"A little ice should help with the swelling," he said. "She didn't give me the chance to patch her up. She was rearing to come home." Jax came down the stairs and the two men nodded to each other. I heard Isaiah coming down not far behind and the doctor's eyes flickered to her, but only just for a moment. He beckoned me out to the porch with him. "Should I notify the sheriff?"

I shook my head. "It won't do any good." He waited for me to say more but I didn't, so he tipped his hat and made to leave.

He paused on the steps. "Please let us know if you need anything," he said. I waved him goodbye as he pulled away.

In the kitchen, I found Isaiah seated in a chair and Jax bent over her, pressing ice to her face, pained expressions on both of them. "Your eye's gonna be good and black," Jax was saying. Isaiah winced at the cold ice on her bare, swollen skin.

"You can't just put ice straight on it," I said, shaking my head. The both looked up at me, their eyes saying *But it's what the doctor ordered.* "Hand me that ice," I held out my hand. I wrapped it in a dish cloth and handed it back to Isaiah. She sat back, pressed it against her face.

Jax poured himself a cup of coffee and leaned against the counter to drink it. He took my hand briefly and squeezed it with affection. I set about making breakfast. It was Sunday, and, once the morning milking and feedings were done, the hands had the day free to them. They moved about the yard, shaving, tossing balls, or just lounging about in the morning sun. Denney knocked on the door once and entered, humming to himself. He took one look at Isaiah and let out a high whistle. She shrugged at him in response and pulled her chair back to the table to join him. Jax filled another cup and joined them.

Denney hadn't commented at all when I told him Jax was staying, he'd just said, "Alright," and left it at that. Come spring, when the others returned, those that had known us for years and stuck with us through Daddy's departure were not shocked to find Jax still there, but were concerned seeing him up on the porch with me during my welcoming speech. Though many of them had known Jax and gotten on with him as their colleague, they still bristled to think he had risen up the ranks so quickly after spending just two summers there.

"This is still my ranch," I assured them. "Still mine and my sister's. And Denney's still overseer." The one's who'd known us, they were content with that. However, the ranch had prospered enough that we could bring on more hands, new hires. It was them we had to cajole.

We had a few who had something to say about working for "an Indian and a woman."

"If you don't like it, you can leave," was my answer. Some of them did. Others swallowed their grumbling and stayed on.

Jax did not ask me to marry him, and I did not want him to. We lived as husband and wife nonetheless. We had not immediately set out to try for a baby again. We were content with each other. After a year, though, I wondered if I would ever have another, and I thought of babies more with each new day. I daydreamed and night-dreamed of them and deep down I worried I'd never have one. And when I had accepted that possibility, it happened.

With the memory of my loss four years before, I was wary of getting my hopes up, but as my stomach grew and I felt the child come alive, I could not help but look forward with eager joy. We would no longer be two orphan girls living alone on a great big ranch and legends of our ancestors. Now we were a living, breathing, growing family.

We ate breakfast together, the four of us, beaming at each other despite the deepening bruises on Isaiah's face. We made no mention of it. Not until the men finished eating and went out. Then, I asked Isaiah, "Is Reuben still alive?"

"Yes," she said. She paused before she proceeded to give me news of the Community—the wall, Leader's crippled leg. She stopped just short of explaining what had happened to cause her injuries. I didn't want to press, but I was afraid something more serious had happened than she was letting on. Leader had always held an uncomfortable fascination with her, from the time she was a little girl. As she'd grown into womanhood, I felt that there was less and less reason for him to contain himself. I'd felt in my gut that, inevitably, he would force himself on her. She picked at the bacon grizzle on her plate and sucked at her swollen lip. "I forgot your gun," Isaiah finally said. She wrapped her arms tight across her chest. "And I don't think I'm getting my knife back this time."

"How bad?" I said.

"I got away before he could..." she closed her eyes.

"You hurt him bad too?"

When her eyes opened, a dark cloud had crossed over them. "Genesis, he's worse than before."

I cradled my belly; she looked out to the sky.

I had grown content. Jax had come back to me, we were having a baby, my ranch was doing well, and Leader had left us well enough alone for nearly three years. In my joy, I forgot about sadness. But deep down, I was starting to feel like it couldn't hold.

And in my seventh month, Jax and Isaiah called to me eagerly from the back porch. I left the ironing and waddled out, expecting a disaster—a trampled young hand, a cattle epidemic, a wolf massacre—but instead I was presented with a cradle and a rocking chair, both crafted by Denney and the hands. I sat in the chair while they all beamed. I thanked them with tears in my eyes. My mother had burned both things after she lost the last child she and my father had conceived, and I hadn't given thought to the fact I lacked both.

"They won't fit in our room," I told Jax when we pulled the furniture inside. We left them in the living room for a few days. As children, we weren't allowed in Mama and Daddy's room, and habit had kept me out at first. After Daddy was gone, grief kept me out. I'd made Denney go in to get the ledgers and the door had stayed closed. I ran my hands over the smooth, varnished wood of my new rocking chair and I was ready to do it, to open the door and air out the ghosts.

The baby I carried, that grew heavy and round in my belly, was not as lively as other women said theirs were. The baby moved, it kicked and stretched and flinched so I knew it was alive. But it was, for the most part, rather quiet. So when I went whole day, two days, not feeling a twitch, I thought nothing of it.

In sorrow thou shalt bring forth children.

That first pain came early in the morning, a month too early, and I said nothing to neither Jax nor Isaiah. I had yet to open the door to Mama and Daddy's room, and the cradle and chair still sat in the parlor. I didn't know what to do so I did nothing; I carried on with my day, barely pausing for the pains as they slowly grew stronger and more frequent. Jax and Isaiah found me in the kitchen, clutching at the edges of the counter, paring knife in one hand and half a peeled potato in the other.

I tried to tell them I was fine as it passed and I could breathe again. I apologized for not having lunch ready, and then I cried. "It's too early," I said and repeated it three or four times. "Something's wrong, it's too early." Jax led me from the kitchen, handed Isaiah the key to the truck. "No, she needs to stay!" I cried out in panic and grabbed my sister's hand in desperation.

"Send Denney for the doctor and come right back," Jax said. Isaiah squeezed my hand and ran out the door. Jax tried to lead me up the stairs, but I froze at the bottom, envisioning the loss of my last baby up in that same room.

"No, not yet," I said. "I can't go up yet." So he sat with me in the parlor instead. Isaiah returned, and we heard Denney start up the truck. I released Jax from my side, sent him to wait outside. And when he stepped out the door, I took Isaiah's hand as another contraction built. "Something's wrong," I said through gritted teeth. "Can you feel it? Will you feel the baby? Please?"

She shook her head. She would not lay her hand on my stomach, she would not confirm the life or the death of my baby. Or maybe she already knew and wouldn't tell me.

The old doctor's wife arrived without either her husband or her son. She asked me to lie back, and she put her hand beneath my skirt. "I believe you've still got a while," she said. "We'll send for the doctor when it gets closer. Now, we'll get you settled. I'll stay here with you." She was calm, soothing, experienced. I relaxed as she took my hand, paced with me, held me when the pains came. She'd been right; it was early evening by the time my water broke and she sent for the doctor. I let her lead me up the stairs. Isaiah stayed by my side, biting her lip with worry.

The old doctor didn't do house calls anymore, but he came for me and brought his daughter-in-law with him. I'd never met her before, but it brought me some comfort to have another woman who'd done this before, and recently too. The doctor prodded at me, laid his hands on my stomach, nodded, smiled. "Nearly there, Miss Genesis," he said. But he was lying. It was another hour still before the pushing came and I thought I would tear in two. The doctors' wives cheered me on, wiped sweat from my brow. It was another hour when the doctor told me to stop pushing, to rest, to gather my strength, while he took Isaiah out to the hall to speak in hushed tones.

When they returned, the doctor's face was determined, and Isaiah sat stony and motionless in a corner. And when, at last, I felt the body slip from mine, and saw the tears falling from Isaiah's eyes, and the weary face of the doctor, I knew.

My daughter was small and perfect and dead.

Still, they wrapped her and I held her, and Jax held her. Then he went outside and as the sun fell and the moon rose. And everything was quiet and I was empty. *Therefore she wept and did not eat.* And I fell into the deepest shadows of sorrow.

ISAIAH

We bury the baby next to the others, the ones that Mama and Gramma buried. Genesis stands in bare feet and her nightgown, propped between Jax and me. Her face is puffy, her eyes red and unfocused. At least she's not crying anymore. The men pass by us with their heads bowed, hats in hand. They squeeze Jax's shoulder and shake their heads.

The coffin is small and beautiful. Denney stayed up all night to make it. He'd chiseled an angel into the top, lacquered and polished it. We didn't bring the bible out, and I don't think any of us know what passage we should read for a baby's funeral anyway. So we stand there silently while Denney places the little box in the earth.

The sun is out and bright and warm on us. The breeze carries the sweet, hot smell of late summer. Everyone grabs a handful of soil and Johnny Connelly starts to hum as they toss their clods in the grave. Nicky Connelly joins his voice to his brother's. *I wish, I wish my baby was born. And sitting on its papa's knee...* Everyone is sniffling. Except for Genesis, who has cried herself dry. She only stares at the dirt falling on her daughter. And when Denney pats down the small brown mound and the Connelly twins' voices are carried away on the wind, Jax and I take Genesis back to bed.

She stays in bed and becomes feverish after a few days. I lay my hands on her, feel her slick skin, think of Mama. I feel nothing but heat. No thump. No Death. I wait and feel again. She is living. She is in pain. I tell Jax I'm going for the doctor.

Doc Jr's wife answers with her own fat, rosy baby nestled on her hip. "She's got a fever," I say, and I can't keep my voice from cracking.

"Robert," she calls back, and he comes down the stairs, buttoning his collar, grabs his bag, kisses his wife and son, and follows after me without question.

"Her milk's come in," he says after he examines my sister. "And with nowhere for it to go..." Genesis's eyes are open, unseeing. "Sage tea," Doc Jr. says "I've bound her chest, and that should help. It will clear up in a few days. Nothing much to worry about."

Genesis closes her eyes, curls in on herself. The doctor sighs. "As for the grief, it will take time."

"Thank you," I say. He watches me a little too long. Like all the other men.

"Well, I think she's in good hands," he says. "If she gets any worse, don't hesitate to come for me."

Word's spread quickly through town, and we're soon bombarded with ladies bringing food. First it's the doctors' wives, then Mrs. Garrett, then the Johnsons and then Keith Feaney himself with his new fiancée, Miss LaRae Kitchens. Her haughtiness is gone as she hands me a bag of cornbread. I believe she's even teared up a bit. "We were devastated to hear of your sister's loss," she says. Keith nods along. A pan of fried chicken weighs heavy in his large hands. The rocking chair and cradle still sit in the parlor and all three of us can't help but stare at their emptiness.

"Thank you," I say, "I'll let her and Jax know you stopped by."

"We'll be praying for her," LaRae says and I think, what good will prayer do? But she is sincere. What else can she do?

I take their food and when they're gone, I carry the rocking chair up the stairs, set it outside Mama and Daddy's room. The cradle is too heavy for me alone. Jax carries it up later and sets both it and the chair inside the room, shutting the door tightly behind him afterward.

I try to make up for Genesis as she mourns. I try laundry and end up with clothes stiff with too much starch, brown spots from leaving the iron in one place too long. I forget to hang a wet basket, and the clothes smell moldy and need to be re-washed, and still smell slightly sour. I forget clothes on the line overnight and raccoons pull them down and scatter them in the dirt.

I forget about the chickens for two days, their eggs for three. I don't even try to make sense of the ledgers. I go to Feaney's and forget half the stuff we need, so I have to go back again in the same day. And Genesis stays in bed, not eating or dressing or washing herself unless I tell her to. I fix her baths, coax her to eat two, three spoonfuls of broth.

The food deliveries are dwindling and I know soon we'll be left with none. And just when we are, I wake to smell bacon frying. I think, finally Genesis has recovered. But I go downstairs to find Jax at the stove. "I didn't know you could cook," I say. He's even made flapjacks just as golden and fluffy as Genesis's.

"It's not much," he says and hands me a plate. "I thought maybe I could help out..." He pulls at his stiff collar.

"I'm sorry," I say.

"You are not your sister," he says with a shrug. He flips a small stack on my plate, and it looks so good I almost want to cry. "You've done your best, but I can do this."

I swallow the lump in my throat. "You're a good man, Jax."

"You are a good sister," he says. He places two pancakes on his own plate and joins me at the table. Out the back window, we see Tommy strutting along with his shirt off, his lightning bruises still stretched blue over his scrawny ribs.. "Can't get that kid to keep a shirt on," Jax says, shaking his head. "Struts like he's some dammed warrior."

"He can't help but show off to all the girls in town, too," I say. "Whether they want to see or not."

"Maybe I should ask if he wants me to tattoo over his lightning marks, so they last forever."

"Maybe you should *threaten* to tattoo over his marks if he doesn't put a shirt on."

"Maybe *you* should do it," he says.

"I did do a good job tattooing the laundry," I say. He laughs. Then stops laughing. Genesis has come down. She stands at the end of the table, saying nothing. Jax gets out of his chair, helps her sit down in it. He makes her a plate, one small pancake and a few strips of bacon. He finishes his meal in quick bites, rests his hand on her head, kisses her gently. He puts on his hat and goes out to work.

Genesis runs her fingers along her fork but does not eat. "What were you two talking about?" she says in a hoarse whisper. She has not spoken a word in more than two weeks.

"How are you feeling?" I say, "Do you want something else to eat?" She shakes her head. Her finger moves up and down the handle of the fork. She stares into her plate, the butter melting soggy into the flapjacks. "Let me get you some tea."

When I set it in front of her, she just stares at that too,

watching the steam rise up and curl before it disappears. I sit with her, watch the men at work through the window. She smells sour. Her tea cools.

I run her a bath, sink her into the hot water. Naked, her breasts are swollen and firm as apples, the veins standing out like rivers. Her stomach is swollen and deflated, lined with mottled streaks. She's still bleeding and the water turns red between her thighs. She pulls her knees up to her chest, buries her face in them. I get her a fresh nightgown. It will be stiff and itchy, but it's clean.

She looks at me with hollow eyes. Her eyes are almost as dark as mine these days. "Where's the cradle?"

"Mama and Daddy's room." I help her dry off and dress. I brush her hair, but I do not brush her teeth. I walk behind her as she climbs the stairs, and follow her to Mama and Daddy's door. The knob clicks and the wood squeaks when it's opened. The room is dim, the only light that's come in the last four years had been filtered through a dusty curtain. The room smells of dust and spice. Genesis pushes the cradle with two fingers so it rocks.

"Do you do it?" she whispers. "Do you bring the Death?"

I can't say anything.

"Leader's wife died like you said she would. Before anyone knew she was sick."

"Why would I want to kill your baby?"

She shakes her head, her voice is angry. "I've told you I won't leave you. Can't I have anything other than you?" She thinks I was jealous, jealous of her baby, of the life she's building. "I hear you two, you and Jax, whispering and joking when you're alone without me."

"Genesis, I don't—I can't—" I am ashamed she would think such things of me. A fire flares inside me, burns at my eyes.

"Get out," she says. I open my mouth, but her eyes bore into me. "Get out," she says again.

I rush from the room. She breaks down and wails from deep inside. Jax is in the hall, he's heard the whole thing. He holds me back, "Isaiah, she didn't mean it," he says. "She's grieving."

I pull away from him, push past him. I hear him sigh before he goes in to Genesis. I saddle Boy and I run him hard, so hard the wind stings. I don't know where to go. My first thought is to go to Reuben, to beat my fists against him and tell him that God's a bastard for taking Genesis's baby. But I don't dare set foot in the Community again. I could go to Robert, but I don't know how to explain myself.

I go to the bar. At first Dickey, the barkeep, tries to refuse me. The last time I'd frequented, I'd made a mess of myself. Daddy and Dickey had been friends, and I think he'd been relieved when I'd stopped coming; he didn't like seeing me like that. But all I have to do is glare at him and he hands me as many bottles and glasses as I ask for, and soon I'm good and foggy. Daddy would have been ashamed of me. Mama would be turning in her grave. Gramma, maybe, would understand. I drink more and forget about them.

I drink and dance and laugh at the men's jokes. Then who should walk in but Aaron Fisher and someone else I can't remember his name. I stumbled to him. "How did you get out?"

"Reuben and me are on guard duty tonight," Aaron says. "It doesn't take two men to watch for something that isn't there." He asks Dickey for a beer. "And on our next watch, I'll let him and someone else through the gate."

"He comes out?" I say.

"Yeah, I'm surprised you haven't seen him here," he tips his beer to his lips.

"I haven't been here in years," I say. And then it sinks in what Aaron's just said. "You mean he comes *here?*"

"Yeah," says Aaron.

"But what about Jesus?" In my foggy state, I've forgotten that Reuben's just about given up on Jesus. He might have even taken a drink or two when he was out on business with his father. I don't know, he hasn't told me.

Aaron chuckles. "I think he's given all that up now," he says. "You know, since his old man just about let him die, he's not been so bad. He's stopped wanting to kill all of us and now only has it in for the crazy old man—I think he's a little disappointed you didn't finish the job." He takes a swig, offers me a drink from the bottle. I take it. "Cause, boy is that old man getting crazy. He's certain the armies of Babylon are coming to us any day now."

I hand him back an empty bottle. "Why don't you all just leave?"

Aaron scoffs and motions to Dickey for another bottle. "Leader doesn't let people leave. You know, Boaz tried to take his wife and kids. But Leader had his children locked up and... well, Boaz agreed to stay." He drinks. "And me, well, I got a mother and sisters—one of them's married to Daniel," he shakes his head. "I can leave for the night as long as I'm back by morning. But I can't leave them there for good." He drops his voice, leans in, "Half the people want out, but we're all in too deep now. Leader's found a reason to keep us all there, if it's marrying our families or taking the kids." He pauses. "It's not the armies of Babylon coming for him. If anyone's coming at all, it's men in suave suits and sleek shoes." He drinks his beer like it's the last thing he'll ever drink on this earth and just as soon as he finishes, he turns to me and says "So are you gonna ask me to dance or what?"

So I pull him on to the dance floor. I'm unsteady on my feet so I have to lean tight to him. He's as tall as Rueben, but stockier, darker. He's always been nicer to me than Reuben and I start to wonder why I didn't choose him all those years ago. "Why aren't you married yet, Aaron Fisher?" I say, my head on his shoulder.

"And give Leader something else to hold over me?" he says. "Nah."

He's musky—hay and horse waft from him. He's warm and solid. I nuzzle his neck and his arm tightens around me. Then I'm pulling him away, out the door, around the side. He's pressing me up against the wall and I'm pulling him into me, opening my mouth on his. He's fumbling with my straps and we're both breathing hard. And then what? *And then what?*

And then I'm crying, sobs in my throat and fat tears rolling down my face. Aaron stops and I slump against him. "Am I that bad?" he says, letting me down.

"I'm sorry." I say it three times. "I should be home. It's Genesis. She's had a baby but…" I go on crying. "I can't make it better. I don't know what to do. I never know what to do."

He lets me cry until I'm all cried out and his shoulder is soaked. "I think," he says. "I think I'm not the person you want right now." His voice is tender, if not a little embarrassed.

"I'm sorry," I say again. "I've ruined your night out."

He shrugs and pats my hand before he stands. "I'm sorry, too." He says.

I sit alone for a while, until Dickey comes out and offers to make me up a cot behind the bar. I take up his offer. "Sorry about this," I say to him. "Let me work it off tomorrow. I promise I won't drink a single drop." He agrees and the next night, I'm helping him behind the bar. And at the end of the night, Reuben walks through the door.

"Aaron said you were a right mess," he says.

We spend the rest of the night on old blankets at the abandoned Miller place, making up for the years we lost, whispering our sorrows to each other. We return night after night. At first he is gentle, but there is a new darkness growing inside him. Each night, he grows more frantic, unleashing all his grievances on me. But I can hurt too; I've got my own demons to unleash.

GENESIS

I was not expecting to see Judith standing in my kitchen, but there she was in her shapeless gray dress, dropping biscuits onto a sheet. "Good morning," she said. "Your husband said you probably wouldn't want to eat much of anything when you got up, but I thought I'd go ahead and try."

I stood there in my bedraggled nightgown, bewildered by her unexpected appearance. "We're not married," I replied, my voice raspy. She wiped her floured hands on her apron and handed me a cup of tea. I held it with both hands like a child and she led me to a chair at the table. When I was situated, she returned to put the biscuits in the oven. "What are you doing here?"

"Well," she said, twisting the timer on the stovetop. "Aaron Fisher bumped into your sister, who mentioned you could use some help. Then he told my brother, and *he* told me."

Guilt kindled inside me at mention of my sister. It'd been two days since she'd run off. Since I'd run her off. "Have you seen Isaiah?" Judith shook her head. She joined me at the table, put her hand on mine. "How are you here?" I asked.

"I still hold some sway over my father," she said. "He's given me a week to return. I had Matthias drop me off first thing this morning. So here I am, at your disposal for a whole week."

We sat in silence. She drank her tea; I let mine go cold. The biscuit timer rang, and she pulled them out. "Shall we sit on the porch and let these cool?"

I followed behind her. I hadn't been outside, not even to the porch, in weeks, and the bright mid-morning sun reflected off my white nightgown, blinding me. I curled into a chair and squinted until my eyes adjusted to the glare and the warm breeze beguiled me to unfurl myself. I breathed deep the scents of manure, of split logs and cut hay, distant pines and spiced sage carried on the wind.

Jax and Denney were bent beneath the open hood of the truck. Big Joe and Tommy were brushing down breeding mares, shining their coats in the sun. Skinny Joe and the Connelly brothers were in one corral breaking a yearling; Robby Burton, Warren Beaufort and Michael Bennett in another. The ranch was alive and going, and though inside me I felt only heavy clouds, I took some comfort that the sun still shined and people still carried on.

One by one, everyone noticed us, and Judith fidgeted when they ventured to speak to us as we sat out on the porch. But she bloomed under their courtesy. She blushed at their compliments, laughed at their silly jokes, and marveled at their concern. "Take good care of Miss Genesis," they'd say to her, "she's like our own sister."

"It's good to see you out and enjoying the air," they'd say to me with tenderness.

"You run this place," Judith said with awe.

"Not alone."

"But you own it."

"Yes," I said.

She fixed me a bath and left me soaking while she set about the house opening windows, collecting linens for wash. I stewed in the warm water, letting it soothe my aches. It was cold when Judith knocked on the door and asked if I was alright. When I didn't answer, she repeated herself. And when I failed to respond again, she came in. She sighed at me staring over the water at her. Seeing I was alright, she turned her back to me. "Isn't the water cold yet?"

It was, and my skin was puckered, but I could have stayed until I dissolved to nothing. Judith unfurled a towel and held it wide to hide my nakedness as I stood. The rust-colored water sloshed. I let her wrap the towel around me and I held it as she drained the water. I shivered, goosebumps rising on my water-logged skin.

"Maybe we ought to rinse off in some warm water," she said. She put out her hand for the towel, closing her eyes. I knew she would not leave me alone until I did as told, so I turned on the shower, let the hot water rinse me. Only when she heard the water stop did she turn back again, eyes still closed.

"Don't you never see your sisters naked?" I said, wrapping the towel around myself.

"They're my sisters," she said and took a second towel to my hair, humming a sunshiny hymn. I let her guide me to my room where she sat me on the bed and opened my wardrobe. "Which shall we wear today?" she said, hands on her hips.

There was no point to dressing. I had no motivation to do anything. The hands had already seen me in my nightgown. Why dress only to undress again later? A bead of water ran down my neck, over the cleft of my collar bone and between my breasts. They'd returned to normal, but they felt hollow, empty, like the rest of me. My stomach, too, was tightening and soon it would be like there was never anything there at all. I put my hand to the emptiness in my deflated womb.

"This isn't the first time," I whispered. Judith folded the dress she chose over her arm—a small floral print—and sat beside me. "There was another one," I continued. My throat tightened, but I went on. "Before Daddy died. But it was so early...and everything was wrong...it was the wrong time." Judith said nothing, she just let me go on. I had not spoken so much in weeks and my throat was dry and haggard. "And this time...it took so long." Tears burned at my eyes. "I've seen my gramma die, my father, my mother. But this time...this time, I can't make the hurt go away." I cried and Judith held me. My hair soaked through her dress.

"*This too shall pass*," she whispered, and let me go on crying.

I slept, and when I woke, the clouds inside me had lifted, just a little. Judith spoke in a stream of bright words. She opened the windows, let in the light. Judith filled the house with the smell of bread and roasts and apple pie and fresh linens. She darned and patched, and spoke to me of books and everything about the ranch that left her filled with wonder. And though my melancholy still clung, I felt a little brighter every day.

I told her she could wear my dresses while she was with us. But she'd always been somewhat plumper than I had been, and she felt uncomfortable in the tightness of the silhouettes. Even those I wore while pregnant, she felt too exposed with her bare legs showing and her collar bare.

At the height of her visit, Judith was cheerful, but as the day of her departure drew closer, I noticed a cloud coming over her. "Why don't you leave?" I said.

"And go where?" she said. "Here?"

I shrugged. Would it have been such a bad idea? But it was still too close to her father. "Your brother..." I said, the one she'd be writing to.

She shook her head. "Father is—well he's... The only people he trusts now is blood and if we broke it..." The thread knotted and she picked at it with the needle. "Who knows what he'd do."

Isaiah still had not returned, and I began to think maybe she'd gone to the Community. Perhaps Leader was holding her until Judith came back? "Have you seen Isaiah?" I asked her again.

"No," she replied again, and sensing my implication added, "She was never at the Community. Reuben and Aaron met her outside."

I believed her, but I thought perhaps there were things she didn't know. That night, I told Jax we needed to find Isaiah. "She's at the bar," he answered immediately.

"The bar?" The relief I felt was brief. The last time she'd frequented at the bar she'd drowned herself in debauchery.

"Denney's seen her there himself. She's been working behind the counter," Jax said.

"And at night? Where has she been staying?" I said. Jax didn't know. "Tell Denney to bring her home." Jax sighed and agreed.

Soon, was Isaiah's response. It frustrated me, but at least I could rest assured she was alright. She was letting me have my time with Judith.

At the end of Judith's week, she brought me a box she'd carried in with her. "I've been holding onto it," she said. "I've had it for a while. I just never got around to getting it back to you." Inside was my pistol and Isaiah's braid that Leader's Wife had so brutally sheared all those years before. The braid had seemed so long back then, but now her hair was twice as long and doubly thick. "I found it wedged under your mother's mattress," Judith said.

I lifted the braid and the gun from the box, revealing Mama's old leather hymnal, where she'd written the names of all the babies she'd born—all but mine and Isaiah's scratched out. *Joshua, Ezra, Ezekiel.* "Thank you," I said to Judith. I imagined my mother tucking these things away, hiding the memories of her children from the other women. It was comforting to know our mother thought of us, but it was odd to think of her as sentimental, and knowing this did not change the past or make me feel any less strained about the relationship we'd had.

"I wish you could have come under happier circumstances," I said, returning everything to the box.

"Someday I will," she said.

Judith returned home and so did Isaiah. I was both relieved to see her home and irritated that she had abandoned me. I rationalized that I could not blame her, I had, after all, thrown horrid accusations at her. We were over-polite, afraid to offend the other.

"Did you know?" I finally asked when I couldn't hold it any longer. I did my best not to sound accusing, but she tensed at the question.

"I—I had a feeling," she said apologetically. "I didn't want to say anything, you were so happy and...."

"I'm sorry," I said quickly. "I'm sorry I was so..."

"Robert's told me about melancholy," she said. "But don't you ever go on thinking that I'd want to take anything away from you, not Jax, not your happiness. I wish I'd never felt it." And for the first time I thought what a burden it must be, to see Death in the shadows, hovering around those you love.

My body healed, and my soul followed slowly, reluctant to return to its former wholeness. I still slept late and spent much of my time lost in bouts of melancholy. I still could not muster up the energy or the care to do much more than pass Isaiah clothes for the line—she was improving in her laundering skills —or sit on the porch staring out at the heat rippling over the dry earth.

It took gunshots and broken bones to snap me back again. We heard the pops in the distance. They lifted my attention from the book in my hands and Isaiah paused her bean snapping. But just for a moment. We turned back to our activities until we heard the horse hooves.

Here came Denney and Jax together on Denney's horse. Jax was slumped forward, his face nearly in the horse's mane, his arm tight to his side. "What's happened?" I said, standing, running down to them.

"Treasure hunters shot at us," Denney said.

"Oh God, no." I gritted my teeth.

"No one was shot," said Denney. "At least none of us were." He slid from the horse and pulled Jax after him. Jax was sweating, his eyes glazed over with pain. He grimaced when we touched him. "His horse spooked and reared. I think he's broke his collarbone."

Jax gasped as Denney and I took him in. "Go for the doctor," I told Isaiah, who was standing, her bean spilled around her feet.

"Sheriff too," Denney said, looking back the way they'd come. Isaiah nodded and bolted. "I told the others to round up the treasure hunters. One of them's not doing so hot..." said Denney, patting his holstered pistol.

Jax bit hard on his lip as we pulled him up the stairs, his eyes shut so tight they puckered. Sweat beaded on his face. I knew what was coming and narrowly avoided it; he vomited just inside the door. Denny and I jerked back involuntarily, shifting Jax's injury and causing him to cry out in a way that rattled my bones.

We sat him down, and I tore open his shirt. I could see the break, the off-kilter angle of the bones, the small angry lump. I sucked at the air. I dared not touch it, not do anything more than wrap ice in cloth and hold it to his bared shoulder. "Hang in there, son, the doctor's coming," Denney was saying. Outside the group of hands were returning with the three trespassers. One was limping, a strip of cloth tied around his thigh, blood oozing down the leg of his trousers. I looked at them and my temper flared.

Before he could do anything about it, I grabbed Denney's pistol, leapt over the puddled of vomit and down the steps. I heard Denney call after me but I ignored him. "Which was the one that nearly shot him?" I shouted at the hands, waving the gun barrel-up. They looked at each other behind the backs of the perpetrators.

"Miss Genesis," the hands said cautiously, but I ignored them too.

"Put them on their knees," I said, and they did. They lined them up in front of me, the three of them with their hands tied behind them.

"You're not actually going to shoot us," the one to the left said. His Adam's apple quivered in his throat, his body shifting for escape.

"Well that one's already shot," I said, pointing the gun at the one on the right, and that one started crying. He was young —Isaiah's age at the oldest, though I suspected younger. The middle one, the oldest, laughed. So it was him I chose. I didn't even give him time to stop laughing. I pointed the gun at his thigh and pulled the trigger. Everyone jumped, but not me. The man's laugh caught in his throat, his eyes widened in surprise. And then the hole in his leg bloomed red and he started screaming and fell to his side. The young one cried harder. The hands stared at me in shock. I don't think any of them really thought I had it in me to shoot someone. It's easier the second time. It's easier when you're leaving one alive. "Someone should probably tie that off," I said, and turned back inside and handed the gun back to Denney. He stared at the gun in awe. I cleaned up Jax and the vomit as best I could before the doctor arrived.

"Shoulder's dislocated," Doc Jr. said. "And collarbone is broken." Jax wouldn't be moved, but his bone needed to be set. The doctor rummaged through once and again to only come up with empty bottles and vials. "I don't have anything for the pain," said the doctor. "But I can shift everything back into place and set it. The break isn't so serious we need to rush to the hospital." Jax nodded and took my hand in his. Doc Jr. removed his belt told Isaiah to hold Jax's head steady. Jax bit down on the doctor's belt.

There was popping and sweating and trembling. Jax grunted and growled. He shook and sweated. Then he vomited and passed out. "Hold his head, Isaiah!" The doctor barked. She was letting Jax's head droop in his unconsciousness. She flinched and immediately firmed her grip. We had both been surprised by Doc Jr's sudden authoritativeness. He had always been so calm and a little shy. Isaiah's eyes widened on him in wonder.

The doctor cut off the rest of Jax's shirt and wrapped him in a long, thick bandage-like cloth, pulling it up and around Jax's shoulder and torso, trapping his arm against his ribs. "Wrap it like this," Doc Jr. said as he worked. "Every day until it's healed."

Isaiah and I both nodded. The doctor went out to tend to the injured trespassers before the sheriff came for them. I mopped up Jax's vomit for the second time as he came to, and he looked at me with sheepish eyes, but I could only smile because there, covered with vomit, having just witnessed my man in pain and shot the man who'd done it, I felt my soul re-awaken and slide back into place. I kissed Jax despite his vomit and sweat and grime.

Two days later, Butter was found dead in the field and several of the hands and cattle fell ill, calling the doctor to us again. Poison. The treasure hunters had not come for treasure, after all. They had come to poison the irrigation stream that ran through our pastures for the cattle. Luckily, the saboteurs had been interrupted and incompetent, leading only to the death of Butter and three calves. The hands and the rest of the cattle recovered.

"Maybe we ought to build the doctor a room of his own," Jax said. "He's here often enough."

We informed Sheriff Burnham and he questioned the perpetrators. All he could get from them was that they were paid to do it. They would not reveal who, but I didn't need to hear it from them. I was already sure who was behind it. We couldn't prove it, of course, but I hoped Leader saw the damage I'd done in return. I hoped he'd see I would not go down without bloodshed if need be.

ISAIAH

Doc Jr. doesn't know about me. I'm sure he's heard the
tales, the rumors, but he has not experienced it first-
hand. And anyway, I'm not sure he believes it.

The first death is Mr. Alvin Coburn. It's really no surprise
since the man's nearly a hundred. He's caught a head cold that
turned into pneumonia. "My father used to drop by every other
day for a decade," Robert says. "And, every day, old Alvin was
up and at 'em. Then I started doing it, and it was much the
same until two days ago. I passed by and he didn't answer."

Robert knocks on the old man's old door before we enter
the house. It's one of the oldest houses in town. It's a large house
for a single old man, but he'd built it with hopes of filling it up.
Mr. Coburn's wife died in childbirth when they were both
young, and he's never attempted to fill the empty space. "Mr.
Coburn?" Robert calls out. There's a raspy groan from upstairs.
"I'm afraid this is most likely what will do him in, and soon,"
Robert says quietly as we climb the narrow stairs. "In this case
the best we can do is just make him comfortable until it's over."

He's right. Though Mr. Coburn is all smiles to see me,

Death dances hard and fast like war drums beneath his skin. It will be tonight. I hold the old man's papery hand while Robert takes his temperature and listens to his lungs. Mr. Coburn already was old before, but illness has made him a warm corpse. His skin sags from his bones, a few wispy white hairs scatter across his chest. He's so thin I can see his heart thumping in his chest.

Robert shakes his head and removes his stethoscope. He takes morphine from his bag, tips a dose into Coburn's mouth. When it takes effect, and the old man falls blissfully to sleep, Robert says, "Not long now." And we sit on each side of the bed and wait.

Robert is starting to gray at his temples, even though he is hardly over thirty. His hair, otherwise, is a deep brown, made darker by his pomade that makes his hair look wet and sleek. He clean shaves unlike his father, though they both share the same nose. "How is your wife?" I say.

"I believe she is past the worst of the morning sickness," he says.

"Another boy, you think?"

"Oh, I don't know," he says. "Anna would love someone to share ribbons and frills and bows with, I think."

"Not all girls are bows and frills," I say, looking down at my overalls. They are old and patched but they are, at least, clean.

Robert looks at me and laughs. It's a nice laugh, higher than expected. "I'll be happy any way it goes," he says. His eyes are blue. Not noon-sky blue like Reuben's, but a deep blue like early twilight. He checks Mr. Coburn's pulse, times it with his watch. Coburn's breathing is wheezing and raspy. Death is drumming so hard, I almost hear it.

"I'm surprised he's made it this long," says Robert. "He was old when I was a boy."

"I think he was old when your father was a boy."

We smile at each other. Mr. Coburn gurgles. It is a sickening noise. "Ah," Robert says, and he moves the pillow so Coburn's sitting up. "How is your sister?"

"Back to herself, I think."

"And your brother-in-law?"

"He hates being broken," I say. "He feels guilty not being able to put in as much work as the other men."

Mr. Coburn starts gurgling again, but he's already sitting up, any more and he'll fall forward. We watch him until the gurgling stops and Robert checks his pulse again. The drums still beat, growing ever wilder. You have held out long enough, Alvin Coburn, I say silently, but he still lives. "What about morphine?" I say.

"I've given him enough to keep him out of pain."

"I know," I say. "But..." I don't dare finish the thought. Is it murder to kill someone already dying? We had to shoot Jax's horse after it shattered its leg in a badger hole. We've had to kill mutated calves, shoot sick cattle.

Robert pauses, talks slowly as if he's working around the suggestion. "Not long now," he says. "He's not in any pain. We have time."

And so we wait. Robert tells me about how pneumonia develops, how to treat it when the patient is healthy enough—young enough—to fight it off. All the while, the drumming is growing louder, more frantic, so I can't pay much attention to what he's saying. The thumping is so strong, I'm surprised I don't see the old man's skin pulsing.

And finally, the drumming comes crashing to a stop. There is no gasping, no crying out, no show of the last breath. I only know it's over by the sudden silence. I wait a few minutes before I say, "I think he's gone."

Robert checks his pulse again, his breath. He lifts the old man's waxy eyelids, looks at his watch. "Four twenty-eight p.m." he says, and he gathers his stethoscope and tucks it back in his bag. "I'll take you home."

"What about Mr. Coburn?"

"I'll let my mother know and she and her ladies will take care of him," he says. "Unless you'd like to help prep him for the undertaker?"

"No," I say. I have enough of death. We walk to his parents' house and he discusses Mr. Coburn with his mother. Two little kids are waiting in the parlor. I assume their mother is behind the closed door of the old Doctor's office. They're dirty and thin, most likely a family from the mountains. There must be half a dozen more of them at home. Their mother is either here to prevent more of them or she's already big with another one. Either way, I don't get to wait around and see because Robert's ready to take me home. "Teach me about babies," I say.

He says *huh* in the back of throat, and I say "About birthing. I sure as hell know where they come from. I've known since I was ten."

He smiles with relief. "Truth be told, around here, most women only call the doctor after things have gotten particularly difficult. The rest of the time, they just have their mothers and aunts and neighbors."

"But you must have some that turn out good."

"I do," he says.

"Genesis and I don't have aunts and mothers and neighbors. She's got me."

He nods and smiles in sympathy. His pomade smells like lemons and oil.

It is not long before he summons me to accompany him on a birth. We don't have to go far, just across our front field to the Darmonds'—the couple Genesis sold the plot to. They are having their second. I was nervous when I entered, afraid of what scene I might be coming into; I'd never seen a birth that wasn't already going bad. But when I walk in both Gertie and Thomas are all smiles. Gertie's mother Mrs. Steinwirth, who's been around to help for a week, answers the door with the little toddler girl on her hip, ready for bed.

When a pain takes hold of Gertie, she breathes through it and comes out of it calmly. As we wait for the birth to progress, Robert tells me the basics of child birthing: how to feel for the baby, how to mark the progress. Mrs. Steinwirth has some of her own words to add now and then, "With my first it went like this..." she says, and "But my last one..."

"The body knows what to do," Robert says. "And in most cases, we're just here to help mother remember that. And catch the baby, of course. In other times, we have to coax the whole body to remember."

All in all, it goes pretty quickly, it's all over in a few hours and Gertie's got another daughter. It's nearly one in the morning when Robert offers to walk me back across the field. "What did you think?" he asks.

"It's horrifying," I say. "And amazing. How can it be normal for the body to go through such...*torture*?" We hop over the Darmonds' fence. "I've only ever seen it go wrong," I say. Only when I'm over do I realize Robert's been holding out his hand to help me. "I never thought about it ending in joy. It looks exhausting though, and I think I'm more convinced than ever to never go through it myself."

I brace myself for the usual that comes when girls say things like that: I'm still young and maybe someday I'll meet a man who changes my mind. Or the other way. Sometimes they say I'd better not have kids because I'm a loose woman and not fit to be a mother. But Robert says none of this. He just walks beside me and lets the crickets chirp over whatever he's thinking. I think back to when he checked me for infection, and how he'd said nothing more than "Be careful," and "Stick to men you know" and just when I'm about to ask him why he's so accepting of girls like me, we reach the house and find Reuben skulking around the corner.

"Reuben," I say, surprised.

He pulls his shoulders back and eyes Robert. "Who's this?"

"This is Rob—the doctor. I was helping him with our neighbor's baby."

"Evening," Robert says, but Reuben does not reply. Robert clears his throat. "I guess I'll leave you here," he says. Reuben and I watch him walk into the dark.

"What are you doing here?" I whisper to him. "We've got patrols now, you know. All I have to do is scream and everyone will come running, guns ready."

"So this is what you've been doing every night?" Reuben says, glaring at Robert's disappearing back.

"What are you even doing here?"

"I thought, you know, maybe we'd be going back to the way we were, but I haven't seen or heard from you since...and now I see why. Some old, shiny—"

"Reuben, he's married," I say. I'm annoyed having to say it, and my temper rises. "I'm learning—"

He's not even listening, and I don't know why I'm trying to explain to him. "What was I just some—some *balm*? Some lecherous balm to occupy you while you were grieving?"

"No," I say, sharp and hard, so he'll stop talking. "But am I meant to spend all my nights with you?"

"You didn't even tell me you were coming back home," he says. "I waited for you."

"Reuben, it's been weeks, and it's not like you're out every night. Am I just supposed to sit around waiting for you? Hoping that maybe tonight's the night? And I don't have to tell you anything, I'm not your wife."

He blinks at me. "You could be."

I laugh. He scowls. "Ha!" I say, "And have your daddy as kin? Never."

"He won't touch you again," he says.

"And you can be so sure?" I say. "Because you'll be there to rescue me? Reuben, he just tried to poison our whole ranch. Where were you then? Why didn't you come then?"

Reuben's shaking his head, his hands in fists. "No one was supposed to get hurt. The idiots didn't do it right. They weren't supposed to put it in the spring!"

I slap him. "You did *nothing*," I spit at him. He grabs my wrists, pins me against the house, the back of my head thuds on the wood. "My sister's baby had just died. I could have died, and you. Did. *Nothing*. You can't save me. You're weak. Weak—"

"You think I'm weak?" He hisses, sliding one hand to my throat. His thumb rests in the hollow of my collarbone, his fingers curled up along my neck. "What about that doctor? I bet he's never mucked shit a day in his life, or thrown hay, or..." His breath is hot and wet on my neck. He lifts me, wraps my legs around his hips and presses into me. I feel my own pulse beneath his fingers. Our blood is running hot. "I thought it was me and you," his voice is so low, it's almost a growl. He's undoing my straps and I don't stop him. I don't want him to stop. "It should be just you and me."

"I'm not yours..." I'm whispering, "I can't..."

I will have bruises on my back, and he will have the marks of my teeth in the meat of his neck. I'm with Reuben, but I think of Robert, and I take the bruises like penance. I shouldn't be thinking on a married man.

GENESIS

I heard the bodies beating against the side of the house, the muffled cries of pleasure. "Who was it?" I asked Isaiah in the morning. She went red. "You were right below our window," I said. Jax had taken to sleeping in the parlor chair while he healed, and I didn't sleep well without him in the bed beside me. "The doctor?"

"No," she said, as if the idea was ridiculous, but she went redder at the mention of the doctor all the same.

"Not one of the hands again, surely?" I said. "We don't need a repeat of *that*." The summer before, Isaiah had taken two of the new hands, and it eventually led to a fight between the two. They'd gotten so entangled in the mud, I'd had to let off the 12-gauge to get them to break it up. Isaiah had looked on stupidly, surprised to see what violence her actions could amount to.

Isaiah grumbled. "No, none of them either."

"Was it Reuben?" I said, not able to keep the distaste from my voice. "Tell me it wasn't Reuben."

The embarrassed red on her cheeks flamed to anger. "It's

not any of your business who it was!" she snapped. She stood from the table, grabbed her hat and the doorknob.

"Isaiah," I said cautiously. "You know what happened the last time he came out here." I stood too, ready to head out the door and see what damage might have been done.

Isaiah scoffed. "Do you ever think that maybe you're paranoid? That maybe you're obsessed with the idea that Leader might still be out to get us? You think he controls everything that everyone out there does?"

"You *know* that he does," I said. "I'm not crazy! How many times has he tried some sort of sabotage now?"

"We can't prove that was all him, sometimes things like that just happen. It might not always be Leader!"

"Why are you defending him?" I said. "You know what he is. You know what he's like. You think he can just forgive us for getting out of his grasp? You know how long he's wanted us and what we've got!"

"What about Judith?" she said. "She was here for a week. And you trust her so fully?"

"Judith's different," I argued, but it hadn't been long after Judith that our water had been poisoned. I shook the doubt away. Judith had no love for the things her father had done. "She's always defied him."

"Reuben's never pleased him, either."

"Reuben's a hot-headed fool," I said. "He squeals like a pig under the slightest pressure. Or don't you remember that?"

"We were ten!"

"The next time he comes," I said, crossing my arms. "You'd best send him away."

"This is *my* house too!" Isaiah shouted and slammed the door behind her.

Didn't she understand? Didn't she see what I saw in Leader? But she thought we were invincible. She thought the ranch could never be taken from us, and I worried about it every day.

I told Jax and Denney to be on the lookout, but there was nothing. And at least once a week, Reuben was there. Isaiah would sneak him past Jax—who'd taken to sleeping downstairs while he healed—and into her room, and I would grit my teeth and wait—wait for the disaster to strike. But nothing happened, and I got to thinking maybe Isaiah was right. Reuben came and didn't cause trouble, even delivering letters between Judith and me, which had come to a standstill when Leader tightened his security. He came late and left early, and I never had to see him.

In October, as per usual, the men went away, leaving Isaiah, me and a couple of winter hands alone on the ranch. I'd tried to tell Jax he didn't need to go—he'd just healed—but he said he was fine.

A week later, I woke in the middle of the night, my nerves on edge. I climbed from my bed and out to the hall. I pressed my ear to Isaiah's door. Reuben was in there. But that was not what woke me. I made for the stairs and saw a faint orange glow at the bottom. Had Isaiah put another log on the fire? My gut told me no. I went down. The fireplace was cold and dark. The glow, then, came from outside. It filtered through the glass in the back door. I looked out, and I froze. It was fire, but nothing so heartwarming as a hearth. The trade-horse barn was enflamed.

The three remaining hands rushed out of their bunk, quick shadows in the burning night. I raced out, barefoot, coatless. Smoke and the faintest smell of gasoline, the unholy shrieking of horses in panic. The entire western wall of the barn was licked in flames. Danny Buckley and Quentin Myers pumped water into buckets, and Benny Carter ran into the barn.

"The horses!" I screamed to Danny and Quentin. They

could do nothing with their infinitesimal buckets. "The horses!" I shouted again, running into the barn after Benny. The noise inside was deafening, the screaming and the hooves beating against the stalls. Benny was busy at the west end, unlocking stall doors and jumping out of the way as frantic horses raced out. The four of us worked fast to unlatch the remaining stalls, the flames burning through the wall, smoke gathering, heat rising. We still had five stalls to go when there was a great *woosh*, and I knew that was the hay in the loft catching. It would burn rapidly and spread the fire like a flood. We freed the horses and grabbed what gear we could as we coughed and sweat.

"Go check all the other barns. Make sure this is it," I told the boys. They scattered, running from building to building, racing in and out. There seemed to be only the main barn in crisis, and for that, there was nothing left to do but watch as the flames devoured it. The fire rose hot and orange, reaching to the black sky. The horses rushed around the yard; there were too many of them and they were too frantic to be dealt with. We could only stay out of their way. I stumbled back to the house, entranced by the frenzy.

"Genesis!" Isaiah said behind me, coming from the house. "Genesis, what happened?"

"Oh my g—" Reuben began to say, and hearing his voice set a bomb off inside me. I barreled into him. Surprised, he fell, and I was on top of him, sinking my fists into every bit of his face, neck, and chest I could. My hands were small, but they were fast and my knuckles were sharp.

"Genesis!" Isaiah screamed. "Stop!" I could barely hear her over my own rage and the roar of the fire. She pulled at my nightgown, my arms, but I was too enraged. "Reuben don't hit her, don't you dare hit her back!"

Reuben could have rolled me over; he was skinny but

bigger than me. He could have punched me back, but he didn't. He tried to squirm away, but I stayed with him. All he could do then was put his hands to his face and whimper "I didn't, I didn't..."

Beefy arms wrapped around my waist and I was wrenched away. Benny pulled me up and into him, my feet off the ground, my fists still flailing. "It was him! It was him!" I screamed.

"I know, Miss Genesis," Benny said. "But you're gonna hurt yourself."

"Isaiah!" I shouted. She was helping Reuben up. "Isaiah, I told you! I don't ever want to see that boy again. I'll kill him! I'll kill him the next time he steps foot here! And I'll toss his head at Leader's feet!"

"I swear," Reuben shouted back, wiping blood from his nose. "I swear I didn't know!"

"But you told him, didn't you!" I struggled against Benny, but he held fast. "You told him Jax and the others were gone, didn't you, you son of a bitch!"

"I didn't tell my father shit, you crazy bitch," Reuben spat.

"Hey now!" The three men shouted back at him warningly, and Isaiah stepped around him protectively.

"Benjamin then!" I shouted, and at that, Reuben only scowled. Isaiah tugged at him, pulling him away, around the house until I could no longer see him. When she returned, she was alone and we knew she'd sent Reuben home. Only then did Benny release me. I slumped to the ground. There was nothing to do but watch the flames go out.

In the morning, the horses had calmed enough to eat what was left of the brown tufts of prairie grass around the yard. There was nothing left of the barn but charred rubble and smoking embers. My knuckles purpled, my hands throbbed. Though we still had hay stored in the mares' barn, it wasn't enough, not for all of them, not for the whole winter.

"We'll have to buy more," I said as Isaiah treated my hands. We'd managed to pull ourselves out of debt, but only just. Each season, we hovered between black and red. Any drastic loss would send us back in the negative. "So much for the new truck." I winced as she tightened linen wraps on my bruised knuckles.

"I thought I was the one who did all the fighting," she said.

I flexed my fingers. She'd put all her violent energy into sex, but I had lost the restraint I'd once had. I had lost the care to remain collected and respectable. "You've stabbed someone," I said.

"You've *killed* one."

"I wished to God you had," I said. "Then we wouldn't be here right now."

Isaiah sighed. "He really didn't know," she said.

I grunted, picked at the wrappings. I was doing my best not to blame her for the fire. I wanted to believe her, for her sake. Why couldn't she just be done with him? We had enough of Leader's meddling to deal with, why drag his spawn to our home?

Tentatively, Isaiah reached into her pocket and pulled out crumpled dollar bills, laying them on the table. "Reuben...he gave me this. To give to you. To help rebuild the barn."

"It's ten dollars."

"It was all he had," she said defensively, crossing her arms. "He feels bad."

"Where did he get it?"

She shrugged.

It was rare that Reuben made an apology. "If he stole it from his father, then maybe I could forgive him," I said. I was not sincere. She knew it.

A week later, Jax and Denney returned. "What the hell?" Jax exclaimed. "Shouldn't we get the sheriff?"

"You know it would do nothing," I said.

Our ranching neighbors, hearing of our disaster, pooled together and gave us what little hay they could part with. They came together and we rebuilt the barn in the better part of three days. It was not nearly as nice as its predecessor, but it made do. We checked our losses and barely made it out clean. We had to branch out to further communities to buy more hay, and even then, we had to ration the horses and pray none of it rotted.

Isaiah and Reuben continued to meet, but elsewhere, and she brought me a letter from Judith stuffed with a few more bills. In the letter, Judith apologized and explained *Benjamin must have heard R. and me talking about you all. He had mentioned to me, only me directly, that your men would be gone. It's as much my fault as his. I asked how you were.*

"Alright," I said to Isaiah. "You can bring that little bastard back here." It bothered me still, the thought of him under my roof, but it was Isaiah's house too, just as she'd said. And I thought maybe it wouldn't hurt to try and get information from Reuben as well. Isaiah smiled like a schoolgirl, and she had Reuben grunting away in her room within the day. We got two more dogs and took on another winter hand.

Not long after the New Year, I thought I might be pregnant again. I felt only anxiety. I had so recently lost a child, I wasn't ready to deal with the possibility of it happening again. I said nothing to either Jax or Isaiah and I went to see the doctor. I'd wanted to see the old doctor, given our long-standing relationship. But he and his wife had gone out of town.

I didn't know the young doctor the same way. I didn't know what he'd say about a woman who wasn't happy to be having a baby. But I needed to know. I hadn't bled in two months, but nothing had felt like the other two.

"You are not pregnant," the young doctor told me.

"You're sure?" I said, sitting up. I could barely hide my relief.

"Completely," he said. "How is your diet? Physical exertion? Nerves? Sometimes these things can affect a woman's system."

"I suppose I've been a little strained lately," I said.

"It wouldn't hurt to take some time to relax," he said. "When was the last time you finished a book?"

His blue eyes sparkled with genuine concern. I smiled sheepishly. I understood why Isaiah was always so perked when he called for her, even though he was a dozen years older than her. "My sister talks about me, I guess," I said.

"Of course she does," he said. He opened his medicine cabinet while I pulled my underwear back on. "Now I can give you some sedatives to help calm your nerves—"

"I don't want sedatives," I said cautiously. "I want... I don't want...another baby—I do, but...not right now."

He turned, cupping a small pill bottle in his hand. "You know there's no foolproof—"

"Doctor," I said, emboldened by his lack of surprise. He looked only concerned. "I can't keep filling that cemetery with those little graves. There are too many there already."

For some time, he said nothing. He placed the pills back into the cabinet and locked it. He pulled his chair up and sat, eyes focused on mine. "Have you spoken to your hus—Jax— about this?"

"What's he got to do with it?" I said, my voice rising. "He doesn't like watching our babies die, either."

"I just want to make sure—"

"If I decide I don't want a baby, then he decides it too," I said.

"Alright," the doctor said, the corner of his mouth twitching. Did he think it was funny? He made a phony cough and collected himself. He studied me momentarily, I could tell he was searching for what to say, weighing out the suggestions and concerns and whatever else in his mind. He sighed. "I can get you something," he said. "It will take at least a week, more likely two."

"Thank you," I said, collecting my things. I paused. "You... you take care of Isaiah, don't you?" I wasn't sure what I meant by the question. Did he give her contraceptives too? Did he cure any possible diseases for her? Was he sleeping with her? Perhaps these were all the questions hidden in the one I asked.

He was a deliberate and thoughtful man, and he took his time with his words. "In terms of your sister's spirit, she is a little impulsive, but she's got a good heart and a good head when she uses it. I'm teaching her whatever I think may be useful for her to know, and she's picking it up wholeheartedly. In terms of...other things—medical, habitual—I'm not at liberty to discuss such things with you." I opened my mouth to protest, but he quieted me. "Even as her older sister and former guardian, I cannot tell you. She's an adult now. If she has concerns she'd like you to know, I'm sure she'll tell you."

Don't be so sure, I wanted to say to him. She doesn't think when her fire is burning; she's got no thought for the consequences and the damage she causes, I wanted to say. I wanted to tell him, to warn him to watch himself, not to fall into the flame so many other men had. But I didn't. I slid from the table and wished him a good day. "If you're serious about prevention, I would suggest no intimacies until I get it in for you," he said as I left.

Two weeks later, he called me back and presented me with

what looked like a small rubber bowl. I did not like the look of it or the feel of it and I wondered if I really needed it after all. But I took the crinkled paper bag from him and clutched it in my grip. "Do you..." I took a deep breath, tentative to hear his answer to the question I'd harbored for months. "Do you suppose it will ever happen for me?"

He folded his hands behind his back. "Given your familial history...I don't expect it will be an easy road," he said. "But I see no reason why you shouldn't, in time, give birth to a healthy child. It happens all the time. And I will do all I can to help you through it when the time comes, and I will help you all the way until it does."

"Thank you," I said. The bag crinkled in my hand. At home, I pulled the diaphragm from the wrapping and shoved it under the mattress. I never used it.

ISAIAH

The second death is the old Doctor. I feel it on him the day LaRae soon-to-be Feaney brings the school kids in for smallpox inoculations. Robert's asked me to help the two of them. I check for scars to see who's already been vaccinated and who has not, then I hold their hands and keep them calm while one of the doctors pricks their arms. They each get a lump of rock candy afterward. LaRae and the old teacher Miss Gilbert try to rein the kids in, but they are a handful. And when they are all finally done and on their way out, Doc hands me a dollar for my help. When his hand meets mine, I feel it.

He has seen the look on my face so many times, he knows, even though I try to hide it. He grips my hand a little longer, letting me feel the thump, making sure it's there. My heart sinks. He smiles. "How strong?" he whispers. My throat gets tight and I can only shrug. He pats my head and pulls me in for a hug. "Take care, dear girl," he says. Robert watches with confusion but says nothing about it, only that Ruthanne Baker asked us to look in on her son, afraid he's come down with measles. Doc and I shake hands one last time and I accompany Robert.

It's only when he's taking me home and a silence falls between us in the car that I say it. "Your father's dying."

"My father?" he says. "My father's fit as a fiddle. Only last week I gave him a physical myself."

Doc brought both me and my sister into the world. He'd been there when Gramma got sick, after Mama died. I did not want to know his death was coming. Maybe I shouldn't have said anything.

"Why? Did he tell you something?" Robert says. "Should I examine him more thoroughly? He's my father, he won't tell me he's sick. Not until it's too late."

"I don't think he's sick," I say. As Robert said, Doc's fit as a fiddle, even for a man in his sixties.

"Well I'll check him out, just to be sure." I nod, but I know it won't help. The death was there, strong and sure.

And two days later, when Jax and Genesis and me are sitting around the dinner table, we hear a car braking hard in our driveway, spinning and spitting the gravel. "I'll see who it is," I say. I'm almost done eating. It's Robert, sitting in his car, staring ahead in a daze of emotion. I go out to the car, open the passenger door and slide in.

"Heart attack," he says. "Just an hour ago. They took him over to the hospital, but I already know it's too late. There's nothing to be done." He slumps in his seat, his hands still tight on the steering wheel. "There was no way I could have known." He sighs deeply and drops his hands. Not thinking, I take one up in mine. He isn't crying, or maybe he's already cried. "How did you know?"

"I just do," I say.

"What do you mean you just 'do'?" He slides his hand out of mine.

I sigh and tell him about Death, how I feel it, how it lurks and plays beneath people's skin, how I've dreamt of Death—the sheriff's brother, my father, my mother, Genesis's babies. "And right before we heard of Jax's grandfather," I say. "I sensed that too. Not in the way I do when I dream or touch it with my own hands. But it was like a vibration, like electricity that came off Jax. I'd never felt it like that before and I didn't know what it was, but then we got word of his grandfather and I knew."

"Mr. Coburn?" Robert says.

"It was like a pow-wow," I say, "Playing him like a hundred drums."

Robert is quiet for a long time. One minute, a thousand. "That's nonsense."

"Maybe it is," I say. "But I've never been wrong."

"Dad never said," he says. "All he said was that you were a good assistant."

"Would you have believed it?" I say. He probably still doesn't quite believe it even now. We sit in the car for a while. So long, I know Genesis has gotten the dinner dishes done. She looks out at the car, but it's too dark to see us. I know I should go inside before she gets suspicious.

"Why are you here?" I whisper. "You should go home."

"Yes," he says. "I just had to...tell you." He takes my hand, squeezes it.

I get out of the car, walk up to the porch. I know Genesis is going to ask me what all that was about. Sure enough, her eyebrow is raised when I walk in the door. "Doc's dead," I say.

"Oh," she says in surprise. "Did you know?" And I start to cry. She hugs me.

I can't sleep, thinking about Doc, and about Robert's hand in mine. I've been with no one but Reuben since we got together at the old Miller place. Between helping the doctor and the ranch, I haven't had the time or the care to go off at night. I see Reuben once a week, and every time is the same. He is there and then we're in bed, and when we're cooled, he's gone. More often than not, he goes to the bar before he comes to me, and he is a sloppy, forceful drunk.

But Robert, he makes me feel like an innocent school girl. He tells me I'm smart, and talks to me like a colleague and hardly ever touches me, and when he does, it's brief and casual. I expect Reuben, but I look forward to Robert. I look forward to the mangled limbs and the rashes and broken bones and splashing wombs because it means I get to be there beside him. But, I think maybe he just thinks of me as nothing more than a girl. But I'm nineteen; I've taken more than a dozen men to bed, I've helped deliver babies and watched most of my family die.

And he is married. And his wife is lovely and his children are precious. They are clean and orderly and speak to each other in soft tones. I'm not the girl for a man with a family like that. And Anna is so warm and sweet, she even tells me to stay the night with them when we've been out late. She always sends me home with jars of jam and cobblers, ribbons and stockings and pretty scraps for Genesis. I can't betray her.

Every man I've been with I've just had, with no thought. It's always been easy, all I have to do is say "Yes" or "Let's go" and they fall to me. I could do it with Robert too, I'm sure. Genesis already has it in her head that I might. But I don't want to. I don't want to be thinking about Robert all alone in the dark of my room. He is respectable and a girl like me shouldn't be ruining that.

And there's Reuben. I think Reuben would not take well to my being with anyone else these days. The thought of it used to bother him before, but now he is obsessed with it. Now he asks me every time if it's still him, just him. "You're the only thing that's true to me anymore," he says. "You're the only one who's never lied." It makes me pity him. I thought maybe discovering what his father truly was, and his giving up God would make him less manic. But it hasn't. It's only made him angry—angrier than he already was. And he uses me to abate his demons.

I don't sleep. I lie awake and think of Reuben and Robert, Robert and Reuben. I can hear the creaking of the bed across the hall, the hooting of an owl on the roof.

We attend the old doctor's funeral together, Jax, Genesis, and me; Denney, too. It's at the old church, which is only used for weddings and funerals anymore. The whole town is there, and we have to squeeze into a pew in the back. I can't see Robert until he gets up to give the eulogy, Anna right there beside him. Seeing her there beside him, her arm through his, stabs me with jealousy. I hate that she is there, and I hate that I am jealous. I wish I could be the one comforting him.

By the end, I am feeling too much: guilt, grief, jealousy, anger. I have to take my horse out, ride hard and far, up into the hills, to clear my head. It doesn't help. When Reuben comes to me later, our demons meet and break skin and draw blood.

The third death, I feel secondhand. It hovers, trembling around Robert. It's spring. We have been treating a handful of kids who've caught measles, all making full recoveries, thank God. I've felt nothing on them but fever. He's always careful, clean and careful, but I worry Robert may have taken it home, gotten his little boy sick.

The weather has gotten warm, the sun high and gold and melting away the last bits of winter. Spring is alive and the ranch is filling with hands and calves. It is not a time to be feeling Death lurking over my shoulder.

Keith Feaney and LaRae Kitchens are getting married

tomorrow. Genesis and I have been invited. We laughed at first; Genesis had dated and rejected the groom, and I had taken him to bed. While I'm sure LaRae knows of Genesis, I doubt Keith's told her about me. Genesis says we ought to go, since the Feaneys have always been so good to us and we do so much business with them. It would almost be an insult not to go.

And now I feel Death humming around the doctor. I know it's not him. I've purposely felt his skin, and there's no thump. *Please do not be his wife.* For a moment, though, for one horrible moment I think about how I won't have to feel guilty for the unprofessional and far-from-innocent thoughts I have about Robert. *Oh God, not his wife.*

Robert chucks little Ricky Johnson under the chin. "I think this little man's going to be back to school by the end of next week," Robert says. I pat Ricky's hand. I can't remember which Johnson he belongs to, what his mother's name is. She's not a Johnson, but she's married to one. Robert snaps his bag shut and stands and the Death around him wafts and waves, hitting me like a bad smell.

"You need to go home." I grab his arm as soon as we're out the door. "You need to go straight home."

He takes me by the arm and pulls me along after him to the car. I try to tell him I don't want to go. I don't want to be a part of whatever is going to happen, but I find myself in the car, my head foggy and my stomach rolling. "Drive fast," I say. It's only five minutes, but that's long enough for something to happen.

"Is it Anna? My mother? The baby?"

I shake my head, afraid to open my mouth because I feel I could vomit as the feeling presses in on me. He's not fast enough, and I feel it all release just before we turn onto the street. We hear the wild screech of tires as we round the corner, and I throw my arms around myself, whisper *no.*

We see the car stopped in the middle of the street in front

of his house. We see all the mothers running from the houses toward the accident. We see Anna screaming and falling to her knees on her lawn. Robert leaps from the car, forgetting to turn it off, to brake. I lunge at the wheel as he sprints the rest of the way. I pull out the key and curl in on myself, trying to close out the sounds of Anna and Robert's screaming.

It's their little boy. Anna turned her head for just a moment to hang a sheet and the boy ran after a squirrel. The screeching tires made her run out front just in time to see it happen—the flash of the silver bumper, her son flying through the air and landing on the pavement.

There are sirens and police and the man driving—a guest for the wedding, is vomiting on the sidewalk, his wife pulling at her hair, walking in circles in the road. The mothers pull their own live children into themselves, turn their faces away from the little body bleeding out on the road. Birds fly overhead and the sun shines so bright it's almost blinding.

I find myself there with them all day and long into the night. I hold their baby while they weep; I help their mother make dinner. I help Robert put his wife to bed after he's given her something to help her sleep. Robert's mother deals with the police at her house next door. Robert and I are exhausted. He has cried, more than he did with his father, and I will forever be haunted by the little body under that white sheet.

We sit together on the sofa, minds numb, bodies numb. I want to go home. I need to go home, but I can't ask Robert for a ride and it's much too late to find anyone else.

"You knew," Robert says.

"I'm sorry," I say because I have nothing to say. He cries again, sobs into his hands. We are alone and he needs comfort and I wrap myself around him, pull him close. My heart beats against his temple, and he shakes against me as he sobs, lets himself fall into me. And in our fatigue and grief, our bodies move, open up to each other, pull at each other. The love-making is sad and slow and desperate. We both cry afterward and when he falls asleep, I leave. And as gold lines the eastern sky, for the first time, I truly hate myself.

PART V

FALL 1943 – SUMMER 1944

GENESIS

My son was born squalling and squirming, red and purple, topped with a thicket of black hair. He cried so loud, Jax and the hands heard it down on the porch. They'd been waiting hours to hear it, and they whooped. "Big, strong boy," the doctor announced and handed me my son. The doctor's mother patted my hand, praising my efforts.

Isaiah was by my side, beaming and already shedding tears as she touched his soft hair. Judith was there as well. "What will you call him?" she asked.

Isaiah and I looked at each other. She had said we shouldn't name him before his first year. "I don't know," I said. Jax and I had been so scared we'd lose another, we never even entertained thoughts of possible names. "I guess we'll know when it's right."

The door opened and Jax was there. Doc Robert stood and congratulated him then excused himself to clean up. "He looks just like you," Isaiah said to Jax, and she moved to let him have her space beside me, then she followed the doctor out. Jax cried. Judith and the doctor's mother silently piled all the birthing things in their arms and left us alone.

Jax held our son, kissed him, and sang softly—words far from English. "What's that you're singing?" I asked.

"A lullaby my grandmother used to sing to us," he said. "Would you like me to teach it to you?"

"No," I said. "It's your song."

He ran his fingers over the soft skin of our baby's face. "The others will want to see him," he said. Most of the hands we had that summer were new, young, still teenagers—the younger brothers and cousins of the lot we usually got. Most of our regulars were wearing different boots overseas.

We had less help but larger herds. They should have been gone by then. It was October, and already the highest peaks were tipped white. But there was too much work to be done and not enough hands to do it, then Jax had wanted to stay for the birth. Denney told Jax he needed to stay, that he'd take the hands and the herds and Jax could catch up, but I went into labor soon after that discussion.

They held out and left three days later. "I'll be back in a week," Jax said. "Two at most."

"Don't try to cut through the mountains if the snow's bad," I said. "Come the long way if you have to. We can wait." I had Judith and Isaiah. Judith stayed all the while Jax was gone, over two weeks. No one worried about her running off; they knew she'd be back, so they let her stay all that time.

Again, I asked her why she didn't leave. Again, she said, almost wearily, "Where would I go?" She was thirty-one, well into old maid-hood now. But, though cloistered, her life was somewhat comfortable; she lived in a big house that she more or less ran, and didn't have to do much more work than any other housewife. Where would she go, and how would she be able to maintain the comfort she had without having to work herself to the bone? She had no commercial skills; she couldn't read well or type, her written grammar was poor.

The Community, somehow, still prospered. All the men had been exempted from the war, claiming religious pacifism. Judith knew some things, but she didn't know everything. She knew her Father and brothers to be involved in clandestine activities, but she wasn't told much. "Reuben tells me nothing, either," she said. "He just tells me it's better I don't know. And every few weeks men we don't know show up in the middle of the night and leave the next day." Judith told me. "We're told to feed them, and make up beds for them, but we're not allowed to speak to them." I shrugged, as long as her father and brother weren't bothering us, I didn't much care what they got into. "I'm glad you got out," Judith said. "That you got to come home; that you got away from Benjamin. Now you have this."

Perhaps if I had not been so caught up in my own happiness, I would have been aware of her eyes misting as she watched me with my own child. When Judith held him, I didn't question her tears. I thought, briefly, that I would not have cried over someone else's child, but I figured that perhaps she was just feeling the weight of her old maid-hood. I should have noticed her soberness, the tell-tale roundness of her features. I would have offered her help, offered her my home.

But I paid no attention to any of this at the time. "Thank you for being here, Judith," was all I said and I held my baby close, determined to know and remember every bit of him, his smell, his curling fingers, the brush of his eyelashes on his cheeks; all his toes I counted again and again, the feel of him warm and weighted in my arms. She watched me, and then turned away, biting at her lip.

The day she left, Judith held my hand in hers. I held her hand without thought to the trembling of it, the clammy feel of her palm, and I merely smiled when I thought she might speak.

Was she opening her mouth to confess then? To beg for help? Or just to say goodbye? Her brother arrived and called for her before she could say anything at all. I watched her go and for the briefest moment I felt the urge to call out to her, to tell her not to go, but I didn't, and soon my attention was focused elsewhere.

The doctor came a few weeks later to check on me and the baby. Isaiah was at his side as he weighed the baby. I'd never really seen them work together before. But I watched them then, the way they interacted. They were discreet, and did not display their familiarity boldly, but I noticed it. They didn't touch, but he stood intimately close to her, his chest nearly against her back as he leaned over her shoulder to read the scale. Once, he had looked at her like other men did, with unfulfilled yearning. That was gone.

"And how are you feeling?" the doctor asked me.

"I'm recovering," I said. If he heard the sudden coolness in my voice, he gave no indication. But Isaiah heard it. She stopped cooing at the baby and turned to me instead, panic in her eyes. She wanted me to say nothing. "I think I'll have my baby back now," I said as the doctor removed his stethoscope from my arm. Isaiah nodded and handed me the baby.

"I'll walk you out," she said to the doctor.

I wanted to walk out with them, but the baby whimpered and squirmed to be fed, so I could do nothing but sit with him as Robert followed Isaiah out. She closed the door behind them, and I listened for the footsteps creaking on the stairs, the shutting of the front door, the roar of an engine. But there was none of that, and not the whole time I fed the baby. And I knew. I knew that right then, they had gone to Isaiah's room.

I seethed, thinking back over the last two years to the nights Isaiah spent away from home, saying she'd stayed at the doctor's home because they'd been out so late. "I didn't want him to bother driving me all the way out here," she always said. "Anna doesn't mind."

I thought back to those few nights I'd sent Reuben away because Isaiah wasn't home, and the flash of infuriation in his eyes. "She spends a lot of time with that doctor doesn't she?" He'd once said.

I had seen it coming. I had known it was inevitable, hadn't I? But I had been hoping that Isaiah had her limits. That she had the decency to leave married men off her tableau. That she wouldn't behave like some common mistress.

At last, I heard the footsteps on the stairs, the doors, the engine, the tires on the gravel. The baby had fallen asleep at my breast. I didn't bother to put him down or even bother to button up. I stopped her as she came back up the stairs. "How long has it been going on?" I said. "With you and the doctor."

She wouldn't look me in the eyes. "A while," she whispered. *Years*, she would not tell me.

"Isaiah," I said evenly. "He's *married*."

"I know," she said through gritted teeth.

"She's lost a child and now you're taking her husband too," I hissed, referring to the doctor's wife.

"Genesis, the baby," Isaiah said warningly, trying to divert my attention, more or less telling me to calm down.

"The baby's fine," I said. "*I* can control myself."

"Can you?" she said. I was angry and disgusted enough to slap her. If I hadn't been holding the baby, I might have.

"I'm not the one sleeping with someone else's husband," I said.

"Well it's not like she's taking him to bed," she said. From all accounts, it was probably true. Since the death of their son, Anna had become nervous and gloomy, and was often sedated. She could hardly even bring herself to care for their second child most days. Isaiah faltered under my heated gaze. She dropped her head. "I know," she whispered, wagging her chin. "I know I shouldn't, and every time I feel... but I ...Genesis, you don't understand. He's..."

"Is no one safe from you?" I exclaimed. "Do we all have to turn our men's heads away from you, blindfold them from your gaze? You sweep men up like a whirlwind!"

"Genesis, you know that I'd never—"

The baby woke and started to cry. I bounced him, more forcefully than necessary. "Reuben, Robert. It will end in disaster," I said. "You can be no one's mistress, and you can be no one's wife, but you bed them all like both. Girls like you bring disaster." It was a harsh thing to say, and maybe I shouldn't have to say it. But in the end, I was not wrong.

ISAIAH

I know Genesis is right. I have to end it with the doctor. But I don't. It's just been him and Reuben and no one else. I don't take any of the hands to bed anymore, or go to the bar with them and pick up strange men there. I don't know how to end it with Robert. But I don't really want to; I just know I should.

Where Reuben is rough, Robert is soft. He holds me close afterward, kisses me all over. *We can't keep going on like this*, I should tell him. *Anna is sick, go back to her*. But I don't say it. Instead, we keep sneaking around. It has gone on for years now. I think Reuben knows it's not only him, but he doesn't ask, and I don't tell him. But I think he knows because he clings to me too tight, digs his fingers into my flesh like he's anchoring himself to me. He breaks my skin between his teeth, leaving his mark on me so when I go to Robert, he can see the bruises.

Robert kisses the marks Reuben leaves and asks, "Who does this to you?" I say it's no one, it doesn't matter. Robert leaves me soft and breathing like a dream. He lets loose my hair, and it falls around us like a black curtain we hide behind, where it's only us and he's not married and I can fall asleep against him. Then I let Reuben break me again, pulling at my hair, twisting my bones, dragging his nails along my skin. He is my penance. I match him, using him to beat my guilt away.

Robert has to go away for two weeks. He's taking his wife to see her family. And I tell him, "I think this should be it." He sighs, runs his hand through my hair, down my naked back. We are in his spare room; his wife is asleep in the next room over. "I'm not the type of woman who can be someone's mistress," I say. I've been starting to think I *could* though, I could be some-one's mistress. But mistresses don't bed other men, too, do they? I can't give Reuben up. I can't make him go away. If I do who will bear my guilt then?

"I know," Robert says. "And I'm not the type of man who keeps one."

"Your wife is so good," I say. "So sweet ..."

"I know," he sighs. He lays back, staring at the ceiling.

"I don't want to be a home-wrecker."

He faces me. "You aren't." He puts his palm to my cheek. "You're good, too, you know. You deserve a man who's loyal, and free. Who can be yours completely."

I think he's wrong. I've never been faithful to anyone. Not even Reuben, and he's been loyal as a dog. I reward him by letting him back into my bed when I'm not with anyone else. I turn away from Robert, sit up, reach for my shirt. "Maybe we shouldn't see each other at all anymore."

"You don't think we can't ..." Robert sits up too. "We were just colleagues before."

"You really think we can go back to that?" I say. "If we're still seeing each other every day, working side by side?"

"We can try," he says. "I'll go away a few weeks. We haven't gone two weeks without seeing each other in the last three years. Maybe it's just what we need."

"Alright," I say. And the next day, he leaves.

And for two weeks, I count the days. I try not to. I focus on helping who I can at the office while he's gone. I try to be with Reuben and only Reuben. I think about how I've gotten other men out of my head; I let Keith Feaney between my legs and now we've both moved on. He's married, we're still friends. But Keith Feaney was once, years ago.

"I've done it," I tell Genesis. "I've told Robert we have to stop." I didn't mean for my voice to crack, but it did.

"You really liked him, didn't you?" she says, rocking her baby.

"He's a good man," I say.

She takes my hand in hers. "I know," she says.

And when Robert returns, we open the office together and try to behave. We look away from each other, pull our hands back if they touch. We make it through a day. I go home before dark, and he goes home to his wife. We make it through another day, and I start to think that maybe we'll be fine.

But then we're called out to deliver twins. It takes all day and long into the night, and when we pull into my driveway, we are too excited by the day, too exhausted by it too. It takes only a moment, a brush of the fingers, a small bump of a knee, and we're onto each other in seconds; lips locked, hands unhooking and unlacing, fingers tracing edges. *Damn it all to hell*, I think. I will never give him up. I will take him as long as he'll have me.

And just then, just as I'm wholly giving in, Robert's door opens and he's dragged off me, pulled out and thrown up against the side of the car. It's Reuben, and he's throwing punches, over and over, into Robert's face. Robert tries to wriggle free, fight back, push him away, anything, but Reuben's a rancher. He might not be quite as tall as Robert, but he's much stronger. Robert's head beats against the car in rhythm with Reuben's punches.

I'm screaming at Reuben to stop, crawling across the seat, trying to pull at Reuben. But Reuben brushes me off. I fall out of the car, and by the time I throw myself on Reuben's back, trying to pull him off, beating against his shoulders, Robert has slumped. Reuben throws me off and drops Robert to the ground to continue beating him, punching at his ribs, his jaw. I barrel into Reuben and manage to throw him off. We roll in the dirt, Reuben grappling at me.

He bests me and is soon sitting on my stomach, his fingers around my throat. I kick and claw at him. I flail at him, making three angry red lines across his face. He tightens his fingers over my throat and slaps me, screaming "Whore."

"You're nothing but a whore," he shouts, spitting into my face. My pulse beats wildly against his fingers. I turn my head, trying to pull free. I can see that Robert isn't moving. I struggle against Reuben, but he clenches even tighter, and I can no longer breathe. The edges of my sight start to fade, and I feel him moving, reaching into his pocket and then I feel the point of a knife bite into my cheek. "I should cut up this pretty face of yours, then no one will want you. Then you won't be able to trap men anymore." I'm fading. My throat is on fire, stars in my eyes, shadows moving in the dark.

Then I hear the click of a gun hammer and Reuben releases me. I gasp, cough, sob. "Don't think I won't pull this trigger," Genesis is saying. Slowly, Reuben rises, and Jax pulls me up, back, away. I fall against Jax, gulping for air, blinking at the blur.

Everything comes into focus. Denney and a couple of the hands have got the doctor propped up between them, his head lolls and blood spills from his mouth. I sob and shake and stumble. Jax holds me up. *What have I done?*

Reuben is glaring at me, his eyes flaming with hate and disgust. Genesis stands behind him, her hair loose and wild, her nightgown stretched tight over her milk-swollen breasts. She's looking at Reuben the way he's looking at me. I think she might actually shoot him. The air rattles in my throat and I think maybe I'll let her. Reuben, too, starts to realize his life is in danger, and his rage melts to pleading.

I can't let her kill him. If we kill him, surely Leader and Benjamin would be on us like fire and brimstone, and what will happen then? She'd be labelled a madwoman, sent to some sanatorium. "Genesis, don't ..." I croak. It hurts to get the words out.

"What do you mean 'don't'?" she says through gritted teeth. She jabs the pistol against his skull. "This son of a bitch would have cut you up; and he would have killed the doctor, why shouldn't I?"

"Community..." I say.

Reuben drops the knife in his hand, raises his arms. Genesis stands still. The rest of us breathe, watch. Robert gurgles. Air wheezes in my throat. "Get his horse," Genesis finally shouts. One of the hands runs around back and brings the horse forward. Genesis keeps her gun on Reuben as he mounts. "Get out of here, and don't ever let me see you here again."

As soon as he's thrown his leg over, Genesis shoots into the air and the horse bolts. Reuben bounces in the saddle. "You're a whore, both of you!" He shouts. "And you'll get what a whore deserves!"

Genesis shoots again, in his direction, not truly aiming. He digs his heels and we watch him disappear into the dark. Genesis turns to me, her jaw set tight. She shakes her head, says nothing. She goes to the doctor, tells Denney and the men to bring him inside. I pull away from Jax, stumble after them. Genesis stops me at the door. "I think you've done enough tonight," she says. She goes inside, shutting the door behind her. I sit on the porch, drop my head into my knees and cry.

GENESIS

I would have shot Reuben. I would have killed a man for my sister. I would have killed Reuben, knowing it would give reason for the whole Community down on us and Leader and Benjamin would use Reuben's death as a way to get me carted off, leaving our land free for their taking.

We brought the doctor inside only to find that his nose was broken and his jaw dislocated. Isaiah was in pieces, and I didn't trust her to set them. So we pressed ice to Robert's face and I had Denny and Jax drive him over the hills to the hospital. By then, Isaiah had fallen asleep on the porch and I left her there. I had left her to her own discretion until then, but I couldn't abide her looseness anymore. To sleep with another woman's husband was one thing, but then to get him beaten to a pulp by another, simultaneous lover... And it was me, it was me, who drove to the doctor's house and explained where he was, why he didn't come home that night.

I went with the intention of telling Anna the whole truth, about the whole affair. But when I saw Anna frail and nervous, tears of worry already in her eyes, I held back. "There's been a fight," I said. "Robert's been hurt. But we've taken him in to the hospital. We'll pay all the bills..."

Anna let out a sob and clutched at her mother-in-law. She composed herself. "Robert ..." Her voice was wispy, cracking. She sounded like she could shatter. "Robert doesn't fight. Why would he ...?"

"He ..." I said. I suddenly wanted more than anything to get out of there. I felt I couldn't tell her the truth, but I also couldn't straight lie to her. "He shouldn't have... He wasn't meant to be part of it." This was Isaiah's bed to make; I couldn't be the one to shatter the poor woman.

"Oh," said the doctor's mother, rubbing Anna's back. "You can't ever predict the animality of man, can you? They get going and things get out of hand."

Some women too, I thought. Anna's small son called for her from upstairs. She did not react. Her eyes had glazed over. The baby called out again, and the older woman's eyes flickered toward the stairs. I stood to leave. "We'll pay for everything," I said again. "He should be home soon. My men will bring him back."

"Thank you," the older woman said.

I showed myself out.

When I arrived back home, I found Isaiah on the porch with my own baby. She stood, cradling the baby against her like a shield. "Did you tell her?"

I looked at the bruises on her neck, her eye. How many times would I have to save her? She was by no means stupid, so why did she put herself here? Why did she get wrapped up in such men? Maybe it was my fault. Maybe if I hadn't let her carry on, maybe if I had expected more of her, forbidden her going out to the Community after we left. Maybe if I'd had better control over myself, shown a better example, sent her to school. "No," I sighed, answering her question. I took the baby from her.

"Genesis, I..." she began, but I didn't want to hear her explanation or apology or whatever she had to say. I wanted only to go in and feed my baby and forget about men; the men she'd bedded, or the men I'd killed or might have killed, forget about the things I'd done or should have done.

I didn't divulge the affair, but I didn't have to. The town worked it out themselves. They knew Isaiah's past, her loose ways, the men she knew. They'd seen her working with the doctor, and when he came home bruised and battered after a day with her, they put it all together. The town could abide a freewheeling woman. They could even abide an affair. They could not abide indiscretion. Such things should be clandestine, left only to rumor.

Isaiah was more or less shunned. A week after the fight, she went to open the office and was met with only disapproving glares. The sheriff went to the office and told her that the doctor's mother requested she'd be removed from the premises. So Isaiah left her keys and came back home. She slept late, said nothing, wandered around the ranch despondently. I had disproved of her actions, but as her bruises yellowed and she withdrew, I pitied her. I worried about her. I worried she'd go off and debauch herself again. So I tried to keep her close. I broke my resentment. I told her to help me with whatever I was doing, laundry, cooking. I made her watch the baby while I went over the ledgers. I even made her sew.

"You were right," she said when her voice came back. "You're always right."

"Not always," I said. Sometimes I got tired of being right.

When I went into town, everyone whispered about Isaiah and I found myself getting defensive. I didn't want to defend what had happened, but she was my sister. I decided not to go into town until it had blown over. Jax could turn away from the whispers and snide glances better than I could.

But the baby caught a fever and I panicked. I thrust him into Isaiah's arms. "What is it?" I said.

"I don't know," she said. I wrung my hands as she felt his skin, held her hand to his heart.

"What do you feel?" I asked, barely able to get the words out, afraid of the answer.

"Just a fever," she said. "All I feel is fever."

Jax and I let our breaths go, and he tried to console me saying, "Children get fevers all the time." But I still worried, I wanted to know *why* he was sick. But Isaiah couldn't answer.

"We can take him to the doctor," Jax suggested.

Isaiah frowned, but bit her lip and nodded, "If you're so worried, then maybe you should," she said, handing the baby back.

"Jax, you'll have to drive so I can hold the baby," I said.

I made Jax knock on the door. The doctor called for us to come in. He was seated at his desk, bent over paperwork. He looked up and paused as we entered. He'd healed well. Except for the lump on the bridge of his nose and a greenish tinge in the corners of his eyes, he seemed all well. For a moment, none of us said anything. The air grew heavy between us. "I—" I began, but faltered.

"The baby," Jax said. "He's got a fever." I held the baby against me, his warm head on my chest. He smiled blearily at us while I told the doctor my concerns. "His skin's so hot. I thought babies cried when they're sick. It just seemed so strange that he's still so calm."

"Depends on the baby," the doctor said, standing. "Well, bring him here, let me take a look at him." I laid the baby on the bed, and the doctor unbuttoned his clothes, revealed his little chest. He felt the baby's forehead, turned him this way and that, opened his mouth. "Ah," the doctor said. "It appears the little man is growing his first tooth." He showed me the little white speck peeking through the red gums.

"That's it?" I said. "That's what's causing the fever?" Relief flooded through me.

"That's it. Nothing to be worried about," the doctor said.

"Didn't know babies got teeth so early," Jax said, looking at me with a "told you so" smile.

"A little early, but not much.," said the doctor. "Six months, isn't he? Good strong lad." The baby gurgled at him, pulled at the doctor's finger, laughed as he redid the buttons.

"And..." the doctor said quietly. "How is your sister?"

"She's..." I didn't know how to answer. I looked at Jax. He shrugged.

The doctor pulled the baby up into sitting, the baby pulled the stethoscope into his mouth. "I haven't thanked you for the..." He pulled the stethoscope back and picked up the baby, bouncing him a little "...the hospital."

"It was the least we—considering..." I said. "Isaiah."

He handed back my baby. "I should have known better," he said. Immediately I thought he was going to deride her, and I geared myself to defend her. But the doctor sighed. "I'm older, mature. *Married.* I should have stopped it sooner." He sat back at his desk. "I shouldn't have ...taken comfort in her to begin with. I shouldn't have let my guard down. I just hope she has the sense to find someone better—more suitable." Jax put his hand on my back and we moved toward the door. "Who's the boy?" the doctor asked.

"Um..." I said. "He's—he's part of the Community. They... They're a hard bunch." I said, hoping he would catch the warning in my voice. He grunted and picked up his pen.

Jax pulled out his wallet, but the doctor turned away. "No

need for that," he said. So Jax replaced his wallet. We thanked him one more time and left.

We met the doctor's wife and mother walking up the sidewalk, the little boy between them. Anna pulled her son closer to herself. He looked too clean, too pale, too soft. And so did she. But she was out and standing straight, and I could tell she didn't want to see me. She'd have heard the rumors and known they were true. But she was a respectable lady and, albeit forced, said, "Is the baby alright?"

"Rob—the doctor says it's just a tooth," I said. Her little boy tried to pull away from her, but she pulled him back. "It's nice to see you out, enjoying the weather."

"Yes," Anna said. "I think I've been...sheltered for far too long." She looked away from me, staring pointedly at the office window. She wanted us to go, I wanted us to go, but the old woman broke into the heavy hum that had fallen between us.

"Have you got a name yet?" The old woman asked.

"No, not yet," I said.

"Maybe just Jax, Jr then?"

"Perhaps," I said.

Anna's eyes flickered to the baby. "They are the spitting image," said Anna quietly. Her grip tightened on her little boy, her face paled. The boy she'd lost had been named after his father. She looked away again.

"Or maybe after your own father," said the old lady. "Levi was such a solid, handsome man."

I felt the pain of loss in my own soul and swallowed hard. Jax placed his hand on the small of my back. It was time to leave. The baby whimpered and saved us from having to continue the conversation.

"Looks like, for all Isaiah's done, she did bring Anna out of her stupor," I said once we were in the truck.

Jax smiled, patted my knee. "Yup," he said. "We might as well stop off at Feaney's while we're here."

Keith Feaney smiled at us when we entered, though LaRae and the other two customers inside did not. Keith exclaimed about a new camera he'd just ordered, but I watched LaRae. She was big with their second baby. "The baby's teething," I said to her. "Have you got anything that can help?"

She made a face at the baby and merely smiled at me politely. "We've got gripe water," she said, but didn't move to get any.

"Oh," I said.

"It's on the top shelf. I'll let Keith get it."

"Oh," I repeated. But Keith was busy getting the things Jax needed. I swayed with the baby in my arms. "Where's your little one?"

"Gramma's got her," LaRae said.

I nodded. I wondered if Keith had ever told her about Isaiah, or if she'd ever asked, or maybe even just assumed. "Are you still heading over to the hospital to have the baby?"

"That's the plan," she said. "Isaiah was great last time, but hospitals have so much new stuff. And real nurses, you know?"

I nodded again. And who wants pretty Isaiah around their husbands when they themselves are swollen and deformed? At last, Keith came over and collected the gripe water for me. It was on a shelf lower than his shoulder.

"What do we do with Isaiah?" I said to Jax on the way home.

"What more can we do?" he said. "She's a grown woman, and a wanderer. You'll drive yourself crazy trying to tame her."

"I tamed you," I said.

"I wasn't wild," he said.

When my birthday came, Jax and Isaiah gave me a camera, the same one the Feaneys had in their store. "You really ought to take photographs of the baby," Isaiah said, beaming. "As he's growing. I don't think you've got any of him at all. And besides, we need to replace some of those pictures in the parlor. Half the people in them were dead and gone long before we ever came along."

I pretended I didn't know anything about taking pictures, letting her take the camera around for a couple days to test it out. "Teach me," I said. It gave her something to do. When she insisted I use the camera myself, the first photo I took was of her bathing the baby in a copper bucket out back, the laundry waving behind them, both of them smiling and squinting against the sun. As the summer bloomed, we made use of the camera, photographing everything. The baby, each other, the house, the hands. How little I knew then what those photos would mean to me, to us.

Late that summer, I'd find her standing on the porch, staring off at the mountains. She looked so serene and thoughtful and beautiful I had to photograph her. But she heard me and she turned just as I snapped the photo. She is frozen in that instant to me now. Her gaze—her black eyes boring into me, her mouth slightly open—made me ache. She looked at me and I felt storm clouds gathering. They hovered over us, around us, and trembled.

ISAIAH

One dawn in early June, Jax shakes me softly awake. "It's one of the Community boys," he says. "Says his sister is in labor."

I sit up, rub the sleep from my eyes. "The Community?" I ask, not quite sure if that's what I heard him say.

Jax nods. "He's begging for you."

"Why would they send for me?" I say. There are plenty of seasoned women in the Community, and they must know I don't want to go back there, not after last time.

Jax shrugs. "He's waiting in the parlor."

I dress and head downstairs, where Matthias is waiting, wringing his hat in his hands. When Jax said "Community boy" I thought he must have meant one he didn't know, someone like Aaron or Boaz. I hadn't expected Matthias and I'm thinking I may have heard Jax wrong again. Maybe he said "wife" and not "sister."

"I know..." Matthias says. "But please ... Please, we don't know what else to do, where else to go."

"Your wife's had a baby before," I say. I don't mean to be so rude, especially to him; he's always been friendly enough, but he must know I can't possibly go out there.

He shakes his head. "It's not her," he says. "I wouldn't call for you if it was her," he adds. "But it's Judith."

I almost laugh, it's so silly. "Judith? Judith having a baby?" It sounds like a ploy to get me out to the Community so they could do who knows what to me.

His shoulders droop, "I know it's hard to believe, but ... it's going badly. It's taking so long. And Father, he's not allowing anyone other than the girls to tend to her, but they don't know what they're doing. I—we don't know if she's gonna make it..."

It takes me a minute to get what he's saying. In that time, Genesis comes down the stairs, looks at Matthias, and says "No" before she even knows what's going on. "No, she's not going; you're not taking her back there with you."

Matthias is crestfallen. I sigh. "Genesis, it's Judith," I say on his behalf.

"Well, you can bring her here," she says. "We'll take care of her here."

"She's having a baby," I say.

Genesis blinks, her mouth falls open. She shakes her head. "You can't go," she says softly.

"But it's Judith," I say. "She helped us; she helped you ... I have to go."

"Fine," she says. "But I'm coming too. And we're bringing our own truck." Matthias nods, grateful.

Genesis and I head upstairs to gather our things. She slings the baby over her shoulder, straps her holstered pistol under her skirt. I wait for her on the stairs and she kisses Jax goodbye. "Are you sure?" he says. "Are you sure? Should both of you really go? I'll drive you, or at least take Denney."

"No," she says. "I need the two of you to stay here. You stay and keep the ranch." Jax holds her, kisses her, cups the baby's head.

"You come back by tomorrow," he says. "Or I'm bringing a cavalry after you."

"I'll be back," she says. "We'll be back."

When we get to the house, Leader and Benjamin and Daniel stand out on the porch like guards, their eyes pointed at me and Genesis as Matthias leads us up the porch. Genesis clutches the baby. *Yea, though I walk through the valley of the shadow of death.* I know everyone else is watching from their windows and cracked-open doors.

Jerusha meets us at the door. "It's been a whole day," she says. "We don't know what to do. She's been in pain since this time yesterday." She is exhausted and bewildered, and something about her haggard appearance pleases me, remembering her vanity in her youth. We follow her inside. We pass Reuben in the parlor, chewing on his nails. I look away when he looks up at us.

Jerusha takes us up the stairs, down the hallway to the farthest room. It's hardly more than a closet, barely large enough for a bed and small, spindly writing desk. There's not even a window. The room is hot with the bodies of the sisters— Ruth, Jerusha, Elizabeth, Judith. All the sisters are exhausted and matted, but Judith by far is the worst. She lays sweating in the bed, her face red and puffy, her hair stringy, her stomach stuck up high. When she opens her scrunched eyes, they look at nothing.

"Oh, Judith," Genesis says.

"Father hasn't let her out since—" Ruth whispers.

"She tried to run away," Elizabeth says from her position beside the bed. "And then he found out...about the baby. Is she going to die?" She is desperate and scared.

I kneel down next to her and take Judith's hand, hook my

thumb in hers, palms together, and I feel her head like a mother checking a sick child. I feel her chest, her belly. "She is not dying today," I say.

"Then what is it? Why is it taking so long? Why is it hurting her so much?" Jerusha asks.

I feel Judith's stomach, reach between her legs. "The baby's the wrong way around," I say. "It's sideways." She's been lying in this bed since the pains started, I find out. "Can we at least go somewhere with more space? More air?" I say, scratching at my clammy skin. The sisters look at each other.

"We'll go to my room," Jerusha says. "And if Father has anything to say about it, I'll answer."

So we help Judith up and down the hall. Jerusha's room is almost cheerful. "It used to be hers," Jerusha whispers, and she goes red with shame. These things are Judith's things. Blue and pink curtains hang over a large window, a matching quilt on her bed, a nice desk, a chest of drawers, a cedar trunk. There is room for Judith to walk and we get air moving in from the open window.

"We should walk her around a little," I say. "Try to get the baby to move." I think of Jerusha as a girl, haughty and beautiful and I expected her to still be so, but she is changed. She is eager to help, to bring comfort to her older sister. She takes Judith by one arm and I take her by the other, we walk her around the room a few times, stopping to let Judith curl in pain when she's hit with a contraction. Genesis sits in the corner, nursing her own baby, scowling. Nothing here seems happy, no one is excited. They are only anxious and ashamed.

Eventually, we let Judith lay down and I end up having to push at her stomach to get the baby to the right place. It makes her scream, and her sisters whimper, but I get it done, and soon her water breaks. Still, things move slow.

It is a long day of waiting, of picking at cold biscuits, of polite small talk and encouraging words to Judith. We take turns pressing cool wet cloths to her skin, playing with our baby. Genesis and I don't leave the room—we don't dare to. Judith, all the while, says nothing and doesn't seem to register that we're there. We talk about her like she's not there, because it's almost like she isn't. She's a changeling Judith. A changeling that's had the soul sucked out of her.

"Who's the father?" I whisper to Jerusha, who shrugs.

"We thought maybe you two would know," she says. "We thought maybe it was someone ... from when she stayed with you."

"She was already expecting by then," Genesis says, overhearing us. "I might have noticed, but I didn't. It makes sense now." Judith whimpers as another pain comes over her. Genesis squeezes her hand, coos at her.

The father is someone in the Community then. Didn't I see her sneaking out one night, when I came for Reuben? "I need some air," I say. The room is too close, too heavy, too full. Genesis looks at me, a small shake of her head. "I'll just be in the hall," I promise.

The hallway is dark and cool. I shuffle along the wall until I can't hear Judith's whimpering anymore. I close my eyes, press my fingertips to the wallpaper. "Is she going to live?" Reuben says in a whisper. My heart thumps low in my chest. I don't have to open my eyes to know he's moving close to me, standing right there in front of me.

"She'll live," I say, opening my eyes to his. "But she's... what's happened to her?"

"We thought he'd kill her," Reuben says, he's so close, his words breeze on my lips. "When he found out, she was trying to leave. She couldn't hide it anymore. He caught her. He screamed at her, threw her to the floor. Matthias and I stopped him before he could do too much damage, but he hasn't let her out since. He ordered us to keep her out of his sight." He leans in, so his lips brush mine. My heart thrums. Is it fear or desire? Both? I haven't been touched in months. I've been rejected by just about everyone I know; but Reuben still wants me, and his want reaches for mine, pulls yearning from my depths. "I came to tell you, but..." he raises his hand, and I flinch, but he only tucks loose hair behind my ear. "I was already so angry; I couldn't believe Judith, my Judith had been so...*unvirtuous*. And then to see you, to see you..."

"You could have killed him," I whisper. "You could have killed me."

"Why can't any of you be true?" He groans, rests his forehead against mine. When I breathe, our chests touch and I feel like I'm trying to breathe underwater. "Isaiah," he breathes, and I catch my own name in my mouth.

A scream pierces through us and Genesis shouts my name. Reuben steps back, and I gasp for air, slide away from him. "Please," he says, tugging on my hand. "Please don't let her die. I don't think I can handle it." I hear what he's not saying: he won't be able to control his rage if she dies. I nod and slip back into the room of women.

The time has finally come, and as Judith screams and grunts, I'm pleased to know Leader must listen to it over his dinner. I'm the one who pulls the baby from Judith's body. "A girl," I say. The baby wails; she's fat and copper-haired. She reminds me of someone I can't remember. Judith falls back in exhaustion, and I hand the baby over to Jerusha. Genesis brushes back Judith's hair, praises her. But no one is laughing, no one is smiling, no one is crying in joy.

Ruth leads me to the bathroom to wash up. "What's to happen with them?" I whisper in the hallway.

Ruth wrings her hands and shrugs. "Who knows," she says. I don't believe her. She knows. Maybe I know too. I doubt

Judith will get to keep the baby. I doubt Judith will ever be let out alone again. As we go back to the birthing room, Leader and his sons gather at the bottom of the stairs.

"Well?" Leader shouts up. I shudder at the sight of him, the sound of his voice. I am glad for all the steps between us, for Ruth beside me, for Genesis on the other side of the door. I stand tall, speak clear.

"It's a girl," I say.

"With red hair," Ruth says.

Something flashes in Leader's eyes, something dark and cruel, and something cackles in the shadows, my pulse rises. "It couldn't be helped, I suppose," he says.

All of them seem to realize something at once, they shift and glance at each other, some worried, some angry. Reuben breaks away, rushes up the stairs, brushes past us to the room. Leader turns to Benjamin and Daniel, mumbles something, nods. The three of them move to turn to leave, and only Matthias is left. "It's time you go," he says.

GENESIS

It was hard to leave Judith like that, broken and hollow. She was too exhausted to hold her own child. She had looked at me without recognition. When Reuben came in, he dropped to his knees at her bedside, saying "Judith, Judith" and she turned away from him.

Isaiah returned, gathering her things. "We have to go," she said. I didn't need her to tell me twice. I sensed an electric buzz in the air, something cloying and unholy. Quickly, I told the girls how to help with Judith's recovery. I brushed the tiny girl's coppery hair, picked up my own son, clutched him to me as I hurried after Isaiah.

Matthias led us out the back door, and we tried not to look left or right, tried to ignore Leader's fiery words booming through the air, the breaking in of someone's door, the clanging of the church bell calling all to come witness a sinner's punishment—a warning to those who'd meddle with Leader's family. I tried not to think of Judith, of the baby that would be taken from her and placed with another family. I tried not to think of the man surely being dragged from his home and forced to his

394

knees in front of the church. I tried not to think of the execution taking place that very moment.

The scent of rain hung in the air, the smell of waiting soil rising up to meet it. We were in the truck before Matthias shut the gate, and on the road not a moment later. We did not hear the gunshot, but by the way Isaiah flinched, I knew it when it was done. "William Jepson," she said.

He had been Little Mary's father, the red-haired girl who'd died while we were confined there. The girl Judith had borne had the same red hair, the hair of the father. William had committed adultery, deflowered Leader's favored daughter. The worst sin, of course, would be trying to leave and take said daughter with him.

Judith had been caught, but William had not, not yet. Perhaps when she failed to meet him, he knew his time was short. Perhaps Judith did too. Perhaps that was why she'd turned into the shell of herself, given up.

"We could tell the police," Isaiah whispered. But we knew that, even if they went out there, Leader and his gang would have hidden everything by then, and no one would betray him —he'd make sure of that.

I beat my palms against the steering wheel, exclaiming "Dammit!" and thunder rumbled in the distance. Clouds were gathering over, jamming at the peaks, turning black. Just as we arrived home, the rain fell in fat, round drops. Jax was waiting for us. "That whole place should be burned to the ground," I said to him.

"Maybe it will be," he said.

The storm hit hard, but it was quick, and the next morning the sun rose hot and grew only hotter by the day. For weeks, the sun rose hot and high. We had no rain, no clouds, only hot, white sun that baked our skin tight. The earth turned dry and cracked and broke apart. The garden withered and shriveled, the streams and springs diminished to trickles. The air waved and shimmered in the distance. Hot winds blew and offered no respite, only more heat, more dry.

Until at last, the wind shifted and blew in heavy and laden and stuck to our skin, weighted in our lungs, and it grew heavier still. The horses became skittish and the cattle moaned like the souls of the damned; the birds chirped frantic, flitting across the blazing blue sky; the hens cackled and the rooster crowed and cawed. The dogs paced and whimpered, licking at the earth. The baby whined and the tips of our hair curled, and we knew rain was coming.

We watched puffs of white appear over the peaks, and we gathered lamps and candles. We checked holes in the roof, pulled the laundry in. The clouds burgeoned and billowed and soon the tallest peaks were all but obscured. We cooked enough for us all, for all day and night, and the clouds coagulated, turning gray and heavy as the wind kicked up, hitting us like a wave. The dogs howled and sprinted across the yard, kicking up dust in their wake. The world darkened quickly, and we were shrouded in gray that cast a shaded glow.

Then everything was silent. The dogs stood still; the hens cloistered themselves. The cattle were quiet, the horses too. The birds were nowhere to be seen nor heard. And we knew the storm was coming. We called the hands up to the house, pulled the dogs in with us. They laid out wherever they found room.

In minutes dusk became night, and as the thunder began to rumble, we paused, as if holding breath, and listened for the first patters of rain. The tell-tale *tick-tick-tick* on the windows prompted us to look outside, to see the dark spots appearing in the parched soil, one then another, another and another, until, like someone cutting open a sack, the water fell all at once and continued for hours.

We ate food, played games and music. We danced and sang and stayed dry. All the while, flashes of light grew brighter, cracked ever closer, until we were blinded and deafened, our bones rattled. The baby slept through it all in Isaiah's arms, while the rest of us were too electrified to doze.

The thunder rumbled away, but the rain stayed. It undulated, from deluge to lullaby and up again. And in a lull, we heard a great, sudden rush and jumped to watch at the windows. A gush of water—a swell of a river, came forth from the gorge. We watched it rushing and spreading over the land, carrying logs and leaves. My garden was washed away. The graves in the cemetery stood like islands in the deluge. The water rose and rose, and we held our breaths as it lapped at the house, licked the steps on the porch. But the parched earth opened up and drank and the water receded.

In the morning, the storm passed over and the sun rose again, shimmering on the skein of floodwater the saturated earth could not take. We stepped out into the mud and breathed through our lungs, through our skin. We set about clearing the debris, churning mud beneath our heels. The sun was bright, the water receding, and all seemed righted in our world.

ISAIAH

I feel Reuben calling to me, yearning for me across the night. I watch the moon rise over the mountains, haloed against the black night. It moves up the window until it is up over the house and I can't see it anymore. He is aching and in turmoil. And I know, like a wounded animal, he is lethal. I know I shouldn't go, but my heart sits heavy in me, throbbing in my gut, weighing me down like stones in water. I am drowning in Reuben's sorrow. Something has happened.

In the morning, when I hear Genesis go down to make breakfast, I sneak into her room. The baby is awake in his crib, babbling to himself. He hears me come in and squeaks at me, pulls himself up to standing.

"Look at you getting so big," I say and ruffle his hair. "One second, little guy." I go to Genesis's bedside table. She keeps her revolver in the dresser. Loose bullets roll and knock against the sides. I jam my hand into the drawer to catch them. I grab the pistol, check the barrel. All loaded but one chamber.

Gun in one hand, I swing the baby onto my hip and take him with me to tuck the gun under my mattress. I kiss him and he takes his finger from his mouth, smears his spit across my eye. I make a face at him and he laughs.

Genesis is frying sausage and eggs. "Both of you are up," she says when we come in.

"I heard him babbling to himself," I say as he gets hold of my hair.

"Do you mind watching him today?" she says. "I've got a meeting with Mr. Garrett. I'll be back in time for lunch."

Jax comes in, kisses Genesis and joins us at the table. The baby reaches for him, pulling himself onto the table toward his father. Jax takes the baby and kisses him too. Genesis brings over plates of eggs and sausage and toast, takes her seat, unbuttons her top and pulls the baby to herself. She eats while she feeds him; his little legs kick in satisfaction. Jax and Genesis discuss business, what numbers to report to Mr. Garrett. It is just another day.

The summer morning sun glows through the windows, lights up the whole kitchen and dining table, halos the family in dusty golden light. I am flooded with affection for the three of them. My family. Genesis smiles at me across the table, feeling my eyes on her, maybe feeling the rush of warmth gushing through me.

But looming in the background of my mind is Reuben, lurking in the corners of this sweet image, threatening to take it over with his own image. I hardly notice Genesis saying good-bye. "Isaiah!" she has to snap at me. She's holding the baby out. "I'll be back soon."

I hold his little palm against my face. "Auntie Isaiah," I say.

"Ba ba," he burbles, and bounces in my arms before he opens his mouth wide and sucks on my chin, his version of a kiss.

"Auntie," I say again and squeeze him tight against his wiggling. We watch the horses and the cattle grazing, the hands moving back and forth through corrals and stalls and barns. We watch the laundry curling in the breeze, point at birds sitting on the fence posts, and feel stones in our hands and everything is new and wonderful. But as the day wears on, I feel only heavy clouds despite the sunshine, despite the laughter and the love.

And when night falls and the family is tucked away in their sleep beneath the high moon, I pull the revolver from under my mattress and slide it into a satchel. Boy is sleeping in his stall, his head bobbing, until I open the gate and wake him. His ears turn and twitch as I saddle him. I know I shouldn't go to Reuben, but he won't leave me alone.

I ride out to the Community—to Reuben. It is the same. The same wall, the same gate, the same church, the same cabins and houses and barns. But something is changed. Is Leader sleeping soundly in his bed? And Judith? Is she decaying back in her tiny room? Is she gazing out at the moon? Which one of these cabins houses her daughter? An owl hoots. It echoes in the silence. Death is here. He is lurking in the the shadows, little by little creeping toward me, smirking. The owl calls again, she is perched atop the church steeple.

I feel the blood of William Jepson calling from the ground, just near the door of the church, where they made him kneel before everyone and confess; where they sent lead through his skull and his blood drained into the dust. Now, last night's storm has turned the dust to mud. It squelches beneath us, each step slides back a little. We carry on. I go past the church and the cabins, past the dining hall and women and children's house. The shadows follow, watching me. I know where I'll find Reuben.

The limbs of the old juniper tree rise in the moonlight, but they are all wrong. The tree is on its side, uprooted and toppled by the storm. The roots splay bone-like in the milky light.

Reuben stands at the edge of the gash in the earth, a shadow in the night, staring in the hollow where the tree once took root.

I dismount and step up beside him. "I'm here," I whisper, sliding my hand into his. It is cold. He says nothing, and I look where he is looking. At our feet lies Judith, her skin blue and puffed, her eyes not quite closed. Her nightgown is sodden, her hair tangled with mud. She could be sleeping. "Oh, Judith," I sound far away, my breath like wind. I can't take my eyes off her, but I don't want to look anymore. The tree creaks, a shadowy figure rests in the gnarled crooks and elbows, humming.

"She got out during the storm," Reuben says. "A tree fell on the back of the house, broke through the wall. She climbed down."

When I close my eyes, I see her, still alive, in a trance, making her way through the storm, the wind whipping her hair and lashing her body. She fills her pockets with stones as she nears the swelling river. I see her sliding into the roiling water, taking one last breath as she lays herself down. I see Death watching from the opposite bank, his eyes blue in the white lightning.

My hand in Reuben's turns sticky, warm. I open my eyes, look down. Blood oozes between our palms, trickling over our wrists. I twist our hands to see where it's coming from. Reuben has etched my name in the flesh of his forearm; the letters stretch crude and oozing from his wrist to his elbow. He has called to me with blood.

"I didn't know where else to take her," he's saying. "I found her, it was me. Everyone else stopped looking. But I found her. I can't take her back up there. Back to them. To *him*."

His hand grows too warm. I have to release it. I step forward and kneel in the broken, upturned soil. "Bury her here," I say, reaching to close her eyelids, but they slide back up.

I try to brush the mud from her hair, but there is too much of it. I try to cross her arms, but she has started going stiff. How long ago did Reuben pull her from the water? How long has he been standing over her? I can do nothing but straighten her dress, removed the largest clumps. The owl has followed, and hoots from a nearby tree.

"He has to die," Reuben says. The voice is his and not his. It is venomous and pierces my soul. I turn to him, and he looks at me. His glass blue eyes are shadowed and wild. "You need to kill him."

"Who," I say, not "no." The word echoes in my head. Why do I not say no? Because I know who he means. Because I agree. Because I have wanted to kill him myself for years. But now to say it, to really say it, fills me with dread.

"*With the breath of his lips, I shall slay the wicked,*" Reuben says. He looks at me, but he's no longer seeing me.

"Reuben," I say, trying to talk him down. "The police, maybe if you go to the sheriff ..."

"No!" he says, and he reaches for me, grabs my wrist, pulls me up. His fingers burn my skin. "You call down Death, you bring him here. It will be you," he says, "You and me."

"I can't..." I try to say. He pulls me into him, clutching my waist. He breathes hot and heavy into my ear, my neck.

"You and me," he says again. Every place where he's pressed against me feels like I'm burning. I cannot bear to touch him, to have him touch me. I try to pull back, and when I look into his face, I no longer see Reuben, I see only that white, cold mask of Death. I see ice-blue eyes in dark hollows. "It has to be us," he says. "We have to kill him."

"No," I say. A shiver knocks through me, my stomach sits heavy in my hollow gut. He means it. He really means it.

"He's murdered. God, Isaiah, you don't know how much he's murdered. Why not end him the same way?"

I cannot be the one to bring death. I feel it, see it, dream it enough already. "Then we would become like him," I say.

He squeezes me, tighter and tighter. "No," he breathes in my ear. "No. We're better."

"Reuben ..." I try to say, but it's barely more than a squeak, he's holding me so tight. "Please let me go." He only pulls me closer, wraps his hand in my hair, tilts back my head. Then he kisses me hard, suffocating me. It is not a kiss, it is a brand.

"It's you and me," he says again, reaching into his pocket. He pulls out a knife—my knife, the one I'd left in Leader. It's sheathed, though, and I see he's only holding it out to show me, to let me know he's serious. But I don't hesitate to think he'll turn the blade on me if I don't follow him. I shake my head, try to pull away.

Rueben shackles my wrist in his grasp and drags me after him. I try to pull away and look back at Judith's body as if she'll rise up and stop him. But I can only stumble after. Tears of panic bite in my eyes. What will happen after? When Reuben's done and his senses return, what will happen then? Will he run? Will he try to take me with him, will he leave me there? Death chuckles in the dark.

Reuben spouts scripture as he drags me along. "*Destruction shall be to the workers of iniquity.*" I thought he'd given up all the bible and Jesus stuff, but he's calling out to the God of destruction now. "*Surely thou wilt slay the wicked, O God.*"

Boy trots along after us. I've nearly forgotten about him, but he snorts, and I remember the gun I'd put in the satchel knocking against his side. I try to reach back, to grab Boy's reins, but Rueben yanks me forward. As we near the church, Reuben goes quiet, looks up at the steeple. It is a brief pause, but it is enough for Boy to come within reach, and I pull the reins, bringing him close enough to reach into the satchel. I wrap my fingers around the gun and pull it out just as we reach the house. Reuben's foot lands on the first step, and, when he hears the hammer click, he stops and turns.

"Reuben, you let me go," I say.

He drops my wrist, and I immediately steady it on the pistol. He glares at me. "Whatever you've got in your mind to do, you're doing it alone. You're not taking me with you," I say.

He rubs his thumb on the hilt of the knife in his hand. "I thought you loved me."

"I've never said that."

He looks down at his arm, the crusting letters of my name glint in the moonlight. He runs one finger over them. "Then why are you here?"

I cry. The gun shakes in my hands. I'm asking myself the same thing. Why have I come? Why couldn't I just leave him alone? Why couldn't I lose myself in someone else? Even with Robert, I could not forsake Reuben. "I don't love you," I say. Love is what Genesis and Jax have, it's not this; it's not pulling blood from each other.

Reuben looks up at me, sneering. "You're just a whore then?" He spits, it lands at my feet. He unsheathes the knife, I steady the gun. "A good-for-nothing pair of legs," he says. "Nothing."

"I was everything you ever wanted," I say.

He laughs. "You say you don't love me, but you think you'll get away from me?" He points the knife at me, I hold up my chin. "You always come back to me. I'll always be etched in your flesh like you're in mine."

I know he's right. The tears come fast now. I don't want to care about whatever he's about to do. I wish I hadn't come, but I know this is it. I'm never seeing him again. "I'll forget you," I say, though we both know I'm lying. The owl hoots, the coyotes howl, Death passes in the shadows, and we watch each other.

Reuben drops his hand. The knife is not for me. "Go then," he says. "Can't expect loyalty from a whore."

Keeping the gun pointed on him, I mount Boy and tug up the reins. I hesitate, thinking maybe I should go back for Judith's body. But when Reuben breaks the gaze and turns back up the steps, I know I should be as far from here as soon as possible. I watch Reuben enter the house and I spur Boy. We slip through the gate and race into the night, my blood quickening as I get further from Reuben.

And though he's out of my sight, I see him still. I pull Boy to a halt. I sway in the breeze; my mind turns and aches, all my hair on end and my skin crawls electric. I could turn around and stop Reuben. Boy twitches beneath me, his ears flicker and turn, the bit rattles in his mouth. I am deaf with the sound of my own rushing blood. My vision fades in and out—the darkness in front of me, and Reuben; Reuben and the darkness.

I'm there in the room with him, I see him standing over his father's sleeping body. I hear him chant, *"I will kill you with the sword and your wives shall be widows, your children fatherless."* I see him bring down his arm in one swift motion, cutting hard and fast and deep. I see Leader's throat spill open, blood gushing, his eyes open in surprise. In anger. In hatred. I see him grasping for Reuben with one hand, using the other to grip his splayed throat. Reuben pulls him off, and Leader falls from the bed, slumps twitching on the floor. And Reuben watches. He watches until the body stops twitching, until the gurgling stops and the blood puddles on the carpet.

I lean to the side and vomit. Trembling, I wipe my mouth and pull Boy's reins the direction home and ride hard the rest of the way, everything whirls inside me, building like a storm. I get close enough home to see Jax is on the porch, pulling a shirt on. "Isaiah?" he calls, coming down the stairs. I all but fall from the horse. "Genesis said you were in trouble..." I hear him say before my vision flashes back to Reuben, and I see only him. My own house and Jax right before me disappear.

Reuben still stands over his father's body. He turns, opens the bedside table, smearing blood on everything he touches, and pulls out a gun. He turns it over in his hands then looks up, looks across the room, looks at *me*. He's staring me right in the eye. He grins, his teeth blue white, and raises the pistol to his temple. My name crosses his lips.

Then I hear the gunshot like it's through my own head, like it's me bursting. Everything goes black, and the earth engulfs me.

GENESIS

J ax scooped her up, and brought her in. I knelt beside her, laid my hand on her head. She quivered beneath my touch. I ran my fingers over her scalp, lost them in her thick black hair. *What has happened, Isaiah? What have you done? What have you seen?*

When her eyes opened, she winced as though the dim room was too bright, as if my touch pained her. "They'll come for me," she said. I ran my hand over her hair again. Her eyes are red. Red and black. She sat up, Jax's shirt falling into her lap. "Reuben..." she whispered and pressed her face into her hands. "I didn't do it. I didn't do *anything*." I let her tell me when she was ready. I asked no questions. "Judith is gone. Leader is gone. Reuben...gone."

"How bad?" I said. Her eyes welled and she dropped her head in her hands, pressed her palms into her eyelids. Then she told me, achingly, what she'd just witnessed—how she'd witnessed—Leader's murder and Reuben's death. She told me she saw Judith's dead and drowned body. As Isaiah spoke, her words soaked through me like an icy stream. Everyone knew the knife that killed Leader was Isaiah's; they'd see her name etched in Reuben's skin. Everyone knew Isaiah was a *witch*—and if they didn't, Benjamin would convince them of that. I turned to Jax. "Go wake the men," I said.

Upstairs, the baby cried. Isaiah stared blankly into the cold fireplace. I pulled my son from his crib, he nuzzled against me and shut his teary eyes again, whimpering. I stood in the parlor, rocking and swaying with him in my arms, my eye on Isaiah, who stared beyond us. The back door opening made us both jump. Jax came in, Denney behind him carrying a shotgun.

"They're set up around the house," Jax said.

"Those bastards aren't getting anywhere near this house," Denney assured us.

"We'll be on the porch," said Jax, picking up the rifle he'd left by the door on his way out for Isaiah.

There shall be wailing and gnashing of teeth.

The star-speckled sky fell inky blue. A haze of pink rose over the sharp, black peaks. The thin white-gold of first light broke. We watched the sun rise and we waited.

ISAIAH

We wait all morning. The air is alive and buzzing. The sun is hot—hotter than it has been all summer. The ground ripples and rises. I am twenty-three today and, for the second time, Death has overshadowed the counting of my days alive. Again, there is no cake. Instead, there are guns and images of blood playing over and over in my mind. I close my eyes and see it all again—the gash in Leader's throat, his eyes wide and wild and surprised, blood seeping between his fingers and down the front of his nightshirt. *And I will kill you with the sword and your wives shall be widows...*I hear Reuben saying over and over again. *Your children fatherless...* I see him kneeling beside his father, his palms red, my bloodied name, the bloody handprint on the gun. The thud. I could have stopped him. I should have tried.

The sun is up and high and hot and still I have not slept. Genesis naps with her naked, diapered baby on her breast, her buttons all undone. They are peaceful in this image, mother and child. He knows nothing of death yet. She has borne it twice.

It is too hot in the house.

The hands patrol in the sun, sweat soaking through their shirts, their hats, guns on their hips and slung across their backs. Most of them are hardly more than boys, still too young to join their brothers in Europe, too young to be shot at, to end up with limping limbs and missing chunks.

"It's not your fault," Genesis tells me, but we know that doesn't matter.

How long does it take to gather a mob? They'll have collected themselves by now, Benjamin standing at the pulpit cursing my name. The sisters will prepare their father's body, their brother's corpse. Leader's laid out on his bed, his face gray, the gash in his throat gaping. Reuben is laid out on the table. The men will get their guns and their righteous rage and come like avenging angels.

How long does it take to gather a mob?

Until lunch.

They come massed together in the backs of their pickups, Benjamin at their head. We sit around the kitchen table, nobody but the baby really hungry. While he eats small pieces of bread and soft potatoes, we chew our lips with anxiety. The rifle leans against the wall; the revolver rests on the table.

The warning whistle cuts like a cannon blast and we eye at each other. Jax takes the rifle, heads out the front door. We hear voices—Benjamin shouting, Jax calling back calmly. Genesis picks up her baby, she picks up her revolver, she pulls open the door. I catch my fingers in her elbow.

"What are you doing? You can't take the baby out there," I say, but she just brushes me off.

"You stay in here," she says.

I watch from the window, hidden, listening through the open door. All the men look at her when she comes out, raising their firearms. But then they are taken aback by the baby. The men all look to each other. Jax's eyes narrow but he hides his anger. "You sons of bitches aren't welcome here," Genesis says, wielding the infant and the gun like she was born to do both just like that, as if it was the most natural thing in the world.

Benjamin's eyes shift from the baby to my sister, to all the men around her. Maybe he had it in his mind to come in like an avenging angel, guns blazing. Maybe he thought to come here and force my sister, take revenge on her rejection all those years ago. Maybe he thought to come and burn our home to the ground, to drag me away and strip me naked, walking me through the streets before throwing me to the dogs. Maybe he wasn't expecting the baby. He might take away a woman's baby, but he wouldn't shoot at one. All he has to fight with now is words. "Your sister's a murderer," he says. He pulls my knife from his pocket. It is still rusted with blood.

"You know my sister had nothing to do with it," Genesis says, her aim still steady.

"She bewitched Reuben," Benjamin shouts, his men holler in agreement around him. "She bewitched him, possessed him —branded him with her name, told him to kill his father! She's an enchantress and a succubus. A Jezebel! You give her to us to pay for her sins!"

"And what of your sins?" Genesis, standing on the edge of the porch, looks down on him. He shifts under her gaze. He looks from her to the baby and back. "Who answers for Judith and William Jepson? For my mother?"

Benjamin spits and sneers. "I know you're in there!" he shouts to the window. He takes a step forward and there is a bang and his hat flies off behind him. Guns are snapped up, fingers trembling over triggers. Benjamin freezes, clutches his own gun, glaring at Genesis.

"That one was a warning," she says. "The next one won't be." The baby barely jolted at the gunshot. He is calm on her hip, watching. "My sister has never killed a soul," Genesis says, "But I have." Now even Jax and Denney turn their eyes on her, not quite sure if she's telling the truth. She holds the baby steady, the gun even more so. "And I'll do it again." Already she's pulling back the hammer. But all other gun barrels are lowered. Benjamin taps his finger against the butt of his rifle. Sweat runs down the side of his face, and Genesis is cool in the shade of the awning.

"We don't want to hurt no one," Benjamin says, lowering his gun. "We only want the witch, Just send her out to pay her debts, and we'll leave you and your little family alone."

"Never," Genesis answers without hesitating.

Benjamin sneers. Then he throws his head back and laughs. "Alright." He waves to his men, and they start backing into their vehicles. I slump from the window, my back against the wall. We have reached the peak of this feud.

Goddammit, Reuben, Goddammit.

GENESIS

T he Community men left, but I knew they were not gone. They'd be back, trying to catch us off guard. They left a few men to watch the house, watching for any sign of Isaiah attempting escape. Jax, understandably, was livid I'd used our baby as a shield. But I had worried one side or the other would start shooting if I hadn't stepped out there. Jax and Denney were really all that stood between us and them. The hands were all just boys.

"They wouldn't shoot when there's a baby," I said.

"You don't know that!" Jax said. "Men have done it before —murdered women and children. They've done that and worse!"

"Benjamin's bad, but he's not *that* bad," I said. He wasn't interested in hurting babies, he just wanted to win what he thought he deserved. "And no law, not even one in the pockets of murderers, will protect a man who kills a baby."

The baby, upset by the tone of our voices, began to cry and Jax yanked him from my arms, comforted him. He took him out to the back porch, away from me.

413

"I'm not letting them have my sister," I said, following after him.

"But you'd risk our son," he said. "After all it took us to bring him here. You've lost one, how could you risk another one?"

I am pierced with a knife of hot shame, but it only angers me. "You think I'd just throw my child to the wolves? You think I'm just some crazy woman?"

"You used him as a shield," Jax said through gritted teeth. "And then you shot. You shot and egged them on. Sometimes you're too strong for your own good." He stormed down the back steps and across the yard, kissing and bouncing the baby with soft words.

"He's right," Isaiah whispered beside me. "You shouldn't have taken the baby out there." Her black eyes were sad, weary. My throat tightened. I nodded.

"I was just trying to buy some time, to make them leave," I said. "I'd never let him get hurt."

"I know," she said. "But they'll be back."

I joined Jax on the porch. The baby had fallen asleep, his cheek pressed against Jax's chest. I knelt, ran my fingers through the baby's soft hair. "I'm sorry," I said. "I shouldn't have done it. I just..." I sighed, looked out at the little cemetery across the yard. The headstones were plain, just stones etched with names and numbers.

Sheriff Burnham came first. He held his hat, twisted the brim in his fingers. "They're going to the county," he said. "There's nothing I can do. They've got evidence, witnesses, records of past behavior. And they've got money."

"We've got money," I said.

The sheriff swung his head. "They've got more." He sighed. "The county sheriff. He doesn't know you like we do, and he doesn't care."

"But they've committed crimes!" I said. "They've actually murdered!"

"From what they say, you have too," he said. He went apologetically red. "I don't mean to sound so callous, Miss Genesis, but that's what they're saying."

"It's true," I admitted, throwing my shoulders back. "If you searched hard enough, you'd find the bones—if they're still there, given the wolves and the storms. But that wasn't murder. He was a vagrant; he tried to attack me, and he was trespassing on my land."

"It's true," Isaiah said quietly from her roost on the sofa arm. Even though she was listening, she wasn't looking at us; her attention was somewhere beyond the window.

The sheriff pulled at the brim of the hat in his hand. "Listen," he said with a sigh. "The county sheriff, he'll look at those Community boys and he'll see men who've been lining his pockets. He'll look at you and see..." He cleared his throat, clearly uncomfortable with the words he was compelled to explain. "He'll see two...young ladies and...one with a reputation."

It wasn't really me that was the concern, he was telling me. It was Isaiah. It was me who'd once killed a man, it was me who'd threatened Leader's sons. But I'd settled down, found a man, had a baby. But Isaiah, she was enchantingly beautiful and freewheeling. And Benjamin knew I'd fight tooth and nail for her, and if he got her, he could easily drag me along too. He could pay me back for the humiliation I'd caused him.

"I wish there was more I could do," the sheriff said, placing his hat back on his head. "But I wanted to let you know that they'll be here by tonight." I thanked him for letting me know, and we watched him leave.

That evening, the county police arrived while we just sitting down for dinner—me, Jax, Denney, and Isaiah. They knocked on the door, and we paused. They knocked again. "We'll open up this door ourselves if you don't," someone shouted. Isaiah stood and let them in. The county sheriff and his deputy enter, followed by our own Sheriff Burnham, who held back with his head hung low.

"Can't you see we're in the middle of dinner?" Denney said. Though his tone was still even, and soft, it was harder than I'd ever heard from him.

"Carry on," said the county sheriff. "But we need to speak to the ladies. So if you will just come on over here and take a seat on the sofa beside your sister." Jax and Denney stood when I did. "Nah, nah, just the girl," said the sheriff. I shrugged and handed the baby to Jax. I joined Isaiah on the sofa.

"What are they doing? What's going on out there?" Denney said from the table. More of the county lawmen were walking around the yard, making their way over the property.

"Just doing a routine search," the deputy said. He went to the table and sat himself down, made himself at home with a biscuit.

"Isaiah didn't kill anybody," I said. And before I knew, I was telling him everything. I told him about all the things the Community had been up to, about the bootlegging, and locking Judith up, about burning down our barn and trying to poison us and run off our herd. Isaiah told him about the night Leader died. She admitted she'd gone out there, but that she'd left when she refused to comply with Reuben.

"Even after all they—allegedly—revenge never crossed your mind?" the sheriff said when I was done. I sucked at my tongue. Of course revenge had crossed our minds—or mine at least. And how many times had Denney and a few of the other hands heard me claim I would kill Leader? How many of them saw me attack Reuben the night of the fire?

"Wouldn't anyone?" Sheriff Burnham spoke up for me. He

finally lifted his head and stood straight, facing the county sheriff head-on. "Come now, Sheriff, I've known these girls all their lives. I can guarantee you neither of them has it in them to commit cold-blooded murder—vengeful or not."

"And you don't think that perhaps your own relationship with them is clouding your judgment?"

"Not as much as that bootlegger's money is clouding yours," Burnham said. The two men eyed each other. Isaiah and I both went stock-still. A chair squeaked in the kitchen beneath one of the men shifting. The baby babbled. Jax *mmhm*ed in reply.

The county sheriff cleared his throat. "Well, I hear tell this one—" he pointed at me, "Has in fact killed. That she admitted so herself."

I will admit I faltered a bit then. I *had* said as much. I had been so proud to say it then. Puffed up in my own power, riled in my sense of familial protection. But just as I was thinking about lawyers, Sheriff Burnham spoke up again, "Case closed there, I'm afraid, Sheriff. Girl told me herself right after it happened. Came to me all shaken up about it. I investigated. Nothing more than self-defense. A trespasser who attacked her on her own property. Doesn't a man—or a woman—have the right to defend themselves on their own land?" It took all my self-control not to let my mouth drop open and give away his lie. "You've come down here, you've interrogated them. You've got no evidence, but you've got a pocket full of cash I'm sure the boys at the marshal's office might take an interest in, and the boys in *my* office are mighty gossipy. Who knows what they might let slip in the next few hours?"

The sheriff's mustache twitched. "I think we're done here," he said. My heart leapt. He called for his deputy. The two of them returned their hats and I showed them the door. "You girls best watch yourselves," the county sheriff warned with sincerity, and I closed the door behind him.

I thanked Sheriff Burnham, then I took my baby in my arms and held him close and Jax held me. Denney went back to his biscuits. Isaiah stood by and looked on, her face unreadable as stone.

ISAIAH

I feel Death again, lurking and looming in every corner of the house, following me like a black cloud. But he won't tell me who will be taken next. It could be me. It could be any of the hands. It could be Jax or Denney or even Genesis. I try to tell Genesis. But when I do, my throat catches and my breath leaves me. For seven nights, I curl up in my bed and cry, the weight of Death bearing down on me.

It takes seven nights. Seven nights from Benjamin showing up with a posse at our doorstep. Seven nights under the cloud of Death, and then I know. I barely sleep all those nights, sitting in the window and watching the moon grow fat and whole. And then, deep into the seventh night, the cloud lifts. All at once, the weight of Death lifts as clouds part and the moon illuminates me. I hear Death laughing as he leaves, and my guts drop. I want to vomit. I know what's coming.

There's commotion from Genesis and Jax's room. Their door opens, I hear footsteps in the hall, on the stairs. I rise and follow. My heart pounds in my ears, deafening me. "What's going on?" I say, my voice shaking. Both Genesis and Jax stop on the stairs. They are both alive and well. "The baby...?"

"He's asleep," Genesis says. "Somebody's just pulled up." She nods to Jax. He carries on, no doubt to go gather the hands. I feel my knees buckle, and I ache to breathe. *Don't let him go out there!* I want to shout at her. But I don't know. I don't know if it's him that Death has come for. Genesis catches me. "You alright?"

I can only nod. I steady myself and follow her down the stairs. She picks up the shotgun by the front door. We peer out the window at the vehicle idling outside. The moon is bright enough to see it's a truck, but the headlights blind us against seeing inside it. The headlights flicker. A message to us, or a sign to anyone lying in wait to ambush us? The backdoor opens and Jax comes in, followed by the dozen hands, all of them guns raised.

The headlights flash again. Then they turn off, and the driver thrusts an arm out the window, waving a white cloth in the moonlight. Jax opens the door, and we all step onto the porch. The driver sticks his head out slowly, both arms raised. It's Aaron Fisher.

"I got your man!" he says.

Genesis and I look at each other, confused. I do a quick headcount of the men around us and realize...

"Denney," Genesis says. We are off the porch running to the truck before anyone else can make a move. Aaron stays in the cab. Genesis and I reach the bed and there's Denney, crumpled up. Genesis jumps up beside him and his tugging at him, "Denney!" she wails. *No, no, no,* I'm saying to myself. "He's alive, he's still alive." Genesis is saying, almost begging, weeping. But I know it's no use. He's beat badly, his face is unrecognizable, there's a dip in his skull. I know it's him Death's taking.

Genesis is weeping and the rest of the men rush forward to help her take him inside. And I am empty.

All the while, Aaron sits behind the wheel, hands gripping at it. I stand at the window. Aaron looks straight ahead. "They found him at the bar," he tells me. Denney liked going there to listen to the radio. They aired updates from the war. "They found him there and brought him back—out to the cabin. I didn't—they tried to get me to, but I—they left him there, and I brought him back."

"He won't make it through the night," I say. We watch the others carry Denney across the yard and into the house. I know by the time the sun rises, so will Denney's spirit.

Aaron faces me. "I tried to stop them. I tried...Leader was crazy, but he still had some self-control. Even at the end. Benjamin on the other hand..." He shakes his head. "I'm leaving. Me and Boaz. I'm taking my sisters, he's taking his wife and we're leaving."

"You think Benjamin will let you go?"

"He can try to come after us, but he's not as clever as his daddy was," Aaron says. "And their connections have been shrinking for years. Doesn't matter. I'm leaving. And you should too."

My heart clenches. It's a thought I've had almost every day in the last week, but I haven't been able to say it out loud. "Where will you go?"

"They're still taking men overseas," he says.

I reach in and touch Aaron's face. I imagine this will be the last time I will ever see it. "You take care of yourself."

He takes his hand from the wheel and cups my chin, then leans out and kisses me, rich and deep. "If only Reuben hadn't caught you first," he says when pulls back. He pulls the gear to reverse and salutes as he rolls away.

Inside, the scene is bleak and frenzied. Denney is laid out

on the couch, his breathing ragged, blood trickling from his busted lips. Genesis is doing what she can, dabbing ointment, setting bandages and splints. The men bring her water. They heat knives for cauterizing. Someone suggests going for the doctor. Someone else suggests taking Denney to the hospital. But it is agreed another car ride will surely do him in. So someone is sent for the doctor. But it's no use. I do not tell them this. Instead I cry in the shadows, wrestling with must be done.

The doctor doesn't come. The sun rises, and Denney is dead. We sit, staring at his body. For hours, none of us has spoken, and all we hear is the clock tick. I am the one who breaks the silence. "This won't stop," I say. My throat is so dry it aches to speak. "Not until it's me. Maybe I should just...I can give myself up."

"No," Genesis' voice flares. "I will not give you up to Benjamin."

"You think he'll kill me?"

"If he doesn't, he'll make you wish you were," Genesis says. The others chime in, saying they'd fight to the death before they let that happen.

"I can't stay." There, I finally admit it. To stay means to start a feud. A bloody capture the flag—that flag being me. Benjamin can't claim Genesis, but he can claim me.

"No," Genesis says again, shaking her head. "No." She tries to say something more, but the baby cries from upstairs.

I follow her as she goes for her child. She lifts him from the crib, and when she turns, I see she's crying. She knows I'm right. I have to go. "Where will you go? Who will have your back out there?"

"You," I say. She clutches the baby close and I wrap my arms around both of them. "I'll always have that bossy voice of yours in my head, telling me to watch out." My tears mix with my sister's. She kisses my head.

A coat, socks, Daddy's old hat, pistol, canteen, food. We collect these things and more, tie it all in sacks and satchels. If I go when it's dark, they won't see me leave. I laugh to myself, thinking that if Leader was still alive, I wouldn't be running. He'd never have gone to the authorities. *Damn you, Reuben.*

The hands saddle Boy in the barn as the sun starts to set. The Community is out there, watching. We can't let them know I'm running. I know the gorge well enough that I can hide out there until the snows come.

"We'll send food for you," Genesis says. "And when the first snows come, move on. Don't try to brave the winter."

"We'll get you money," Jax says. He hands me a slip of paper with his sister's name and address on it. When things settle, I can go there. I'm taking Honcy, the last of Denney's dogs. Genesis makes us dinner, but she and I are not hungry. Jax eats, the baby eats. Genesis and I do not eat. She clasps my hand on the table.

GENESIS

The smell of sage was sharp on the warm evening breeze. The sky turned from blue to purple, the mountains from purple to black. The baby should have been put to bed, but I couldn't lay him down without seeing Isaiah again. Benjamin would come back, and he and his men would search for her. They thought they'd rattle us. Let them come, I thought. They would keep trying to tear us apart, to bring me into submission. To sully my name and my sister's. Let them try to drag me through the mud, I though. It would only swell our legend. Were we not the daughters of a lawless man? We would only be carrying on his name. The same town that had turned cold to Isaiah would keep her like a hero; they'd tell her story, and they'd fight for me. The Community would come for us and only burn themselves down. Benjamin would destroy them and they'd crumble and fade into the history of our lives.

It was Big Joe who brought out Isaiah's horse. Joe had a bad limp now, thanks to a bullet that took his knee. Jax tossed the bags over the saddle. The hands stood around like a funeral party, hats off, hands solemnly clasped in front of themselves—

we had just buried Denney hours before. Another headstone for the cemetery. A couple of hands would ride out with her to the mouth of the gorge, make sure she made it there unmolested.

The baby heavy on my hip and my revolver heavy in my hand, I held my breath—each one I took was another second, a second that came closer to taking my sister. She would have to protect herself now, be smart for herself. She turned to me, to say her goodbye. I dared not speak, afraid my emotions would burst if I did. I held my gun out to her. My trophy-winning gun.

When she threw her arms around me, around us, I bit back against the tears. I bit my lip so hard it bled, but it did not keep the tears from flowing, one right after the other, raining down onto my sister's shoulder.

We heard a shout. *Headlights coming.* We had to pull apart. "Ba ba," the baby said as Isaiah kissed him, breathed him in one last time. She whispered a single word in his ear. She mounted her horse, held up her chin. The moon was just starting to rise, certain to be bright and white enough to light her way. She tugged the reins, and we watched her rock away, her braid swinging, taken away into the night to be delivered unto the black and jagged mountains. I held my son close, his head on my shoulder, his hair soft and black as my sister's.

And when the wind blew, I heard his name, the name Isaiah gave him; the name given to my grandfather.

Isaac.

AUTHOR'S BIO

Shay Galloway began writing stories as soon as she knew how to hold a pencil, and before she even knew she wanted to be a writer. She studied creative writing at Utah State University and received her Bachelor's degree in 2012. She received her MFA from Roosevelt University in 2017. She currently teaches English at Pierce College and resides in Washington State with her husband and son.

ACKNOWLEDGMENTS

So much of my adolescence was spent sitting beside my grandparents as they told me stories of their youth in their small Rocky Mountain towns of their pioneer ancestors who settled those towns. Many of their tales featured mothers and grandmothers of steely dispositions as they weathered the harsh landscape of the high mountain plains, often alone with their many children as their husbands worked out in fields or chased jobs around the region. So first, I would like to thank my grandpa, whose storytelling voice inspired Isaiah's.

April, Jess, Stephanie, Huong, Sam, and Keili; all the "sisters" I picked up all the way who have been—and will be—forced to read and talk about this book for years. You have all been my rock.

To Kyle and Christian, who encouraged me to write beyond what I thought was "literary." And to the rest of my Roosevelt crew who, too, had to endure years of hearing about this book.

To Lawrence, who has always praised my progress.

And to RIZE and Running Wild Press for taking my debut into their care.

RIZE publishes great stories and great writing across genres written by People of Color and other underrepresented groups. Our team consists of:

Lisa Diane Kastner, Founder and Executive Editor
Mona Bethke, Acquisitions Editor
Rebecca Dimyan, Editor
Abigail Efird, Editor
Laura Huie, Editor
Cody Sisco, Editor
Chih Wang, Editor
Pulp Art Studios, Cover Design
Standout Books, Interior Design
Polgarus Studios, Interior Design

Learn more about us and our stories at www.runningwildpress. com/rize

Loved this story and want more? Follow us at www. runningwildpress.com/rize, www.facebook.com/rizc, on Twitter @rizerwp and Instagram @rizepress